Jennie Cooper

Those Orphans

the trials of a stepmother

Jennie Cooper

Those Orphans
the trials of a stepmother

ISBN/EAN: 9783337387334

Printed in Europe, USA, Canada, Australia, Japan

Cover: Foto ©Andreas Hilbeck / pixelio.de

More available books at **www.hansebooks.com**

THOSE ORPHANS

OR THE

TRIALS OF A STEPMOTHER

CLEVELAND, OHIO

WILLIAM W. WILLIAMS

1883

PREFACE.

Our book is a history of the married life of a stepmother. It contains facts which we have gleaned from our Diary, put into shape, and through the request of many friends, present to the public. Trusting, however, if any of our lady readers are contemplating matrimony with a widower who has from six to twelve or more children, she will not be discouraged after reading the life of our heroine. For should the novelty of a young wife die out with the gray haired old man, like a little boy's whistle; should frowns instead of sweet angelic smiles that won her come to his fair countenance, and he grow sullen and morose after a few years of wedded life, the best she can do will be to work more zealously in her missionary field with those large boys and girls under her care, and she will surely reap her reward when they have grown to manhood and womanhood, ornaments to society; when she hears them call her mother affectionately, and knows they feel a reverence as divine as though she were their own.

Many of our readers may be stepmothers; the sunlight of a happy home illuminating their lives. If so thank God, and pray to Him that the olive branch of peace may continue green in all your hearts.

To those who have a seemingly hopeless task—the care of an ungrateful father's unruly children—we would say faint not by the way ; but imitate the example of our heroine, who though dead yet speaketh through ''Those Orphans,'' so tenderly cared for, so early trained in the paths of virtue and Christianity.

THE AUTHOR.

CONTENTS.

CONTENTS.

THOSE ORPHANS

The Young Stepmother.

THOSE ORPHANS.

CHAPTER I.

Elice Woodville is seventeen years of age. We will now introduce our readers to her home—Woodville Grove, a name given by herself to a cheery little place on the banks of the beautiful Cohocton River, in the town of Lepser, New York; the price of which her father had managed to save from the wreck of a princely fortune, where in his old age he had settled with the intention of spending the remainder of a life made useful by a strict adherence to business, as well as many praiseworthy and heroic deeds.

There are but three members of the family at home, Elice, her father and mother—Mr. and Mrs. Woodville. It is the early dawn of a cold December day; Elice is in a room assigned to her by her parents on their removal from one of the eastern States, where she had spent the most of her life at school, her education superintended by the best of masters; where she had been faithfully trained, morally, physically, and spiritually, as well as intellectually; and although she had left a home of far greater grandeur, she did not feel to murmur; but a sweet contentment stole through her heart when she looked upon the faces of her loved ones, and thought how good God was that He had given them to come with her to this quiet spot.

A bright fire glows upon the hearth; and though the winds

are whistling wildly without, and piling up the snow against the bay-window, her flowers blossom on the same; and her bird, whose gilded cage is hanging in the midst, sings just as sweetly. She is seated upon a low arm-chair listening to the little warbler, whose notes seem to be more exquisitely mellow than ever, upon this morning.

A few oil paintings are scattered about; hitherto she had taken much pleasure in working her improvement in this art. Her books she did not care to peruse at this time, for all such delights were swallowed up in the great happiness that permeated her whole being—the consciousness of loving and being loved; that the following day the fruition of her fondest hopes would be realized—she would become the wife of the wealthy, talented, and kind-hearted Walter Clayton, and oh! so affectionate and devoted.

True, she knew little of his former life; but his address was so pleasant, and his voice modulated to such a degree of sweetness, that she verily believed him the impersonation of all that is great and noble in this world.

·He was a widower; talked long of his angel wife that lay beneath the cold sod; told how he had loved her; what she had said in her last moments,—"Prepare to meet me in Heaven above;" and he was striving to be a good Christian, that he too might go to that happy place; of his cherub children, Charlie and Blanche, the tender buds, who so much needed a mother's care; all together they had been one of the happiest families in existence.

Then wonder not that Elice, who was but a young girl uninitiated in the wiles and intrigues of the world, should believe this man, who had so insinuating a smile, could shape his words into such honied phrases, that she poured out the wealth of her love upon him who had scattered roses all along through the life of a former wife, and could not fail to fill hers with peace and sunshine, to satisfy the cravings of her soul with an entire devotion to her happiness.

"Thinking, darling," said her mother, entering her room, "and of what?"

The face of Elice, already radiant with hope and joy, kindled anew at the words of Mrs. Woodville.

"Yes, mother, how good and true he will be, how much I love him, and that you will be so happy because I am."

"Oh, yes, Elice, I honor your choice; and although you will not be free from care, in him you will find no dictatorial master; howbeit should the future prove that there are two sides to our picture, we have nothing now to do but look back upon the bright one."

"Darling mamma, there can be but one side—and that so bright, with such a man as Walter Clayton."

"I hope not—I hope not," replied Mrs. Woodville, and stooping kissed her, but in spite of herself the tears fell like rain upon the pale face of her daughter.

"If I only knew," she thought, as she passed out of the room. "Oh, my little one—my pet—she has thus far been shielded from all the storms of life; and of the rough gales that so often blow up suddenly to overturn our pleasure boats, in which we feel securely gliding, she knows comparatively nothing. But I can only pray that none of those things come upon my Elice—my beautiful child."

The eyes of Elice wandered out over the huge drifts of snow, through the tall, leafless maples and horse-chestnuts, whose branches were swaying to and fro in the cold December winds, to the river—the Cohocton—whose murmurings were now hushed beneath a thick crust of ice, and in a delicious, half-wakeful dreaminess in which the past and future blended, she was roaming in the springtime with the old friends and new, gathering the lily of the valley, the trailing arbutus, and lovely violets that bloomed in solid masses all along its borders; or sitting upon some drooping willow bough angling for trout; again, discussing a favorite author, or with pencil in hand sketching the scenery that made the place so attractive. And as she thought how soon she was to be removed from these, her reverie was overshadowed; and she made a wish that she might not be obliged to leave the pleasant home that she loved so well, and her dear parents in their old age; that Walter would find business in the large town close at hand; and she believed he would, for he loved her so dearly that he would do anything consistent with reason to please her; but she would not be unreasonable, and would sacrifice everything for his sake; she would do for him just what she knew he would do for her.

Then she took from her private drawer his letters that had been written from time to time, and read many of them over. How deep and passionate and fond were his words. In them she beheld herself mirrored an angel of light; and when she perused passages like these: "My thoughts are alone of you, darling;" "How happy we will be when we are wed, my angel;" "This earth would be very drear without you, love;" she believed every word expressed, and felt that she could lay down her life far sooner than lose the smiles that emanated from his true, honest eyes, the love of the great noble heart she had won, the good opinion of him who had singled her out from all the world to bless his home, to cheer his life and those of his little ones.

CHAPTER II.

Lavarre, the birth-place of Walter Clayton, like all towns, had its good with its bad inhabitants.

It was here that he commenced business a poor boy, working his way up, until he had become a man, by which time he had amassed a fortune. Here he had lived a few years a married life, been blessed by the birth of two beautiful children, Blanche and Charlie, and laid away a lovely companion in the little cemetery called Wild Rose Glen.

Far and near he was known as the "rich widower;" and many an ambitious mother tried hard to secure him for a son-in-law, so intent are some upon having their daughters marry wealthy, although this may be the only recommendation a man has. Poverty is a crime with them, and sooner would they subject their children to a life of sorrow, than have them lose the golden opportunity of being rich and grand.

Among those who figured conspicuously at Lavarre was the Tattum family, which consisted of Mr. and Mrs. Tattum with their daughters—Minnie, Augusta, and Vina.

Mrs. Tattum was termed the "Town Gossip," as she usually became acquainted with the business of her neighbors; and possessing a very fertile imagination, a little truth grew into great stories. Was there a funeral, she knew the moment the deceased died, how much he was worth, all about his will, and made herself peculiarly odious oftentimes by her officiousness on such occasions, thrusting her presence upon the survivors, asking a multitude of questions which she had no right to know, then coloring and shaping into falsehood such as suited her own particular fancy at the time; and yet in spite of her ignorance and boldness, of her habits being so thoroughly known, she had a degree of influence and held many in awe in the immediate vicinity of her home; for her intrigues, plottings, mischievous tongue, were objects of fear. Deceitful to her friends and revengeful to her enemies, she helped largely to turn the little town of Lavarre upside down, although if a person were asked what he or she thought of Mrs. Tattum, they would answer, "She is an old mischief-maker to whom no one pays the slightest attention."

Mr. Tattum never thought of engaging in the slightest business until first consulting her, and then usually did as he was bidden; for if he failed, to use his own words, "I know'd Mary Ann, and know'd the red hot sparks I'd strike lively off that hot temper o' hern."

He was under the influence of intoxicating liquors the most of the time. "Just enough," as he said, "to drive off the blues, and help me tolerate life with that woman of mine."

Frequently, however, he imbibed so much as to be quite boisterous on the streets, which subjected his wife and daughters to much shame. The daughters had received an education, limited, however, by their lack of means. Two of them, Minnie and Augusta, were very vain of the knowledge they possessed, and also of the wit and beauty some had accorded them. Further, like their mother, they were bold and impudent, and given to prevarication.

Vina, the other daughter, was different; her loveliness of character shining out more conspicuously in contrast with the mean, driveling disposition of the other female members of the family; a christian, and a lady in all the relations of life; they insincere, unjust, always stooping to conquer.

All belonged to a popular church. Each child in its infancy, having been dressed in costly robes, was carried to the altar by its hypocritical mother, and there christened, and at a suitable age persuaded by her to join the church of which she was a member; and to them her unanswerable reason was, "It is a grand stepping stone to fashionable society, and will pave the. way to the most aristocratic circles."

The father seldom had any voice in the matter—never, unless under the influence of an extra amount of stimulant, and didn't mind, as he called it, "a little row," as it was "sort o' spicy," when he would say, "Nonsense, Mary Ann, now what's the use of that child jining the church? 'twon't make her no better; 'taint got no more religion nor I have, and don't know no more about creeds; nor that muss they're into up to their eyes about the Trinity and Unity, nor I don't believe any on 'em knows a bit more nor that old brindle cow o' ourn. Poor little young ones! what's the use starching 'em up and taking 'em to the meetin' house where they've got to set up like so many mummies; can't sneeze, nor wink, but ha' got to pretend paying desprit 'tention. Goodness gracious, but don't I, Hezekier Tattum, git desprit when I hev to go without victuals fur half a month to save money to flam 'em out with furbelows! and that's just what they're thinking on instead of the sermon. Nonsense, Mary Ann, I won't 'low it to hev 'em go there and answer 'yes' to all them are ringamajigeries about church doctrines what they don't know nothing about, nor can't know nothing about, nor nobody. I won't hev it, I tell ye, I won't."

Whereupon Mrs. Tattum raising her voice would reply, "I can't see, Hezekiah, what business it is of yours. I just wish you wouldn't interfere with my authority, and I won't put up with it."

. By which time Mr. Tattum, willing to do anything to insure peace, and feeling that his wife was getting the better of him in the fray, and thinking how many days would elapse before he would be free from her tongue lashings unless he "caved," as was his word, he would say,

"Well, well, hev it all your own way, Mary Ann; mebby 'tis

best arter all—a sort 'o comfort to hev a lot uv leetle pious souls around ; let 'em go to meeting all they wan't to ; 't has made a saint o' you, mebby 't will o' them ; but with my con-science wide awake, I couldn't recommend any o' you fur your goodness.　Well, take it all in all, if you go to heaven, I've no fear—that's all there is about that."

The Tattums—mother and daughters—were very much dis-tressed on account of the illiterate husband and father.　He was a plain, outspoken man.　In spite of his lack of culture, he possessed a liberal amount of good sense ; disliked hypoc-risy, and did not believe in stealing the covering of any church as a cloak for sin ; and offended his wife by a frequent allusion to the subject, threatening to inform the pastor if she did not behave better—did not stop playing off so many tricks on her friends and neighbors, and being so "uppish" and "waspish" to him.　"Taint what a Christian orto do," he said, "they orto set a good example afore the world ; but for my part I don't see much difference between saint and sinner.　If I want to trade hosses with a saint, if 'tis heavey at all, they keep 't on straw awhile so 'twill appear all right and cheat me, if possible. If a sinner has a lame one he palms it off the same way, and 'twould take a smarter man nor I am to distinguish one from t'other.　Then, there's Mary Ann, goes to all the meetins there is, brings up the gals to go, has 'em jine the church afore their baby close are off, makes folks b'lieve she's jest the thing—and a good many do think so, I suppose, and a good many don't agin—when, to my certain knowledge, she does wus things than I'd ever think o' doing—backbites her neighbors, toles their chickens into the back yard, ketches 'em on the sly, and thinks she's doing a Christian act, cos she makes the preacher a present o' 'em.　Then that big turkey she killed didn't belong t' her—only jest strayed onto our side the fence, then to keep all right and pop'lar, gin that fur a New Year's gift.　Ha! ha! wasn't Parson Gray profuse o' his thanks—telling folks what a good and liberal soul sister Tattum was ; that if all the sistern tried to help sustain the gospel like what she did, he'd hev no trouble gitting his salary. Didn't I wan't ter say, Guess they wouldn't if they paid it out o' other people's hen roosts; stole the last nickel out of their husband's pockets, after they was abed and asleep, so they hadn't as much left as ter buy a little tobaccer."

CHAPTER III.

"She has always been a good child to us," said Mr. Woodville, addressing his wife, "and I shall be very lonely when she is gone. To-morrow she will be hundreds of miles away. We will miss her so much, won't we, mother?" and here the old man bent his head upon his cane while he looked as if twenty years had been added to his life.

"Yes, she has always been the sunlight of our home; no one can tell my grief as the hour approaches that takes my darling from me."

"It has been a wild, bitter night; the winds have whistled and moaned without any interruption, which seems almost a prophecy—a warning of the future."

"What do you mean?"

"Well, nothing, mother, nothing," he answered as he looked upon her eyes red and swollen from weeping.

"I must know all you think!"

"If you must—why, it is just an old man's whim that takes its coloring from the anticipated hours of loneliness; our home will be very desolate when she is away, you know."

"But if it it be her future that thus forecasts its shadow, ah me! ah me!"

They then looked out upon the sky, black as night, the blinding storm and the great banks of snow piling up against the house and covering the fences as far as the eye could reach; and, added to this, a beautiful young evergreen that had protected the window of Elice from the scorching rays of the mid-summer sun, had been uprooted and thrown directly across the path that led from the house to the gate.

"Fearful sight!" escaped them simultaneously, while their lips were tremulous with suppressed emotion. Then both were as silent as though the angel of destruction had spread its broad wings over their dwelling, or the finger of death had been pointed toward the idol of their household.

After a time, when Mr. Woodville could command himself enough to speak, he said, "Is it a voice from on high? Now I do not really like Mr. Clayton. I fear he is not all he professes—he talks fair, and smiles sweetly; but an unguarded word here and there discloses a nature too grasping to be altogether honest, apparently so, at least. Now I did not like the way he managed with those parties where he took advantage of a technicality of law to rob them—that is what I call it; with him it was a clever business transaction whereby he cleared a 'cool thousand.'"

To the reply of Mrs. Woodville, shaped to favor her daughter's betrothed, in which the tones of her voice were freighted with the same distrust that weighed so heavily upon her husband, thereby contradicting words intended to soothe the "dear heart," he answered, "I know it is the way of the world, but the world's way I do not like—to lie and cheat, the more the better, let it be inside the law, which, haply, cannot always bear the strain. But if I really believed all this of Walter, though her heart were broken, I would not allow Elice to marry him. Yet, he may be all that a trusting, loving husband can be; but I do wish I had not heard him talk so much about money and his lucky speculations."

Elice, who was passing through the hall to her own apartment, hearing a portion of the conversation, became pale as the lily bells that trembled in her fingers.

"Poor dears!" was her mental exclamation, "can it be that the thought of losing their Elice is so appalling that its shadow falls upon Walter's integrity?   I will go and comfort them."

Yet, upon entering she did not allude to the subject, but, exhibiting her flowers, she said, "They are the gift of our friend, Mrs. Lane.   Are they not lovely?"   The lilies she handed to her mother, but a sprig of orange buds, two of which were more than half blown, she laid against the glossy braids of her luxuriant hair.   "Is that becoming, mamma?   Walter will think it a happy omen;   her orange trees have never bloomed before, and now this, just for our nuptials."   And she spoke so trustingly and looked so happy, that her father tried hard to put away all unkind thoughts, and to feel he had passed a too hasty judgment upon her lover.

Mr. Woodville drew her upon his lap, then kissed her again and again.   He pressed her to his bosom in a long and silent embrace, when, unable to restrain his tears, the pent up flood rolled down his furrowed cheeks.   Clasping her closer and yet closer, he exclaimed, "My daughter! oh, my daughter! and must I give you up?   Cursed be he who dares harm one hair of your precious head."

Elice patted his cheek and told him not to fear; that while she regretted parting with her friends, she knew that her future home would be all that a loving heart could make it.

Still the winds whistled and shrieked; still the hurricane beat wildly against the windows, while ghostly moans fell upon the ears as the great trees, swaying to and fro, struck their leafless branches against the eaves.

Then, as if looking outward—on—beyond the storm to that Power who alone can control the winds, Mrs. Woodville said, "God rules, father; soon, very soon old Boreas will be driven back into his cold lair, where he will be as quiet and peaceful as any lamb."

Elice catching her manner continued, "Yes, and the frost king has bound our buds in his cold shrouds; but a little while, and they will burst their icy cerements to gladden all our spring time;" and, pointing to the lilies full blossomed, still in the hands of her mother,—"See, he cannot hold them; no more can any stormy wind or tempest bind our joys."

To which her father added, "You are right, my child; though the world is full of tribulation, in Christ there is sweet peace; moreover, it is whimsical, to say the least, that we burden the present with fears of future ill. Strange, is it not, how our thoughts take coloring from the weather?"

The three then knelt together, Mr. Woodville placing his hand upon his daughter's head, while he prayed so fervently, as if his words were burdened with a great agony—"'If it be possible, let this cup pass,'—but no! Thou wilt keep our Elice in the hour of temptation; in thy secret pavilion keep her from the 'strife of tongues';" and his prayer seemed almost a prophecy.

The three then conversed of the responsibilities Elice was about to assume; her relations as wife, particularly her trying position as step-mother. "But," said Mr. Woodville, "should the noisy undercurrent of popular prejudice set in against you, do not be discouraged; love for your husband and the little motherless ones will lift you above the petty caviling of uncultured natures. The most turbulent streams sometimes wash down the purest gold, and often gems of priceless value. But it is only through prayer and much rugged persistence that you will be able to gather them up and wear them in your woman's crown of rejoicing. And now, darling, I commit you to the care of our dear Father above, of whom it is said, 'A sparrow falleth not to the ground without His notice;' and 'Ye are of more value than many sparrows.' Come here, mother, place your hand with mine upon her head. Our blessings upon you, child! Go forth; battle with all a woman's fortitude in the great warfare of life, but in the fear and love of Almighty God."

CHAPTER IV.

Walter Clayton was seated in the old stage-coach bound for Cambden, where he intended to take the cars for Woodville to claim his promised bride.

He had just bidden adieu to friends on the porch of the hotel, and little aside was talking confidentially to another, telling his plans; and, oblivious of the fact that the town gossip, Mrs. Tattum, was standing just within his shadow, was enjoining the strictest secrecy.

She had seen him the moment he stepped into the sleigh, wrapped in his huge shawl, with satchel in hand. Surely, she thought, there must be something going on—a journey to be taken, which meant—a new wife, perhaps, and moreover, she was quite sure of it; for, hadn't it leaked out through the village postmaster that Walter was daily receiving letters superscribed in a lady's hand? the woman's he meant to marry? Of course it was, or they wouldn't be coming like snow flakes, thicker and faster; and she was going to find out all about it.

She listened for a time disappointed, when she thought, "Well, this will never do; I'm only having trouble for my pains: I will walk slowly by where I may hear enough to give me the drift of their conversation, for I'm bound to know all about this mystery. When people try to keep so mighty sly, they don't want to forget that Mary Ann Tattum is after them," and she gave a little chuckle, as much as to say, "I shall catch you yet; it's no little pussy that's after you now, old rat."

She heard Walter say, laughingly, "I am suspected of matrimonial intentions then, Hal? Well, you just tell them I am going to New York to replenish my stock of goods. Good-bye."

"All right?" inquired the coach-driver in the blandest tones, after having waited half an hour beyond his usual time. He then tucked the robes more closely about his passenger, handling them carefully as would a father had he been wrapping them about a favored daughter.

They were soon riding rapidly along, unmindful of all that was passing. Walter was thinking—was it of Elice, that dear loving soul who was about to launch the barque with him upon the uncertain seas of matrimonial life; how happy he would strive to make that child, who so implicitly trusted him, that she promised to become his wife; that was so soon to leave her father and mother; to separate herself from all other earthly ties for him?

No! While he wrapped himself in his cloak of selfishness, he mused thus: My ceaseless expenses are now about to end; this having so much extra help is what eats up a man's profits —a kitchen girl, a nursery maid, sometimes a woman to sew, and all to board, all to pay. But with a man's wife it is different; she can take the place of all three, and more. A married man has another advantage a widower has not; if he feels crabbed after a hard day's work and snaps at a servant, she will say, as pert as can be, 'Look for another girl, please,' perhaps throw your squalling baby into your arms, and tell you to take care of your own brats; dare not open your mouth even to advise her, so must smother down your rage, when you feel like pitching her into the street. Why, servants think they can run right over and trample down a poor man, who is so unfortunate as to lose his companion, and leave him alone with little children! But it doesn't mind what you say to a wife; however tart, she hardly dares resent it; and while she accomplishes more work than the whole complement of girls, it's all right; true, their tears fall like rain sometimes, but that's nothing; like flowers washed in a shower, they look the brighter for it. I wonder if Elice has a good disposition. If a shrew, I can tame her. I don't care only so she's tough and hearty. Oh, dear, I presume I shall be obliged to keep one servant for the looks of it." Then Walter Clayton commenced musing upon his speculations, and to count his gains, in the midst of which he reached the railway station, where he was to procure tickets for his eastern trip.

When evening came he was folding his betrothed to his bosom, and telling her of the beautiful home over which she was so soon to preside as mistress, of his little ones who were waiting to give her a welcome, and kissing away the tears that fell so fast at thought of leaving her other darlings behind, and assuring her of his ceaseless endeavors to make her life as pleasant and happy as the old one.

CHAPTER V.

"I declare, Hezekiah, you can't guess what I've heard!"

"Don't know, Mary Ann, when you stays so long, I makes up mind you'z smellin' out somethin'."

"Hang up that frisky old tongue of yours, and I'll tell you. Walter Clayton is surely going to be married—started off to-day for his wife. Now, my mind was made up to have him marry our Vina."

"What! that old miser? Jakes! and 'tis a mighty mean one that he is; afore I'd see him marry our Vine I'd let her rot, and wots more, I'd go and help the sexton dig her grave, fur it wouldn't be many months afore Clayton wud give him the job."

"But he's rich, and riches is power, and power is an elevator; and for my share, I'd like elevation. Now, if Vina could have married Walter, she could well nigh support us, and we wouldn't be obliged to work so hard; at all events, there would be one less on our hands—one less to dress, and that's a mighty big thing I'd have you to know."

"To buy ribbons and furb'lows fur. Why don't you put your gals to doin' somethin'? Y'u'r too pesky 'fraid they'll sile their lily-white hands, and so you wash an' scrub and do nigh onto everything yourself, so they can set 'round like so many ladies; that's no way, Mary Ann; set 'em to work; 'tis no determent to any one to know how; any feller, if he knoze shucks, 'll take em off your han's twict as quick. I ruther the

2

gals, all on 'em, w'u'd take care o' 'emselves than to marry that man."

"Innocent old Hezekiah! where's your brains? you don't know any more than our little banty rooster; don't know that somebody that is worth while will be taken with their soft ways and delicate hands. No! Kiah, no! I'd work my fingers down to the hubs, before my daughter should take up with one of your clod-hoppers. They shall marry rich, for, as I said before, I want to be elevated."

"And," added Hezekiah, with a peculiar shrug, "'twould histe the hull on us, to have Vine marry old Clayton!"

Whereupon, enraged, she moved backward, and unmindful of the trap door, fell headlong into the cellar.

"Elevated, Mary Ann? sure how do you like it? Hev you hurt you much?"

"Oh, yes, come quick! I think I am dying! don't you see the blood all over me?"

"Burst an artery, mebby?"

"I guess so and broke my foot!"

"Wish 'twuz your tongue, so you couldn't use it on me again, or yer neck—ha! ha! Who's got the brains now, Mary Ann? as little as Ize blessed with, I'd know better nor to shove my chair off a trap door when it was wide open."

"If you are not going to help me, say so, and go to Guinea and never come back again!" Then she sprang to her feet and commenced ascending the stairs.

"Oh, you be hurt, aint you, Mary Ann?" he added in all meekness, frightened that she was indeed upon her feet, and hoping to ward off the storm of bitter words by making hasty atonement for his cruel taunts. "Let me git the camfire; where's the gals? tell 'em to bring the hartshorn. Shan't I go directly for the doctor? I'm so sorry you be hurt, Mary Ann."

But ever after, when he had drank sufficient brandy to make him courageous, he would inquire, "How do you like your ele-vashun, Mary Ann?"

CHAPTER VI.

" Whew! what a blustering storm," said Mrs. Tattum the following day. "I hate to travel way up to Clayton's; but I must know whether Walter is going to take a wife. I have been to all the neighbors, and into most everybody's house in town, and no one seems to know a thing about it. But his mother will know, and I'll get it out of her through strategy; it takes me. I'm as good as the chief of police to find out people's secrets."

Once making up her mind, nothing could change her purpose; so, in a few moments she was on her way, now and then trudging through snow-drifts that reached nearly to her waist. A man came along with a horse and sleigh, and asked her to ride; she was glad to accept the invitation, as it was a mile from Mr. Clayton's, and she was now but half way.

An Irishman just going to shovel snow: "The rig I have, ma'am, is a gentleman's, shure," he said, "who is sick, and sent it home by me."

It was not long before the snow was so deep that it was impossible to proceed further without clearing the way; and as Pat was about to alight, his horse reared, plunged, and upset the sleigh, turning them both into the deepest of the snow. Once relieved of its burden, it was soon through the drift, and running with its utmost speed in the direction of home.

Pat was soon upon his feet and looking for his companion, but he could only see a portion of her dress above the snow.

Clutching at this and giving it a pull, he hallooed at the top of his voice, "Come out of this, laddie, and be quick wid yerself!" But she had become so benumbed she could neither speak nor stir.

"All Holy Saints! she's did thin.   Och! the poor soul; I'll make her hear me now, if she's alive." Then again grasping her dress, he screamed at the top of his voice, "Come out uv here, I tell yez;" still she did not move; she moaned slightly.

"Do ye hear, Patsey; I tell yez now, boy," he said to himself, "get yer spade and dig the laddie out, an' who knows but she might be a rich laddie, and will give yez a hansame christmas gift?"

It was not long before he succeeded in getting her into a sitting position; but she was unable now to rise to her feet. Just here he bethought himself of his flask of whisky, and, uncorking it, pressed it to her lips, saying, "A drap uv the crayther, dear laddie, 'll set yez all right agin. Ize a temp'rance mon an' so are yez ; but it's wondrous revivin'."

He had not anticipated her ready acquiescence, or he would not have made the request—and certainly not to the extent of her grasping the bottle and swallowing its contents to the last "wee drop." "Och! och!" he exclaimed in anger, snatching it from her, "Yez can walk now, sure, or I'll lave yez here to die."

She once more put forth an effort, but failed.

"Well, well, then!" he said, relaxing his frigidity of manner, "I see yez can't; but faith, that whisky arter put a head on old Gerliar; well, I've strapped mony a hog across my shoulder, and can do it agin, sure. So yez jest clapse yez arms about my neck, and I'll carry yez into yon house."

Mrs. Tattum did his bidding. A moment more and he was striving to gain the opposite side of the drift. Though it was a heavy load for Pat, yet, puffing and blowing, with the great drops of sweat falling from his red, round face, he would have succeeded had she not relaxed her hold and fallen back heavily into the snow.

She had espied the pastor of her church in the distance, and not wishing him to see her in this situation, had dropped herself purposely from Pat's neck. But she was a little too late; and though he was aware something strange and mysterious had happened, some serious accident, perhaps, he could not help laughing at the ridiculous figure before him. He was, however, soon out of his sleigh, and helping Pat to place her between two nice, warm robes, with a soapstone at her feet, and hurrying his two fleet ponies as fast as possible towards her home.

" I was going to visit the sick, or I should never have ventured out into the storm," she feebly remarked.

" Very kind—very kind, indeed, Sister Tattum."

" You see, a particular friend lies at the point of death, and sent for me."

"You got into the snow, Sister?"

" Well, yes, yes, I did," she replied, looking confused.

" I am glad I happened along. By the way, Sister, I must thank you for that fine lot of poultry you sent me. Do you raise turkeys?"

By this time Pat's whisky was running riot in her brain, causing her to tell more truth than she had for many a long day.

" That are turkey I sent you over, Parson Grey, was a pesky, wesky, mean, aggressive beast of prey, what belonged to that close-communion, tight-fisted Deacon Jones, and was continually bothering the life and soul out of me; and so I thought the best Christian act I could do towards promulgating the Gospel, was to kill it and send it to you. And them are four chickens was worse on me all summer, than the turkey— stole all their feed out of my back yard; so I took out a big pan of corn, and hadn't no trouble catching them at all, as I guess as how they knode me, for I was always throwing them out feed, whenever I saw them coming in sight; but, when I got them killed" (slapping her breast), "my conscience give me a great big thump right here, and I couldn't eat them after all, for I thought it might be a sin to wring the heads off of other folk's property, and so I sent them to you." (Crying)— "Oh, the poor, benighted heathen, how I wish I could help them more than what I do! When I see them are fellers in heathenish darkness, how I pray for money to get them out! Don't you think, Parson Grey, I'd make a good missionary?"

Then changing her voice to a sing-song tone, "I like to forgot to tell you, Parson Grey, that Hezakier and I had a big rowdy, de, dowdy, de dow, yesterday; and he knocked me down cellar, back-end-to. I believe I'll get a divorce, wouldn't you? But he couldn't kill me; I jumped up and told him I wished he'd go to Guinea and never come back. I'm the boss of that old feller, after all!" Then returning to the sorrowful tone, she said, "Poor Hezakier, he's so sinful and grovelling! but if he'd only join the church and go to meeting with me, I'd forgive him for all he has done; but the poor, old, drunken cuss, you needn't never expect nothin' good from him!"

"When rum is in, wit is out,' thought Parson Grey. "The poor woman is intoxicated, but she is not to blame; and, as for all this idle talk, I shall never speak of it, for, of course, it is not true. How kind of her to expose herself in that wild storm, for a friend; 'tis just like her! Strange, strange, she is a poor woman, but she gives far more liberally than many of our more wealthy members."

CHAPTER VII.

The wedding is over and Elice is seated in the cars by the side of her husband, bound for their future home. She was happy, and who would not be in possession of the love of a great, manly heart, with the pure kisses of his devotion still warm upon her lips?

True, she had left a home of plenty; never in all her life had she known what it was to want; never had she been sick, but a mother's gentle hand had ministered to every wish; a father's loving arms thrown out at all times to lift her out of her distress, to gather her to his bosom. But, if they had been kind; if they had been so anxious for her welfare, how much more would he be, who, as he said, was henceforth to live only for the love of his wife; who would worship her as the star of his life and home.

These were her thoughts as she rolled away on the train bound for Cambden, as her dear old home with all its pleasant associations as left in the distance—that little nest, as she termed it, upon the banks of the Cohocton—the centering point of all that had made life worth living for; but never more dear to her than on this morning when her idols were left behind her, and forever; and she was to make a home for all future time among strangers—"in a strange land."

And what were they like? she thought. Would they take her to their hearts, would they love her as her own in the sweet valley of Woodville? How did the children look? Would they like her ?   She did not doubt it, for they usually did.   But then, she was a step-mother ; she had seen something of their trials ; but it would be different with her, for she would strive so hard to do nothing for which she could be blamed.

They had not yet reached Cambden when she had a hard headache.   "Oh, dear!" she said, pressing both hands upon her burning brow.

" Are you sick?" said her husband, looking coldly upon her, " I thought I had married a healthy woman."

"Oh, no," said she timidly, "not sick, only—only—you know it is a great deal for a young girl to leave all her friends, and I did not get much sleep last night."

Had an arrow pierced her, she could not have felt so badly ; every vestige of color faded from her cheeks and lips, and she looked as if she might have fallen dead, then and there, at his feet.   Not heeding her agony, he still kept on reading his newspaper.

Soon they they reached Cambden, the terminus of their railway journey ; and though the winds blew high and the snow came whirling down so that it was almost blinding, it was a sweet relief to Elice to alight, that she might feel the cold air once more upon her cheeks.

Being obliged to remain an hour or more at this place, he ordered a coachman to drive them to a hotel.

Arriving there, he asked carelessly if she still had the headache ; he hoped she would not be a sickly woman, for they were no comfort to themselves nor anyone else about them. Then excusing himself for a few moments, to arrange some business matters, he left the room.

When alone, Elice wheeled a rocking chair around to the window, and throwing herself down, gave way to a burst of grief such as she had never known before ; and exclaimed in all the bitterness of her soul, "Mother! mother!" and then her thoughts turned backward to her childhood, to the cooling draughts and soft hands upon her fevered brow, the tender solicitude of that dear one who, she remembered, had so often arisen at the midnight hour, and trodden upon tip-toe, so that if asleep she might not awaken her, to tuck her in more snugly if the night were cold, and then leave with a kiss upon her cheek.

"I wonder if Walter Clayton will always remain as he is now; what could I have done to offend him?"

Soon her husband returned, and approaching Elice, said he hoped she was better; but the fact was he had this little business on his mind and she must excuse him for his seeming lack of attention; it was very hard to be sick, and wished to know if he could do anything for her.

With her eyes cast down to the floor, she aswered meekly, "I was afraid you did not love me."

"Well, to tell you the truth, I did feel a little out of sorts when you commenced complaining so soon; for when a man gets a wife, he wants one that is not everlastingly in the dumps; and I thought, supposing you were one of that sort, what would become of me and the children! Now, my first wife was never sick a day in her life, and she was such a busy little body, always seeing if there were not something to do; and it would seem kind of awkward like if—well, if I had got one that was not healthy. You look so pale and—and—well, I thought you could not be very stout, to say the least, and it made me feel badly."

CHAPTER VIII.

"Well!" exclaimed Mrs. Tattum, rushing into Mrs. Jones's, her favorite resort, who lived just across the garden, "they do say Walter Clayton has just arrived with his new wife; that she was a widow, and had as many as two or three children, and is as homely as a hedge fence, and her folks is not rich either; and they say—well, they say—they say—they say—"

"Why! do tell!" responded Mrs. Jones, "I wonder if he had to go way down there to get him a woman, when there are so many here that are just crazy to have him for a son-in-law."

"'Tisn't me," answered Mrs. Tattum.

"You're the very one," said Clorinda, one of the daughters, "and, furthermore, I was very near Walter Clayton and his wife; saw them through the window of the old stage coach as they turned up to his brother-in-law's, Major Cliffton; and she does not look a day older than seventeen, and is as fair as a lily; and I don't believe she ever could have been a widow."

"Well," Mrs. Tattum answered sarcastically, "she isn't an angel like his first one; for all she lacked was the wings, that is, some folks said so; and now that she's dead and gone, she surely was. For my part, looking out of my two eyes, I could never see that she was any better than I am, or most any other kind of a good body."

"Nor me, either," replied Mrs. Jones; "but I kinder liked the woman, though, because she was real industrious; and somehow I take to folks who know how to work and keep their house in order; and they did say that she was as neat as a new pin, though I wasn't myself acquainted with her—wasn't never in her house in my life; but as for her being any better than other folks that are just as good as she is, I don't believe it at all,—good enough, but no better than your daughter nor mine, Mrs. Tattum. They say that she nor her husband didn't agree none too well, anyway, though there were very few what knowed it; but who was to blame, I don't know, nor don't care; though you never see two people what didn't live agreeable but what one was to blame as much as the other, or very nigh on to it. Although I never liked him since he came and took the last cow I had for store debt, when I told him if he'd wait about two weeks I'd have the money to pay him; and, of course, I hate him like pizen."

"Me too," said Mrs. Tattum; "we were in the same box— we owed him a little bill; and, because we couldn't get around just at the time, he cleaned us out, 'bag and baggage.' I'd liked awful well, to give him a dose of ratsbane; but I've got over it now, though I always think of a snake when I see him; no one knows when they are going to be bitten by it. We've never traded one cent with him since, though he's come around as sweet as peaches and cream. But I'm going into Major Cliff-ton's this evening, to see Walter and his new wife; I can pret-·ty soon tell what kind of stuff she's made of."

"She ought to be made of forked lightning and bullets," spoke Clorinda. "I happen to know all about Walter Clayton; and any woman would have to be iron-hearted and iron-framed to get along with him. I'd like to have him to deal with, I'd kill him if I could. I worked for them three weeks, and I was exasperated with him the whole time the way he treated his poor wife; she was one of the dearest little creatures that ever lived; she never gave him a cross word—never said anything to hurt his feelings; and seemed to strive so hard to keep him good natured. But he was continually finding fault; she did not do this thing right, nor the other thing, and it was fret, and fret, from morning till night, whenever he was in the house."

"Come, Clorinda, we'll go and get a squint at the bride this evening; we'll make some excuse and they'll never know our errand," said Mrs. Tattum.

"No, ma'am! now, I'd as soon meet the devil as that man, for I hate him—I loathe him!"

"Well, well, then I'll go myself."

"Be sure and come back then, and tell us all about her, won't you?"

"Good evening, Mrs. Cliffton," said Mrs. Tattum upon entering that lady's domicile, "I hope you are well: I came over to see if you would lend me your last magazine, to look at the fashions and read the stories; I am very much interested in Knickerbocker Moses'—la! me! you haven't got company, have you? If I'd a known it I wouldn't have come, no how; why didn't you send a little bird and tell me? who are they?"

"My brother Walter and his wife."

"I'm so sorry I came. I wouldn't have come for anything if I'd a known it; but seeing I'm here, introduce me. You see I knew his first wife and always liked her so well! I feel wonderfully interested in the family; no doubt he's got a nice woman—one that will be good to those poor little orphan children. Is that she?" glancing into the room where she was seated.

"Why! she's as pretty as a pink, and she looks as if she might be good enough;" she was going to add, "a thousand times too good for Walter," but remembering to whom she was talking, said—"good enough for any man living!"

"Yes," said Mrs. Cliffton, "I knew her when she was a little child, and have known the family ever since."

"Was she a widow?"

"She was not."

"I guess I'll just step in and speak to her, if you've no objections."

In a moment more she was in the parlor, face to face with Elice.

"Mrs. Clayton, I s'pose—I am Mrs. Tattum. You see I come over here for a magazine, and nothing would do but Mrs. Cliffton would have me come in and see you; I'm not dressed up much, but I s'pose you'll excuse me; I didn't know you were here, or I'd slipped on another dress. I'm well acquainted with your mother-in-law, and she'll be tickled almost to death to think you've come"—then to herself, "in a horn." "Does she know you're here? You know, I s'pose, she's got those children of his. I suppose you'll go to keeping house right away and take them from her; or, are you going to board? Were you ever to Lavarre before? How do you like it? You will probably wait till morning before you go up to the old man's? They live about a mile out in the country. I don't like the old woman much, because I think she is very deceitful; but may be you'll like her—I hope so. She pretends to be terribly attached to those young ones, but she whips them once in a while, for I've seen her do it; but it won't do for you to touch them, or the fat will be all in the fire; and when it's there, it will flash up and scorch those pretty fingers of yours. Well, I don't envy you old Walter Clayton, if he is rich. Did you know he was rich? May be you married him for his money? He tried awful hard to get one of my girls, but there wasn't one of them would have him: they call him an old sharper about here, and worse too—an old miser."

"What!" was the simple response of Elice, confused and indignant, that any one should dare to speak thus of her husband.

Mrs. Tattum saw this, and said, "Well, little one, you needn't get your back up, for it's the truth; and if you are not sorry before the year is out, you set yourself down along side of Walter Clayton, my name isn't Mary Ann Tattum. You are too pretty, and too fresh, and too innocent-like, for that man; he wants one that'll scratch his eyes out, and put them in again, if necessary.   But I guess you'll get along very well; I hope so, any way.   You were never married before, were you?   I heard so, but I didn't believe it—I said so to Mrs. Jones.   Is your father and mother living?   Are they pretty well to do in the world?   Oh, I suppose so, or that old miser wouldn't wanted you.   Did you leave them well?"

Not waiting replies to her many questions, she bade Elice good night, repeated all she had seen and heard, and more,— that she imagined.

Elice thought her intoxicated, and asked Mrs. Cliffton if this were the case.

"I think so, by the way she talked and appeared; if not, I have been deceived.   She does imbibe occasionally, but is very sly about it."

CHAPTER IX.

On the following day, as soon as they had breakfasted, Walter and his wife started on their way for the farm-house, the residence of old Mr. Clayton. It was a pleasant place—a large, square stone, surmounted by a cupola, overhung in summer with green vines and climbing roses; shaded by tall maples and huge old apple trees, within whose boughs birds of almost every name and nature built their nests and reared their young. Then there was a large orchard, and great, green meadows, grazing fields of lowing cattle and sheep and horses; the old spring down in the valley, whose stones were covered over with mosses; the woodland, just at hand, filled with violets and all manner of sweet wild flowers.

Elice had heard a description of the place before, and, oh, how she wished, as she rode along through the deep snow, that spring had come; and in imagination she was roaming over those fields, gathering daises and buttercups, listening to the sweet chirping of the bluebird and robin, as they poured forth their notes from the twigs of those ancient trees. As they neared the house, she felt her heart warmed in a strange degree towards its inmates.

"And so you've come?" said Mrs. Clayton, "and this is your wife, Walter?" as she met them at the door. "Come here, children, this is your mamma." The elder, Blanche, a girl of four summers, stood back, and with her dark, expressive eyes, scanned Elice for a few moments, when she abruptly broke forth with the words, "No, 'taint nuther; my mamma's in the ground; big man covered her all up with dirt and green thods, and s'e couldn't get out no how. How can s'e be my mamma?"

"But this is another one," said Elice, taking her upon her lap and kissing away her tears, "You will love me, won't you?"

"Will you be dood to me and not stold me, nor whip me? My mamma was angel; s'e's angel now, ain't s'e?"

"Yes, sweet," said Elice, clasping her more closely to her heart, "I believe your mamma is up in heaven—a beautiful, shining spirit; that she watches over you, and sees all you do. You will one day go to her; you will sometime see her."

"Oh! will I ever see my mamma again—my dear, dear mamma?"

"Yes, God took her to himself to live in Heaven, where all good little children go when they die, and every body who loves the Saviour and will my little girl love him?"

"What did he do that for? What? do you ask me to love thutch a man as that ith? I was always mad at that man what frode dirt all over my mamma. Now, if you say Dod took her away from me, when I loved her so—oh, I loved her so!— I hate Dod, and I won't never like him."

Elice drew her head upon her bosom and remained silent, while the child gave vent to an uncontrollable torrent of tears.

She knew it was better to say nothing more to her at present; in fact, what could she say? Not anything that would reach the little one's consciousness; she could only lift her heart to the great God above, to pour the oil of peace and consolation into her sorrowing heart.

She had hardly framed her prayer before Blanche had fallen asleep. She laid her away in her little crib and then, taking up Charlie, the baby-boy, she showered his face with kisses; and while he laughed and crowed in her arms, she felt what a sweet responsibility had fallen upon her—the care of this darling child;

and how proud she would be of them both, and wished from her inmost soul that they were indeed her own, and then, she could rear them untrammeled by the cold eyes of suspicion, the fear of which had suddenly stolen upon her.

Dinner over, the mother-in-law brought out several dress patterns for the children and showed them to Elice—said, "They have been lying in the house a long while, and I couldn't get time to make them up. Can you sew any? I hope so, for it cost so much to hire it done ; and as you are going to live in town, and won't have anything else to do but your little house work, and take care of the children, you can do it just as well as not. Of course, Walter always keeps two cows, but you can do the churning and take care of the milk when the children are asleep, in the morning, and all the sewing at night after they are gone to bed ; and then, you will have lots of chances between times, for the children isn't no bother at all ; sure, Charlie will want to be tended a considerable, he is so small, and Blanche took up now and then, for she ain't much better than a baby, for they were both always rocked asleep here—father takes one, and I take the other on our laps; and the little things are not very heavy, and you're young and strong and can hold them both."

" Yes, certainly," said Elice with a slight smile she could not suppress, " I could take Blanche on one knee and Charlie on the other, couldn't I, pets ? Come here and let me see how heavy you are—now spring, Blanche ; well, you are quite light. Bring Charlie, too ; come, black-eyes—well, I've a lap full of babies, havn't I ?" And the children laughed till they cried, they thought it was so much sport.

" How much do they weigh, mother ?"

"Oh, I don't know how much ; I wouldn't think more'n a hundred pounds, both on 'em."

"That's not much," said Elice, striving to be composed.

" Wall, you see," continued the old lady, " their own mother dressed 'em up twict every day. She said she 'druther do it than not have them clean and neat; and my darter Ann has some little fellows she keeps awful tidy. Of course you are a good washer and ironer? I hope so, because it costs a good deal to hire it done, and you know you'll have nothing else to do, as I said before, only your little house work and to look after them poor, little motherless children."

"Yes," said Elice, not knowing whether to laugh or cry, "we'll manage that, won't we birdies?" giving each of a them a kiss.

"Wall, I'm glad of it," she continued, "for I told Walter that I always heard you had been brought up to go to school, and I was afraid you didn't know nothin' about work; and you was so kind of white looking like, I didn't know but you might be sickly. You know, Elice, that would make it bad for poor Walter, and them little motherless things. Can you knit? Now the fact is, I've had so much to do, that I hain't had no chance to knit the children any stockings, and my darter goes to the 'cademy, so she has to study her lessons, and she don't have no time to help me much; but you'll have lots of time. Now, when my children was little I used to keep a big bag of stockings all the while—all kinds of knitting in every hole and corner of the house; these was for ketch-up work, evenings and when I went a visiting. You see, if one employs every minute, they can accomplish more'n than any one would dream of; then, if they're kinder lazy and good for nothin', everything kinder goes to loose ends—now ain't that so?"

"I suppose it is," answered Elice.

"Wall, one thing more, I happened to think of: if I was in your place, I'd make the children some sunbonnets right away so to have them ready for hot weather. You know it will be kind of nat'ral like fer 'em to want to run out and play a good deal; and Charlie'll be so he'll want to run around by that time and they orto wear somethin' on their heads to keep the sun from burning up their faces. I was going to make 'em hoods all winter, but the fact is, I haint had a minnit of time, the little things hev kept me so busy waiting on 'em, and they're so mischievous, I had to watch 'em a good deal too; so you see its took me all the while to look out for them."

"Without doubt," replied Elice.

Some ladies called, and Elice was glad of a respite from the unceasing tongue that had so skilfully and, as the old lady thought, so successfully, planned for her future employment.

It is bed time; Walter had returned to town where he was extensively engaged in mercantile operations, and had not yet arrived. And as Elice felt fatigued, she went to the room appropriated to her use, and lay down upon the sofa awaiting his arrival.

Reader, imagine her feelings, if you can. Do you think they were such as to produce sweet sleep and pleasant visions?

We will see. With eyes closed—but whether awake or not, we scarcely can tell—a great panorama spread out before her, in which more sorrow was pictured than happiness. Beautiful streams and winding paths; on either side lofty trees covered with rich foliage; all along, green grass and flowers, so varied in their hues—beautiful enough to deck the fairy bower of a queen; bird notes floating in perfumed air, filling her soul with rapture as she listened. Looking again she beheld huge serpents, with slimy breath and forked tongues, coiled or dragging their length through and over them all; while all the flowers were withering at her feet, and the songs of her gay, plumed darlings were no more heard. And she uttered a cry so piercing, that it startled her husband who had just entered the room at the time.

"What is the matter, Elice?" he said.

"Oh, nothing," she replied, rubbing her eyes, "I guess I was asleep. I'm so glad you have come!" But she did not tell him her dream, for thus soon she had learned it was not to him she could confide her troubles expecting sympathy.

CHAPTER X.

"Mrs. Clayton," said the old gentleman, addressing his wife, after they were quite alone, "what made you go on with such a tirade to Walter's wife, and expatiate so largely on her duties —the poor, little homesick child? I consider it an insult to any sensible person ; I believe in every one keeping his own door-yard clean. Did you ever read your Bible, 6th chap. Matthew, 3rd verse?—'Cast the beam out of thine own eye, then shalt thou see clearly to cast the mote out of thy brother's eye.' Now you know as well as I do, that these children are kept none of the tidiest; they oftentimes go ragged and dirty, and with their hair uncombed. No longer ago than this morning, the baby's face was smeared two hours after you had given him bread and molasses to keep him quiet; and you never washed it until you saw Walter drawing in sight; and Blanche was like a little house pig."

"John," she replied, while she was vexed beyond all description, "I consider it a Christian duty to look after those poor, little, motherless children. Didn't she, their own mother, on her deathbed, ask me to watch tenderly over them ?"

"She said simply this, and nothing farther, 'Oh, who will look after my little spirit angels when I am gone ? who will train them for that happy place ? I trust they will be brought up in the fear of Almighty God.' These were her last words, addressed to no one in particular."

"Wall, wall, who could she mean unless she meant me ? For my part, I intend to look after their welfare ; and then, another thing, when I see a woman come into the family with soft, white hands like that one, I like to sound them."

"You do not wish her to think you would make an old drudge of her? you planned more work for her to be done in a week than you would ever do! The children have been here six months, and you have complained every day that they were so much trouble; when the most you have done is to prepare their food."

"Think what she's a mind to, I don't care! One thing I know: after she gets to house-keeping, I'll be just the person that'll pay the lady a visit, and see how she treats them children—of course she'll abuse them. Wall, there is one thing about it, and that is this:—what I can't see way off up here, sister Tattum can; for Walter told me to-day he had rented that pretty, white cottage on the corner just across the way from her; and she'll tell me if anything goes wrong with that woman and the children."

"How sorry I am that you are so meddlesome! you and Mrs. Tattum are off the same piece; and two-thirds of all the rows kicked up in the neighborhood where she resides, have been through her instrumentality. Why can't you stay at home and mind your own business? I wish you would let that busybody alone."

"But it is my bounden, Christian duty to do just as I am doing; and you, nor no one else, has any right to interfere with a person when they are trying to do just as they orto do. Now if I should neglect those little motherless children, which, you know, would be one of the sins of omission, how could I ever kneel with you around the family altar? and how would I feel, when I was reading out of the Bible this express commandment: 'Train up a child in the way it should go?' Now, John, let me alone; let me have my own way, for duty I will do, and duty I must do, as I expect to escape punishment at the last day."

"Thank God, I do not see mine as you do!"

CHAPTER XI.

After a week spent here, it was decided that Walter Clayton and his wife should board through the winter, and commence house-keeping in the spring. So they took rooms at the residence of their brother-in-law, near his business, a comfortable place, and always cheery on account of its happy inmates, which consisted of Major and Mrs. Cliffton, and a little daughter of three summers.

All settled, Elice determined, though not happy, to make the best of circumstances; to always wear a pleasant smile; and, under no provocation, to allow herself to rebel against any of her husband's wishes; for, had she not promised to "love and obey?" And her life, she thought, would be much more peaceful, even though it seemed exacting and tyrannical; for after all, it might mean nothing, simply a pressure of business and his great care, that made him sometimes appear what he was not—her great, noble, manly husband—taciturn and sullen; and at any cost, she would bring back those smiles that had won her heart.

But the more she yielded, the more she had to, until her identity seemed likely to be swallowed up and lost in his iron will; while he laid down rules, only for the purpose of having them obeyed, continually alluding to his first wife, telling with much pathos, how she did this or that; how much better way it was; how industrious she had been; how useful; and, finally, winding up by saying, "If she had only lived, it would have been so different with me and the children!"

One day he went to 'a desk and brought out a gold locket containing her miniature. "Dear little soul!" he exclaimed, "we never had a word in our lives."

Mr. and Mrs. Cliffton, who were in the adjoining room, heard every word that he said.

("Listen," said she, '"We never had a word in our lives? Now, if they did not, it was because she would not quarrel with him. But you remember, Cliffton, when they boarded with us, they would sometimes go three days without speaking to each other; but I always thought it was his fault—in fact, I knew it was.")

"I always let her do just as she had a mind, and never undertook to dictate her; but she had so much more sense than a common woman," Walter continued, "that it was unnecessary."

("Listen again," said Mrs. Cliffton.—"Now you mind the terrible scolding she got when she dressed a little different from what he told her, at the time they were invited to that party at Mr. Simpson's? Although she said she was sorry, and if he would wait a moment, she would change to suit him, he turned contemptuously upon his heel, went off in another direction, and left her at home to weep over his abuse and neglect.")

"I always told her to come to the store whenever she wanted money or anything else, and she got it, if I had it; and I had it you may be sure, generally."

("That's enough, now," said Mrs. Cliffton, vexed beyond measure, "and it's a falsehood too; for she worked for the store for most everything she got; and he knows it as well as we do, don't he?")

"I think he ought to," replied Major Cliffton, "for I knew it; and, still further, that she went beyond her strength trying to do her own work to please him; and lost her life at last in the vain endeavor; and he never appreciated her until she was laid away in the silent grave; and so it will be with this one, I fear, for she is altogether too good-natured. I wish he'd got some one like old Ketchum's wife; wouldn't she make him walk the chalk line, and 'no tripping either, Jack Ketchum'?"

"But he would not live with such a woman a month; they would quarrel and fight, and then separate."

"No, they wouldn't either. I know him like a book; he's like a big hound, the more you box him, the better he is."

"Not exactly that either; if a woman would assert her rights, and let him know she was determined to have them, she would be treated far better. I do not believe in being trodden upon: I do not believe in a tame submission to all the despotic claims a man may assert. Each has rights."

"And you would fight for yours, wouldn't you, pet?"

"I never had occasion."

"And if you had?"

"I'd box you, right and left," she said, laughingly—"see here; and pull your ears just like this"—reaching forth her soft hands toward his head, which, however, he caught and kissed, telling her to be very careful how she waged war upon him; for every offense she would receive like punishment.

Still Elice stitched away on a dress for Blanche; she had it almost finished; she held it up and showed her husband, and asked him if he did not think it was pretty.

"It looks well enough," he replied. "Where did you get the cloth to make it of?"

"But is it not real nice," said Elice, trying to smile.

"I told you it was well enough, for all I know; it is not as her own mother would have made it, though. Now, if I remember, the child's dresses were all low necks and short sleeves; and she didn't put on so many flummydiddles—but you didn't answer my question."

"I took the five dollars you gave me and bought it; dear little Blanche needed it so badly."

"Needed it! quite likely she did. Why didn't you ask me, before you went into this piece of extravagance? Now, I gave you that money just for a trial. If you knew enough to save it and show it to me again when I asked you about it, I would have given you as much more sometimes, perhaps; but all you will get out of me in the future will be a caution. I want you to understand that my wife was no such spendthrift as that; and I always, as I said before, gave her all the money she wanted. If there was anything she needed, that our store could not supply, she would tell me so, and I would hand out ten or twenty dollars; as I knew that every cent would come back to me, to the last penny, of what was left after she had made her purchases."

("Another falsehood!" said Mrs. Cliffton, "he never gave her twenty cents in her life without a fuss; and she was heart-broken over his penuriousness and dogged selfishness. It does excite me, when I know Elice has been striving so hard to please him; spent her own money for this garment; sewed on it when he was abed and asleep; and then, to hear him talk so insultingly to her in reference to it.")

CHAPTER XII.

"Would you like a ride?" said Walter Clayton, coming in very early one morning, and tapping his wife on the shoulder.

"Certainly, nothing would please me better. Are you going immediately?"

"No, I have a little business to attend to, which will take me half an hour."

"Well, that will please me, as I have one room to adjust, and several other matters to see to." Then unclasping a little jeweled time piece, a gift of her mother, said "It's now half-past six; I will be ready at seven o'clock sharp—don't come before."

Fifteen minutes, however, only passed, and Walter made his appearance.

"Back this soon?" Elice said gaily.

"Of course. Didn't I tell you to hurry up?"

"You know you said half an hour; but give me but a moment longer, to attend to my birdies, and then we'll away."

Elice ran, rather than walked; but as she had to go to the pump for fresh water for her canaries, she was longer than she otherwise would have been.

"Mrs. Clayton," Walter said vexatiously, "you are slower than cold molasses! Now, my other wife would have been ready long, and long ago; she was the spryest person I ever saw; all I would have to say was, 'Come, wife, do you want to go with me?' and she put on her things in a jiffy and went."

He had a spirited horse, and he had tied it to a small tree; and while he was talking it tore up the sapling and ran away. No damage was done, however, only to the tree, for he could not get far with this cumbrous weight; but it proved of sufficient magnitude to cause Walter to pour out his invectives on the horse and Elice in particular.

"This is all your fault, Elice, and now you can stay at home. What made you keep me waiting so everlastingly?" said he, with the most intense passion. "I never could have believed there was such a difference in women! Now, Lola would have watched out of the window every minute, after I told her we were going, and the moment she saw me drive up would have bounded out to meet me like a deer; she wouldn't have waited for me to hitch up, I'll warrant you; and then that tree wouldn't have been ruined, and—well, I wouldn't have it to pay for."

"I am very sorry," said Elice, "but let us drop the subject and have our cozy little ride."

"If you will promise never to keep me waiting."

"Not for one moment, if I can help it; but the half hour you assigned me has not even yet expired."

Soon they were on the way to his father's. A mile was passed in perfect silence. He then broke forth by saying, "Do you always intend to be as tardy as you were this morning, Elice? Now, supposing the horse had succeeded in getting away, had injured himself and broken that elegant, new sleigh of ours; don't you see what a string of accidents we should have had? and you would have been all to blame—such a wife! As mother says, marriage is all a lottery; nobody knows just whom he is getting."

They were soon alighting at the residence of old Mr. Clayton. Once in and seated, Walter told the whole of the morning adventures, laying the catastrophe to Elice; no one responding, however, but the old lady, who occasionally broke in with, "Dew tell! Wasn't that awful? You don't say! La! Sus!"

Once alone, however, she freed her mind about her daughter-in-law. "Now, wasn't that a shame, father?" she said, "the way that woman treated poor Walter?"

"I don't see that she was at all to blame."

"Why! why! and keep him waiting an hour and a half, when he told her to hurry up? and she must know what a frisky, wisky horse he has, by this time. I declare to man, I believe she is as lazy as that old cat yonder! But who ever saw a girl brought up like she, to go to school all the time, that ever was good for anything?"

"What about your own daughter, that is constantly in attendance at the academy?"

"Wall, that's different, you know; you couldn't spile her, no way you could fix it up; but she's no common girl."

"No," he replied, "a mother, and a mother-in-law are two different and distinct people, also; their own children are angels—others—well—devils. I like Elice; I always did from the moment I first set eyes upon her. I took (and have seen nothing to change my mind since) her for a rare woman. If Walter would do anything near right, I believe she would be one of the best wives in existence. See how patient she was under his censures."

"But you know, John, she is nothing like the other."

"It is very strange that death will transform a person the way it did Lola. When she was alive, you found as much fault with her as you now do with Elice."

"Humph! John," exclaimed the old lady contemptuously, and left the room.

CHAPTER XIII.

The winter with its days of shadows and storms has passed away; the heart of Elice has grown wondrous light within a few days, for she has been promised a visit to the home of her parents; and, as she sits and listens to the chirpings of the birds, which tell how near the summer is at hand with all its array of light and beauty, she forgets the lack of sunshine in the long, cheerless months that have just passed; she forgets everything, but the pleasant, sunny home of her girlhood, the faces of those that have become a thousand times more dear to her since her absence from them; and she looks forward to the hour when she will turn her footsteps thitherward, with a yearning she never felt before; and she can scarcely wait for the moment to arrive when she may be permitted to clasp her loved ones once again to her bosom, and feel their warm kisses upon her cheek.

But the time came at last, and it was decided that little Blanche should bear her company. So she started on the journey with her for a sole companion; but she was not lonely, for who would be with such a great pair of black eyes as this little darling possessed, that drank in all the beauty with which they came in contact, and such a chatterbox to tell what she saw and heard? She rehearsed in glowing colors, her adventures of the past season, when she was taking a trip with her own mamma, and was lost in the great city of Rochester, at the time of changing cars.

"I wath tho skart; and I fot I never should thee my mamma again in my life long; and I cried tho hard, and big man athed me who I wath, and where I wath going; and I thaith to grandpapa's; where doth you s'poth a little girl would be going? and my name is Blanche; and I got out of the carths yonder; and, oh, dear! that very minute my dear mamma was looking all over for me; and I tell you, she got right fast hold of me, and kithed and kithed me, and then s'e cried. What made s'e cry?"

"For joy, I suppose," said Elice, "she was so glad her darling was not lost."

Blanche than sat for an hour without speaking; after which she looked up angrily, and said, "My grandmamma theth s'e speths you'll lick me like blazes, sometimes; and if you doth, s'e ith going to tell my papa. Be you going to do it?"

Elice answered her by drawing her little lips to hers a dozen times. "Like this, and this, and this, darling little one," she says. "Is that what grandmma meant?"

"I dunno, only s'e said you wuth my step-muzzer, and they wuth awful hateful; and s'e told me about one little dirly, what had one of zem fings, and s'e shut her up and spanked her, and all for nossin at all. Be ye going to shut me up?"

"You will not need it little one; you will be so good, won't you?" said Elice.

"Not if you stold me, nor lick me, I wont!" said the little thing with her eyes flashing wrathful sparks.

"But if I should buy you big dollies, and pretty picture books like this?" as she took one from the hand of the book agent, who just then happened to be passing.

"Wy zen I'd like you, and tiss you, and be so nithe to you."

A lady attracted by the prattle of Blanche, came and took a seat just ahead of them. She looked at Elice, and then at Blanche, her curiosity alert to find out the relationship existing between them; and began to think she might be a little sister.

Soon, however, hearing the child call her mamma, she enquired if, indeed she was her mother.

"Do we look alike?"

"Yes, I see a great resemblance; but did not think you could be a mother, and so young."

"I am one of those hateful creatures people call a step-mother."

"Be assured of my sympathy, then, for I know what it is. You are young, little girl, but don't let them run over you. Let them know, just half the time, at least, that you are mistress, yourself. We read great books about step-mothers —their cruelty to poor little helpless children; but never a word about their vexations. One would think they had nothing to do but recline on a bed of roses. If so, there are many thorns to pierce their fingers, and tear the hands; arrows aimed straight at their hearts—if they can dodge them, well and good, if not they must submit with a quiet Christian grace, for who ever had any sympathy for such monsters as step-mothers? They may be angels, they may strive with all their powers of heart and mind to do right and to please all parties concerned, but it would be just as easy for a 'camel to go through the eye of a needle;' to remove a mountain and cast it in the midst of the sea. I know, little one, and when you have had my experience, you will know too; but I trust you will not reap tares where you expected to gather wheat; that no deadly asp with its venomous sting will coil among your house plants. But you have no cause, I presume, to worry, for without doubt you have a kind and loving husband, and a good mother-in-law."

Elice smiled.

"If I can read character from the face of an individual, I should take you to be one of the mildest of children (excuse me for the appellation, for you look so childish); you might be buffeted, kicked, and cuffed around, and no one would be any the wiser for it; you would clasp the hand that smote you,

and kiss the lips that pronounced their words of vengeance ;
but hours would drag their weary lengths along, your sky would
grow darker day by day, until the sun to your childish heart
would have ceased shining ; your eyes would have become
sunken, that pretty rounded cheek lose its pink and grow as
white as this cluster of snowdrops in my hand, but you would
smile just the same, and, while people were admiring your
cheerful disposition and wondering you could always be so
happy, your heart would be breaking. Finally, and not very
long before the shroud and the coffin, the tuberoses and daises
would be substituted for the beautiful orange blossoms, and
bridal veil. Isn't that true ? "

Elice did not reply ; the picture was one upon which she did
not care to look.

The lady continued,—"We are different. While I do not
court the storm, I should not mind it as you would. You do
not wish to hear my story ? It is too painful."

"Yes, yes ; go on !"

" As you desire. I was younger yet than you are when I
was married. I idolized my husband, for I thought him everything noble and good. He was a widower with three chidren ;
had one of the loveliest homes in the world, on the banks of
the Hudson river, where we could sit, if we chose, and see
the steamers glide over this beautiful stream, fish, or go sailing ; while we had music of every description in the house to
help beguile the hours in his absence. He was wealthy—my
wishes only thought seemed gratified—never returning from
his visits to the city of New York, where business so often
called him, without bringing me costly, even extravagant presents. This man, Roderick Augustine, was my first, my only
love; I saw with his sight, his words inspired me, I lived for
him and him alone, for he was the personation of my ideal—
tall, handsome, witty, social, genial, and so kind and good to
me. You know how bright the whole world was to me, I
know you do, for you have felt the same silken cord drawing

you closer and closer to another, the same link binding and cementing you, till your whole being was lost and swallowed up in that of your husband; so it was with me. With the love of the children and their father, what more could I desire to make my paradise? We had a sail-boat constructed purposely for ourselves, and oh, so often, times without number, did we explore every nook and crevice all along the banks of the river, bringing home the loveliest flowers, stones, and shells, rare birds and insects, to place with other things in his cabinet, of which he was so fond.

"And so time winged on, for about three years; then some acquaintance, from maliciousness caused from an envious spirit, grew meddlesome, and poisoned the minds of the children, setting them up against me, until their actions became almost intolerable. Through these it at last extended to their father, until he at length became cold, then morose, and did not treat me even civilly; but this did not drive from my breast the love which had so inspired me; in consequence of which I bore my agony and grief for years, without the slightest idea of rebelling; when one morning, after being closeted an hour with his mother, he came out and struck me a blow in the face, which nearly stunned me, uttering an oath at the same time, and calling me hard names.

"Stung to the heart, and maddened to a degree I never had felt before in my life, I rushed out of the house, and in a paroxysm of woe, resolved to throw myself into the river and end my sufferings. It was night—ten o'clock—oh, what a lovely sky! the moon was at its full; and the stream, as far as the eye could reach, was but one silver crest of beauty. I was on the bank, just about to take the fatal leap, when a voice, as from Heaven, bade me stop. It was my mother's, my darling mother's; there was no mistaking it; an angel had come to deter me from that fatal step.

"I had not been here long, before I heard footsteps in the dis-

4

tance, and, hiding behind a group of trees, I thought I would wait and see who it was.   As I anticipated, it was my husband in search of me.   Becoming repentant, I thought he had come to find me to ask my forgiveness for his cruel treatment—not so; he spied me and bade me go into the house, at once.   I asked him what I had done, and why I was so ill-treated. 'Enough,' he answered.

"'But I will never step my foot beneath your roof, unless you tell me what is the matter, and on your bended knees ask my forgiveness.'

"'Your forgiveness, demon! one who has been striving so hard to kill my children?'

"'Kill your children!   You are certainly insane!   What can you mean?'

"'I was so informed,' he replied.

"'A base falsehood!' I cried passionately.

"'Didn't you purchase arsenic at the drugstore and spread it on bread, and lay down purposely for the little girls to get hold of?'

"'Never! never!   Who told you so?'

"'I will not tell.'

"'But you shall tell, and you shall prove it!   Husband or devil, whichever you are, the law shall settle this little slander! Now tell me who was your informant, for I will not rest under this vile calumny—tell me, and tell me instantly.'

"Frightened by my manner, and fearing consequences, he told me all, keeping nothing back, but the author of the mischief.

"I proved to him my innocence, but took the next train bound for New York, where my father resided, and have never seen, or heard of the family since.

"Thus ended my dream of happiness; thus, quickly, turned my cup of joy into wormwood and gall.   The world is all changed since then ; and oh, how changed! But don't mind this little bit of my life's history.   Do not let it worry you, for yours will be different.   Do not look so disconsolate, for you will have no such bitter experience. Forgive me, if my tale of sorrow casts a shadow over your young heart, for it was not intended. But I could not help speaking; I could not refrain telling it, when I saw you with that child, and found that, like me, you were a step-mother."

By this time the train had reached the depot at Rockville, and the passengers had commenced to alight; and, after bidding the strange lady adieu, Elice and little Blanche started for the hotel, to await the early morning train bound for Woodville; and as Elice laid her head on the pillow, she felt a strange restlessness, still a happy consciousness that only a few miles were to be travelled, before she should behold the ones that now, of all the world, she held most dear. But when she did, she was roaming over the fair woodland and bright meadows, or holding sweet converse with her darlings in that bright and cheery home whither she was bound.

Morning came—it was so long in coming, she thought. Several times she had mistaken the straggling moonbeams that quivered through the shutters, for the dawning of daylight, and had arisen to find herself mistaken; but now it was surely here. The porter had given the signal to make ready for the departure, and not an hour would elapse before she would be on her way.

Joy! joy! Was anyone ever so happy before? the bright present shut out all the gloom of the past.

But the time passed in rosy anticipation, and found Elice and her little charge seated in the cars ready to make the last point in their home-bound trip.

On, on, sped the iron horse which soon brought them to Woodville.

"Just as I expected, darling," said Elice, kissing Blanche again, scarcely knowing what she did, "papa is coming for us with my own pet pony and the phæton—dear, dear papa!"

"Where, mamma?" said Blanche; but ere she could reply, they had alighted from the cars, and were folded in the embrace of her dear father, Mr. Woodville; and as they drove away to their home, it was hard to tell which of the party was the happiest, he, Blanche, or Elice. Mrs. Woodville was at the gate with arms open wide to receive them. Elice, on seeing her in the distance, began to hum "The Beautiful Gates Ajar;" when Blanche, with her sweet voice, chimed in.

"Oh mamma! mamma!" she cried, on alighting and throwing her arms about her neck, "the gates are indeed passed, and Heaven is won; would that it were forever and ever."

Each wept and laughed alternately, their rapture was so intense. When Mrs. Woodville could sufficiently command her voice to speak, she said, "Thank God! thank God for this blessed moment! I did not know I should ever miss you so much, my darling; it seemed as though you had been gone for years, and would never come back to us; but here you are, the same Elice as ever, only paler and thinner. Are you not well?"

"Certainly I am."

"And happy?"

"Most assuredly," replied Elice, determined that a knowledge of her troubles should not come to the ears of her parents to mar their happiness in their declining years; praying that the canker worm that was sapping the life from her young heart should never be revealed to them.

CHAPTER XIV.

A few weeks of uninterrupted pleasure have passed ; Elice returns again to Lavarre.

As the elder Mrs. Clayton had remarked to her husband, Walter had rented a house across from the Tattums. Elice was sorry for this; for, from what she had herself seen, and still more from the gratuitous information of the old lady, she had not formed the best opinion of them; but still she said nothing, as fault-finding made up no part of her nature; and, when the household goods arrived, she commenced arranging them with all possible speed, turning this bit of soiled carpet and that, so all might appear at its best, and revarnishing each separate piece of furniture, while everything brightened as if by magic. Then the beds and bedding must be renovated ; the curtains hung and draped; the unpainted pantry and kitchen floors scoured until they were white as snow.

Once finished, Elice took a survey of her work, and although everything was of the cheapest material, she had the satiefaction of knowing that the whole house was clean and neat ; and yet, there were several rooms for which there were no carpets ; but she thought her husband would attend to this upon his return from his business journey to Philadelphia.

" He will be pleased when he sees how nicely I have everything arranged; even his first wife or mother could have done no better."

He came at last, and she met him at the door with a kiss— her usual custom.

"Don't you see papa, what we have been doing? isn't it nice?" and taking hold of his arm, said, "Come, let me take you over our cozy little house."

He shook her off, and gruffly said, "Can't you let a person alone, when they are tired and hungry? I can see from here. Is supper ready?"

"No," said Elice, "it is not yet time by a whole hour and a half."

"Not ready! you knew I'd be hungry!"

"How should I know that?"

"Oh, you don't, of course, but Lola would, mighty quick."

"Not unless you told her."

"Know! know! Why she knew everything without telling!"

"Doubtless. But be a little patient, and we will have your tea in less time than we have been talking about it."

"Hurry up, then; don't be fooling around here! I wish you weren't so slow!"

"I never was called that," said Elice."

"For you never did anything in your life, I suppose."

Elice did not reply. Another arrow had been sent; she felt its sting, and laid her hand upon her wounded heart. All night long she tossed her restless head upon the pillow.

"If I could only be appreciated," she thought. "Must I drag out this miserable existence? Are all my beautiful visions to vanish? Would that I could die!"

In the morning her cheeks were flushed, her lips red and swollen; she had a burning fever. Her husband did not know of her illness, as he left his bed when he found she was so restless, declaring he could not sleep a wink, wishing she would lie still and not disturb him. So she told him nothing of her terrible headache, lest he should be more angry than ever.

Business called him out of town that day, and when he returned she was delirious. All the long day she had been uttering incoherent sentences; sometimes hurrying to have all the work done up so nicely before papa returned; again, scouring the tin, wondering if it would ever be bright; then mending the carpet; but all the time so fearful she would not be in readiness to receive her husband.

"All done at last!" she murmured; "and now we will make some nice cake—some of those tarts, you know, he likes so well, Bridget.'

"What does she mean?" said Mrs. Clayton, who, with her daughter, Mrs. Cliffton, had just called.

"She means, mum," said Bridget, crisply, who had watched over her all day, "that she has worrikt so haird, and been so ill trated she got sick. If it had been me that had jist sich a mon, I would have broak his back bone. Why, afther we ware all through, mum, and the poor little dair wus jist as tired as could be, she wanted him, whin he came home, to go over the house, and see jist how nice we had got things; and, troth, he wouldn't do it; and ordered her to go and get supper for him, en I dun know what all, mum! Fath, he may be your son, but if he ware mine!" and she clenched her fists with rage.

Mrs. Ashton, another lady, called; said she had heard of the illness of Mrs. Clayton, and had come to see how it was.

"Quite sick," said the mother-in-law. "The truth is, she has taken a severe cold; and her health hain't no time none the best; she's a poor, sickly creetur, anyway, to make the best on't."

"Sickly crathur, mum!" said Bridget, "and is that what yer afthur calling the mistress? And its yerself would be sickly, if ye'd worrikt so haird as she for the past thray wakes. Ivry thing out of rig, mum; the children, bless their little souls, had to be looked afther; their clothes to wash and mend; the house to rid up from top till the bottom; and what, mum, was wust of all, the masther was so cross; and the poor thing not been used to the likes, it hurtted her, I'm sure, thin. So, fath, whin she was so used up like, afthur puttin' to right thim old fixins of hisn any dacent mon would a' pitched into the street, she got sick."

The old lady strove hard to deter Mrs. Ashton from entering the room where Elice lay; but, the door being slightly open, she caught sight of her, and begged her to come in. As Mrs. Ashton entered she cried, "O, mamma! mamma! I'm so glad you have come. Why did you wait so long? dearest, sweetest mamma! Come, lay your hand upon my head just as you used to do, and kiss away my tears. Don't you see how I have been weeping! Not one of them love me, and I tried so hard to please them; but it's no use, at all. Take me home again, oh, won't you?"

Mrs. Ashton smoothed her hair caressingly, and kissed her fevered brow, and thus she soothed her.

"Have the birds built their nests under my window yet, mamma? Oh, they have! they have! I hear them singing so sweetly. Why, yes, we're home; I'm so glad! Do not let me go away again, will you, mamma?"

By this time Walter had finished his supper, and waited to smoke his pipe, as usual, after meals; he then repaired to his wife's room, to see what all the ado was about.

Finding Mrs. Ashton there, he assumed a look of anxiety; and, approaching the bedside, attempted to take his wife's hand; but she drew it away, and, uttering a faint scream, asked if he had come to take her away again.

"Why, Elice," said he, "don't you know me?" She pressed her hand to her head and answered, "I believe so— yes, I do. You came into my garden and robbed me of all my flowers. Why!—why!"—and, quivering from head to foot—"you set me in a scorpion's nest. When you told me you loved me so much, you said I was your idol, didn't he, mamma? But you won't let him take me away again!"

When he found he could not pacify her, he hastily said, "She must be kept quiet; we had better go out of the room."

"No, no, mamma, stay with me!" she piteously cried.

"I will stay with her all night; she is very ill, and needs the strictest care."

"Thank you," said her husband, "but we will not trouble you; I will watch by her myself,"—wishing her to believe him so tender and true.

"No trouble, I assure you; I can soothe her, and that is what she needs."

"Now the fact is," said Walter, "Elice is not strong—she never was; now it's a bad thing for a man circumstanced as I was, to marry a sickly woman."

"I believe her work had something to do with her sickness; for I was at your house several times, and she was hurrying as fast as she could to get everything arranged. She seemed to be very well then; but extremely fatigued."

"There was no need of that; she had a servant."

"But one servant cannot do everything. At such a time, Mr. Clayton, there is no end of work. She is far too ambitious; the whole cause of her illness is overtaxation of both mind and body."

"She has no need of any trouble or worry, as you well know, Mrs. Ashton."

"I hope not," she answered, with the slightest smile of scorn curling her honest lips.

"I know she has not!"

"You know best. If you have not always done right, pour on the healing balm from to-night."

"What do you mean?" said he angrily.

"Oh, nothing; the whole thing rests now between your conscience and your God. But I will stay to-night," she said, laying aside her bonnet and shawl; "I am used to the sick room."

All night long she sat by the bedside of Elice and gave her medicine. In the morning she recognized her and was so happy that she was with her.

"I must have been dreaming," Elice said in a whisper, "or has my mother been here?"

"No, Mrs. Clayton, do you wish to see her?"

"Oh, yes," she replied; "my sweet, sweet mamma!" while the tears sprang to her eyes and rolled down her face, which was now pale as death.

"You see, Mrs. Ashton," she said in a whisper, "I worked so hard and had none of the best of treatment, and so I got sick. Oh, dear, I didn't mean to tell it; I never do say anything; but it's out now, and I cannot help it."

"How is Elice this morning?" said the old lady coming in with one of her most hypocritical smiles.

"A little better," said Mrs. Ashton; "but she must be kept very quiet. You had better take the children home with you, as their noise will disturb her."

"Wall, certainly—poor child! I am so sorry for her! Do you think she will get well? Isn't it a pity she is so sickly like?"

"It is really a shame she has had so much to worry about," said Mrs. Ashton.

"Oh, she's had nothing to fret her. Don't you see how well she has been provided for?—the hull house carpeted from head to foot. Walter is such a liberal, hull-souled fellow; there never was nothin' too good for his wives; it's a lucky woman that got my son, I tell you, now."

It was neither the time nor place to discuss the matter; but Mrs. Ashton resolved she would have a talk with both mother and son some time—not that she wished to interfere, but for the sake of Elice who, she knew, had been downtrodden ever since she came into the family.

CHAPTER XV.

Six months have passed. The honeysuckles and wild briars that shade the windows of the sick room are putting forth their buds and blossoms; the bright scarlet geraniums and fragrant heliotropes are bending and bowing with the delightful breezes of a June morning, while the dew is yet upon the grass. Elice is well again, and her heart goes out in thankfulness to the great God above for all his tenderness and watchful care of her, through the long weary days and weeks that she has been obliged to stay within doors.

Early in the spring she had visited the grave of Lola, and for the interest she felt in that child wife who died while yet in her teens, she had covered her tomb with pure white daisies, and planted lovely roses at her head and feet; and then each morning, until she was taken ill, had either gone forth at an early hour, or sent some one to water them. And her heart went out to this beautiful spot, wondering if the grass were not choking out all those flowers, and if they were not already dead for want of attention. So she thought she would take the children by the hand and go to the cemetery, and show them the grave of their darling mother, who, had she lived, would have loved them more sincerely than any other person, no matter how strong her depth of affection; for she wished them to cherish a remembrance of one who had watched over their early infancy; who had sung for them the lullaby, and soothed all their little troubles on her loving breast. She wished them to imitate the example of one whom, though never knowing in person, she believed, from all she heard, to have been one of Christ's loving chosen followers, and who now was wearing a crown of rejoicing at His right hand.

They entered the cemetery and wound their way to the trees overshadowing her tomb, and sat down to rest. As had been anticipated, the grass was growing rank among the flowers, and they were parched and withering under the strong rays of the summer sun. After a few moments Elice brought water from a crystal spring that bubbled near, and sprinkled them; then, with the help of the little ones, pulled out every blade of grass from among the mosses and daisies, after which they all seated themselves once more near the grave to talk of the loved one that lay beneath the sod; the children, to hear more of "the bye and bye," and how they might live to meet their mother at the breaking of morning into beautiful dawn, beyond the river of death, when the night is past. She told them of the Heavenly City—the new Jerusalem—whose streets were paved with gold; of the blessed Jesus who had died for them; and in the simplest manner possible, the story of the cross on Calvary's rugged mountain; and while Blanche seemed to understand, the boy, who was too young to know all she said, was just as earnest a listener.

"Up there, mamma? Is that where Heaven is, among the tlouds? Ith my other mamma up there, and the Thaviour too; and dothe He love all the little childrun, and bruver Charlie, too?" said Blanche.

Elice answered that he did, and told her how He was once here upon earth, and laid His hands upon the heads of little boys and girls and blessed them.

"And how will we get there, mamma? Will papa take us with a horse and tarriage; and will dolly horse go too; and all these big birdies and little birdies, too?"

"Buddies," lisped baby Charlie, while he rolled his great, black eyes toward the trees, where the robins were flitting from limb to limb, and piping forth their plaintive notes, as if singing a requiem for the departed, and sharing with the little group their sorrow.

"Mamma cannot tell you, love, of all the beauties up yonder." "'For eye hath not seen nor ear heard,'" she added to herself. "'In this world ye shall have tribulation, but in me ye shall have peace.' Oh, the bright, bright beyond! how well we can bear all our affliction here, if it only helps to give us an entrance into Heaven, where Jesus is; our dear, dear Saviour who gave himself a ransom for all the world!"

After another long, sad look at the grave of Lola, they turned their footsteps homeward.

"Dathes, mamma, 'fore do!" lisped the baby.

"Yes, sweet," said Elice, breaking a few from their stems, and placing them in his hand.

"Now dint, mamma."

Elice went to the spring, and got him water, and, smiling— "What next, pet?"

"Buddies—tat home wid me."

"But we cannot catch them."

"Me tan," he lisped, and, breaking loose from her hand, ran toward a bush, where one had alighted—"Oh, dear! dot way!"—when he commenced to cry.

His tears were soon dried, however, for he had the promise of a picture book, a doll, and a lot of pretty toys; while Blanche assured him that he should have the first bird she could get anywhere, to put in his little gilded cage.

Baby's eyes sparkled—"Won't that be nithe?" said Blanche.

"Et," he replied, holding up his ripe, rosy lips to kiss her.

All that night Blanche was dreaming; but she verily believed the little story to be true, that she told on the following morning.

"I thaw thuch lots of anthels—oh, they were tho butiful! and the blethed Thaviour, and my thweet, thweet other mamma! S'e took me in her armths, and asthed me if I did not want to go wis her.   And we all that down by a great, big, bright river, where I tood thee over into Heaven—I dess—that's what my mamma thed it was; and I heard musit—oh, thuch a big, big, band! and they were all dresthed in white; and birdies and flowers, more than I ever thaw before in my life; and Jethus thed, 'Be a dood little dirlie, and thumtime I will take you over there, and you thall have a dolden harp like thothe bright thpirits you thee yonder.'   Will he tum for me?   He thed he would; but I want you to go too, mamma, and baby Charlie, or elth I rather stay here alwayths."

CHAHTER XVI.

"There are so many things we need," said Elice to her husband, "to make us comfortable and respectable. I have repaired the children's old clothes until I can do it no longer. They need hats and wraps, shoes and stockings, in fact, everything that constitutes their wardrobe."

"I presume so. Always wanting something. I never saw just such a woman as you are. Some folks need so much more than others, and you, Elice, are·just one of that sort; now my first wife seldom asked me for anything—was one of the most economical women I ever saw, and could make cloth or groceries go the farthest of any one in the world, I believe."

"What would she do, if, as in this instance, the children's clothes had given entirely out, and they were hatless and shoeless?"

"Why! why! she would mend them, and keep mending them and no one would ever know where the patch was put on, she was so neat about it; made all their shoes, and her own sometimes; although I told her she need not and should not, for I much preferred to buy them, than have her work so hard. Why! why! I always got her everything she asked for, and more too. I tell you she was a great wife to me. If she only had lived."

"But you say she never wanted anything at one time, and then at another you got her everything she desired. Now it seems strange that a young person like Lola, with all the hopes and aspirations of a mother, would not want to see her darlings neatly clothed."

"Can't you understand, she scarcely ever asked me for anything—wasn't eternally and everlastingly dunning me, day and night, for everything she saw. It would take an independent fortune to keep you in what you wanted. I'll tell you just how she did get the most of her things—industrious little body—sewed for our store; for she said she rather do it than to take that much out of the business; and then—dear little economical creature—kept every penny of her hard earnings; I verily believe she was more saving than myself, and when I went off to buy my goods, would say, " Here now, Walter, is my money; take it and get so and so, and so and so—I can't tell all what—for the children and me. I'd never spend any of it for myself, do you suppose I would? Why, no! but have often put as much as a dollar or so with it and surprised her by bringing home more than she expected. Let me tell you a little incident that occurred, for it may do you good. One time after I got to the city, I thought I would get a nice present for her, she had toiled so Hard, been such a good little wife, done without a hired girl, and had work-hands into the bargain; and so I got her one of the prettiest dress-patterns I could find at all. Well, I thought she would go off in ecstasies, as I had not purchased anything for her in a long, long time, but she said, 'Papa, put it in the store and sell it; the money will help you along so much; I can do with a cheaper one. Now what do you think of that? Don't you feel ashamed of yourself when you see how far you come behind her in almost everything?"

"Oh! wouldn't it be nice if, like the sheep, our wardrobe grew upon our backs, then it would not cost anything?"

"You'd manage somehow, then, to get rid of money, always spending, but never earning a cent."

"What would you have me do? I would gladly toil from morning till night, if I knew just what avocation you wished

me to follow, if you think I have not enough to do to take care
of the house and children; shall I take in washing?"

"You could at least do your own work. Lola never kept a
servant, nor ever hired any of her sewing done—dear, dear, if
she had only lived! How different, oh! how different it would
be with me now."

"What could she have done better than I do? Now, Walter, if I err in judgment, please inform me of my error, and I
will correct it if I can—I do not doubt that Lola was a good
woman, and made you one of the best of wives, but certainly
she never tried harder than myself to please you. But just
turn your thoughts back to the time when she lived, and see if
you were not as hard to suit as at the present. The grave,
you know, covers a multitude of faults, and I am glad it does,
for I should grieve to hear that dear one censured whose lowly
head now rests beneath the sod, and who could not come forth
if she would to speak in her own defense—no, talk to me as
you will, but never breathe one defamatory breath of her who
sleeps in the silent city of the dead."

Overcome by her feelings she left him and went to her room
—but adding to herself, "Where, oh, where I would fain follow were it the will of my Heavenly Father, for Walter makes
me so miserable. He strews my way with thorns which pierce
my heart each day, and casts a blot upon my otherwise happy
existence. Pretty birds, how I envy you, free from care; sing
on in your glad joyous strains and be merry, while my poor
heart is breaking—it cannot be otherwise. Only in Heaven can
I find rest to my soul. Beautiful sunset! once you gladdened
me with your brightness; the glorious halo that surrounds you,
the soft fleecy clouds, were a thing of joy; were there a black
one, it had a silvery lining; but alas! alas! there is no help
only in death. Blessed God, let me be faithful to Thee, and at
last—oh! at last, I shall have that peace of which I am here denied; a sweet rest at Thy right hand in Thy kingdom."

5

Morning came, and she resolved to muster courage to assail the "lion in his den"—she would go to the store and see what could be done.   So kissing each of the children a good by, she said, while tears ran down her cheeks, "You are his own bairns, and it's strange he would not dress you like princes; mamma is going to get you some pretty things, so you stay with Bridget until she returns, and be good little darlings—will you?"

"Yeth," answered Blanche, clasping her arms around her neck, "but you wont be don lon?"

"Eth," echoed baby Charlie, "tiss ou too."

"What do you want Elice?" said her husband after she had entered his store and stood before him trembling like a culprit.

"You know of what we were talking yesterday.   I thought I would fix up the children for the Sabbath School and church."

"Well, well, the babies must be dressed; if you see anything at all, you want for you or them, get it of course."   Then he turned to a bystander with the remark that he didn't want his family to be at all behind the times in dress, for he was able to give them everything for their comfort, and his money was always free as water, as far as they were concerned.

"What a good man," said a little boy, "how I wish I had such a papa."

"And I," remarked another, "and then I could have so many nice things."

"He is not as liberal as he pretends," said Mr. St. John, "I happen to know him, and I'll lay a wager that his wife does not get five dollars worth to-day."

"But he told her to take just what she wanted; what more could he do?" answered the gentleman addressed.

"But keep quiet and see I lose nothing.   Did you notice with what timidity she approached him?"

"That is her way, I presume."

"If you are not in a hurry, wait a bit, and see if my words are not true.   You take one of these papers and I will the other, we will be very much engaged with them; pretend to see, and hear nothing: but to satisfy yourself of his character, keep an eye out, just the same, all the time his wife is in the store."

"I will take a dress of this pretty cashmere. It's but a small pattern, but I think I can make it do."

By this time her husband had come within whispering distance, and asked her if she knew how expensive it was; that it was as much as fifty cents a yard, and she could not have it.

"Then this cambric, papa, oh, it's such a lovely pink! how well it would become our little Blanche!"

He gave her a look that well nigh demolished her, and said in an undertone, "You are satisfied with only the very best, I see; I'll select myself at my leisure and bring to the house, although I am very sure the children do not need a thing."

"Well, but please give me money to purchase hats."

"How much do you want?" he said very pleasantly, but loud enough to be heard all over the store at the same time—drawing his portemonnaie from his pocket.

"Three dollars, for both—I'll make this sum answer."

Really, I forgot about that large bill I settled yesterday; but I will draw on the bank and then you shall have all the money you desire. You had better go home now," with a hypocritical smile. Elice, heart-sick, left the store; she had been subjected again to mortification and grief by her husband, and where would it end?

"Oh! mamma is tumming wiz our new fings," said Blanche, clapping her hands in a perfect paroxysm of delight. "Now we is doin' to Sabbath Stool and to meetin'; ain't we, Charlie?" and she clasped him around the waist and held him up to the window where he could see as well as herself. "What you dot?" she asked, as her mother entered the door.

"Nothing, pet, but papa will bring you something, I guess."

"Oh, dear, but I fot I sud have sum new suse, an' a new bonnet; thee here how my tothes are sticking out."

"Yes, dear, I see it all."

Sure enough, Walter brought a large bundle, and, oh, how the heart of Elice leaped for joy! "I am so glad, so glad," she said.

He opened it and took out some faded remnants of goods which had been in the store for a long time, which no one would purchase, some coarse shoes, a cheap hat for the baby, but none for Blanche.

"How do you like my selection?" he asked.

"Not at all," replied Elice.

"Just as I expected, you always want the dearest of everything. You have high notions."

"You may think so; but supposing I have this cloth made up, which you ought to know is not at all suitable—a person who has been selling goods for so many years—besides the poor little dears being mortified to wear them, *we* would be censured, and justly. I would like to avoid this, would you not, papa?"

"I don't care; it's nobody's business what we put on our children, and I have got independence enough to tell them so, if I hear anything said."

"But it is not what other children wear. The cloth might be made into wrappers for the morning, but for no other time. I guess we will have something better, wont we, papa? Daughter must have the pink silk hat, and the pretty white Swiss for these hot days, for the Sabbath School ; and our bonnie Charlie, the little white chip trimmed with blue ribbons, the linen suit with the snowy pearl buttons. What do you say to that, duckies?"

The children actually danced with delight.

"Can't you see," said Walter, "how you are bringing those children up ? When they become grown, there will be nothing good enough for them."

"It is natural for little folks to have pride as well as older persons, and, to a certain degree, it is quite essential for their good."

"To bankrupt their fathers?"

"No, you cannot say this, for you have no cause. Now see here: I have made over my own clothes for them; that silk sacque worn by Blanche this summer, was one of mine; the lawn dress and aprons from garments that I had when we were married; and I have turned and twisted every way to save your money, so you cannot think I wish to waste, or be lavish at your expense. All I desire is, to see the family respectable."

"Well, there is one thing I want to say to you, and that is this: if you ever come into my store again, and there are customers in, and ask me for anything before them, you'll not get one penny's worth; for of course you know I wouldn't refuse you before them, but that is the way you take advantage of me; and I despise any one's playing such little underhanded tricks."

"I never thought it would make any difference."

"Well, it does, and don't you do it again. Now, seeing you take on so terribly, about dress, just tell me how much money you want to make your purchases, and if I've got enough to satisfy you, why, you can have it; but mind now, you must not ask me for anything again very soon."

She then made an estimate of the cost of some of the articles they most needed; then rolling a bill in his hands for some moments, as if hard to part with this portion of his treasures— but only a small portion of the amount desired—he handed it to her, but with a look so sour it haunted her all day, and took away much of the pleasure she felt in getting gifts for the wee ones; and when she had it spent and the things in her possession, she used the utmost care to get the most she possibly could out of a small pattern.

The faded garments were made into pretty little wrappers for the morning; the muslins and cambrics for afternoons and the Sabbath; and never was an own mother prouder or fonder than she, when she took her darlings by the hand on the following Lord's Day and went with them to church and Sabbath-school, dressed in their new suits which she had planned, and made; how many times an inward prayer went from her heart for this Divine favor, and how she thanked her Father above that had opened her husband's heart, and deprecated her lack of faith in Him who said, "Consider the lilies of the field how they grow, they toil not neither do they spin, and yet, I say unto you, that Solomon in all his glory was not arrayed like one of these. If God so clothe the grass of the field, which to-day is and to-morrow is cast into the oven, how much more will He clothe you,"—and she thought as she wound her way on that beautiful morning to hear of Christ out of His word, that trials of this life should no longer weigh down her spirits; but, like the clouds that floated along before her eyes, looking so like things of life, and drifting away from the dust and dross of earth, so should her heart rise above all sorrow and be fixed more steadily upon Heaven. And as she listened to the sermon preached from these words: "Forgive us our trespasses as we forgive them who trespass against us,"—another prayer went up that God would examine her heart, aud if she cherished a spirit of hatred, or revenge toward any person, that He would banish it at once, no matter how much she had been wronged or ill-treated by him—that perhaps it had been suffered for a trial of her faith. And she went home better prepared to bear the ills of life, with more of the subduing influences in her heart that keeps the Christian from retaliating in anger, when he is assailed, when he is persecuted, and obliged to bear the weight of the oppressor's power.

CHAPTER XVII.

"Good morning, Mrs. Clayton," said Mrs. Tattum, as the former lady appeared at her front door one morning. "You see my sleeves are rolled up ready for the washtub; but that's no difference; I am so glad you have come; now we will have a little cozy chat. Sit down."

"Wall, I don't want to hinder you, and wasn't intendin' to stay but jest a minute when I came in, and don't let me bother you."

"No bother at all; I've been wanting to see you this good while, and have a long conversation with you; for you are just the person I can free my mind with, and so of course, you are just the one that is never afraid of hearing the truth, and I've got so much to tell you."

"Wall jest so, I thought likely, mebbe you would have, and that's jest what I came in for; and I have things on my mind I want you to hear. You see, when any body has any trouble, they do like to have some one that can sympathize with them; and, as you was always one of my best friends, I never had any fear that anything I said would go any further. Of course you won't tell; for I don't like to have any disturbance with any body, and will bear most everything before I will say anything. Father says I am a fool for not pitching into folks and telling them just what I think; but you know that ain't me, Mrs. Tattum, and I can't do it. Now, I have lived a great many years in this town, and never had a word with nobody. Why, father says that's what no other women would have done, and he thinks—why—I don't want you to think I want to praise myself, or set myself up in no way; but I'ze telling just what he thinks—that I was almost a saint."

"Yes, I think myself you are. Now, see what care you took of those children, and what good care you took of them, too; and they were a world of trouble to you, and you never got one cent for it, did you?"

"Wall—no—yass—no—well, no, I didn't get much of nothing of any account."

"As much as eight dollars a week for both of 'em?"

"Why! who told you that? That ain't so; I only got six dollars, and then that wan't just nothin' at all, for all the trouble them children give me; but you know I didn't take 'em for money, poor little orphan, motherless children!"

"Ha! ha!" is Mrs. Tattum's inward ejaculation, "that, my lady, is what has roiled the water between you and your daughter-in-law—the loss of that six dollars!" but she said, "I know well you didn't, and it would be a great while before anyone would do just as you did. Why, I don't believe I would myself, and I've a pretty clear conscience as to what I ought to do."

"Wall, I come to ask you how you thought they wus gitting along over there; you know where I mean."

"To Walter's, I spose. Of course I know."

"The truth is, I haven't been there much lately, for the hired girl is so dumbed sassy, and snubs me at such a rate, I stay away. We had a little squirmish, and she hasn't treated me any too well ever since; and betwixt her and Walter's wife, I don't go any oftener than I can help; though I shall allers go to see those poor little, motherless, orphan children, jist as long as they live, for all of them."

"Why, of course, what was the muss all about?"

"Why, she was sassy and abused my son, and tried to make

out he didn't use his first wife well, and so on, when you know he's one of the very best men in the world."

"Certainly I do; and what's more, Clorinda Jones does; for I heard her say she worked for his first wife, and he was dreadful kind to her, and would be to this one, likely, if she were deserving it: but you know, sometimes step-mothers are not deserving."

"Well, that's jest what I wanted to get at—whether, living here as you do, so near, you thought she did use them children good or not."

"Now, I do not wish to make a fuss in any way; but I hear them crying a good deal, and what could they be crying about unless they were getting whipped?"

Mrs. Clayton, greatly excited—"And who could be whipping them, if it wan't that good-fer-nuthin step-mother of theirn?"

"That's so—that's just so—just exactly as I thought. Now, I'd be the last one to accuse anybody wrongfully, for you know I belong to the church in this very place, and it wouldn't be me that would tell anything but the truth."

"Wall, no, I don't believe you would," answered Mrs. Clayton.

"I'm sure you wouldn't tell to make me trouble, so I'll tell jsut what I do know."

"Sartinly not."

"All right, then. One day (I think it was in the morning) I heard a child scream; I went to the front door, and what should meet my astonished eyes!—well, no, I wasn't much astonished either, after all; it was just what one would expect of her; but, as I was saying, I went to the door and saw your daughter-in-law with a whip in her hand and Blanche by the side of her, and it was she who was taking on so. Now, you can be your own judge of what had happened."

"Wall, now, you don't say!" said the old lady, hitching up a little nearer. "Poor child, how she misses her own mother what's up now in Heaven!   I don't think she jest orter gone off in that way and left 'em poor leetle things; wall, no, that ain't jest what I mean after all; but I mean—"

"Well, I'll tell you what you mean,"—with an inward giggle, as she afterward said of the "old fool,"—"My daughter-in-law is in league with the evil one against those poor, little, motherless, orphan children!"

To which she made answer, "Jest so—I couldn't spoke my own mind any better."

"Another time I was going along and the baby was out on the front steps, and I just thought he would go into fits, he was crying so hard.   I stopped and asked him what the matter was; and he said something about mamma, and I thought he said (but I couldn't tell for certain; you know I can't tell you a lie or misrepresent anything, because the communion is next Sunday); but I thought he said, 'Mamma spanked baby.'"

"Wall, wall, wasn't that terrible!   and nothing but a baby, neither; it makes my blood bile! and I shall jest inform Walter—I consider it my duty, don't you, Mrs. Tattum?"

"I guess I do; I wouldn't let the sun go down before he should know all about it.   Of course you won't bring my name in; and I'll tell you what's more: if I were dead and those were my children, I couldn't sleep in my grave when she was in her tantrums with the little dears; but I'd walk right up to her in my shroud, and let her know what was what. I've heard dead folks did do that sometimes."

"Wall, them's the times they orter come, I'm sure."

"I ain't told you all yet: another time that little dear had the nose-bleed very bad, and she never offered to stop it; and I went over there and listened around, and when she saw me coming she might have hid, for all I know, for she was no where to be seen.   I took him in my arms and went to the pump, and pumped water all over his little head and it soon stopped it, I tell you; and she never put in an appearance all this time.   Perhaps she does not like me, but I don't care for that. If I see anybody abuse other folks' children, I'm the one to take their part, no matter who they belong to. But friends like your son, Walter, and his first wife, my, though! do you think I'd stand by and see a cross word spoken to them? No, indeed!"

"Wall, that's jest doin' as you would be done by; and I am so thankful for the interest you take in them poor, little, motherless orphans. If you don't get your reward here, I know you will hereafter; and she—why, she will be punished, and she orter be."

"That's jest so, Mrs. Clayton—she ought to be; but I've a plan, and it is a good one: I'll go to the hired girl, and find out everything—now see—and then I'll tell you."

"No use, you couldn't get a word out of her, no how; and I'm going to have her ousted and get some one in her place that won't be all on one side like a jug handle. She wouldn't say one word against her mistress to save both of our lives."

"But I can manage her, I know just how; leave it all to me, and when you come again, you will say I am nobody's fool."

"Wall, if you can and will, I'll send you down two bushels of the best harvest apples you ever put your teeth in."

"All right, but I don't want any pay; I'll do it jest for humanity's sake; and what better reward can we have than a clear conscience?"

"Wall, that's so, but I must go; I hope I hain't bothered you."

"No, you haven't, for I was just dying to see you."

"You are so good," said the old lady, taking her hand and giving her a parting kiss.

That afternoon Bridget passed the residence of Mrs. Tattum, whose garden displayed a profusion of choice flowers. Stopping for one moment to indulge in a look at them, she was seen by Mrs. Tattum who straightway called to her and invited her to enter.

"Oh, no, mum, I can't tarry, I'm in sich haste, going on an irrend fur the mistress."

"Well, then, if you can't stay, I will gather a nosegay of these choice lilies for Mrs. Clayton."

"She's very fond of purty flowers, sure; so, mum, if you please I'll take them to her."

Opening wide the gate she bade her enter and, while cutting and arranging her boquet, she made all possible haste to open up her business, which she did in the most artful, insinuating manner.

"And your name is Donnelly?"

"It is thin, mum."

"And are you from Dublin?"

"Sure, thin, mum, thot's the thruth for yez."

"I am of Irish descent, myself; my name was Donnelly, and I have friends living now in the city of Dublin. How strange if we should find out that, after all, we were relatives."

For a moment the loving, honest heart of Bridget warmed towards this woman, when, from some inexplicable reason, she started up in alarm, exclaiming, "I must go; the mistress will be waiting for me."

"I will not detain you," she said, handing her a bunch of lilies and roses beautifully arranged; for in this little transaction she had an eye to capturing the mistress as well as the maid.

"Give them to Mrs. Clayton, and tell her to call over and see me; and you get leave of her and drop in to-morrow, and we will talk it over; I wouldn't wonder if we were closely connected—perhaps cousins."

"Well, mebbe," said Bridget, who had already started.

"Come at five o'clock; otherwise I might not be here."

"Sure, mum, I'll see if the misthress is willing."

"Oh, she will be willing," and feeling that her only hope for the success of her plan lay in diverting the mind of her maid to Mrs. Clayton, she added, "She's the sweetest, bonniest mistress in the wide world, eh?"

This praise of her mistress seemed to quiet the feelings of Bridget, for she added, "I'll come thin, sure."

"How could you, mother?" said Mrs. Glenn, her daughter, a real lady, who married some years ago, and was now home from Brooklyn on a visit.

"Could I what?" answered her mother, laughing.

"Why, bring yourself down on a level with that Irish girl!"

"Why, what's the difference?" seeming to enjoy her joke hugely; "it's only a little play acting—the price of two bushels of delicious harvest apples—don't your mouth water already?"

"O, mother! how can you? But I know you will do nothing dishonorable."

"Of course I won't, you chit, you; I only want to find out something I really desire to know—something necessary, and has nothing to do with the Claytons." And thus she deluded her daughter.

She talked it all over with her mistress who, unaware of the pitfall set for her, could see no reason why Bridget should not go; and she even reminded her of the time when it had almost elapsed, and she saw that she was making no preparation to start.

"On time!" said Mrs. Tattum a few minutes after. "You see I got rid of the girls and all my visitors so that I could have a good visit with you. I have been studying over the matter since you were here, and find that your uncle Donnelly at Dublin is a first cousin of mine."

"Sure, thin!"

"So you see, that makes us blood relatives, don't you?"

"Mebbe, mum, and mebbe not; I don't jist see."

"But I know to a dead certainty; I can't just explain, but it's the truth; and I had a letter from him a while ago."

"You did, thin!" said Bridget, looking at her incredulously.

"Yes, I've been looking for it, but I can't just lay my hand on it. You don't think I'm lying to you, Bridget?"

"And I hope not, mum."

"Are you fond of strawberries and cream, Bridget? Here is a dish I prepared purposely for you ; I do think so much of my relations. And here is another dish; we will eat them together in token of a lifelong friendship."

They conversed a few moments on different subjects, but mostly in reference to their relationship. Mrs. Tattum finally brought it about naturally, to ply her with questions concerning her situation.

"How do you like your place?"

"Iligant, sure, and why shouldn't I, mum?"

"The old woman tells great stories about you ; said you and she had a regular pitched fight, how is that?"

"Fath, thin! I niver heard of it afore!"

"Well, I made up my mind she was lying; I don't believe much she says, any way—a regular mischief-maker. Now she came to me yesterday, when I was up to my eyes in washing, and I as good as told her I had no time to spare ; but it didn't make any difference, she's got lots of cheek; she cuddled right down in the kitchen, and began to talk about the folks over there—you know whom I mean?" she said, shrugging her shoulders and winking.

"I don't think I jist understand, mum."

"Well, you and your mistress, she said, abused the children ; and that you were a good-for-nothing Irish trollop that hadn't any soul; and she was going to have Walter discharge you, and wanted me to watch you and Mrs. Clayton, to see if you didn't whip those children. Just think what a shame! I was fearful mad, I tell you, and told her as much. That was one reason why I wanted to see you, to set you and your mistress on guard against the old huzzy. Now, Bridget, keep shady, don't say a word ; although your mistress ought to know just what she says, I wouldn't make mischief for the world ; but our being relatives, so I thought I would tell you. Do you get treated well yourself?"

"Well, thin, and I do, sure. Mrs. Clayton is the same to me as my mither, and I love her."

" I am very glad of it ; because if you weren't, you would have to be looking up another place, for I couldn't bear to see any of my kin ill treated. Isn't Walter Clayton an old miser ? and do you have enough to eat? I heard you didn't ; I know he's the meanest man that ever breathed—just like his mother."

Bridget arose in great wrath, threw her saucer upon the table, and replied, " If, thin, ye are a Donnelly and kith to me, I will change my name ; for ye are a liar, and know it too. There never was a tattlin' vein run through their bodies! Now, don't niver bid me to yez house agin, for ye are naught but a meddlesome old body; yez took me for a fool, sure, and it's yez own sel' that's a fool!" And at this she rushed out of the door, shaking her feet and garments, as if she would shake off the dust of deceit, hypocrisy and lying that had gathered upon them.

CHAPTER XVIII.

A large concourse of ladies was in the habit of assembling at the church parlors every week for the purpose of sewing for the poor children of those parents who chanced to belong to this particular denomination.

Mrs. Tattum, ever ready to attend to its calls, had canvassed the town thoroughly, and brought a list of the names of those who could not attend the Sabbath-school for want of proper clothing ; and herewith she made a move, that all the stores and houses in town should be visited, and whatever money could be collected, should be brought into the treasury to await the wants of the poor "heathen children," as she was pleased to call them; that she would take upon herself the task out of love to the poor creatures to whom poverty had denied the privileges of the gospel. She was an active worker in the church, and not wishing to offend her, she found an acquiescence in her plans; although the most of the ladies would have preferred another person, they did not say so.

Persistent in her wants, eloquent in her appeals, she succeeded admirably; every man, woman, and grown up child being asked to give something. Of some she got clothing, of others money, of merchants, goods and groceries generally. Of all these she pretended to keep a record, but only about one-half of the receipts were accounted for; but at home in secret, she reckoned her ill gotten gains and put them to the use of herself and daughters.

"Why don't you visit the Claytons and put their children on the list?" said Augusta Tattum ironically to her mother at one of these social gatherings.

"Why! why!" spoke several voices, "and they so wealthy?"

"Yes, rich enough—very rich, I suppose, but their young ones are perfect tatterdemalions."

"That's not so, now," answered Mrs. Tattum, "you might take them for a poor man's children, however, sometimes,"—trying to smooth the matter over as she was too far-sighted to tell all she would, when she saw any of the friends of the family around; for she did not know, but, as she had often before remarked, she might have "a little axe to grind," and some one of the Claytons might assist her.

"Well, now, mother," said Augusta angrily, "you needn't try to oil up matters, for you know that was just what you called them yourself, yesterday, when they passed our house—and worse—you said, 'If their own mother had lived, they never would have been in the street with such patched clothes, and their toes all out of their shoes.'"

"I saw them myself," answered another, "and I almost cursed step-mothers in my heart, and should, had it not been the children were so very neat and clean. I thought she must have some redeeming qualities. Of course she has no reason for allowing them to go looking so, when their father would get them anything she desired, he is so very wealthy; I wonder that he allows it!"

"Yes, anything but a stepmother. Those poor little things are really to be pitied; they might just as well have no one to take care of them at all as this new wife," said Augusta Tattum.

"Hush up, now," whispered her mother, "or you'll be sorry for all this freedom of speech."

"I saw the children at home very recently," spoke another voice, "they were not at all ragged or dirty, but their raiment

6

was more like Joseph's of olden time than anything else—of many colors ; and I thought then that she either did not care how they looked, or was very odd, to say the least."

"Ladies," said Mrs. Ashton, while her voice trembled with the deepest emotion, "if you will allow me, I think I can explain matters to your satisfaction, and perhaps clear up the character of her who, whether intentionally or not, has been so slandered to-day by parties of this sewing society. I was at the residence of Mrs. Clayton when her husband brought remnants to make up for the children, which looked more to me like curtain calico than otherwise. She told him it was not at all suitable and did not wish to use it. He flew in a passion, as he always does, when he cannot have his own way, and said it would be the very last article he should ever bring to the house, as it was impossible to please her. I told her to use the cloth, and when he saw how ridiculously the children looked in suits from this material, he would never bring the same again. She said she would be censured, but I told her not to mind that. I think she did perfectly right."

"And I—and I," was heard in every part of the room.

"I don't believe a word of it," said Augusta Tattum in an undertone to a lady who sat near her. "She could have just what she'd a mind to, but she's a stepmother,'and don't care anything about those poor little orphans."

Mrs. Clayton had the sympathy, however, of most of the ladies, while some of them were incensed beyond endurance by the slanderous remarks that were made. One of them turning her flashing eyes upon Augusta Tattum, an elderly lady who had known the family since she was a baby, said, "You can't remember, perhaps, how you used to go looking. Half the time you had no hat nor shoes on at all ; and it was not patched clothes you wore, but those that were tattered and torn ; and you looked like a beggar; and you had an own mother. Now when you talk about Mrs. Clayton in the way you do, I believe you only intend to blacken her character. And I would say to these ladies in her behalf, that she does everything in her power for the whole family. She has sat up all night long with those children when they were sick, and taken the very best of care of them ; and further, she would be as glad as any mother present to see them neatly dressed at all times. You are not aware how hard it is for her to get the necessaries of life. Now, Miss Tattum, would it not be better to tell things just as they are, and not take advantage of an innocent person in her absence to bring her into disrepute? I have seen you meet her on the street, and one would judge from your manner that you were the very best of friends ; but I know, now, you are a Judas; your kisses the same as his ; and there is not one in this company who might not be a target for the shafts of your unruly tongue in her absence."

"Good enough—good enough," whispered Mrs. Tattum to her daughter, "Now keep your tongue to yourself, after this, and don't go talking about folks at sewing societies; you better go home about your business!"

"Not till I give that woman a piece of my mind, now I tell you."

Her mother then said something else to her, which seemed to have the desired effect, for she flew out of the room, put on her things, and left without replying.

"Well! now! Walter, my son, is one of the very first-class providers, and has the best of taste, and don't bring nothing to the house but the prettiest he has in the store," said the elder Mrs. Clayton, putting in an appearance from an adjoining room where she had been an unknown listener to all the conversation.

"That's so ; those dresses are nice and stylish too ; I don't see why there is so much fuss about nothing—now my daughter has just come from the city, and says, ' Rainbow cloth is all the fashion,' and I presume as Mr. Clayton has just been there, he got this goods on purpose for the children—trust to his taste every time; he knows," said Mrs. Tattum in the slightest tones of raillery, perceptible to every one but the old lady.

"Wall, he orto know,—I don't see why he shouldn't," she replied.

"How long has he kept store?"

"About ten years."

"I saw that goods there upon the opening," said Mrs. Ashton, determined, if possible, to open the eyes of Mrs. Clayton to the deception of her double-faced friend.

"And no one thought enough of it to buy since? Is that it? Well, that is the best of policy—just what I'd do myself, and every one that is not very well off ought to do. He's a first-class financier. It is not half the folks that know how to keep money when they get it,—but he does—and that is right," answered Mrs. Tattum with a smile and a shrug of the shoulders, which Mrs. Clayton did not see,—nor did she intend she should—for she wished her to think she was in sympathy with her; and while her words conveyed this meaning, her appearance, more powerful than these, told the other party that she held him in derisive scorn.

"Wall, he's made what he has got himself, for he was nothing but a poor boy in the first place, and he's worked his way up," said the old lady.

"Honest 'Old Abe' was a rail splitter and he got to be President; there's nothing like ambition and perseverance; wouldn't wonder if we should see some of our citizens in the White House yet—wish we might, they'd give us all offices like enough, and then we'd all get rich," said Mrs. Tattum.

One of the Committee announced tea, and here the conversation closed in reference to the Claytons. More gossip than work, as usual, had been accomplished; some of the ladies, disgusted, had the audacity to say that the Sewing Society had got to be a great sieve, where each one's character must be riddled; and they believed they would stay at home and give directly to the poor, and then they would be sure they got it.

CHAPTER XIX.

A year has passed since Elice entered upon her duties as wife and mother; and sad as the twelve-month has been pictured, the "little mother" at times longing to loose the tether and, unconstrained, lie silently down in the arms of the Good Shepherd—the snowy fleece caught and in many fragments hanging upon the rough thorns of vituperation, of cold, cruel neglect, and miserly wrong. Yet she felt her married life had not been altogether unfruitful. She had learned many lessons of faith and quiet endurance upon the way that had seemed to her an untrodden, trackless desert, where burning sands had blistered her bleeding feet; and dense clouds shut out every ray of sunlight, so that she neither saw nor heard aught but the raving winds and tumultuous hurricanes that beat with pitiless destructive force, uprooting every green plant, each beautiful germ that might have struggled to life and growth and strength in the desolate garden of her soul. And had it not been for the glimpses of the "bright beyond," the finger of an Almighty Friend pointing through the mists to the azure gates, her temptations would at times have led her to put an end to her unhappy existence. It was in one of these fits of despondency when she felt so much the need of sympathy and did not get it; when another was to become a living soul and take its place upon her bosom, which she felt was to be buffeted about like herself on life's stormy sea, without hope, without love; which, although waiting and striving, and begging for, never came, nor never would, that she penned the following:

"How shall I cool my fevered brain?
  How shall I break this cankered chain?
  Though scattered here and there a gem,
  Rich settings for some diadem,
  They rankle in my aching heart,
  Till tears in quick succession start.

  My idol brought the choicest flowers
  E'er culled in Cupid's rosy bowers,
  And bound them in my tresses gay
  Upon our happy wedding day;
  And said that years with rapid flight,
  These flowers of love should never blight.

  In me he'd found a blossom rare
  That he should guard with jealous care;
  That mildew breath or blighting worm
  Should ne'er destroy this precious germ
  Of beauty, innocence, and truth;
  That love grown old should crown our youth.

  My flowers are withered, every one;
  The fabric, beauteous begun,
  Of threads on threads of golden light
  Dissolved in darkness and in night;
  And lines of grief alone are traced
  Upon the spot they were effaced.

  Sweet mother, on thy loving breast,
  Thy weary child again would rest;
  For oh, my husband loves me not,
  And long, so long ago forgot
  The sacred vows he made to thee,
  That he would love and cherish me."

When she had finished writing, she folded the poem and laid
it in a box containing papers which had not been opened since
the morning she started from home, when, in the excess of her
joy, she felt that she had won a priceless treasure, a heart
above suspicion, a friend who would protect, cherish and love
her through all the vicissitudes of life; one upon whom she could
lean in sickness and in health, that would sustain and shield her
in all the trials that might await her; and thus they would pass
down the stream of time, encouraging each other with pleasant
smiles, and tender words, until they reached the valley, when
they would pass over gently, conscious of no unpardoned wrong

that they had ever done each other to mar life's transitory note book.

Such wild visions did her fancy picture ; such beautiful dreams of future bliss came to her childish imagination. With a mind thus exalted, and overshadowed with happy expectancy, who could wonder that, while waiting in the depot for the train which was hours late, she should take from her pocket a note book and pencil the following : "To my husband ;" not for the eye of the world ; not for his, but simply an outburst of enthusiasm and love, converted into a pen picture, mirrored upon paper and there it lay—the same, identical words that she had that morning—her wedding morning—traced. Oh, how it thrilled her as her eyes fell upon this, and what memories it brought up, while every letter burned upon her bosom like blistering lava ! for she could not recall that time without feeling that the weight of years of suffering had been crowded into the brief period that had elapsed since then.   She took it from its hiding place. however, and read, while her agony was too great for utterances :

> "Thy love is sweeter, far to me
> Than breath of jasmine flowers,
> That in their brightness gem the lea,
> Or Flora's dewy bowers.
>
> 'Tis sweeter far than sunset glows
> 'Upon the clouds at even,
> When every gentle breeze that blows
> Is telling us of Heaven.
>
> 'Tis sweeter far than violets
> That lift toward the sky
> The drooping lash, the velvet lids,
> The soft, the pale blue eye.
>
> A day beam from the realms of light,
> A tale as sweet as morn,
> Where Angels bathe their pinions bright,
> And happiness is born."

When she had finished reading, she folded the paper and laid it away again in the box, hardly knowing what she did, for her head reeled and shadows flitted before her eyes, so that she could scarcely see.

She thought she heard some one addressing her, and listened to hear what it was, but only a confused humming, as of bees, sounded in her ears, and she knew nothing more until she found herself upon the bed with some one bathing her temples. It was her husband. He had stood in the doorway behind her screened, as he thought, from observation, certainly from hers, all the time she had been reading, with flashing eyes and demoniacal glare, reminding one of the wild, frightful, imaginary pictures of the infernal one. But this was not fancy, for it was a living, terrible reality. When she had finished and laid the poems away, he broke out with these words: "Caught at last! And is that where you hide your love letters from me? I have long suspected that you had a favorite correspondent, and now I'm glad I found it out. An old lover, eh? and you have stolen away to peruse his tender missives?" And not till she had fallen to the floor did he cease his furious reproaches; and then a dim perception of something in her appearance while he had been talking revealed the fact that she had been unconscious of everything he had been saying to her. He took her in his arms and laid her upon the bed, and applied restoratives to recover her from this death-like swoon, after which he went, unperceived, and slid away the box containing the papers, opened and read, never wasting a moment until he had taken out each separate one and perused it sufficiently to satisfy his mind that he had been mistaken. He then shoved them lightly aside into a niche near where she had been sitting, as if they had fallen there, and took his station again at her bedside.

When she revived she desired to get away somewhere from this sense of suffocation—to the garden, she thought, and she asked her husband if she might go. With a heart humiliated and warmed towards her by defeat, he lifted her up, and, placing his arm about her, led her to a little rustic seat—her favorite resort—under the maples, and went away feeling chagrined that he should pour forth such invectives on his faithful wife,

and made up his mind that in future he would not let his diabolical passions get so much the mastery of him.

"But she did not hear me," he said, "and I am glad of it;
She is a good wife, and I know she loves me, but I am a bear,—
worse than that—a born devil. "

Now, it was very seldom that these glimpses of himself made
even a momentary impression or gave any direction to his
outward manner ; and if he had lifted up the weakest prayer for
Divine guidance, of which he had no thought, he might have
been lead in plain paths approaching to the true, beautiful life
of his wife ; and together they might have grown up a harmonious, perfected family, not only loved of God, but respected,
and a blessing to all men. But this was not to be, for ere the sun
went down, he was again throwing out cruel insinuations to
Elice concerning her lovers, although he knew his accusations
were without foundation, as he had proven conclusively to
himself in the mean, niggardly manner he had taken of testing
her in the morning.

Elice had been seated in the garden but a short time, when a
fawn leaped through the half-open gate, and rushed to her side
as if for protection from it's cruel tormentors. It had been
wounded, and the blood was flowing freely. Her heart was
touched at sight of it's distress, and she took cold water from
the well and bathed the wound, and then brought milk to feed
it.

"Poor little thing! how I pity you!" said Elice. "You
will come and live with me now; I will put this silver chain
about your neck, and you shall eat out of this pretty cup."

The fawn answered by allowing her to draw its head upon
her lap, and looking up into her face with it's soft, languishing
eyes so full of distress that it made her hot tears flow, which
fell upon it's neck, soft and silky as the finest velvet.

"My pretty dear," she continued, patting it caressingly,
"here shall be your home beneath this tree ; you shall be my
companion ; the hateful gash will heal, and should I have but a

pittance, you shall share it with me." It rolled its eyes to her again like a creature of reason, fell and expired.

"Oh, why was this!" thought Elice, again caressing it; and wondered if it was not a premonition; and felt that it was in some way connected with her own future. Then her mind went forward to a not far distant time, when a pair of eyes—not fawn's—not birdling's, but real human eyes, should look out of their depths into her face; when a human form should lay its head upon her breast, its snowy arms encircle her neck; and then after a time, her name lisped by rosy lips; and already she began to feel a secret spring touched in her heart, a mother's love bubbling forth from a hidden fountain of which she had never before dreamed. And then she thought, would she, like Lola, find a premature grave? and her eyes turned to the little mound in the cemetery, which was visible from the spot where she sat, where the roses and daisies had again commenced putting forth their blossoms; and she could not help feeling that it would be so sweet to lie down by her side; for her rest was so calm, her slumber so peaceful; while a thorny, rugged way, all untravelled, she had left behind, for a seat in Paradise, a golden harp, the society of angels, and her dear Redeemer. And the picture was not a sad one to Elice, who had only commenced her journey through this "vale of tears;" had just entered upon a dark and gloomy road, overhung by frowning precipices, beneath which were deep morasses, slippery paths, and angry streams. But she hoped that, if God should call her hence, that her child would die too; that they would be buried in one grave, and that should be with her dear ones at home in Woodville; in a quiet little nook by the river's side, where the white lilies sprung spontaneously, the perfume of wild flowers greeted the senses, weeping willows overshadowed the spot, and the rippling waves of her favorite Cohocton mingled its tones with songs of the summer birds.

CHAPTER XX.

Although she had drifted down to the Jordan, so near she could see the angels beckoning her from the other side; could hear their songs: "Unto Him who hath loved us and washed us in His precious blood," and knew they were waiting to receive her by the gates that were open wide to the "evergreen mountains," through her spiritualized consciousness felt the delicious Heavenly breezes stealing upon her senses, locking them in sweet, mysterious obliviousness of all earthly things. Yet she did not die; though almost over, earthly loving ones weeping, looking momentarily that "the golden bowl be broken," yet there were angels here, as well, that held the precious crumbling vessel,—her mother—her own true-hearted mother, who with faithful hands and loving prayers, ministered at her bedside by night and day, scarcely leaving it for a moment,—a little heart throbbing against her own,—a rounded, dimpled cheek, contrasting strangely with the pearly whiteness of hers,—a little hand lying within her palm, a head of glossy black, as soft as eider down, and rosebud lips resting upon her bosom, wooing the life tide from its outward flow; and for this, for these, she opened her eyes upon earthly things, and the picture was more dear to her mother heart than aught she had ever seen in earth or heaven; and the first words that opened her lips were, "Life, after all, is worth the living." Then she called for the other little ones; "Oh!" she said, "I had forgotten, but I could not go away and leave these. I will try and live for their sweet sakes too."

Although she felt a tenderness for Lola's little orphans of which no one knew, and would have experienced untold happiness with them, supplying their wants, directing and entering into their childish recreations, yet the drops that fell from envenomed tongues into their cup of pleasure made it very bitter to the taste.

"But," she says, "I will drink it, for love must sweeten all at last; but if it does not, my duty is plainly written; God has given me to be their mother, and as I do to them, so let it be done to mine."

One day after she had so far recovered as to leave her bed, her mother noticing her in a meditative mood, inquired, "What is it, Elice, my darling?" She was about to say, "Oh, the burden of life, mamma!" but for her sake she threw off the sad wistfulness that had settled upon her countenance and replied, "My one great thought was of my jewels. Oh, the resplendent gems in a mother's crown! Pray every day and every hour that God may gather up each thread of the lives of my precious ones and weave them into sunshine. I know you will not forget the 'little mamma.'"

Here the tones of her own voice thrilled her, for she realized so much more in that word "mamma" than she ever had before; not so much that the little one, bone of her bone and flesh of her flesh, filled it with tender sweetness; but through it were clearly revealed her responsibilities and her vow, "So let it be done to mine."

The little stranger was an angel to be entertained, at least by one of its grandmammas—a gift from Heaven; and one hearing her would think a special shower of pet names had fallen to bless the darling, for, though ready with a new one every time she looked upon the dear little face, the supply seemed inexhaustible. The other, looking out of jealous eyes, saw no attraction in the child. One day Mrs. Woodville with great pride and tenderness brought and laid it upon her lap saying, "You have not seen it lately; look at its little face like a great, round pearl without a flaw upon it. Do you see any?"

"Wall, I dunno ez I do; p'raps it'll be passable yet; I hope so, for Walter's sake; and I 'spose Elice would feel proper bad to see the difference between it and the other children." But to Mrs. Tattum, to whose house she soon after repaired, she said, "Miserable little pinched up thing. I'm so sorry for my poor boy, for he can never set the store by that one he does by Lola's orphans."

Now her listener was of the same mind, but changed it whenever she came into the presence of Elice, when she said, "It is the sweetest little thing I ever lay my eyes upon; looks just like its mother!" but if Mr. Clayton happened to come in while she was talking,—"Well, I don't know which it does look the most like—its papa or mamma; and it don't make any difference, for it is pretty—just as pretty as can be." While her daughters praised its eyes, its wondrous growth of hair, the dimples in its cheeks, and usually wound up by kissing it several times, and laying it back, as they said, "in its cozy little nest by the side of its mamma."

Elice was happy when, for the first time, she dressed her child, which she named Robin, after the birds that had cheered her lonely hours so much through the spring months with their songs, that she had watched through the long, weary days that otherwise would have been gloomy enough, at times, had it not been for them, when she was obliged to keep her room; when she was alone with no companions but these, with nothing to break the dull silence but their lovely notes, which they seemed to pour forth with more exquisite sweetness than she had ever heard before. And so its baby name was Robin, which, she said, could be changed when it got older; and she took it in her arms and carried it out to the garden, her favorite haunt, which she had not been able to visit for more than a month, not since the morning her husband had assisted her to the rustic seat beneath the maples. And, for the time, she believed she was as happy as any mother possibly could be, with her darling fast asleep, and watched it with the fond delight that no one ever can experience, but a doting mother, gazing upon her first born child—a comforter from Heaven—a well spring of inexhaustible love. And silently, with no eye upon her, as she thought, but God's, beneath an arbor of wild grape and fragrant climbing honeysuckle that hung above her head, laden with its fresh blossoms, she dropped upon her knees, thanking Him for a happy deliverance from the perils of her past sickness, dedicating her little one to Him, asking Him to make it a blessing to her, and to enable her to bring it up in the love and admonition of the Lord, and closed her prayer in tones and words so touchingly pathetic:

> "Oh, Father, grant that he may be,
> When years have winged their flight,
> His locks of black have turned to gray,
> As spotless as to-night."

When she took her little Robin again and went into the house, she felt stronger and better prepared for the day's care; and she would try, she thought, and throw off the gloomy looks that hitherto had rested upon her countenance, and assume cheerfulness, even though she did not always feel like it, and meet her husband with the old-time smile which his coldness had entirely driven away, and take up life anew. And she went to bed that night, feeling that He who commanded the winds and the waves and they obeyed Him, was able to quiet, was able to smooth the seas of sorrow; and so, with little Robin upon her arm, she slept a peaceful sleep, and awoke in the morning with the same earnest resolve to rise above the mountains of trouble; to subject her heart, through prayer and meditation, to a submissiveness to her lot; to be doubly meek and obedient to the wishes of her husband;—"And, after all, what a small thing for me," she thought, "compared to the great hope that fills my heart, that hereby I may be the means of leading him into the beautiful paths I was early taught to tread—the way to Christ."

Love's eyes had been forced to see the utter selfishness of his nature, and would have looked hopelessly, but for this one light ahead, this one director, in which, if prayer availed on high, she would lead him; but it was a question with her whether, surrounded by such adverse influences, she could live in such a manner as to insure an answer to her petitions. But, in one of these struggles between faith and despair, a dear old friend in the church came in, to whom she disclosed her lack of trust, not, however, naming its object. "Why," says the friend, "be sure you know that God wills your petition. Is it your husband to be saved, or your children;—is it anything you might properly wish to gain;—anything you might conscientiously work for, remembering always that love is the fulfilling of the law, then go to God with the assurance that you are heard. But often, after having done the will of God, 'ye have need of patience that ye receive the promise.' Do not look for the leopard's spots to be changed at once; but I do believe by praying and waiting you may hope even for that."

So after she left, Elice went away to her room, knelt there, and prayed as she had never before, that her husband might be changed; that a new life might be begotten in his soul—a life of honor, of truth, of generosity and love; and a sweet peace stole into her heart—the assurance of hope fulfilled. But afternoon came when her hope wavered; why, we shall see.

A poor forlorn beggar made his appearance, and asked, "Will the lady be so kind as to give me a bite to eat? Not a mouthful has touched my lips for these two days; I have been sick and obliged to give up work; and I could not make up my mind to die for want of a little bread, though I have never begged before. It is only a short way home, but I shall not live to get there without something." And he sat down on the door-step exhausted and apparently ready to faint.

"Yes," thought Elice, "this is the same old story, but I do not believe he belongs to that class of beggars."

Now she had been told never to feed tramps,—that they were vagabonds and thieves;—that in every instance she must turn them away. She had been greatly tried upon this point, whether she should heed her husband's commands and withhold that of which they had plenty and to spare, more than they could ever use, or give to them secretly. Here was the injunction: "Inasmuch as ye have done it unto one of these, ye have done it unto me." And could she turn away her Lord and Master? This was the form the question assumed in her mind; and so, while it was pending, she occasionally poured her fragrant coffee, and gave a morning roll to these poor outlaws, without her husband's knowledge. But she discriminated, she thought, and fed only those who were really needy,—and secretly, because she did not think it necessary to place herself in a position to listen to his bitter, violent imprecations on the account.

As soon as the beggar sat down, she hastened for a glass of water and placed it to his lips, and then went for a cup of wine and some chicken. At this critical moment, her husband made his appearance, wishing to know who was there on the step, and what he wanted.

Tears sprang to the eyes of Elice, and she said, "He looked so pale and sick, I thought I would give him some breakfast. If I turned him away, he might die by the wayside."

"Ahem! little madam," he said sneeringly, "I'm just in time to witness the consummation of your good intentions." This was but a faint rumbling—precusor of a fearful storm of wrath. Taking the poor fellow by the collar, he lifted him clear off the door-stone, and applied his foot. "Go," he thundered, "go, beggar, vagabond, or I'll have you arrested and thrown into prison." And then to Elice, with cruel oaths, and threats, and imprecations upon her defenseless head, "This is the way you entertain these pests to society; you squander upon them my hard earnings. I will not endure it."

The man arose from where he had fallen, and staggered, and fell again just outside the gate, from sheer hunger and exhaustion, his great, shrunken, lusterless eyes portraying the agony of his soul—his hopeless condition. "Oh, God!" he said, "has it come to this at last; must I die for the meagre pittance that will keep soul and body together?"

Elice could endure his pleading looks no longer, but arose in the majesty of her womanhood, and went quietly to her room —to her private medicine chest, and poured a glass of wine from a bottle—the gift of her mother the last time she had seen her, which she had placed in her hand ·with these words: "This is the pure juice of the grape; use it whenever you are sick, my pet;"—and humorously, "It will be more tasteful when you remember the sun of Woodville sweetens your cup."

With it she took some water which she sprinkled upon his face to revive him, and then held the wine to his lips and told him to drink it all. He obeyed her mechanically, and this pure invigorating draught warmed in his veins and gave him strength. She then took from her pocket a handful of small coin,—and this, too, a portion of a gift from home, and the very last, and which she had intended to lay out in something nice for the children. "But," she thought, "he needs it more than they, and he shall have it to provide for the remainder of his journey."

She was not mistaken in her estimate of the man. He was a gentleman in the truest acceptation of the word, as her acquaintance with him afterward proved. He thanked her, and left with an inward prayer for God's blessing upon her and hers.

Under no other circumstances could Elice have gone contrary to the wishes of her husband; but led by the impulses of her generous nature, and the commands of God, written upon her heart, and flaming out like fire upon a consecrated altar, "As ye would that men should do to you, do ye even so to them." And her faith was so exalted at that moment she forgot, entirely, the wrath of her offended master, and he, ashamed of himself, had stolen away where he could see, unperceived by

7

her, all that she did; seemingly powerless to make' any effort.
Like a lion whipped, he had surrendered to the foe. More
than that, he watched her with an admiration he had never felt
before,—not for the crown of noble daring that, like a halo,
encircled her brow; but simply, he had been beaten—conquered.

CHAPTER XXI.

A boy made his appearance at the door of Mr. Clayton's residence; he had no hat on, nor shoes, and was very poorly clad. He held in his hand a bunch of flowers, composed of marigolds, poppies, nasturtiums, and peonies. Bridget, who answered the bell, after looking reprovingly at the little beggar lad for daring to come in at the front entrance, asked him what he wanted.

He dropped his head on his breast and said, "Please, ma'am, and will some one buy my flowers?"

Her heart softened at once when she saw his tears and heard the sad tones of his voice. "P'r'aps thin the ladies inside will take them; will yez come in and see?"

She then conducted him into a room where Minnie Tattum and Mrs. Clayton were. Minnie laughed so loudly when she saw the child and knew his errand, that he dropped his eyes to the floor, while his face at first crimsoned and then turned very pale, and he started to leave the room.

"How ridiculous!" said Minnie, "what made you suppose one would buy these weeds? Why, I pull all such from my garden and throw them away."

"Come back, dear," said Mrs. Clayton, "and tell me all about it; why you wish to dispose of those flowers which are quite pretty and favorites of mine."

"I thought you never prevaricated."

"Neither do I mean to, Minnie; those flowers, indeed look

beautiful to me, for they take me back to the earliest recollections of my childhood—to the days of my dear old grandmother, whose garden was full of them, and I have ever felt a love for them since. Where did you get them, my boy? What made you think to bring them here?" said Elice, patting him on the head.

"Oh, I don't know, guess the angels; you see my mother is sick, and we are both starving. She taught me to ask God for what I wanted, and so I asked him for bread. Then I thought about these pretty flowers and maybe I could sell them. They are nice, ain't they? I heard you say so; won't you buy them?"

"Don't you believe a word he says, for he is making it up," said Minnie. " Now, did you ever hear such a pretty story from such a small boy? Where do you live? What's your name? Ain't you telling us a big lie?"

"I ain't told anything but the truth," the boy said meekly.

"I believe you, dear," said Mrs. Clayton, "and I will go with you and see your mother. Will you accompany us, Minnie?"

" Why, yes, to be sure. We will take little Robin and have a jolly time."

" A basket of fruit, some bread and butter and wine."

" You're a ministering angel! I wish I were half as good, and yet, I don't believe in following up these worthless vagabonds; let them take care of themselves. But I'll go with you just for the adventure. Perhaps I'll get an item for my book—don't look so incredulous, for authorship runs in the family. My grandfather was an own cousin to Sir Walter Scott, ha! ha!"

"What was his name?" said Elice smiling.

"I don't remember, but mother knows."

"Och! Donnelly, shure, thin," thought Bridget, not forgetting the relationship that lady claimed 'to herself. "I guess yees can match her for telling a whoppin' story."

" You have never seen any of my manuscript," continued Minnie. " I'll bring it over and read it sometime."

"We must hasten, or the poor woman may die," answered Elice, sadly, not heeding the remark.

"Oh, fie! die? I presume we shall find no such woman as the boy represented. It is certainly a sin to be so credulous. Now you believe all the pretty stories these beggars tell you—too lazy too work, while they live by just such people as you are."

"I can discriminate, and it is necessary so to do. I never yet was deceived; while many of them are as you represent, there are more worthy of your assistance. 'Be not forgetful to entertain strangers, for thereby ye may entertain angels unawares.'"

"Harbor thieves, who would pick your pockets."

"I do not intend to give them an opportunity to take anything from me, and if I did I should not fear it. I believe it is our duty to help the needy, to relieve the sick, to encourage the down trodden and oppressed by kind words and a portion of our means. We know not how soon the wheel of fortune will turn with us, and if we disobey the commands of God in neglecting to administer to the afflicted, he will visit us in judgments."

"Poh! where is there a man more prosperous than Mr. Walter Clayton? and he never gave a cent in all his life to a pauper, and it is not at all likely he ever will. Just look at his houses, farms, and money at interest! I only wish I had one tenth of his income;—wouldn't I wear diamonds and point laces? Oh, how I wish I were rich!"

"You would then give a portion to the poor?"

"I'd give them a wide berth,—they don't trouble me now, and they wouldn't then. Whew, how hot it is! we've walked a mile I do believe; well, there's the hut, and there are more of those lovely flowers you love so well. What would Mr. Clayton say, if he saw us here? He wouldn't give the woman a penny to save her soul, and you would divide the last cent—more, give all you had and go without yourself. Well, he's the sensible one, after all ; he looks out for number one, and that's the way to do."

A wild shriek rent the air; then piteous moans fell upon their ears, while they heard the words: "Mamma, oh, my mamma is dead!" which came from the lips of the lad who, hurrying, had arrived some time in advance of them at the house.

They passed to the bedside as quickly as possible and strove to revive her, hoping she had only fainted; but all to no avail; life was indeed extinct.

"What do you think?" said Elice, her eyes brimful of tears.

"It is a sad sight! I must have the air," Minnie replied, and immediately passed out of the hut into the garden.

Elice consoled the child as best she could, but he would not be comforted.

"How I wish I could give him a home!" she thought,— "yes, every poor little boy and girl in the country. Oh, for the means to rear asylums for these creatures of starvation! Not the idlers, the loafer, nor tramps that infest the land like locusts,—but poor unfortunates, the old and infirm; and they should have nice homes, comfortable rooms, and books and pictures; the sick should have delicacies, attention, and companionship; and I would like to see that their wants were supplied; no poorhouse with its insufficiency of food, its lack of ventilation, its cruel taskmasters which are sometimes found." And then she shuddered when she drew the picture, lest some of her loved ones might become inmates of these gloomy prison walls; but oh, she hoped not; she would willingly go to service, if necessary, to keep them from it,—she would do anything rather than see them obliged to ask alms.

The doctors came and held a post mortem examination and said she·came to her death by starvation. And it was not in the city, but a by-way hut in the country—just in sight of waving grain, fields of corn, and acres of potatoes. Too proud to beg, too conscientious to steal, unable to work, and so she had died for the lack of nourishment.

"Dear little fellow," said Elice, pushing back the flaxen curls from the child's forehead and imprinting a kiss,—"how much like your mamma!"

"Oh, oh, my mamma—mamma—and will she never come back to me?"

She drew his head upon her bosom; showered it with tears, while she repeated these beautiful lines:

> "Mother, come back from the echoless shore;
> Take me again to your heart as of yore."

"I know," she added, "sweet child, your grief is boundless, which I gladly would assuage." And then she breathed a prayer so touching, to the God of the fatherless for that poor orphan boy so suddenly bereft of this last earthly friend.

"Isn't she beautiful?" said Minnie,—"fit for the model of a statuary. A very princess in this disguise—these rags. Do you notice the material of this once lovely dressing gown? 'tis of the finest satin. Who is she? Where is she from? I'd give much to know. Here is a letter,—look at the superscription. May we read it? It will give us some clue, perhaps, to this poor, unfortunate woman."

"Oh, yes, read it—read it—for my mamma said 'twas to her papa way over the waters; that may be he might forgive her and send us something, or come for us and take us away; 'twas just for my sake she did it, for she was going to leave me soon; she was going to a beautiful place up yonder"—pointing to the sky,—"and then she gave me this little locket with this pretty ribbon, and said, 'Tie it round your neck, put it in your bosom, Sammie,—never—never, part with it.' You may see it; but don't take it from me, will you?"

"What else did she say?"

"Oh, that it was a likeness of herself before she ever saw my papa; and she was so sorry that she ever did see him—then she might be living in a lovely castle over—over the Atlantic."

From an outburst of generous sympathy, from enthusiasm, Minnie grasped the locket, and kissed the miniature again, and again, exclaiming, " ' A very divinity of charms.' Who ever saw a person half so lovely? Fair young creature! little did she know, at that time of squalid poverty,—but the letter : "

" MY DEAR PARENTS: Can you—oh, will you, forgive me? My only crime has been worshiping 'at an earthly shrine,' and not heeding the kind admonition of friends who knew so much better than myself. But 'tis past. I would not burden you with my griefs, nor a recital of wrongs inflicted by him who lured me from my beautiful home of peace and plenty by his syren songs of devotion, which fell upon my ears, entrancing my soul like sweetest strains of music—yes, yes, it was all the comfort I had; for I had only been gone a short time before remorse seized me for so bold an act, and I desired above all things to retrace my steps and throw myself into your charitable arms, and beg you to receive me. But then it was that the bird of hope and love nestled in my bosom and warbled its sunniest notes, tightening the fibres of my heart which was breaking for my loved ones left behind, and wooed me on—on —away—so far away, from them over the trackless waste of waters—the great Atlantic ;—as Theodric Rathbun said we were only safe from my father when the great deep rolled between us. But he—my husband—is dead, and I am dying of want and starvation. I ask nothing at your hands for myself, for I am not deserving ; but it is for my child who is so soon to be left in this strange land alone—my blessed, beautiful, darling Sammie, the sole companion of all my lonely hours—whose sweetness and attention have held already the threads of my life together for a long time. I am forgiven of Heaven—say, oh, say I may have your pardon, for these words of comfort, like golden light, will illumine my tomb.   ·

"I hope to live to receive an answer to this missive, and believe God in his love will spare me till succor comes to my poor innocent boy, who weeps night and day with his heart-broken mother.   Your loving daughter,

FREDERICA RATHBUN."

"Her people probably never knew her fate," said Elice, "this letter, tattered and torn, blotted and tear stained, she repented likely having written, and made up her mind not to send it."

"Here's a book," said the child, "I found under the trees in the garden. My mamma lost it there, I guess."

It was an old diary, the name of the owner with date on the fly-leaf. Turning over its pages they read with the greatest excitement: "Morning—Never dawned a more lovely day; never such wild conflict raged within my breast. Which shall conquer, duty or love? My proud old father has driven Theodric Rathbun from his house and forbidden my speaking to him—but he is my idol; to hear his voice, to know he is near me, to listen to his oft-repeated tale of love, is dearer to me than all Count Parloe's wealth. Shall I stay where even the flowers are a mockery? for do not their buds open leaf by leaf, and revel in the sunshine, while a drapery as black as night overshadows my life? The rippling of the waves of the beautiful Thames, upon whose glassy surface I have taken so much delight, only speaks to me of buried hopes. I see it from my window—the little boat which but a month ago bore us away on a pleasure ride, when we both were so happy—so happy. My parents have been kind—never lived truer friends. My sisters and brothers love me, I know; but they are opposed to Theodric—and so I shall bid them all good-bye.

"Evening—Come to my aid precious tears, nor blister upon my aching, bleeding heart, for to-morrow's dawn will find me far from all my darlings, save one, for whose sweet sake I would fling my jewels—all—all to the winds, and pass through life a beggar, only so to quaff the air he breathes, to share with him his fate, be it for name and fortune or the reverse, it's enough. This is a magnificent old castle; my room is not equaled for grandeur; its pictures, statuary, books, birds and flowers were bought at fabulous prices; but at night it is my prison, for here I am locked in for safe keeping, and watched by day. My brain is on fire! I see a loop-hole for escape; I clutch at it. Haste, Theodric! Haste! and we'll away ere the morning breaks. Holy Saints! Here he comes! Can I steady myself to descend that ladder? Once with him I am the happiest of mortals. Poor boy! how he has risked his life for my sake! How still it is! Not a breath of air, sound of ripple, nor a bird note. The birds are asleep. Good-bye, my sweet little pet canaries, mocking-birds, orioles. How glad am I you cannot speak! for now you will not inform on me. I leave you and forever—everything I leave for him—for him —adieu! adieu!—so soon will 'fade o'er waters blue.'

"Oh, agony! Could I only steal to my mother's chamber, clip but a lock of her silver threads, imprint one kiss upon her precious lips—but no, no, 'twould awaken her. But there he is!—my Theodric on the top round of the ladder, and awaits me! My treasure! My all! Ready; wherever he leads I will follow."

"I could cross the ocean to know more of her," said Minnie. "I would like to adopt the child. Will you go with me, Sammie?"

Elice saw that the poor woman was respectfully interred in the little cemetery—Wild Rose Glen.

Minnie took Sammie home with her and plead with all eloquence of words that she might keep him, picturing in strong language the merits of her protégé—not forgetting to speak of his noble lineage, of which she had no reason, after what she had herself seen, to doubt. Her mother acquiesced in her plans, but her father said, "I've enough lazy young ones around already to support, and you can send the brat to the poorhouse for all of me. I'm not one o' the kind that runs after kings, nor queens, nor none o' their relations. I don't alwers have jest what I want myself and I have to work pesky hard for what I do git."

Minnie coaxed, then pouted, and finally declared he should stay—she'd give him half of her allowance, and if that was not enough, go begging for more; that her father was a very mean man to turn up his nose at this lovely little boy, and wouldn't wonder if he got to be a beggar himself—in a low tone,—didn't care much if he did.

But it was at last decided that he should remain with them until another place could be secured, which was sufficient excuse for Mrs. Tattum to circulate again a subscription paper —"For this dear, little, destitute boy, bereft so young of both his parents, for which I and my family are doing so much, and for whom we are all willing to make great sacrifices."

And so she collected enough to dress him very comfortably, while she replenished once more her private purse, which those extravagant daughters could soon empty, do as she might, she said; which end satisfied her conscience about the means she took to fill it.

CHAPTER XXII.

"Elice, what does this mean?" said Walter Clayton very angrily, handing her a paper and pointing to the article entitled "Death by Starvation," in which was a full account of the incidents named in the preceding chapter, which wound up by speaking laudingly of Mrs. Walter Clayton and Miss Minnie Tattum, who were present and gave so much assistance in this terrible hour of agony and distress; particularly of the poor little boy left to the charities of strangers; that must have died, had it not been for the timely succor rendered by these estimable ladies, who would care for him until a good home could be elsewhere secured.

"Now all this is true, I suppose? Mrs. Tattum is telling that you took a wagon-load of provisions to the house, and other things. How is that? Why, you'll beggar me and my children by your extravagance—you've pauper on the brain and no mistake, for I've heard that you let none of this class pass without feeding them."

Elice did not reply; she feared to speak while her husband was in this terrible state of excitement, lest anything she might say by way of explanation would only be as fuel added to fire.

"Do you hear me? Have you nothing to say? Haven't I told you to let this low-born class alone; that you only encourage them in idleness and vice by any assistance you render them?"

"I could not resist the pleadings of that sweet, innocent boy; supposing it had been Charlie?"

"Charlie—Charlie—he'll never come to want, for I shall train him up to industrious habits, and to take care of himself." Then waiting a few moments, biting his lips to suppress his wrath, he said, "Bridget must leave this house to-day."

"My faithful servant! for what?"

"Helping you with all your deviltry and keeping it sly from me. Now, I have been told, and on reliable authority, that you and she are in the habit of feeding all the worthless paupers that make their appearance; which, when questioned about, she stoutly denied."

"She never gave a crust of bread to my knowledge, for she is too conscientious to appropriate a farthing's worth that does not belong to her."

"I see—I see, you stand up for each other; I don't believe a word either of you tell me. I was going to let her stay till she finished up your washing, as I see she has commenced, but if I hear you take her part once more, I shall dismiss her this evening."

"Oh, Walter! what will the children do? She thinks so much of them, and takes such good care of the little darlings!"

"I don't care what they'll do, nor you either; she's got to go; and when I get another—if I do at all—it'll be one that won't be all on one side—that'll tell me what's going on in the house. Now, I hear lots of things more than you think for about you, madam. Well, of course Bridget must know all about it, and when I come to ask her she says, ' 'Tis false;' and 'That's not so;' and 'People have been speaking untruths'— when it's herself that tells falsehoods. And another thing— that Minnie Tattum that used to book me more'n all the rest, has been plastered up by your sweet tongue, and set up I s'pose by you, till she keeps everything to herself now, and makes out to folks that you are a clear angel, and I—well— everything but a good, kind husband, as you know I always have been, Elice. I'll give her a piece of my mind about things, and she'll have to stay away from here, after this, too."

"I am so sorry that you are so credulous. We can never live happily while you believe everything that is told you. I did not know I had so many enemies."

"I'm glad I've friends enough to tell me—oh, I know everything; but here, on this book you pretend to love so well, your Bible, you swear you'll never, in no way, give assistance to these detestable vagabonds that live on charity, either in town or out, and I'll keep Bridget and make up once more, and let Minnie come here if she wants to—no, I won't, for she's got to be such a mischief-maker and tattler I will not have her around."

" 'Cast thy bread upon the waters, and it shall return to thee after many days.' I must do my duty as I see it, or have the displeasure of God."

"Cast your bread to a dog, and he will bring a dozen with him next time he comes," answered Walter, and left the house.

He had only been gone half an hour before Minnie Tattum surprised Elice, by rushing into her presence in the deepest state of excitement, her great black eyes flashing wrathfully like some hunted panther.

"Your husband is a devil! Mrs. Clayton, how you can live with him and ever expect to be a Christian is beyond my comprehension. I'd—why—I'd—What's the matter with you, poor soul! You've been crying! he said he'd been giving you a blessing for your tricks; but let me tell you my story. He came along just a minute ago—I had started to go into the house— he called me. I turned around and said pleasantly, 'Good morning, Mr. Clayton,' and he never answered to it, but angrily exclaimed, 'See here, young woman, I want you to stay away from my house after this, setting my wife up to all sorts of mischief and coaxing her off to look up paupers.' I thought instantly of our many conversations and your good advice—that when I felt my temper—my dreadful temper—getting the mastery of me, to lift up my heart to God, and he would help me. I guess 'twould have been all right if he hadn't said any more;

but just at that moment, when I was trying to pray that I might answer him calmly, Sammie ran to the front door and called my name—O Mrs. Clayton! our dear beautiful child, dressed so sweetly and looking just like an angel—you remember what you said about 'entertaining angel's unawares?' and he's one if there ever was one—then Mr. Clayton spoke up and said, 'Is that the dirty, little scullion there has been so much fuss about for the past week, and that you and Elice are taking care of?' Oh! ho! ho! didn't the hot blood dance in my veins, while all my prayers went straight out of my heart; and all I desired or thought of was strength to give Walter Clayton a black eye; and I stepped up to him with my fists doubled up. 'See here Mr. Clayton,' I said, 'I'd like well to level you and grind you under my feet! If I were your wife I'd sew you up in a sheet when you got soundly sleeping, and whip you to death; for I would prefer to be hanged than to live with you, if the law took cognizance of the crime, which it would not, as it would only be ridding the world of a public nuisance!' Two mountains of wrath had come together, spitting and pouring out red hot lava; he was too mad to answer me, but I thought for a few moments he'd eat me; when he turned on his heel and went off swearing. Don't waste your breath any longer on me, for it's no use. I'm certainly ashamed of myself, but am satisfied that prayer will do for cool heads like yours, but not for hot ones like mine. It's only an offense to heaven and punishable as a great sin committed against God—a mockery, for he has said, 'Thou shalt not take the name of the Lord thy God in vain, and if, while I am calling upon Him, everything wicked, as in this instance, runs through my mind, I am certainly one of this class and will not be found guiltless. So save your prayers, which I know are well meant, for those of whom there are hopes, but not for such a sinner as I."

"It was for just such that Christ died; you surely are not worse than the thief on the cross."

"I believe I am ; for, while he never made any pretensions to piety, I have belonged to the church for years ; and when I should have been a burning and shining light, am only a stumbling block, and scarcely understand the first principles of religion ; only this I know, that a church should be as a city built on a hill—and what influence for good have I exerted? I am wilful, revengeful, with feelings that could almost annihilate a person that stands in the way to keep me from gaining an object I desire ; and yet, I am put forward as a teacher of those dear, tender buds, who, if they knew me as I am, would have but very little confidence in me or the doctrine of the blessed Book that I endeavor to explain. I believe I will give the whole thing up—leave the church, for I am not worthy to belong ; and then, if lost, will not drag so many to perdition with me."

She then rested her head upon her hands, while tears commenced to trickle down her cheeks. Neither spoke for a few moments—then Minnie broke the silence by adding :

"Mrs. Clayton, some are born good ; they have no such passions as mine to contend with—Vina, for instance, has no inclination to sin, while Augusta and myself are full of evil. Her hopes and desires only run in a right channel, so it is no trouble for her to be a Christian. Now, why does God, who is said to be no respecter of persons, deal so unfairly? giving her one of the sweetest of tempers, a love for the lowly path of holiness, a character so Christlike, that shines out beautifully through all the daily walks of life, to which the rest of the family could never aspire, even through prayer and tears."

"The desert may blossom as the rose. Where barrenness prevails, there may be fruitfulness. The highway is within the reach of all, and when we really have a desire for holiness, then God will baptize us with his spirit and transform our natures, so that which we once loved we would then hate. Do not despair, dear Minnie ; there are yet hopes for you in the precious blood of the Redeemer, who came not to call the righteous, but sinners to repentance."

"God's promises are not for me," she said, weeping more bitterly, and left the house.

"Dear girl," thought Elice, "she is under the deepest conviction for her sins; if she could only see the precious balm extended by the Divine Master who died for her as well as all the rest of mankind; but she will go to the ball chamber, the theatre, any place of amusement, perhaps this very night, where the voice of her conscience will be hushed by their festivities."

8

CHAPTER XXIII.

If the conversation of Mr. and Mrs. Clayton were a subject of anxiety to them, they had a listener to whom it was none the less so. Bridget had heard all his plans, and the tears and prayers of Mrs. Clayton, begging that she might remain; which latter had quite as much to do in influencing her objections to going away, as her own interest; and this involved so much to her—no less than home-leaving, and separating again from friends, as these were all she had known after having left her own in "swate Ireland."

Moreover, she had a certain regard for Mr. Clayton—a loyalty as against the world; would always defend him, unless at times, to excuse his own wrong doing, he had thrown the blame upon those whose interest was identical with his own—upon the altogether guiltless.

"There be places, sure," said Bridget, "but where will I find anither sich a misthress? Where be one like herself, the darlint?—wid come and sind me abed wen my head be nigh onto bustin wid the ache thot's in it, and doctor me up so swate like? and when I be bether to come again, to find ivery thing ran hither, I niver do; but the kitchen as bright as a bran new pan, bless her thin! and the children—Holy Saints bless all their swate souls!" And here, breaking down with sobs, she dropped upon her knees where she stood, and pored over her prayer book, and counted her beads until midnight.

When morning came, she found it necessary to do something

more than bathe her eyes to remove the tell-tale traces of her last night's vigils.

"It be half an hour," she thought, "till the time I be risin ivery morn. I'll wet this bit of cotton as the misthress do fur me, and lay it ferninst my two eyes and, sure, the masther'll niver know that I be sheddin tears afther lavin, and he niver shall at all—at all!"

When she arose ʼthe second time, she found the delicate, thread-like vessels that had distended the eyelids, emptied of their surplus blood, for which again she raised her eyes upward and said, "Blessed Virgin, now, and always be wid and bless the daire wise misthress. Och! she knows ivery thing, indade she do."

Thus closing her ejaculatory prayer and praise, she went down about her daily labor, as if nothing had happened.

In this last, long conversation between Mr. and Mrs. Clayton in reference to Bridget, she repeated instances of her faithfulness, and told him how, never sparing herself, she had given soul and body to their service; and begged him, by her love for them all, to let her remain. Wisely dwelling upon her fealty to him, she almost gained her point.

"But, you know, she has a terrible temper," he said.

"Yes, but would in no wise tell a falsehood—not even to screen herself from blame."

"But would do anything to help you out of a scrape; see how she lied about those tramps. I'll have no man, woman, or child about that will not tell all that's going on in this house!"

"You may bring one here who will tell you untruths."

"I will look well to that. I know a girl who will answer our purpose much better than Bridget, who has been here quite long enough—so long she has become independent and saucy."

Though his reply was direct and sharp, yet there was the least something in his voice, that gave signs of his relenting; that in his inmost soul he had been made to know he would never find another faithful soul like Bridget—another so capable of rendering them intelligent service.

But when his wife said, "She is always pleasant to the children, and never spoke to me unkindly," his relaxed features took again a harder look than ever, and he replied, in tones of the most insolent wrath, "That's it, now—just it, and shows she is in league with your deviltry! She's ugly and cross enough to me, God knows!"

"Never, unless you fly into a passion and abuse her without cause."

"You stand by her and she stands by you—I see! I see!" and here he arose and paced the room, looking much like a madman who needs to be confined in an asylum. Finally, turning to Elice, he said, "Madam, she shall go now, sure." Then leaving her, went to the kitchen and, as Bridget said, "With villainous tongue bad me pack up my duds and lave."

"What fur, thin?" she inquired.

"Why, for not letting me know what is going on in the house. If Elice whipped the children to death, you would put your heads together and smother it up; so, between you both, those poor little things suffer alive."

"Indade!" she answered, "and what would I be smuddering about the wee bairns? for it is she that trates them much the likelier of the two, little jewels; she never kicked them till they were black and blue, and never struck 'em a blow. If ye war half as dacint as herself, or the other swate wife, ye'd be much the better than ye be; and if ye'd not trate her like a baste, she'd a been wid ye now, to look after her own."

"Moses! Jupiter! How dare you insult me!"

"It's no insult, nor no lie, but God's blessed truth. If it's a lie I'm after tellin' yez, wot wus it thin, when yez good old father-in-law looked down into the coffin upon the snow white face of his swate child?"

"You must get out of this house, or I'll help you out!"

"But not till I tell yez. The poor old mon said, 'I bees

happier now than I've been in mony a day, for she be gone, swate one, where she can get no more abuse.' He didn't know that I heard him ; and troth, I be not the only one that did. If ye'd got divils instead o' saints, 'twould be better fur 'em, sure."

By this time Bridget had settled down into a calmness that nothing could move. Going quietly about, she gathered up her clothing, and when all was ready she visited the room of Elice, which brought to her dazed senses the first glimmering that her faithful servant, her friend, was really about to leave them. Having been so accustomed to her husband's passionate words, she thought he would at least allow her to remain ; and she could not see why this great infliction could be permitted. However, she accepted the situation, having faith in the promise that what we know not now shall be revealed hereafter ; that somehow, forth from the wrath of man, should flow praises to the Most High.

While Bridget was taking leave of the panic-stricken children who, though so young, seemed to realize something of the great calamity which this foreshadowed, Elice, with characteristic thoughtfulness, was penning a short note to her friend Mrs. Ashton, commending her dear servant to her care, until she could arrange her own household matters, so as to be able to give personal attention to securing her a suitable situation.

The last farewells had been said, and having returned to the kitchen, she had bestowed a lingering look upon her household gods ; her feet were pressing the threshold as if glued to the spot, when Mr. Clayton made his appeaaance.

"You might have remained," said he, "had it not been that you were always taking sides with my wife, against my interest ; otherwise the neighbors are given to fearful lying, which I do not believe. You are all for the mistress and not at all for the master."

" I'm for the right, and it's not meself that could be guilty of berating an innocent person ; and if any one axes me, I shall tell them the truth, that yez trate yer family like bastes. Yer nasty tricks I've always kept, and dropped a word of praise when, had I told what I knew, it would be, yez never like to see them ate enough. The mistress, dare crature, I shall love her thin till I die, and if she should iver want, it's me two hands that would work to buy her bread; for she's always been good to me, treated me like a mother. I'd die over the washtub to support her and dare little Robin!"

Here her handkerchief came to her eyes and, breaking down entirely, she went away.

"Old fool," exclaimed Mr. Clayton, "I'd like to give her the toe of my boot;" then banged the door, and locking it, went to look for Elice, whom he found trying to comfort the children.

"You can do the work now, yourself," he growled. "You are always kicking up some bobbery to get me into trouble."

CHAPTER XXIV.

Scarcely a month had passed, when Sammie Rathbun was adopted into the family of Professor Wilmington, a teacher of the languages in the Academy at Lavarre and his name changed to that of his own.

"I am not wealthy," he said; "can never, I fear, be able to leave the child a legacy; but he shall share equally with my own little daughter. I will carefully superintend his education, for I see in him germs of great promise."

It was not long before he astonished them with his brilliant genius; especially his musical talent, and completely charmed them by the wonderful sweetness of his voice as he sang some beautiful little Scotch or Italian airs, taught him by his mother.

He would blow through his fingers, so closely imitating the horn, that a listener would think he was playing upon one, providing they did not see the performer; and it was but a very short time before he brought out the most exquisite music upon this, as well as other instruments, which no one ever seemed to have heard before, and which were really melodies of his own improvision.

The family fairly worshiped him. He filled, to a great extent, the niche in the home made vacant by the loss of their darling; and while Mrs. Wilmington mourned for her own as a fond mother only can, she loved to watch the lights and shadows play upon his countenance, as she rehearsed some of the pretty stories she used to repeat to Willie.

Sammie loved his new home, and, young as he was, seemed to appreciate the kindness of the family; but oh! how often he would steal away, and wander back to the hut or to the grave of his mother, who, he said, was so beautiful, and whose likeness he was continually tracing on slate or paper.

"Now, don't that look like her?" he would say. " Here are the curls, and here the eyes, just like mine; but they were always so full of tears! I wish I knew what made her cry so much; but we did not have enough to eat, and she wanted to die; and once, a good, long time ago, she said she believed she would drown herself. And she went out one bright, moonlight night, just like now, and sat down by the lake up yonder for a good many hours, and wrung her hands, and said,—well, I can't remember all she said; but she wished she hadn't been so foolish to run away from her home—her 'sweet, sweet home,' and she wished she was back again; but her father and mother wouldn't forgive her; and she'd just like to be in the bottom of the lake, and would, if it weren't for me; and then she kissed me, and kissed me as much as a hundred times, I guess. But she's up in heaven now, ain't she? I wish I was there too, with her."

Everybody loved Sammy; he went by the name, sometimes, of the "Lute," as his voice resembled that instrument; again by the "Mocking-bird," as he imitated every sweet sound he heard. All predicted a bright future for him. His life had been rough thus far, they said; but with his talents, his disposition, energy and ambition, he was sure to make his mark in the world.

.   .   .   .

Three years have passed; Sammie's birthday has come again, and with it the remembrance of other birthdays, and the sweet words of his loved mother, who was laid away to rest where the chilling frosts and winter snows would never disturb her. Picking up his hat, he started in the direction of the cemetery. It was but a few moments before he reached the spot where, to his great surprise and joy, he found a lovely monument erected to her memory. Evidently it was that day's work; on it was the simplest inscription, "Frederica, my beloved;" and this was all. He went up to it and looked it over and over, when, sinking into a deep niche, beneath a cluster of rose buds, chiseled in the most delicate style, was the miniature of a young and lovely girl, apparently sixteen; it seemed but a copy of the same picture which he had now in his possession, guarded as closely as ever miser his gold.

"My mother!" he cried, "my sweet, sweet mother!" and looked away as far as his eyes could see, as if to catch a glimpse of some fairy who, with but a touch of her magic wand, had converted one of these bright, clear, shining pebbles at his feet into that lovely stone that rested above the remains of his darling.

For weeks people gathered around the grave 'of Frederica Rathbun, so curious to know the history of the beautiful girl who had so entranced them, as they gazed with tearful eyes upon her sweet face nestling away beneath the finely chiseled flowers, as some lovely bird in its downy nest; so deep it could scarcely be desecrated by a wicked, ruthless hand. But these were the queries: "Who the friend that loved her so much as to go to the expense of this work of art? Who so wealthy in all the country around as to afford anything half so elegant." All minds were busy with their conjectures; but none more wildly enthusiastic than Minnie Tattum, who declared she was a princess or daughter of some duke or lord of fabulous wealth; and they had sent this as a token of their love.

"I will find out all about it," she remarked to Elice; "I can never finish my book without it."

"Have you learned anything?"

"Nothing! But that the monument is Italian and sculptured in Rome, is evident, for it bears the name, also that of the artist. But the purchaser! that is the mystery—a father, brother, or lover? I think the latter. Have you seen the statuette? It is more beautiful than my imagination could picture. Our protégé is no pauper's brat; you might have known that by his looks. I am so glad we picked him up. See here, I have written several chapters about this matter, which I have guessed at as being correct. I would like my story to be true, but, if I cannot get at the facts, shall substitute fiction; but it would be so much better to say, 'A true story, etc., etc.;' people would be so moved by the narrative; I do hope it will make a sensation! Wouldn't it be fine to stand behind the scenes and see folks crying at the production of your brain?"

"Pooh! Nonsense, Minnie Tattum," cried her mother, rushing into the room; "I'll throw all that heap of paper in the fire. Do have common sense; if you'd do your sewing you would please me better. Writing, writing, all day long, something that no one will read!"

"O, mother, dear!" cried Minnie, jumping up and clasping her arms about her neck, "You'll be a sorry woman some day for underrating your daughter's abilities; when her name is wafted by every breeze that blows over land and over seas; when the high and mighty do homage to her talents—and—and—"

" And what, simpleton?" said old Hezekiah, thrusting his head into the door. "Let me finish that pretty speech. When folks want to know, who is she? Why, old mother Tattum's gossip—that's who; that laze abed in the mornin' till breakfast is ready, and pores over novels a part o' the day, and gads the street the rest o' the time."

"Fair play," answered Minnie. "It would have pleased you if we had never been sent to school, I suppose; if we had gone out as servants; no education yourself, you would like to have had all books excommunicated from the Tattum family. But here's our mother, bless her big heart, that has made the ladies of her daughters; she talks now and then, but does not mean a word she says about our wasting our time foolishly over

Shakespeare's plays, Moore's melodies, and Byron's beautiful lays. But she's proud of us; ain't you, 'darlint?'" And here Minnie gave her another kiss, and asked her if she would please waltz with her for a little exercise; or, if her father and she would step to a tune, she'd play "Fisher's Hornpipe," or anything they most liked; whereupon the old lady laughed till she declared her sides ached, and went out of the room, leaving her and Elice to continue their conversation.

.CHAPTER XXV.

A few days pass, and Walter Clayton enters his residence accompanied by a servant girl—a well-formed, buxom, country lass, altogether inexperienced in household matters, so much so that she was unable to take charge of the plainest baking, and as for cooking a meal and arranging it properly upon the table without assistance, it was quite out of the question.

"You will find Hettie a good girl," he said, addressing Elice, "one who is willing to do what she is bidden; and, better still, she will be ever so kind to the children."

"I hope so," she replied, but sighed when she thought how far short she would come of the trusty, efficient servant who had just left them.

"You can work?" inquired Elice.

"I make out, but I s'pose I don't do as well as I might; the fact is, mother never put me to it, and I can't wash nor iron, nuther, and I told your man so, but he said that needn't make no difference for you could do it yourself. I'm afraid I won't suit you; mebby I hadn't better stay."

"Yes you will; what you can't do may go undone, unless my wife can take hold and do it herself. The little work we have is nothing but play, and for the life of me, I can't see why we need any servant. Only three children and my wife and I; any woman ought to do it, and would if she weren't so confounded lazy!" said Walter, looking toward Elice, "and that is what I expected when I married you!"

Hettie was not naturally bad; however, was as plastic as clay in the hands of the potter; did not mean to do wrong, but she did, as she said, because she couldn't help it. This want of resistance in her character gave her a prey to the designing who were constantly leading her into trouble, when, to screen herself from blame, she would, if necessary, tell the wickedest falsehood. Consequently she became one of the best subjects the enemies of the family could find to aid them in their plottings, and could be bought, soul and body, with the least expense.

She had been there but a few weeks when Mrs. Tattum was as well acquainted with her as though she had known her all her life; and with blarney and smiles, cake and ice cream, kept her for hours, sometimes, prying into the affairs of the Claytons, and planning in her own mind how she should turn this knowledge to the best advantage.

She asked her if Mr. Clayton bought his sugar by the quantity, tea by the chest, coffee by the sack, and if he did not keep barrels of pork and beef in the cellar. Said she, "You might make nearly enough to buy you as fine clothes as any body has, without being at all suspected. Poor hired girls are kept under too much, and it is no sin to steal from your employers; it is only taking what you really ought to have. I will buy everything you have or can bring, and will pay you well for your trouble. However, you must be extremely cautious, otherwise you will be caught, which would be a very grave offense, and punishable by the law."

Hettie consented, although she felt that she was doing wrong, but stilled the voice of her conscience by thinking it was no harm to take from this rich man, as he would never feel it. So every week there was filched from the family stores, a little of everything in the line of provisions and carried over to the Tattums to be used as quickly as possible, lest these articles should betray them.

Mr. Clayton thought his grocery bills rather large, and laid it to the extravagance of his wife and her feeding everybody that came along; so he fretted and fumed and swore whenever he was requested to bring anything to the house. He said, " You will surely bring me to ruin, Elice, if you keep on being so wasteful ; will have us all in the poorhouse at last."

" I have had all the sewing to do, as you know, and Robin has been ill so I could not pay the attention to Hettie that I would like; and you told me she was so honest, of course it did not seem quite so necessary," answered Elice. " Hadn't the storeroom better be locked? then when any article is needed, I will deal it out; by this means you can tell where the fault lies."

" Yes, I presume that would suit you; but Hettie would leave if this were done, for it would be a direct insult to her, as much as to say she was dishonest. But as I know her to be every way trustworthy, I will give her the key and tell her to be very careful and not leave the door open, and then—then —well, I might as well say it—you won't get your fingers on very much to give away; for I believe you know where everything has gone, yourself."

Elice was full of grief, as she had been a hundred times before—too full for utterance ; and went away by herself—not to weep, but to think what could be done to remedy the evils that were crushing out all their pleasures, and making a foothold which, she feared, could never be removed. She took up the Bible and opened it ;—this blessed book had brought consolation in many a trying hour, and it would now, she thought. The first words upon which her eyes rested were these : " Cast thy burden upon the Lord and He shall sustain thee." That promise was sure ; and it was hers, for she had felt its truthfulness and power before. Again, "Whom the Lord loveth, He chasteneth, and scourgeth every son whom He receiveth." Oh, was it she that He was bringing through the furnace of affliction, to make her better? She turned back to Psalms, where she read, "They that trust in the Lord shall be as Mount Zion which cannot be removed, but abideth forever."

"I will not doubt, my Father," she murmured,—"help! oh, help!"

She went about her duties once again, cheerfully, feeling that He would take care of all her troubles. "In His own appointed time and way," she thought, "my deliverance will come; these crooked paths will be made straight; but, if not here, in the glorious hereafter; praises to the most High God!"

And here she rested as a weary traveler that had reached an oasis in a barren desert; like him, she had tasted of sweet waters gushing freely amid burning sands, and her soul was soothed; and she had gathered strength to take up the staff anew and go on her journey, striving to endure everything that was heaped upon her defenseless head, in a spirit of meekness, feeling how much better it was to suffer than to do wrong.

A few weeks passed; Mr. Clayton came into the room where Elice was and sat down.

"How do you like Hettie?" he enquired. "I think her a splendid girl, and capable of doing more than I thought. I don't believe anything goes to waste now, nor slides out in any shape. She says she is very particular to keep the store room locked, as I told her, and the windows all fastened. The truth is, I have so much confidence in her, I have not paid attention how things were going."

"By refering to our grocery bill, you must know all about it; is that satisfactory?"

"I don't know. Haven't thought to look it over since she came, not feeling in the least worried, for Mrs. Tattum and mother both give her an extra good name; and I am so glad she has more than borne out the report of her. Steal! by no means; she would not take a farthing that did not rightfully belong to her. I thought I'd test her: I was counting over my money one evening and dropped a dollar bill—did it purposely, of course ; she noticed it in an instant, and called attention to my carelessness, as she thought, and established her reputation for honesty with me. If you had found it, you would have kept it, and as much more as you could have laid your hands upon."

Elice did not reply to this insulting remark, nor did she tell him of the bits of ribbon, silk, velvet, etc., too numerous to mention, that this servant had managed to purloin from her drawers, for she felt he would not believe it; and further, thought he might learn a good lesson yet, from his misplaced confidence; that God himself would teach him; yet, how, she could not see. It would all be right.

In a few evenings, Walter came to the front door, and found it locked. He rang the bell furiously, when Elice hastened to open it. In great rage he demanded the cause of its being barred against him. "You never care how much you trouble me—why do you keep so closely?"

"This was one of your orders, you remember, papa, long ago, and I have fulfilled it ever since, as I felt it was necessary for the safety of the house."

Her words were lost, however, or the most of them, as he went straight through into the kitchen, knocking over every chair that came in his way, catching up the cat and tossing it through an open window, and taking up a poodle on the toe of his boot and sending it quite into the street; while Charlie and Blanche ran for the bed-room, and only felt safe when they had hidden under the bed, wondering what was the matter now.

"I have just heard," he said to Hettie, "that those children are abused, and shamefully, right before your face and eyes. Why did you not inform me of this?"

"Who told you?"

"Mrs. Tattum, who said she got her news from you."

She was about to say, "She's an old liar;" but remembering their confidences, replied, "I do not recollect having said any such thing, and had rather not be questioned any more about it."

"Why do you wish to keep this a secret from me? I pay you good wages, and you ought to appreciate it. Do you know what Bridget was, sent away for? Simply because she kept everything to herself, and under no circumstances informed on her mistress."

Hettie hesitated; it was not a correct statement of matters that he wanted. If she told him the truth, he was far less liable to believe her than a falsehood; and she did not wish to lose his good opinion, so replied, "I might have said as much, but it was so long ago I don't remember. What did Mrs. Tattum say about it?"

"That Mrs. Clayton kept the children all one day in that dark cellar-way, never giving them a mouthful to eat, and promised them a whipping if they informed me. She heard their cries herself, and mother was passing that very day, and thought she heard them sobbing; and was very sorry she had not come in to look after the poor little things."

"Ask the children."

"Don't play up Bridget Donnelly with me now," he said angrily; "but answer me at once."

"It was true."

"Why didn't you tell me before?"

"You's gone so long, I forgot," she answered petulantly.

He then found Elice upon whom for one full hour he poured a continued volley of abuse, swearing and raving like a madman, finally saying, "Were it not for the law, I would horsewhip you!"

The moment she found an opportunity, she answered, "Call the children, and ask them if such a circumstance ever occurred."

He questioned them closely: "Why, no, papa, when did mamma do that?"

9

" Are you so afraid of that woman that you dare not speak the truth ?"

"No, thir, I ain't afraid of my dear, good mamma!"

"Well, then, tell me all about it, or I'll shut you up in the cellar-way myself, and whip you to death in the bargain."

"Yeth, she did, I geth.   I don't remember."

Frightened by his manner, little Blanche did not know what to say, so told a falsehood, but not intentionally.

"A precious good thing for you, little lady, that you owned it.   Now will you let me know hereafter when your mother misuses you?"

"Yeth thir," she answered in a trembling voice.

Turning to Elice, he said, "Now, what about it?   Oh, dear, I wish I had never seen you; to think I should bring a devil into the house to take the place of their angel mother; it is more than I can endure; and I will not much longer, you may depend upon it!"

After her father had gone, Blanche threw her arms about her mother's neck, and, with sobs and tears, asking for forgiveness, said, "I did not mean to tell a lie, but papa made me."

"I know, and God knows all about it, little one," and Elice took the child upon her lap, and told her pretty stories to divert her mind from the painful subject.   She then listened to their evening prayers, and tucked them away snugly in their little bed.   And as she gave them the last good night kiss, scalding tears dropped upon their upturned faces.

CHAPTER XXVI.

It is midnight; Walter Clayton has remained at the store to ascertain how his accounts stand with the firm of Clayton & Coon. It has been three years since he cast this burden from his mind; but they were now about to close up the business, for a time, at least, and it becomes necessary to turn his attention again to the subject. He looks over the long columns of his grocery bills, and wonders if it can be true that all of the searticles could have been consumed by his family.

Some of the items were in his own hand-writing; some in the clerks, while others were in the partner's. Of course there could be no foul play unless, indeed, Mr. Coon had entered more than was taken, to defraud him; but that was not probable, for he would not dare to do it; there was no one to blame but himself, if Hettie had got things that were unnecessary, or more of them than was needed, for he had given express commands, if she came to the store in his absence, to give her what she called for. But no one else was allowed that privilege, not even his own wife; so, if the bills were large, it must all be right, for Hettie was as honest as the day was long. Elice had no access to the store room, therefore she had no chance to give away, to be extravagant, or to feed all the beggars that came along, for which she had such a terrible propensity.

He proceeded to foot up the account—"Great God!" he ejaculated, "can it be with all my caution, that I am fifteen hundred dollars extra indebted to this firm for the last over the former three years? is it true? it is true," he sighed; "here it is, all in black and white. What can it mean? Elice must be to blame. I wish I hadn't got married. Of course she's had extra keys, and stole out of the store room ; she's always raising the devil with me, someway; she'll ruin me yet, always wasting something, but never doing anything to help along in the world. If it were not for my little children, I'd run away. She's as sly as a fox and sharper than lightning, or I'd catch her, sometimes, at some of her tricks. She lets on to me that she is so saving, but it is false ; she is not—is not! Curse the women! not exactly that, for there are some good ones in the world. There's Hettie, and she's pretty, too ; but how those things could have been taken and she not know it, is a mystery to me. I'll go right home and ask her—put her on the watch the rest of the night ; for it must be done when we are all abed and asleep. Oh! what won't a treacherous woman do? But if I catch her, she'll wish she had never been born! I've half a mind to play spy on her myself; between us two, she'll be caught, and no mistake; if it is not to-night, it will be some other time. I'll tell her we are afraid of some one breaking into the store, and I'm going to sleep there all the week. Capital! that's just what I'll do, and she'll never mistrust. I wonder what the lady will say when she finds herself in my trap at last."

He went home. Elice was still up waiting for him. She had been cutting over some of his old clothes for a suit for Charlie, and had commenced making them ; she showed it to him, and said, "Do you not think it will look pretty well? I have sat up to get them as far along as possible ; for he must have them to-morrow afternoon, as some of our friends have sent word they will take tea with us. I had hard work to get them out at all; but by management I have accomplished it. Now, do not forget, and say, papa, that I gave that suit of yours to old tramps, as you have sometimes before," smiling and going up and patting him on the cheek; "for you know your own little son will soon be wearing them;—but I must hurry up; I will sit up as long as you do, and then we will go to our dreams."

"Go to the d———l!" he replied, his brow lowering.

Elice saw a cloud gathering and said nothing further. She sat down to her work, when she tried to think what possibly could be the matter; but she had not the remotest idea.

He heard Hettie in the kitchen, and wondered what she was up for at that hour of the night, and asked Elice if she knew.

"She has been to a party," I believe, "and has just returned."

He hastened to see her.

"Do you know why it is, Hettie, that our grocery bill since you have been in our family, should so exceed that of the former three years?"

"I do not, sir; it is none of my business. I suppose you have had more to feed," she replied, coloring. "I have taken as good care of things as I could, and if you don't like my style I can go home."

"Why, now, don't be angry, Hettie; I'm not blaming you at all, unless, as I have thought perhaps, you have been careless and left your keys around where other parties could make use of them—you know whom I mean."

This little talk gave her new ideas, but they were several moments revolving in her mind before she replied. It was a grand opportunity to shift the loss upon Elice, but it would be too mean; she did not like to do it; she could steal, for she had been made to believe it was no sin to take whatever she could turn to advantage, providing it came out of Mr. Clayton; for he would do the same had he the chance,—not exactly that; but, what was the same thing, he would take every advantage in his power of a lack of penetration in the man, woman, or child—rich or poor—to drive a good bargain; and, were they silly enough, like the poor little fly that was enticed by the silky web of the spider and was caught, it was ten chances to one if they ever got out again.

Mr. Clayton walked the floor uneasily. Hettie felt that he was waiting for an answer, but she did not know just what to say; finally he looked up coaxingly, and told her to tell him if she knew "all about things," and it should never go any farther; if it were as he at first suspected, he would like to know.

She feared to tell the truth; and she had not strength of character to resist the temptation longer, of shifting this loss from her own to the shoulders of an innocent party; so she said, "I have suspected as much."

"Don't you know? Tell me the circumstances."

"I have missed my key very often from its hiding place; when I did, I could hunt up another; after a while I would find it again. Sometimes I've seen ragged boys go away from the house at a very late hour with baskets; I didn't know what was in them; it was after I went to my room always."

"Of course it could be no one but Elice."

"It was she; but you've promised not to tell."

"I'll say nothing to her about it—but curse her! curse her!" he muttered, as he went out of the house and on the sidewalk; "I believe I'll get a divorce."

It was neither moonlight nor starlight; the sky was covered with black, floating clouds; now and then a bit of blue was visible; but it was so dark a person unused to the town could not tell in what locality he was. But it was not much matter to Mr. Clayton; he knew every foot of soil upon which he was treading, for he had traveled over it for years; whether it was night—pitchy night—or daylight with all its effulgent charms; whether a howling winter had set in with maddening fury, or a glorious summer had arrived, redundant with birds, balmy zephyrs and beautiful blossoms, for he had lost, or as good as lost, fifteen hundred dollars, and all by an intriguing wife, as he had worked himself up to believe; and he wished he was dead.

"I might as well be dead," he said, "for what does a man amount to who has to live with such a woman as that?"

He heard voices. "Where am I?" he said to himself. He put his hand out and touched a house. At that moment a faint light glimmered through a window, and then, in a moment was gone, but was sufficient for him to tell that it was the residence of Tattum. Two of them were in earnest conversation about something; and, as he heard his own name mentioned in connection with that of his servant girl, he thought it was a fine opportunity to find out what was going on; if gossips were busy at that hour, it must mean something, and he was going to know all about it.

It was one of the daughters and Mrs. Tattum, that was evident, for the former said, "Oh! can it be, that you, a church member, and of good standing, should connive with that girl to steal from the family who have employed her? It is a heinous sin; and, when you do such a thing, you are directly violating a commandment—offending the master whom you profess to serve; and if found out, laying yourself liable to a punishment by the common laws of our country. Dear mother, break off from your sins by way of repentance, and never be guilty of so debasing an act again."

"She brings these groceries in a basket and leaves them," answered her mother; "and I do not see the harm to take them, inasmuch as they come from a rich, old man that wouldn't give a person anything to keep him from starving to death; it's all right, Vina, you've got too much conscience, and it goes in the wrong direction. Nobody will ever find it out, either, and we are poor, we're very poor; and what are we to do?"

"You pay Hettie for these things?"

"Yes, a little something; it don't amount to much, what I give her—sometimes the girls' old, cast-off flowers they have worn on their hats for several years; then again, one of their old silks to make over; so you see we live pretty well out of it, without costing much."

"Let this be the last night you ever do the like; promise me, or I'll return home to-morrow, and never darken your doors again."

"Oh! don't take a little thing like that, so to heart; old Clayton is worth an even million, and can never feel it; and what do I care if he does? Why! I come honestly by them; I pay for them. I do not go to his house, and get them; and am not supposed to know they come from there, either. Go to bed, and go to sleep!"

"No, not till you say you have taken the last farthing's worth you ever will, from that servant girl."

"May be you'd like me to swear to it?"

"Yes, here's the Bible—say solemnly, with your hand upon this blessed book, that you will never take, use nor conceal anything that is not your own."

"Here it goes, then—I swear." Aside to herself—"Just to please you, little goose. Well, I believe I'm worse than what I used to be; once that would have made me feel solemn, but now I don't care! What's the use of trying to be good? somebody is all the while stepping on somebody's toes, and everybody is all the while slandering everybody. If you are an angel, folks don't like you any the better; if you're a devil, you are respected none the less; and I'm going to get all the good out of the world that I can, and just where I can, that's all there is about it, if I be a church member. But I don't mean to be caught at it, at all, mind that; Mrs. Tattum, don't get caught at it;" and then, laughing at what she imagined her own witty thoughts, she turned over in bed and went to sleep.

Mr. Clayton was confounded at what he had heard; he did not know what to do. "Is it possible," he said mentally, "that Hettie could do such a thing as has just been alleged to her? I will go and see her. May be she and my wife have connived together; it would be just like Elice, she'd do most anything to get a little money ahead; and what in the world she wants of it, is more than I can tell; what any woman wants more than just enough to eat and drink, is beyond my comprehension. Well, besides clothes to make her comfortable, a good calico for every day, and then a slick-up dress that's a little better, and one meeting dress ought to satisfy her. I'll make it warm for her now, if she's helped to steal from me these past three years! but then, it couldn't be, for old mother Tattum just said that she paid Hettie in ribbons and old dresses; and I vum! my wife is too high-toned to take anybody's old trumpery, so I rather guess she hadn't anything to do with sending off those groceries. But there's one thing she's been to blame about, anyway, and she'll get a piece of my mind about it; and that is, that she didn't see to things better; and to punish her I'll not get her that new bonnet I promised her, nor the children any Christmas presents either. Why, when a new girl comes into a house, it's a woman's place to keep an eye out on everything there, just as we merchants do when we get new clerks. I'd like to see a clerk of mine that could take a cent's worth and I not know it. Well, women are curious creatures, and no mistake; and my wife beats them all, to let fifteen hundred dollars slip out of the house and she not pay any attention to it, or even know it! But I guess the best way will be not to say anything about it; for she'll ask me why I took the keys away from her, and gave them to the hired girl; that she couldn't help her taking things, when she had the keys and slept so near the store-room; and then she'd boohoo and cry, and that'll be all there is about it. And if I go to Hettie, she'll be mad and get up on her ear again, and say she'll leave; and I don't want her to go, anyway, for she's good to the children, say what you've a mind to, and pretty too, and generally pleasant; and I like someway to have her around the house; it would be lonesome without her, she's been in the family so long."

So he made up his mind he'd try to forget all about it; went home, and in a very kind way, told Hettie that he guessed he'd take the keys, and take care of them; then, if there were anything missing, it wouldn't be laid to her; he should dreadfully hate to see an innocent person blamed for what they were not guilty.

CHAPTER XXVII.

"I'm afraid there is going to be a terrible thunder storm!" said Mrs. Carlyle upon entering the residence of the Tattums.

"What! what! There never was a fairer day, nor never will be," said Mrs. Tattum.

"That is, if the lightning can be drawn from the clouds."

"Oh! I see what's up now; don't keep me in suspense. There is no one around to hear you; go on with your gossip, my dear, old news-bearer," Mrs. Tattum said, laughing.

"Not quite so pointed, or you may not hear what will be lucky for you to know."

"Nothing about me, I hope, nor my girls? they're always getting me into some scrape."

"Just what you've helped me out of many times, and that's the reason I came to let you know what was going on. You've got a pretty mighty long tongue, you know, as well as myself, and in case of any trouble arising therefrom, any contest, you've always been smart enough to stack your cards and throw out trumps to yourself and partner, sometimes accompanied with a V, or an X, which brings you success every time. Are you prepared?"

"Why do you keep me waiting?" Mrs. Tattum said impatiently, "if you have anything to say, speak out at once. If bad comes to worse, I'm ready for anything, and not without."

"You remember what you and Augusta were saying the other day at our house in the presence of Mrs. Col. Thompson?

—that Deacon Smith got drunk sometimes, and his wife was an old spinster before he married her that nobody but he would have. Now you thought she was such a friend to you that she wouldn't tell, but she did, and there is a great row about it; old Smith has been to the minister's and told him, and said if you did not go before the church and confess to the lie, he should compel a meeting to be called, and bring you and Augusta forward to prove what you said, which could never be done, for he would never rest under the stain of your vile lips ; and then, if they kept two such busy bodies—meddlesome, mischief-makers in the church, he should call for a letter."

"Oh, grief! my good friend, what shall I do?"

"I told you, shall I repeat it ?—stack your cards, and throw out trumps to yourself and partner. Your fertile imagination will tell you better than I can just how this is to be done."

"But I must first have a partner."

"I am at your service ; if not sufficient, another can easily be obtained; that will be two against one."

"What is your plan?"

"When Mrs. Col. Thompson is brought forward to give in her testimony against you, she will probably be asked when and where the slander originated, and who was present at the time. She will tell, and this will give me an opportunity of laying her in a falsehood; you then can bring up that little sewing woman, who was there—over the left; between us both she will be excommunicated instead of you and Augusta."

"Capital! capital!—what can I ever do for you."

"I don't want anything at all—only—well—if Augusta would embroider my baby a suit throughout, I'd be so glad."

"Agreed! but how lies the land?"

"All right for you."

"Then you know?"

"I was coming from prayer meeting last evening—you remember how dark it was—well, I heard a couple just ahead of me in conversation—'twas old Smith and his wife—from whom

I learned that Parson Gray favored you and Augusta; said he hardly believed you would be guilty of such a thing; that you had always seemed to have a strong desire for the 'blessed cause,' and he considered it very slanderous to accuse ladies of your standing in the church, of so base a thing as falsehood. Don't let it worry you, sister Tattum, for all will yet come out right."

"Have you the cards? You know you put them in your pocket after we had finished that game of euchre at your house yesterday."

"Why! why! look out! don't speak above your breath, for you know well 'tis against our creed to amuse ourselves by any games of chance, but just draw that bolt; we will then be safe from intruders and I will shuffle my cards, which I brought purposely, and tell your fortune. I can do it you know, as aptly and truly as any gipsy."

"What you can't think of no one can."

" Here, cut them now ; the king of spades is old Smith—how I hate him—the queen, his wife, remember. I'll put you in hearts, as I always have, because you are so large hearted. The club woman is Mrs. Col. Thompson, and the diamond myself."

"And our minister? You forgot him."

"Oh, yes, he is the king of hearts, and if we don't see all the black ones in a muss, we will steer our boats in another channel. Well, look here, you and I are together surrounded by all the light cards; there is a little trouble for us, but the king of hearts, bless him, is near to help us out, while the rest are wading through fog. You see them right in the midst of the ace, face, six, nine and ten of spades—the worst in the whole pack, and I'm glad of it. I've been aching for just such a chance to pay them off for the way they have treated me, and now I've got it."

" The trial, of course, will not be till after the donation," said Mrs. Tattum ; " can't you wait for your suit until then, for there will hardly be time to embroider two, and Augusta must present the minister's wife with one for her baby, and I — I — well, I must do something handsome, for you know it don't make any odds how good a person is it tells on their decisions."

"And what you do now must tell, Sister Tattum or — maybe ——"

"Spit it out; cut my head off or leave it on, for the minister is invested with power. Well, you asked me if I was prepared ; I have just received my rent money with which those long promised silks for the girls were to be purchased; I'll give it as free as air, and they must go without until I —" She was going to add, "am paid for next quarter's rent," but was interrupted by the well known voice of Hezekiah who had been now some time listening at the keyhole, where he heard the most of the ladies' conversation.

"Kin go round with a subscription paper for poor children, or git into somebody's hen roosts, and now you're goin' to take all my rent money—blazes ! let me in and quick, too, or I'll tell on you—you be sure ! — then to himself, "That woman o'mine gits herself into more fusses nor I ever seen a body, but she crawls out o' the smallest holes ; dear, dear, I didn't think when she's regrettin' to that old elder how her husband was sich a sinner, and she felt so bad about his playin' keerds, she'd do the like herself. Talkin' about trumps, she's one, that, Mary Ann. But blixun ! why can't I get into that 'ere room ? Mary Ann!"—shaking the door—"you better, now, let me in or I'll push the pesky thing over."

"He's drunk ! I must conciliate him, or he'll rush into the street and tell all he knows," said Mrs. Tattum.

"Well I'll go home, and you hasten, for it will be quite a puzzle now to carry out all our plan ; and if we have old Hezekiah against us, still more difficult. Hurry up, or he'll pull the door down !"

"Dear husband," said Mrs. Tattum as soon as she had let him

into her presence, "you always were just as good as could be, especially when any of us got into trouble."

"Going to give us taffy—that tastes better nor sass—but go on."

"Don't be foolish; you know just all about this piece of business as you heard all our conversation; we talked loud on purpose—or I did—now you don't want us to be disgraced by being turned out of the church, as we surely will be unless—"

"You kin stack yer keerds."

"Well, yes, anything you like, only so we're shrewd enough to hide the cheat."

"But I ain't going out o' my vittalls for no donation to keep yer to the head o' the heap in that ere church."

"But I'll promise if you don't pick up a fuss in any way, to make it up—every cent that I give; you've pretty good sense, my dear Hezekiah, and know 'twould disgrace your unsullied reputation, as well as ours, not to see us safely through this terrible muss."

"Go your own way, Mary Ann; I know o' three or four new porpers that you can begin to clothe up to go to the Sunday school."

"Now, dear Hezekiah, don't be ridiculous! I don't ask you to help me in any way, only to keep your mouth shut."

"Fur you know mighty well I wouldn't lie fur yer—don't yer? How sweet you are! just like winegar and molasses—ain't that what they ketch flies with? it's good just for the skercity o' the article."

Here he staggered to the closet to take another drink. "Well," said he, "I should think I were—hic—'toxicated if 't-wa-s-a-n't I ne-vr take the s-t-u-ff, only fur med'cin, and Mary Ann does that h-e-r-s-e-l-f."

CHAPTER XXVIII.

There is a series of meetings being held at the church of which Mrs. Tattum and her daughters are members. The celebrated Dr. Adams, from New York, has come to assist them in a revival, and there is a great commotion in the little town of Lavarre.

People who were in the habit of attending upon divine service went regularly each evening, to listen to the burning words that fell from this great man's lips; not for the good they might receive; not that they cared to be benefitted particularly by his teachings, but for the same reason they would go to a celebrated play or theatre—just for amusement, from a curiosity to hear what new thing he would have to say.

They were in from the country in large sleighs drawn, sometimes, by four horses; and from far and wide, wherever they heard about the meetings, flocked to the church, filling up the seats, then the aisles, next the vestibule, while hundreds went away for want of standing-room in the great brick church, where this man would talk for hours to the excited throng, striving to lead them to Christ, first, by the love that He bore them in coming to the world to die for them, His great goodness in giving His own life to save perishing sinners, then by the tortures and torments of hell, where they would surely go, unless they repented of their sins. And, as he portrayed the beauties of heaven, the glories of that blissful place, to which they might all have an entrance, and then the darkness of the yawning pit, he seemed to move the throng as though it had been but one man ; and many, when he had finished, were ready to gather to the anxious seats, kneel lowly down, and ask mercy at the hands of their offended Judge. Among them was Hettie; she had been as attentive a listener as he had ; there was no meeting that she had not attended. She had heard him read the commandments, then take them up one by one and explain them, dwelling largely on the sin of theft. She never saw it in the light she did then, her eyes were opened, great scales, as it were, dropped off; and in an agony of mind she was ready to ask, "What shall I do to be saved?" Night after night she went to the altar with others; she tried to pray, but the heavens were as brass ; she got no consolation from this source.

The days dragged their weary length along. It seemed as if the clouds of perfect despair had settled over her life, and the fires of endless torment were leaping up to consume her. "I will go to church, once more," she said. "Oh! if I could but have the prayers of my dear mother, and her advice at this critical period, how glad I would be! for I believe she is a Christian; I know she is, for her life and conversation show it."

The bells rang; she put on her bonnet and shawl, and wound her way along, with many others, with whom it had now become a serious thing, to the house of God, to hear more of the way of salvation. Mrs. Tattum was among the rest; Walter Clayton went also.

Never had there been a more solemn congregation; and, as the Rev. Dr. Adams arose, his face beaming with love divine, it seemed as though one of the old prophets had been sent to earth to preach the everlasting Gospel to the children of men. He took for his text, "Confess your sins one to another." He said, if a man wrongs his brother man, he should ask his forgiveness; he should not be ashamed to go to him and say he was sorry for what he had done. If he had been slandering a person, he could not be blessed of the Lord unless he confessed the sin, and strove with all his powers to undo the mischief that his

10

wicked words might have caused; that no person could ever enjoy religion, if, after a duty had been made clear to him, he did not hasten, with all diligence, to perform it; that it was an obligation he owed his Almighty Father and Friend, who stood with open arms to receive and bless him when he should have done all his will.

Hettie felt that the words would apply to herself, and she resolved that she would be led by the teachings of the Spirit; that then, perhaps, the great weight which, like a mountain, rested upon her heart and conscience, would be rolled away; and, when invitations were again given, she was among the first to seek the enquirers' seat.

Mrs. Tattum, in the meantime, was all through the congregation inviting souls to Christ, trying to induce them to go to the altar for prayers. She could talk well, that is, she could make a free use of her tongue, and those unacquainted with her thought her a very pious soul, a zealous Christian woman and a faithful worker in the vineyard of the Lord. She came forward; two young ladies from the country following her, and took her seat by the side of Hettie. When they knelt, she dropped upon her knees by the side of them.

After a season of prayer, the enquirers were invited to speak; the minister talked again of the importance of confessing their sins one to another; hoped there was not one there, but would take up the cross—that was the only way they might expect to be blessed; that he would not take the time, himself, but sincerely wished he would hear from all, and then sat down.

Hettie was among the first who arose. She said, "I have a weight upon my soul, for I have sinned, and I wish to take this opportunity to tell the whole congregation all about it; and, as Mr. Clayton is here, I will this blessed moment crave his forgiveness. For the past three years, I have stolen provisions, and carried them in baskets to the house of Mrs. Hezekiah Tattum, there to be used by her family; this lady made me believe it was no sin, but I now have my eyes opened, and I feel that I have ·committed one of the most atrocious of crimes— theft! But what troubles me more than all the rest, when questioned by Mr. Clayton in reference to the missing articles, saying he knew they never could have been used in his family, I told him his wife stole my keys from their hiding place, went into the store-room, and took out those things, a portion of which she gave to old tramps and sold the rest, all of which was a wicked lie! Oh! what shall I do? for this last sin can never be forgiven me!" And here she broke down, and sat down, sobbing and groaning, as though the bottomless pit was opening to receive her; and she felt there was no escape.

Before Hettie was fairly seated, Mrs. Tattum was making her exit from the front door; she had pulled and pulled her shawl all the time she was talking, thinking to make her hold her peace, but all to no purpose; so the next best thing she thought to be done, was to make her way home. But, on rising from her seat, she found her little terrier puppy had followed her, and taken up his temporary dwelling-place in the spacious folds of her dress. Unintentionally she had aroused him from his slumbers by treading upon his toes, when he set up a howl, attracting all eyes in the direction; but she hurried along, the rougher of the men joking and laughing, one of the boldest ones speaking out as she passed, "Come back, old hypocrite, and get your dog;" another one actually humming in a low voice, but so she could hear, "Keyser, don't you want to buy a dog."

Mr. Clayton, too, went away muttering curses on protracted meetings, where people go to make fools of themselves; and resolved he would give Hettie a good blowing up for raising such a breeze, and getting up such commotion among such a crowd of people.

Mrs. Tattum passed out of the church into the street, into the darkness of the night, alone and unattended. In her great hurry to get away from the scene of her dishonor, she had forgotten her lantern, and as her sight had become somewhat dimmed by age, she did not make much headway over the pavement, but slipped and slid, till at last, making a misstep, she plunged headlong into a ditch between the walk and the road.

"Merciful heavens!" she groaned as she found herself going, "What shall I do?;" but before she could recover her foothold, she was immersed in the mud and mire.

Walter Clayton came that way at the moment, and at a glance saw just who it was. He bit his lips with rage, walked the faster, cursed her for bringing so much trouble to his house, and stopped long enough to say, "You can lie there and drown, for all me. I would not help you out if I knew you would die!" But the barking of her little dog soon brought assistance, however: two gentlemen who of all the world she would have preferred not to have seen her in such a distressed state—her pastor and another brother in the church. They had been away on very important business, on the cars, and had but a few moments before returned, and thought they would go over to the church, as they might be in time for the conference and prayer meeting after the regular service.

"Why! Sister Tattum, is that you?" they both exclaimed at once, after they had got her out of the ditch, and she was fairly on her feet once more.

"Oh, yes," she said, while she proceeded to spit out the dirty water, "you see I was taken with one of my sick spells while I was in the meeting, and thought that I'd go home—oh, dear! oh, dear!

They asked her if she was much hurt.

"No—oh, no," she said; "a little jarred, like; that is all— but only see my terrible condition!" while she picked chunks of ice and mud out of her hair that had fallen down, and hung around her neck.

They assisted her to her own door; told her how sorry they felt for her; wished it would not make her sick; and sincerely hoped it would not frighten her away from the meetings.

Hezekiah meeting her in the hall, said, "It's good enough for you; no business going off every night, leaving me alone, and I hope every time you go you'll git the same sass!"

In a short time, Minnie and Mrs. Glenn entered the house. As soon as they discovered their mother had left the church, they followed her, but not in time to render her any assistance. When Minnie found her mother was not hurt, she commenced laughing at the ludicrous figure she cut, and going up and taking hold of her, she insisted that she was never in a better fix in her life to dance a jig; that it would do her good, stir up her blood, and keep her from taking cold.

Mrs. Glenn sat down and wept, simply saying, "O, mother dear, you did get caught after all! 'the way of the transgressor is hard.' 'Man proposes but God disposes.' I trust you have learned a lesson that will last you all your life."

There was great excitement the next day about the revelations of the past evening, as well as the accident that occurred. It was in the newspapers, and little boys had commenced selling them before it was hardly time to be up in the morning.

Mr. Tattum was an early riser, and generally had five cents tucked away in one of his pockets with which to buy a paper.

"Hello! my man, you see, if you git here the fust, I'll take yours; so hurry up," he said to one of the many boys.

The first thing upon which his eye rested was this, headed in large letters:

"SHOCKING ACCIDENT!

"Mr. Hezekiah Tattum, a prominent man of our town, from too free use of spirituous liquors, of which he is said to be quite fond, lost his gravity last evening in coming home from church, and went, head first, into a big ditch; and, had it not been for the prompt assistance rendered him, might have expiated his sin of intemperance, by losing his life—a warning to all men who are so unfortunate as to yield to their morbid tastes and passions for rum!"

"Me? me?—liars! thieves! vagabonds! I haint been in no ditch! They'll take that back, or I'll take the law on 'em!

Here, boy, go up to the editor of that paper, and tell him if he don't make it right in the next twenty-four hours, I'll horse-whip him; it's 'bout as nigh as newspaper men git at things! Tell him 'twas my wife, nor she want drunk, nuther—not—well —not as I knowed of. I wont tell no lie to him; tell him to come to her, and she'll relate the circumstances jist as they ware, won't you, Mary Ann?"

By the next day they had the truth, made their retractions and concessions; and the whole matter—her exit from the church, accident, etc.—was heralded in the "Daily," much to the mortification of the Tattum family, with these words added: "All of which sprang from misplaced confidence. If men would only learn to appreciate their kind, industrious, frugal wives, instead of wresting from them their rightful authority, putting it into the hands of strangers, they might, in a few years, save, instead of lose a fortune."

Mr. Clayton did not pay much attention to the gossip that was afloat; he was too busy trying his powers of persuasion upon his servant girl, who had fully come to the determination to quit the place of her temptations, and lead a different life, although he affirmed that they never had a more trusty girl, and told her there would be no further trouble about things; that she was a silly little goose for exposing the matter, but to never mind, now, that it couldn't be helped, and threw the whole of the blame upon Mrs. Tattum for coaxing her into it, and his wife, for not taking better care of things.

Elice knew nothing of what had taken place,—the wonderful *denouement* that had come to the, ears of the public, all of a sudden, as she had been sick for several days, unable to leave her room; and the matter heretofore had been kept quite secret; so she asked Walter why it was that Hettie had made up her mind to go.

Taking advantage of this ignorance and seeing one of her friends seated by the side of her, he thought this a fine opportunity for bringing Elice again into disrepute, to lessen her in-

fluence in a certain direction, and to shift the blame of the loss
of their servant on to her ; so he replied, '' When you get a
good girl like Hettie, you ought to treat her better ; but, inasmuch as you have a tyrannical disposition and a bad temper, I
never expect to be able to keep good help when we get it, long
at a time ; so you can do the work, yourself, and see how you
like it. It will be a good lesson for you."

These words were spoken in such apparent good faith, that a
a less experienced person than Mrs. Ashton might have been
deceived ; but she answered him by saying—'' We know all
about it, Mr. Clayton ; we were all at church last evening, and
we all take the papers. I brought one with me, to show Mrs.
Clayton."

Mr. Clayton was about to leave the room in a hurry—said,
'' I have very important business that needs my immediate attention."

Had it been any other than the lady mentioned, he would
have stood and argued the matter, but her husband occupied a
very important position at court, and he had so many lawsuits
that he feared to offend the family, lest their influence might
sometimes weigh against him, and injure him pecuniarily ; so he
thought best to keep silence.

'' But a word before you go," said Mrs. Ashton ; ''don't tear
yourself away. I was never so happy as last evening, when
this whole community, from words uttered by that simple-
hearted servant girl of yours, operated upon by the spirit of
God himself, which every one in the house felt were as true as
the Bible, was brought to feel how much and how deeply you
had wronged as good a wife as man could ever have ; for many
there had been made your confidential friends long enough, for
you to pour into their ear tales of her dishonesty, her waste-
fulness, lack of interest, etc., in her domestic relations when,
indeed, whatever loss you sustained was not by her, but by
your own mismanagement, and, as the *Herald* remarks, ''misplaced confidences," and a love of listening to anything that

may be said against her by her enemies, and working yourself
up to a belief of the same, when your own better judgment
ought to teach you that a house divided against itself cannot
stand; and that a woman with but a small portion of common
sense would know better than to squander the earnings of her
husband, lest they might themselves come to want and beggary,
by the means."

He did not venture a reply; but walked out of the house
into the air, to cool his smothered wrath, wishing that woman
was some one else—that some one else was a man; then, how
quick he would horsewhip him for his impudence! It was not
the first time that Mrs. Ashton had rebuked him for his growing propensity to bring disrepute upon his wife, and he felt the
sting most keenly; and wished, he thought, he could see her in
as good a position as Mrs. Tattum, the evening previous, and
no one to extricate her from her troubles, he'd serve her as he
did that venerable lady; and then he smiled, when he thought
of her position, and verily wished she had not been blessed
with a little dog, even, to give the alarm, and—and—well, never
mind the rest; he would not like us to tell, for he certainly
would be ashamed to have those thoughts published to the
world.

CHAPTER XXIX.

"Good morning, Sister Carlyle," said the Rev. Dr. Gray. "I am glad you have called, as I wish to have a confidential conversation with you in reference to a little church business; and, believing as I do, in your sincerity as a Christian, your words and advice will go a good ways with me. Now, Brother Smith urges a church trial; he says he has been slandered by Sister Tattum and her daughter, to a painful extent; yet, upon their confessing to the falsity of their statements before the church, he will forgive them; otherwise, he must establish his character by requiring them to prove what they have said; if this could not be done, they or he must leave the church. 'Tis a sad state of affairs—one which I deprecate exceedingly; I wish to do what is right with both parties; I am for reconciliation without the matter being made public, as it will injure our influence as a denomination. Is there any way, think you, that this can be brought about? Living close neighbors, could you help me in this good work?"

"I had rather keep aloof, lest blame be attached to me; yet, if you think it is my duty, I am willing to sacrifice myself for the good of our church, and the cause of Christianity. What do you propose?"

"Inasmuch as you and the family are friends, go to Sister Tattum and Augusta, and ask them to call upon the slandered brother and his wife—or, who think they have been (of course I know nothing about it), and, in a Christ-like spirit, strive to make it all right with them."

"But our brother is so obstinate, I think nothing would satisfy his selfish nature but seeing them excommunicated. It pains me to say this, and should not, if I did not feel the utter hopelessness of arguing the matter with him; and, without wishing to advise, I think he is a man who adds but very little lustre to the position he occupies; and it would be better, were it filled by some other person. The wiser course for you, is to let him have his own way, as he will have, you'll find at last—grant a trial, and let him prove slander, if he can. Sisters Tattum certainly should be chastised for their evil doing, unless they can prove that he is in the habit of getting intoxicated. If so, he has no business to have his name enrolled as a member; if not, let them suffer the consequences. I am no respecter of persons; all I desire is to see justice. It may be, however, the whole trouble rests with the informant, Sister Thompson; if so, let the blame fall upon her head."

"Let us strive, to follow the teachings of the Spirit in this matter; to make it a subject of prayer, sister. I am willing to forgive seventy times seven, if I thought, at last, a person would do better."

"Yes, yes, we are all sinful, and need sympathy; but is it best for the upbuilding of the glorious kingdom to tolerate vice in our midst? if, after we have been and labored with an erring brother and sister, then taken two or three more as our beloved discipline enjoins, there is a continuation of some heinous sins, such as profanity or drunkennesss, should we not rid ourselves of that evil, even though we root out the cause? lest the tares destroy the wheat, or our influence as a Christian church ceases to be felt."

"Your argument is good; but it seems like taking out an eye to lose a member."

"True, but what saith Holy Writ? 'If thy right eye offend thee, pluck it out, and cast it from thee,' etc. But do not understand me that I desire to see any person turned from the church and the holy communion, unless he continue to follow up certain vice after their salvation has been sought through tears."

"No, sister, I cannot think you do; I know how you feel. But now a few words in reference to the scandal of the other evening. It does seem that Sister Tattum has much tribulation for so zealous a follower of the Master. Of course I believe in her innocence; but how came that servant girl to make such confessions, if there was nothing at all in them?"

"She has spells of derangement; the excitement brought it on at the time, and she did not know of what she was speaking. Mr. Walter Clayton told me they were making arrangements to send her to the lunatic asylum."

"Dreadful! I think me now, that I saw aberrations of mind, but attributed it at the time to an undue excitement. I'm sorry for the girl, but it clears up the character of our worthy sister."

Mrs. Gray heard the well known voice of Mrs. Carlyle, and went into the room. "See here," said she, after the usual salutations, "have you seen this little suit, this beautiful gift from Augusta Tattum? I have brought it in purposely to show you. Wish you had come a little sooner, as I have been trying it on to baby, and it's a perfect fit; and oh! so lovely. Isn't she a a dear, good girl? Was it not thoughtful of her? Nothing could have pleased me better."

"I know about it, sister, and gave her the patterns of the embroidery."

"She is possessed of patience."

"Yes, for it took her a long time to do the work; beside that, you notice the material is quite expensive."

"Indeed! indeed, 'tis very nice throughout, and I thank her very much for her kind remembrance."

"Her mother gave us a very liberal donation, beside," said Dr. Gray. "I felt that she was robbing herself, and would not have taken it, only I knew she would feel so hurt if I said anything.   It is a generous family; there are none in their circumstances that pay as liberally.   And then, see how much they do for the poor every year, and from purely disinterested motives! but a glorious reward awaits the faithful.   'Inasmuch as ye did it unto one of the least of these, ye did it unto me.'"

CHAPTER XXX.

Mrs. Carlyle went directly from the parsonage to the residence of the Tattums. "I think," she said on entering, "your troubles, Sister Tattum, are nearly at an end. I've been over and had a long talk with Brother Gray and wife, neither of whom have been influenced in the least, by the gossip which has been afloat."

"Just step into the other room," replied Mrs. Tattum, and led the way, once more into the parlor where, a few weeks before, they had held their private tête-a-tête in reference to the same piece of church scandal. "Now we are safe from intruders"— bolting the door—"and you can speak your mind freely, without being heard."

"And you're sure old Hezekiah is not around?"

"Not a bit of it. He went fishing early this morning, and will not return till evening."

"So far, so good."

"Any new plans?"

"Some improvements on the old one is all; but we are sure to have it all our own way, for I have made the minister believe that is the only way."

"How now?"

"Well, old Smith, the old villain, is sure to take you for slander; you will prove you never said anything against him; that will lay Mrs. Col. Thompson, the low-life 'creature, in a falsehood, and put her directly into your shoes,—either an open confession which her pride will not suffer, or be excommunicated. Having disposed of her, we will inform on old Smith for repeated drunkenness and profanity."

"But your witnesses?"

"You, Augusta, Mrs. Jones,—you know she has got all her buttermilk at our house for these three years, and would swear to anything I said, if necessary—Jonas Carlton, that drives a team for us; he's in regular standing and his word is as good as any one's—Mrs. Jinks, my sewing woman, who would rather die than offend me, for she couldn't live at all outside of our house—and myself. By the way, has Augusta commenced that new suit yet?"

"Yes, and has it nearly half finished."

"Oh! how sweet Lillie will look in it, won't she? Bless her little heart!"

"Well, now, are you sure no one is in the house but ourselves? You had better take a survey, lest we might drop something we would not want the world to know."

"None of my family would tell a word, if it were going to implicate me."

"Unless it were the old man."

"Ole man—ole man; now it's a wonder to me that woman's so respectful!" thought Hezekiah, who had been listening at the keyhole for some moments.

"No danger at all of him, for he'll not be in before midnight, like enough. If he comes, we can hear him."

"I've brought over my cards again, just to show you how the thing is coming out; and I wouldn't want any one in the wide world to know, only you, that I had anything to do with them. What do you suppose Parson Gray would say if he knew we actually indulged in games?"

"Turn us out, probably."

"Yes, I think he would, for I believe he is a conscientious man, and acts from pure principle; and we would have but a slim chance, only he is so easily deceived."

"But here, now, the cards are shuffled—cut them. Do you see? here is Mrs. Col. Thompson, with her back turned upon the whole congregation; following close at her heels, with excitement and tears between, are old Smith and his wife, which shows that they'll all soon be marching along out of our midst, to the double quicksteps that we shall give some day for their especial benefit." And hereupon she went to the organ and played "Yankee Doodle," and Mrs. Tattum got up and tried to dance.

["Wuss nor me, I vum!" said Hezekiah in an undertone; "an folks don't think o' calling me nothin' but, 'that ole sinner'—and, 'that ole drunken cuss'—an' 'ole d–l,' an' a heap o' pet names, just like 'em"—taking out his bottle of whisky from his pocket—"I bel'eve I'll go in and ax 'em don't they want a drink."]   .

"This being settled, don't you feel better?" said Mrs. Carlyle.

"I trust to your shrewdness, or I should fear of being swamped. You must have help from some unknown source."

"Indeed, I do—from a good many dead friends whose spirits come and tell me just how to manage."

"And they speak through these cards?"

"Appear in most every form imaginable. Sometimes there is a white hand laid upon my shoulders; again, a face appears. Now I should fear to do as I do, only they tell me the Bible is untrue. Discard this, and we have no hell nor heaven; and I am in doubt about the existence of a God!"

"Oh, dreadful! you never said so much before."

"It is only recently that my eyes have been opened."

"And why do you still cling to the church?"

"A sacrifice of opinion for popularity, that is all. If I should openly avow my principles, a finger of scorn would be pointed at me at once."

"Horrors! Ain't you in league with the Evil One?"

"I think I am, if there is such a creature," and here Mrs.

Carlyle chuckled inwardly to think she could arouse the fears of such a woman as Mrs. Tattum, and get the start of her for once. Then, fearing to go too far, lest there would be a break about the church business, she laughed aloud and said, "You needn't believe me, for I do not mean half I say. Can't you lend me twenty-five dollars?"

"Yes, if I had so much."

"You have more than that. I heard you counting it, and saw it through the open door, when I first came."

"You are mistaken."

"You have a hundred dollars in the bank, and fifty in your pocket."

Mrs. Tattum turned pale; she knew this was true; but how that woman came to find it out, was the mystery.

"Don't be frightened, if I know everything that is going on; why, I can read your thoughts! but I'll not hurt you," said Mrs. Carlyle.

"You impose upon me."

"No more than you do on other people. Where do you get the most of your change?"

"Out o' subscription papers, and my pocket," thought Hezekiah, placing his ear still closer to the keyhole; "but it's none o' her business; notion to pitch her out doors. Now Mary Ann an' me has a heap o' skirmishes, now and then, but I don't want the likes o' that critter to come right inter the house, pertend great friends, and then want to rob her; an' I'll show her as mighty glib as that wife o' mine uses her tongue on me, she ain't going to make a fool on her, any way.' He raised his fist to knock against the door, then thought he would wait to hear what more she had to say.

"Will you let me have it?" she said coaxingly; "you know I will have to pay the witnesses something; and then, can't you see the trouble I've been to for you? That will be nothing; you make it so easy. I'll return it again, or what I'm not obliged to use on this business of yours."

"Well, here it is; but your promises ain't worth shucks," said Mrs. Tattum, angrily.

Bang—bang, went the door—off came the bolt! Hezekiah could hold his peace no longer. He grabbed the money, and said, "Now, woman, unless you take one o' them double quicksteps I heered you talking on, in one minute, I'll give you the toe o' my boot; and furthermore, I'll report on you myself, and get you all turned out of the church."

She made a hasty exit; but as soon as Mrs. Tattum could pacify her offended master, Hezekiah, she hastened to the house of Mrs. Carlyle. They talked up their business and arranged everything with perfect satisfaction, to their own minds, inviting in their witnesses for the evening, and after giving them a grand supper, proceeded to instruct them on all points necessary to the consummation of their wishes at the coming trial.

Mrs. Tattum was the last one home; and, when she parted with Mrs. Carlyle, she gave her not only the twenty-five dollars, but promised her as much more if everything turned out satisfactorily.

11

CHAPTER XXXI.

The day of the church trial came at last. It had been long talked of and much gossip was afloat, not only going the rounds of all the members of this particular denomination, but others had taken it up. Consequently, great excitement prevailed when the time came for these offending members to be arraigned to answer words of defamation claimed to have been uttered against a worthy brother and sister. The church was filled with people anxious to hear what could be said, some affirming that the ready wit of Mrs. Tattum would come to her aid, as it always had, and be the means of her clearance; while others declared that she would surely be excommunicated, as the pastor was so intent on dealing justly and doing right; all that was required was the evidence, and there was enough of this which could not be gainsaid.

The accused and accusers with all their witnesses sat facing each other; while wrathful glances flashed out whenever their eyes chanced to meet, Augusta Tattum so far forgetting herself as to turn up her nose at Deacon Smith, if he ventured to look at her; while her mother and Mrs. Carlyle, each dressed in a becoming robe of black, deeper dyed in hypocrisy, endeavored to appear very saint-like, and did deceive a good many, as they put on their solemn faces, and sweet, dignified bearing, keeping, a portion of the time, their eyes closed, as if in prayer and meditation. The minister noticed all this, and his large heart, previously warmed by the liberal donations that he had received, went out in deep sympathy for the accused; while occasionally he wiped tears that welled up in spite of his great effort to restrain them, with a snow-white handkerchief, his initials beautifully embroidered in the corners—a gift, too, from one of those generous ladies.

After a time he arose, and, with solemnity said, ''I regret exceedingly that anything should have transpired among the beloved flock, of sufficient magnitude to call us together in the capacity for which we have this day assembled. The accusation alleged to have been made by these sisters in the church, who have heretofore sustained an unblemished reputation, who have led a truly exalted and Christian life, living up to all the ordinances of the church, conforming to the rules laid down in our discipline, so heroically offering their services on any and every occasion required, and sustaining the Gospel, is a very grave and serious matter; and one which involves loss of character, a position of influence in this church, which they have held so many years.''

By this time, the sobs of Mrs. Tattum were audible all over the church, while it seemed very hard for Mrs. Carlyle and the rest of her witnesses to restrain themselves sufficiently to keep from following her example. A lady on the opposite side sent a note to Augusta; she had something to communicate which would be of service to them, and desired her to come and take a seat by her side. It was directly back of Deacon Smith, and, as she passed along, she could not restrain her temper, now that so good an opportunity presented itself to satisfy her wicked and mischievous disposition. Having to pass near to him to take her seat—so near that she could touch him if she chose, and no one know but it was purely accidental, she gave his wig a little twitch, when it fell off and down directly under her feet, giving him somewhat the appearance of a shorn lamb; some given most to merriment calling him ''Mary's little lamb.'' Vexed beyond endurance, his hot temper gaining the ascendancy, and without heeding the beautiful words, ''If a brother have aught against a brother, forgive," which had been so wisely explained the Sabbath previous, and which had seemed to him so easy to perform, and such a little thing, turned around and boxed her ears soundly; while she ground her teeth in rage, but what he considered still worse, tramped upon, and scoured his lovely locks of black, for which he had paid a goodly price, and considered very fair to behold, with one of her little feet until it was not fit to be again worn.

The back door being but a few steps from him, he beat a hasty retreat, not knowing what to do hardly, as he could not absent himself from the church trial very long, and he did not wish to stay under the appalling circumstances. He bethought him, however, of an old wig locked up in a trunk with other antique relics, which would be better than nothing, and perhaps look very well when he had oiled and combed it. But it was a very bright red, while his was coal black; and after placing it on his head and doing his best, it had so changed his looks that his nearest friends would scarcely know him. But it was. not for the better, and, as he took a survey of himself in the mirror, great oaths came into his mind which, however, he did not utter, while he asked, mentally, "Am I Deacon George Washington Smith, or some other man? Now, this hair belonged to that aged man who died here a long time ago, and I look every moment as old as he did then, and he was well nigh onto one hundred years. My own wife would think it was his apparition if she should see me. Why, where is she? Had not got to the church when I left, and and I am glad of it, for she would have felt so badly to see me insulted by that good-for-nothing. Well, well, well, stop, George Washington Smith, don't say what you think (putting his hands over his lips), for you know you profess better things; you are the deacon of that great church over yonder." He then tried so hard to repeat the words, "Forgive us our trespasses as we forgive them that trespass against us;" but, for his life, he could not say it, for the thoughts of the saucy, arrogant, mischievous

Augusta Tattum and his once beautiful but now tattered and demolished wig kept crowding them out.

He glanced again into the mirror—"Oh, fury!" he exclaimed, "I'm a fright: I believe I'll stay away from the trial entirely, for I shall be nothing but a laughing stock when I get there; for some will be sure to recognize me. But no—that will never do! I must hear what all those dirty, lowlive, blackguards on the other side have to say about me." "Be still, deacon, be still!" his conscience again whispered; "be more respectful: do unto others, as ye would that they should do unto you: say nothing about them you would not have them say of you;" and so he repeated the sentence again: "I must hear what all those," etc., to see if he could not put "dear brethren and sisters" in place of the harsh names he had uttered. But they had got to be such hard words to speak, he could not do it; and he made up his mind whether a person were a saint or a sinner he could not very well help his thoughts; and so brought relief to his mind in this way. But, inasmuch as he could not absent himself from the church, he said that he would make his disguise perfect; so he put on a suit throughout—a very odd looking one—that had belonged to the same gentleman, which he thought no one would recognize, perhaps; but if they should, hoped they'd think 'twas this old man's apparition—he had come back to avenge him. 'Twas going to be a dark night, and so he thought he'd better watch for those d-ls (he could not say brethren and sisters, yet; and, as this other word had already escaped his lips, he said, "Well, that's just what I think they are, and I will not be a hypocrite, nor try to be one any longer; so let it slide,") and scare them into fits; make them believe there is a ghost after them, Augusta Tattum, especially. But instead, he went once more to the scene of his distresses and took his seat in the congregation; but as far removed from all the Tattums as possible, lest their keen eyes should discover his trick and they should commit other depredations upon him.

The minister not noticing this little play between these two very worthy members, as he had been so intent on smoothing matters up, continued, "While on the other hand our dear Brother Smith whose name has been enrolled so many years upon our church books, and in all that time been so faithful a servant of the Lord, upon whose fair name no blemish has ever rested, of course, is perfectly justifiable in vindicating his honor and reputation, by inviting an investigation ; which, after having been done, we sincerely believe will feel satisfied that there has been no cause for complaint. We will now proceed to take testimony. Sister Thompson, will you please tell us what you know of this matter?"

She arose, and, after looking daggers at the opposing party, snappishly said, "I cannot see how any person with a particle of observation or sense of penetration can for a moment think that a brother who has been so wilfully and repeatedly slandered, has no cause of complaint."

The Rev. Mr. Gray, fearing he would again be reproached by this one of the "beloved flock," coloring slightly, told her if she had ever heard any slanderous remarks made by the accused—Sister Tattum and daughter—to tell just what they were and when it was, as they had no time to enter into preliminaries.

"Last summer, then, at the residence of old Carlyle himself, I heard them both say he got drunk very often—drunk as a beast."

"Who was present at the time?"

"Mrs. Carlyle, Mrs. Tattum, daughter and myself were all."

"Well, that will do, sister," said the pastor.

She expected to tell the whole story; how, without the least provocation, they had commenced their tirade against Brother Smith; expatiate on the meanness of the assault upon his character, and to plead his cause; but she had to sit down before she had half finished, and she was exceedingly angry.

"Now we will hear from Brother Carlton. Be brief, and tell us what you have heard, in as few words as possible."

He was not considered bright, and people began to laugh the moment he arose to his feet, expecting a rich treat from his testimony.

"Well—well—hic—old mother Carlyle—sister, I mean—has got a stock of the worst cats I ever seen—most as bad as their mistress; for, one day, I guess 'twas last July, I went into the buttery to git me a drink uv milk, an' what should I see, but three or four on em blazen away at the milk, licken the cream clean off on it, mostly; and when I was strainin' it over after um —you see I had to do that before I could eat it at all, you know —I happened to look out on the winder, and there was her hull drove of hens in Miss Thompson's (Sister Thompson's, I mean) posy beds, scratching them all to thunder—kingdom kum, I should have said; then I thought I'd jist go an' tell this worthy sister to jist shut up them dumb'd hens o' hern; so I runs over there in a jerk uv lightnin', and who should I see but our worthy sisters—old mother Tattum and her darter, cummin'; well, I'd jist as live hear 'em talk as to go to a show, any time; and I hear so much news alwers I don't hev to buy any newspapers for a hull week or two, and it's a savin', can't you see?"

Rev. Dr. Gray had been spoken to by a person in the back part of the house, just as he had arisen to tell his story, or he would not have allowed so much preamble; but now, listening, told him to simply state the facts as they were, and to be very brief.

"This is all a fact, sir, what I hev sed, but Ize tellin' about them Tattums. They came to old Carlyle's, an' went in and commenced about Brother Smith; and said he got drunk as an owl—both on 'em said it, an' they can't deny it."

"Who was present?"

"Why! them and me an' old mother Carlyle an' that woman what sews for her—yonder she sits, lookin' as solemn like as them are hens arter I'd chased 'em off uv the door yard—an' Sister Thompson, an' that wuz all."

All of the witnesses on the other side testified that they remembered the time well to which they referred, but the deacon's name had never been mentioned only with the greatest respect. This cleared the Tattums, and they went away very happy to bear the news of their triumphant acquittal; but Deacon Smith and wife, Mrs. Col. Thompson, with as many others as they could influence, left the church, declaring they would not remain longer where there was so much lying, hypocrisy and deceit.

CHAPTER XXXII.

Morning came—the next after Hettie had left for home. It was eight o'clock, and no one was yet astir at Mr. Clayton's. He had been awake for several hours, thinking what an unhappy lot had fallen to him, and wondering why he should have so much trouble; when, finally, he broke forth with these words: "Well, I suppose I'll have to get my own breakfast, or go without any. Elice, how much longer do you expect to lie here—a burden to yourself and everyone around you? I do wish you'd get well, or—or—well, do one thing or another— live or die! Do you 'spose if I'd known that you would be sick in this way, and I'd have to make my own fires and get my meals, I'd gone way out there to Woodville and married you?"

"What do you mean?" replied Elice. "I'm scarcely ever sick, and shall be up now, in a few days, able to attena to my own household affairs, but I cannot rise this morning; don't be so disconsolate, just because I am not around to attend to things. Mrs. Ashton told me of a very worthy servant girl we could obtain; hadn't you better go for her?"

"Who is it?"

"An elderly girl living on High street."

"You don't mean that homely old maid, do you? If so, I'll do the work, myself, rather than have her around. Well," he said, springing to his feet, "I will be servant girl for a few days; the store is closed, and I'd just like to show you how neat and trim I can keep things, and then have two-thirds of the time to myself."

Poor Elice drew a long breath; she was unable to rise from her couch, and what would she do, with no one but him to wait upon her? Still, she said nothing.

"Why don't you speak? Don't you 'spose I could do it? I know I could, and keep the children dressed up every minute; they wouldn't look as they do now, sometimes."

"You might try," said Elice, smiling. He dressed himself and went to the kitchen. Everything had been left the day before in perfect order by the servant girl. He cast his eyes around. "It looks pretty well," he thought, "but nothing to what it will when I get to doing the work. I'll scour this floor with sand every day, dust and sweep, make the beds, get the meals and wash the dishes—that's all there is to do. Why, yes, there is washing and ironing, but I'll put that out. Oh! I forgot—and baking bread and pastry. I can do that; I know just how, for I remember exactly how mother used to do; and I know I can do just like her. Well, to-day shall be spent getting my hand in; to-morrow, baking and slicking up; and next day—oh! I know, now, I'll have company to dinner. It would not be like a woman, unless I invited in guests, so I'll ask some of my gentlemen friends to dine with me. Who will it be? Hon. John Rutter and Attorney Winthrop. They are coming from Cambden to hunt and fish. I'd like to show them how perfectly elegant I can keep house, if I'm a mind to; not that I care anything about waiting upon them, but just to let them know that my argument was sound when we had our dispute in their office about the rights of women, etc., and how true my words were when I said I could do any woman's little housework, providing she did not have more than half a dozen children, keep things tidy, and have two-thirds of the time left, to do what I pleased in. Won't they be surprised? But, inasmuch as I've got so much to think of, we'll take some pancakes for our breakfast—that'll do for the children and me this morning; here are some already light and beautiful—some that Hettie left; they'll be so nice!"

So he baked a plate of pancakes, put on the syrup dish and some butter, and all sat down around the table.

"O papa, these pancathes are thour!" suggested Blanche after she had tasted them.

"I know better. Now you'll eat them, or go without anything, miss; you're getting some like your mother; you like to find fault, don't you?"

"No, thir."

"Well, then, stop your noise!"

When he came to sit down to the table to take his breakfast, he found that what the child said was quite true; but, pretending not to want anything, having a headache, he left his meal almost untouched, and thought he would go to the hotel and get his breakfast; then, thinking that would give rise to so many queries, he concluded he would wait and see if he could not do better for dinner.

He then started off up town, thinking he'd just go and get his morning mail, come immediately home, do up his work and get dinner. Once there, however, he found an old acquaintance from the country, with whom he discussed politics for a while, then went around to a restaurant, took a sandwich and cup of coffee. Here he met some more friends, talked a while with them, taking a few with whom he was most familiar one side, relating his home troubles, at the same time asking advice in regard to certain matters, and forgetting all about the work in the kitchen, until the town clock pealed out the hour of twelve, and he knew the children would be home for their dinner. He then started. The table he found just as he had left it in the morning, only it seemed to him there were not so many dirty dishes; but there were no more in the house, so he told the children it was so late that they could eat off the same plates they did for breakfast, or they might be delayed from school, and it would never do to be tardy.

"But what are we to eat, papa?"

"Why, why, the pancakes are not all gone, are they? We'll have some of them and molasses; they are the easiest got. I'll bake them directly."

" I believe I don't want any dinner," said Blanche.

" Nor I," said Charlie, " for my breakfast made me sick."

" Me nuzzer, don't like yo nassy, sour sings," little Robin ventured to say.

" You are all very particular, just like your mother about that too."

Mr. Clayton went around the second time to the restaurant, bought half a fried chicken, half a dozen eggs and a cup of tea, all of which he partook with a relish, as he was very hungry. After he had finished, he went to the bakery and bought a loaf of bread to carry home, said, " It is too bad for those little children to go to school without their dinner, but I will have a nice supper for them. I will not loiter around, but go straight back, wash up the dishes and have tea all on the table, waiting for them."

He had proceeded but a few steps, however, before he met a gentleman who said, " I have bet five dollars that you can beat the best man in town playing chequers, and, as there is a crowd already assembled in Dunn's store, to witness the game, come with me immediately before they disperse."

He accepted the invitation, and house, children and everything pertaining to his responsibilities as housekeeper were forgotten, till he heard one of the bystanders remark that he must go to his tea, as he had promised to go shopping with his wife directly after, when he hurried home with all possible speed, forgetting, however, the bread he had bought for the children's supper.

" But I cannot go back," he said, mentally, " it is so late now. I can put soda in the pancakes, and then they will be as good as ever. What a wonder I had not thought of this before!"

So he went in, made up a fire, walked to the pantry, took a handful of this commodity and threw it into the pail of batter.

"Now," he said, "I'll warrant them to be good; that is the way mother used to do, and it is a nice way, too."

But he was saved all further trouble, as Blanche came into the room and said, "We have all been to supper, papa. Mrs. Ashton brought some oysters for mamma, and gave us all a dish."

"I'm very glad of that, for I'm tired; so I'll read my newspaper, sweep up a little and go to bed, as I must be up early in the morning to attend to my housework. Things do not look very well here just now, but wait till to-morrow, and then see." And in anticipation he beheld every board in the floor as white as snow; the pantry transformed into a model place of neatness, all his baking done up by noon, at least, and the dinner on the table waiting for the children when the clock struck twelve.

It was nine; the sun was streaming through the shutters when he awoke next morning. Thinking of his day's work he hurried up and went out to his tasks. Breakfast over, the first thing to be attended to was his bread, but on examination he exclaimed, "Oh, how sour! What can I do?" He bethought him a moment. "Why, that is easily remedied, I'll serve them as I did the pancakes—put in soda. Let's see, a teacup full, that is precisely what mother would use for four loaves, and that is precisely what I shall make; but to be perfectly sure I am right, I will go in and ask Elice, for she is a good cook if she has a mind to be, if she is not fit for anything else."

"One teaspoon full," she said.

"Yes, I thought I was right," he went out repeating—"one teacup full—it will be none too much. I knew it would be just what mother would use; just a teacup full will make them light and nice." So he went to the soda dish once more, and, finding a coffee cup, he filled that, to be sure he had enough, and threw it into his tray of bread.

He then mixed his crust and beat his eggs. He had made up

his mind to have custard pies, as they would look so nicely when frosted, and he wished to excel in everything he did.

"A cup of sugar for each," he thought. "Yes, that is the rule that mother has." So he went once more to the pantry; but, as it is quite easy to be mistaken, got salt instead and mixed with the milk for his pies.

"Pretty well under way," he said as he placed them into the large oven with his bread which was now light enough.

"What a wonderful man people would take me for if they only knew what I have been about! Just to think, do business equal to any lawyer, and actually take the place of a French cook! There is nothing like having brains, and your head level. I will go now and get my turkey and oysters, I can cook them equal to the best of them; behind no one in anything."

So he went to the market and selected his fowl; then to the grocery, for other things needed. This time he hurried home, however, as he had the bread on his mind, and got there just in time to take it from the oven, when it had become a lovely brown; the pies were baked admirably also, and never prouder man existed when he beheld everything, as he thought, in such beautiful style.

But it was afternoon already, and no sweeping, dusting or anything had been done to bring about a particle of order in the house, and the children were crying for their dinner, every dish in the house still dirty; while all the spiders, pots and kettles stood in a circle around the stove left there to be handy and still unwashed; but which, he said, must all be put in their places before the company arrived on the morrow.

"Well, well, well," he sighed when evening came, "I never would have believed that the little work there is in this house, could fatigue one so, and see what is before me yet! But I can finish up in the morning when I am rested, and never feel it— bake the turkey, dress the children, and—I don't think the floor looks very badly—sweep up in the dining-room and let the rest go; for where is the man who ever notices a house? if they get a good, square meal, that is all they think of, all I care for, any way." So he sat down again, to read his newspaper and rest, and thought no more about his work, until he was reminded the children wanted their supper; so, putting them off with some of their baker's bread, and butter, he bade them go to bed and not bother him any more with their noise.

The next morning he arose cross and sullen. "I wish," he said to himself, "I hadn't invited people to dine with me; what a fool I have made of myself! but it is done now, and I'll show them yet."

"Children, we shall have a splendid dinner to-day, so you can take a piece of bread and butter again for your breakfast; or, if you rather, some of those pancakes and molasses."

They chose the former; so, after satisfying, as best they could, their appetites with this kind of fare, went again to school with sorry faces.

"Come back precisely at noon, as I wish to dress you up before dinner, which will not be till two o'clock."

"Yes, sir," they all replied.

One o'clock came. "I will now set my table, to be sure everything will be in readiness, so not to delay my company; for of all things I have ever talked about, it was punctuality in meals." But in vain he looked for a clean tablecloth; they were scarce, any way, at his home, and every one was soiled.

"Oh! what shall I do? The very best one is covered with tea stains and molasses! Well, I can put the platters and soup dishes over the worst places, and what does it matter? for it is not the tablecloth they are going to eat, and they will never notice it any way."

So he did his best, which when he had finished, presented the appearance of anything but order or style. He then went for the vegetables and meat. "It is now within a few minutes of the time and I will have every single thing complete, so there will be no ringing bells—bless me, whom would I call?—jumping up from the table after I am seated; and they will never mistrust I have been the getter up of this meal, for I would like, when they have eaten heartily, praising the food, which undoubtedly they will, to tell them it is all of my own manufacture; that my wife lies sick in the bed; girl gone; and it is I, myself, individually." And here he drew up proudly before a mirror which had been so besmeared with dust, that it did not reveal the soot which bespattered his face.

"Just in time!" he exclaimed; "they are coming. Oh! la! sus! dear, me! I forgot the young ones, where are they? ain't washed, ain't dressed, ain't nothing! Here, children, havn't time now, to fix you up, visitors are most here; so you go up stairs, and stay there till they go away."

Then he remembered he had not swept; so he caught the broom just in time to brush all the dust up into one corner of the room, and place the broom in front of it. When they arrived and he went to welcome them with all the blandness of which he was capable, he looked more like a frightened hen than otherwise.   .

"How do you do? looking well, Clayton," said the judge; "but what is the excitement?" while Attorney Winthrop smiled, and asked him if he had been to any large fires lately. ⌐

"No,—no,—not as I know of; the fact is, there have not been any here for a long time!"

"Well, gentlemen, our dinner is ready, and waiting," Mr. Clayton said, after a few minutes had elapsed.

All seated around the table, he commenced carving the turkey, when, to his chagrin, he found he had left the vegetables on the stove, over a very hot fire.

"Excuse me, please," he said, with a very polite bow, and proceeded to the kitchen, where he found they were all burned to a crisp.

He was about to utter an oath; but, remembering the presence of his guests, he restrained himself, and returned to the dining room, saying to himself, "Well, who cannot be satisfied

THOSE ORPHANS.

with what there is left, ought to go without dinner." He looked again over the table and found he had neglected to buy crackers for the oysters. "Well, that can't be helped now; they can put some of this beautiful bread into their soup: it will taste just as well."

They all said they did not eat them, so he removed the dishes and returned to carving the turkey.

He passed this around, then the bread and butter, which, with a few scorched potatoes and the celery, were all that they had for dinner aside from the dessert, which he had prided himself upon with its beautiful, snowy frosting, fit to set before a queen.

The fowl happened to be a very old one, and very hard to be masticated to be made suitable to be taken into the stomach; and so it was but very little of this that the gentlemen ventured to eat; they thought they would try the bread and butter. The bread was pretty highly colored, but they presumed it would be eatable.

The judge tasted it; but when he bit on one of the hard lumps of soda, his countenance wore anything but that serene, placid composure for which it was characterized; while Attorney Winthrop seeing the joke but not feeling it, put on a broad grin, which he could not well avoid.

Blanche thrust her head out of the stair door at that moment and said, "We are awful hungry, papa, please tant we have our dinner?" little Robin yelling, "I mos' starved to deph, papa; don't let mans eat every sing up zere be!"

The jug of molasses he had kept in the stairway, because it was the handiest, and the child's face was literally covered with it. Walter Clayton's rage was unbounded; still he answered them in as gentle tones as he could assume. "Go back, darlings, for a few moments, you shall soon come down;" hoping thereby, that these gentlemen would not only be convinced of his equanimity of temper, but his great faculty for governing

12

his family by the laws of gentleness and love, of which they had so often heard him boast, and whom of all men he would rather impress favorably, for many reasons.   First, one was the high judge of the county courts; much better that he made him believe he was a gentleman, and a good man, affectionate in his family, than the reports that had possibly come to his ears; as they had been afloat in all the surrounding country for years, that he was one of the most miserly, tyrannical, and dishonest men in the world; that the very breath he drew was contaminated with villainy: for then, he might receive favors—not exactly this; but if he was himself impressed with his moral worth, how much easier it would be for him to charge a jury in his behalf, than if his mind had been set against him; while Attorney Winthrop being his lawyer, and as honest a man as ever lived, could plead his cause with far better success, if he felt his client was sound, with an irreproachable character; for truth, or what a person supposes to be truth, pleads far more eloquently than idle words, which a man does not himself believe.   And for these reasons Mr. Clayton wished to do his best, and did try very hard upon this day—memorable to him, never to be forgotten, but which haunted him like a spectre, as long as he lived—to ingratiate himself into the good graces of these two popular men.   But he overdid the matter when he spoke so sweetly to the children, as they were unused to the voice; so, taking advantage of their father's lenity, they began to whine, and finally proposed to go down, whether or not, and get their dinner, thinking papa wouldn't care much, and if he did, would not say anything cross or unkind before those strange gentlemen.

"You halloo again, Robin, and see what he says," urged Charlie.   "Mebby he'll say come down and git somethin', for I'm dying this minit for my dinner."

"Say, papa, tell mens not to eat sings all up, wez awful hundry, tant we tum down now?"

This time he thrust his head out a little too far, lost his balance and came tumbling down stairs, his hair uncombed, daubed with molasses and covered all over with feathers. The two boys had been occupying their time, first with the molasses jug and then jumping into a barrel of feathers, till you could scarcely tell but they belonged to a new race of birds or fowls.

This was too much for Winthrop; he now indulged in the heartiest laugh he ever had in his life. He had been wanting to relieve his proclivities for merriment ever since he had been in the house, but his good breeding restrained him; now, this was a glorious opportunity; no one would consider him rude, especially if he told an anecdote about this same little fellow, or what he did when he was over once before.

"This incident reminds me of the time in the summer when this same little chap came in covered with feathers. His mamma asked him where he had been, when he replied, 'To ze barn settin' on a hen's nest. Will I hatch out boys zer hens?' when he started back to get at his work again."

The judge's dignity gave way; his sour looks vanished, for he had felt a little cross ever since he had tasted the soda, and he made up his mind he would enjoy himself, get a little sport out of the day, for that was what he came for, as well as Winthrop. So the two laughed long and loud, not so much at the anecdote, but at the ridiculous sights that everywhere met their vision.

Robin, frightened, scampered back when his father asked him if he were hurt. Going to the door, he gave them one of his savage looks, which quieted them only for a few moments longer, however. when they all came down stairs, revealing their filth and rags, and with pleading voices and tearful eyes, said, "Please, papa, won't you give us something? for you know we haint had nothin' but sour pancakes and molasses for three or four days, and you promised we should have such a lovely dinner."

"Do, do," little Robin repeated; "for we mos' dead, papa."

This was too much for his rising wrath. He sprang from the

table, grasped the two boys by the hair of the head and thrust them into a dark cellar-way; then ordered Blanche to follow them.

"There now," he said, "judge or no judge, you'll find you'll have to behave yourselves better than you do, and mind what I say. Didn't I tell you to stay up stairs until we were through dinner? You, you dirty little whelps! Never were children so trying as you have been to-day; now peep, and I'll rawhide you!"

His fiery passions had got the ascendancy, and, instead of the angel of all goodness, which he vainly endeavored to show himself, he opened up his heart and portrayed his real character; revealed to these gentlemen his terrible, almost diabolical disposition.

There was silence for a while. At length, his wrath cooling, he said, "It is very trying to have children behave as mine have to-day, and I cannot quite understand it. The only explanation that I can give is that I have been absent a considerable lately, and their stepmother has managed them so badly, whipped them for the most trivial offense, and then, again, let them have their own way, till they are spoiled. She takes no interest in them; does not care in the least for the little things. I never saw just such a woman, she takes the strangest freaks imaginable; providing everything does not go to suit her, she takes to her bed and does not get up in several days. She has one of those spells upon her now. Oh, dear! I do have so much care; I almost fear I shall become insane, myself, some time! Why, I cannot keep a girl very long at a time, she misuses them so, if they are ever so good; and this is the reason they do not like to work for us; and so I thought, for the sake of peace for a few days, at least, I would do the work myself. I could do it well enough, but she needs so much waiting upon, so dreadful particular and whimsical with all the rest, that she is so hard to be suited."

"Very strange," said the judge.

"Quite singular," Attorney Winthrop replied, while both looked incredulously. This Mr. Clayton did not notice, however, and continued, "It is a delicate subject and pains me exceedingly to open up my mind to you; but I trust I have your sympathy, for you can hardly conceive what I have undergone since I was married; and the worst of all, that I was so deceived in my wife, for no one could have made me believe that she was not one of the best women in the world; but she will steal from me whenever she gets a chance, take my money, give away my clothes to every old beggar that comes along, and has proved herself in every way unworthy of the position to which I have raised her."

"A fine looking woman, Clayton, and if I am able to judge from physiognomy, I should say she was directly opposite the character you have given her—but—" drawing a long breath, "we cannot always tell by a person's looks; a very bad one may manage to cover up his sins by insinuating smiles and honied phrases. If such is the case, as you have affirmed, it is a very bad state of affairs, and I am sorry for you."

"O judge," he said solemnly and in such measured, sorrowful tones, "that woman will ruin me! I get her everything that heart can wish, and still she will run me in debt for things unnecessary, and oftentimes converts clothing I buy for the children into money. I will own to you that I am a different person from what I was when my first wife was alive," and here he came near breaking down with crocodile tears. "But she was an angel; all her influence over me was for good; but my disposition, which was once the very best, has soured, as I am ashamed to say was exhibited a short time ago, and which I so regret now-a-days. Would you advise me to live with such a woman? Could I get a divorce under these circumstances?"

"Have you ever tried gentleness and persuasion? A woman will submit to the tyrannical rules of a man, generally, providing he spices them up with love, now and then, makes her believe it is essential for his happiness for her to yield; but you cannot drive her, she will baulk in the harness, and all the powers of darkness cannot get her along; while, if she beholds but one ray of real, genuine sympathy or affection, the slightest thread would be sufficient to guide her; they would go through fire and water, lie down in a dungeon if necessary, die for such a husband. Now my experience is, knowing the sex as I do, having had the opportunity that I have in seeing this tested, that a man is generally to blame in desiring a divorce."

"Sometimes that is so, but not in this instance; for you cannot conceive of the trouble that woman of mine causes me, and such terrible treatment as my poor, little motherless children receive at her hands; why, the neighbors have taken it up, and out of a sense of duty, informed me."

"Your neighbors may have accused her falsely. Who told you? It might help you some, if reliable people should testify to her cruelty."

"I do not like to say, but I can get good proof."

"And who?" said the judge with affected earnestness.

"My hired girl, as truthful and honest a servant as a person could wish to have, and Mrs. Hezekiah Tattum."

"What do they know?"

"That she put them in a dark cellar-way and kept them there all of one day, without a mouthful to eat, and was in the habit of doing this with other cruelties, poor, little, motherless orphans!"

"Where are they now?"

Mr. Clayton colored; he had actually forgotten, through his earnest and exciting conversation, all about their waiting for their dinner under a dark stairway. He did not reply.

"Is that the place you thrust them a moment ago? or have you another jail?"

"The same."

"Get a divorce, of course," he said ironically. "She must be a heathen, indeed, any woman who would be guilty of starving her own offspring and keeping them in such a place as that, is not fit for the name of wife or mother; a man who knows of no better mode of punishment than to lift a child by the hair of its head, is not fit for a husband or father: you better separate."

The children heard the conversation and commenced to whisper among themselves. "It's a bid lie! aint it, Charlie?" said Blanche. "Mamma never starved uth, nor put uth down theller nuther."

"No, she didn't, nor licked us. I wish I dare tell that man so; and I will, see now."

By this time, the father bade them come forth, and said, "I am very sorry I have to deal so harshly with my little children; you can now have your dinner; another time I hope you will behave better, and then I shall not have to scold you at all."

He had occasion to leave the room for a few moments, when Charlie slid up to the judge and said, "Mamma is sick—is awful sick; she fainted clear away t'other night when papa was fighting with us, and cried 'cause he licked us so awful hard; she never licked none of us, and it's a great big lie, whoever said she did; and she never in her life shutted us up, nuther, nowhere. We all love our mamma, we does, and Mrs. Tattum tells big lies about her; and don't believe a word she says. You won't, will you? Blanche told me to ask you what divorce meant. I wish mamma was well, and then we wouldn't have to eat sour pancakes and molasses all the time; but papa ain't used to doin' work much, and he never gits us anything but them nasty sour things. Oh, dear! oh, dear! I do wish my mamma would get well. Papa told the hired girl she needn't mind a word she said if she didn't want to. He used to lick us for sassing her, but let's us sass mamma all we're a mind to; but I don't want to. Robin tells her, sometimes, he won't do it, when she asks him to do anything, and papa says that's right; tell her again so, every time she asks you. Hettie told papa mamma licked us, and he told us to fight her back like blazes, if she teched us again; that she wan't our muzzer, at all

—nothing but a stepmuzzer, and no bizness with us at all. Then he kissed Hettie. Do you know who she is? Why, she used to be our hired girl. He kissed her lóts and bags of times; for Blanche and I seen him; he didn't know it, though, but we peeped through that hole yonder, do you see? what's in the wall that goes into the kitchen; and we heard him say he liked her awful well—a thousand times better than he did our mamma, or any other body. But I likes my mamma the best, for she made me a new pair of trowsers out of papa's old ones; and I was awful tickled to git 'em, for you see these here ones are all wared out, and I never could go to meetin' or Sunday school without 'em. Do you like my mamma? She's so awful good; she setted up most all night to make them pants. Shall I go and get 'em and show 'em to you? She made Robin some out of another pair, and Blanche a new dress out of one of hern. Wasn't she good? Papa jaws her awful, sometimes, and—and (getting up closer) won't you never tell?—licks her, too. I wouldn't told on him, but he uses us awful sometimes when we're at home, and then pets us on the street. I don't like him, if he is my fozzer."

"Children and fools generally tell the truth," said the judge turning to Attorney Winthrop. "I believe every word the child says. That man is a villain; and his wife and children suffer more from his ill treatment than any person is aware. You never saw a greater ebullition of temper than he exhibited a few moments ago. Of course the children were trying, but it was very unreasonable for him to expect they were to stay up those stairs contentedly, when they had had nothing to eat since breakfast."

"True, I am as hungry as a bear, myself. Shall we go to the hotel and call for our dinner?"

"We'll take an early supper; order it by four. Can you stand it?"

"I guess so," said Winthrop, smiling, "I'm better on a fast than eating old fowls and saleratus; I never did like them."

"We must go," said the judge, when Mr. Clayton entered the room.

"Don't hurry," he said blandly; "but if you must leave so soon, call again—both of you, whenever you are over. Please don't repeat what I have said, but ponder the matter; if you think there is any chance for me, please let me know."

"I've no right to meddle with the matter, and would not if I could. Do right by your wife, and I think you will have no further trouble; I have heard her highly spoken of."

"And I," said Attorney Winthrop, "have been often told that she was a very pleasant lady," smiling, "too good for you, Clayton, by far; but a person may smile and smile and be a villain, and who knows what is what? Call at my office when you are over."

"I'll do so."

In a moment more they were bending their footsteps toward the hotel.

"A leaf for your diary, judge."

"And yours," he answered. "Alas! for degraded human nature. If we were in the habit of being bought, we might make a speck out of that chap. The truth is, he has fallen in love with some other girl, and would like to get rid of his wife. I have not the least confidence in him; have seen too much. He would get a divorce, if he could; leave her penniless; and let her go to the almshouse, if she failed to support herself. Knowing him as I do, I have no sympathy with him; for I have it from reliable authority, that she never failed to do her part; and if he was but a tithe as good, he would be far better than he is. It is astonishing to what depths of villainy he plunges, keeping just inside the pales of the law, but doing everything in his power to entrap the unwary; to entice them into his clutches, and ruin them at last. No wonder that such a man has trouble with his family! I presume they do not have what they want to eat half the time, and he a millionaire! Shame on such a degraded specimen of humanity!"

CHAPTER XXXIII.

Walter Clayton went into the bedroom where his wife was. He was not altogether satisfied with the results of the day, and he felt irritable and morose. It was the first time he had seen her since morning, and in that length of time had not asked, or even sent a messenger to look after her wants.

Mrs. Ashton had been with her, however, the most of the day; had brought from home everything in the shape of food for her comfort; had cushioned a large arm-chair with pillows; assisted her to it, and had just placed a little waiter on a stand in front of her, filled with dishes of tempting food, and was urging her to partake. She was better, decidedly, thanks to this kind friend, and her alone, for her husband had not given her a particle of attention since she had been sick, only to come in now and then, and try to pick up a quarrel with her, saying, "I wish I had married some one that was not sick everlastingly; some folks are always grunting around, but they are the kind that never die;" and then repeating words of a low chum who had a great deal of trouble with his wife: "Take a good woman, and she is sure to die; but a mean one cannot be killed with a club!"

"How do you like housekeeping?" Mrs. Ashton asked.

An oath was on his lips, but remembering again that she was the wife of one of the judges, he restrained his wrath, and answered, "All right."

"Nothing to do, I suppose? You had company to dinner?" she continued, smiling.

"Go to h——! You wish to insult me," he replied, and, turning on his heel, left the room, muttering, "I wish I could exterminate her! always around when she is not wanted; always sticking her nose into other people's business. I've a notion to turn her out of the house! No, no, that will not do, either. Dear! dear! if ever a man had trouble, it's I. I believe the world has turned against me ; but let it, haven't I my money left? But what is money without friends?—well, what are friends without money? Give me the latter always, if I may not have but one."

He then went to a large safe that stood in one corner of his room, and counted over his treasures by thousands of dollars. Then his eyes rested on all the gold which filled the little drawers. "I'm all right so long as I have these," he said, "for I can buy both love and friendship when I need them. This will gain my lawsuits, buy up juries enough—the judges—I wonder if I would dare to try them! No, no, I guess not, for I never did. Money! money! that's the lever that turns the world! I can bring thousands within my control with far less than the amount which is now within the walls of this ponderous iron box. Well, well, 'tis good to be rich ; I am rich, and let the rest all go. Mrs. Ashton may mock me with her taunting words, but what care I ? If I choose to be civil, it is my own business ; if not, as I like it ; for it does not make much difference—people will cringe, and cringe, and bow, and scrape the same, no matter how they are treated. Now, the preacher asked me for fifty dollars to help put that addition to the church. I cursed the church and him, before he ceased his importunities ; and I thought I had offended him so deeply that he would let me entirely alone after this, but not so, he was sweeter than ever when I saw him next, and bowed still lower. Then old Green, the father, I call him, of the same church (for it wouldn't have been built had it not been for him), asked me to help sustain the Gospel ; we had quite a long conversation about the matter, and in the round I abused him, I thought, a considerably, but he didn't take it so; and 'twas not long before he actually came to my office to ask my opinion on some point of law; I thought 'twas begging again for the church, and in rage I told him, before he named his business, never to come to me again, for I would not give him a cent; I considered the whole of them nothing but a set of hypocrites. Well, I supposed he would never speak again, but what should he do, but give his hat an extra touch the next time I saw him? Well, I'm some that way, when I meet a richer man than myself, or one that might, some time or other, be the means of helping to fill my coffers a little fuller; so, I do not know as I blame them."

All this time he was on his knees in front of his safe.

"Kneeling to your god?" said Mrs. Ashton, as she passed through the room on her way to the pump to obtain a fresh draught of water for Elice. She would not have said it, but her indignation had gained the mastery of her, when she saw Walter Clayton's hoarded pile, and knew his family often wanted the necessaries of life, when they should be supplied with every luxury.

He sprang to his feet. "What do you mean, madam?"

"That you worship the 'mammon of unrighteousness;' that you hoard your wealth while you refuse to get the comforts of life for your family."

"You are a liar! and if you were a man I would put you out of doors. What do I ever keep from them?"

"Wine and medicine from your sick wife. The doctor said a little tonic would restore her; she asked you to provide it; you told her you would not; and for the past week she might have starved had it not been for me, for you have never taken her a cup of tea or coffee in all that time, nor asked her how she was. Such treatment would drive me distracted, and I wonder she is not dead!"

"She told you all this?"

"No, she has said nothing. I heard you refuse the things of

which I have spoken; and I hastened to my cupboard where I always keep a supply, to procure them for her. You are as heartless as the savage! and it's a good thing that you do not have me to deal with, instead of your amiable wife. Think you I would brook all your ill treatment, and say nothing, as she does? That is where she makes a mistake; knowing as much as she probably does of all your villainy, I would cause you to disgorge thousands of your gold, or I would not keep your secrets. If I lived with you at all, which I think I could not do, I would use them as a whip to lash your treacherous hide; I would bring you down from your lofty pedestal; you'd treat me better, or I'd tell what I knew of you, if it sent you to the gloomy prison; for in my estimation, that is the only place fit for a fiend incarnate like yourself!"

"How dare you utter such words?" he hissed between his teeth.

"How dare you do as you have done? I know more than you think."

"What do you know?"

"That you are one of the vilest the sun ever shown upon!"

"If you were my wife, I'd tame you."

"Do you remember to whom you offered the thousand dollar bill, and what for?"

Walter Clayton turned deadly pale, while he shook like a leaf in the autumn winds.

"Be careful how you tread upon my toes, or you will crouch lower than you ever have before! Do you recall that bribe? You have made the innocent weep; you have wrung, as it were, blood from their lacerated hearts; you have stripped them of their homes; and, as though this were not enough, have taken their last bed, stove, or cow, together with some of their old clothes that were scarce fit for a beggar and flung them into an old garret to rot, having no use for them! And what can you say when you are brought to an account to that great tribunal from whose decision there can be no appeal? So you see, it is not only those whom you should love and cherish as the apple of your eye that you wrong, but every one that gets into your power. I hate you ; I loathe you! I would not eat the bread and butter bought with your money ! I would starve first before I would be your dependent—your wife, if you please ; for you make a servant of her—worse than that, for many of them are better used—a slave to bend and bow to all your whims and caprices ! If she fails, if she does not, it's all the same ; her poor heart must be bled anew, day after day, night after night, week in and week out, through all the year, and through her whole life ! Shall I go? Must I go?" she continued, while her lips curled with the deepest scorn of which a person is capable.

"Stay, Mrs. Ashton ; I have a word to say," he commenced with great meekness. "You do not know all my troubles and trials ; that woman of mine would ruin any man ! "

"Hold ! How so, sir ? I choose to espouse the cause of the innocent, but if the proof can be brought, my mind is open to conviction. Commence ; tell your story."

"In the first place,"—stammering and coughing, as if he did not know what to say. "Well, now. Well, you know, yourself, she has been sick a great deal, and no woman that is all the while grunting around is fit for a wife."

"I will own she has often been ill; then was the time she needed the most tender care. Must she be abused because, for a few days, she is prohibited from being the lackey of a tyrannical husband? What next ? Proceed."

"Elice is awful extravagant," said he.

"Eats the lean meat and leaves the fat, because her delicate organization will not allow her to do otherwise ; protests against frozen potatões ; thinks it's no economy to use them," she answered ironically.

"I don't want her to."

"I know better ; you cannot deny that your potatoes and all

your vegetables are frozen.   You raised a hundred bushels ; for
fear she should give a few to the famishing of the place, you
ordered your man to put them in the cellar of an old store-
house ; your apples also ; both this moment are hard as flint.
Your family must eat them or starve.   Mrs. Clayton remonstrated ; it did no good, you carried the day.   She partook of
that poisonous food (so to her, at least) ; she is sick.   Who is
to blame ?   Have you any more to say ? If so, speak out."

"She gives away more than a poor man can earn."

"Have you ever caught her at this business ?"

"By no means.   I have been told, and I know her generous
nature ; she never saw a dog hungry but she fed it.   Now a
person cannot give to all the beggars in creation without im-
poverishing himself."

"Are you impoverished?   Now, you hold she is extravagant;
that she gives away so much.   How is it that you now count
your millions, where you could not count your thousands when
you were married?   You have been told ; by whom?   Servants,
that you raise to the standard of equality ; set them upon a
throne above your wife ; deliver them the keys, and cause her
to extend the sceptre within her own kingdom.   They dispose
of your goods, to their liking ; say it is your innocent wife ;
afterwards confess their guilt ; you forgive them without the
asking ; conscience-stricken, they go home to their mother.
Another one of your informants—Mrs. Tattum—snake-like and
more to blame than they, lures them on by sweet promises ;
she receives the stolen goods, and to screen herself, pours into
your willing ears a recital of the depredations of your wife upon
the paltry allowance you give your family.   Now, you do not
believe, yourself, any of the stories that sometimes are circu-
lated, that you, and you alone, with some of this class set afloat
respecting her."

"But how little you know the difference between her and
my first wife!   She was an angel, I have often told people ; and

I loved her so, when she died, I would like to have been buried with her."

"Perhaps better than she would have desired you to. I know she was good, for I was well acquainted with her; but she only suffered half as much at your hands as the present one, because she did not live with you half as long. But listen to what she told me but a short time previous to her death: that she could not, nor would not spend her days with you; that you were jealous, abusive, tyrannical and stingy to meanness; while I soothed and hushed her sobs, as best I could, that people should not hear her from the street."

"Are you not mistaken?" he said, with his eyes upon the floor.

"No. I could write a book, myself, of you, and there would not be one line in your favor. Now, look at it, you are a millionaire; you have one old stove in the kitchen, and one in the sittingroom; you have forbidden that a fire should be kept up in both rooms at a time—the former unplastered—the latter but poorly furnished. What can you call yourself but a miser, and a niggardly one at that? I will go, now."

"I hope we part as friends," he said meekly. "I never want any hardness with my neighbors. Come again, Mrs. Ashton; it seems so pleasant to have a person drop in at any hour without formality; and—and—well, don't, for God sake, tell about that bribe! for it really was not intended for that. I suppose your husband told you, did he not?"

"No matter how I knew it; you want to keep your wicked tongue from uttering untruths about your wife, and behave yourself better than you ever have, or, if I know of it, I'll show you that you can be squared by the common law of the land, if you do not choose to obey the moral one!"—she then left.

"Good morning," he said, "step in this afternoon and see my wife; you are always welcome."

She went home; he returned to the kitchen, where he muttered curses upon her interspersed with oaths for an hour, wishing she was dead.   Said he, "If it were not for the law, I'd as soon shoot her as not.   Me, a man, a cool millionaire, to be bluffed by a woman,—it's terrible! and yet, I am beaten, that's certain.   Revenge! revenge! 'tis sweet.   'Twould be sweet to me, but I scarcely know how to get the start of her; I wish I did.   I'll go and tell Elice to forbid her the house; I'll make her do it.   The scales will then be turned.   Ha! ha! happy thought! I'll go at once!" and he, Walter Clayton, actually petted himself as he saw a loop hole so dexterously drawn.

He went to her room.   "Elice," said he, very sweetly, "do you think it quite right to make friends with any person who is continually bringing trouble to our house?"

"Certainly not."

"You know that Mrs. Ashton is one of that stamp; has (could you believe it?) insulted me many times under my own roof; and what I want of you is to vindicate my honor by forbidding her the house."

"Do not ask it, Walter; I cannot do it."

"He took a sovereign from his pocket—"Take this, Elice."

"I can not turn against so kind a friend."

"I will make it double."

"No, papa, not if you gave me all your wealth."

"You shall!" and he started toward her with clenched fists. "Will you?"

"I will not."

Mrs. Ashton opened the door—"Stay thy murderous hand, or I'll cause your arrest before night! I returned just in time. Leave this room, fiend!   Why do you persist in your diabolical course?"

"She provoked me to madness—she always does; never, as in this instance, grants me a favor, not the most trivial.   When she can better accede to my request than otherwise, she says no.   It was all her fault; she has made my disposition just what it is.   When I lived with my first wife we never had a word."

"Strange she would not turn her best friend out of doors; one whom, an hour previous, you invited to come again, saying she would always be welcome! I returned for a letter that I had forgotten, and stood in the hall and heard all your conversation. I was not deceived, for I knew your civility was instigated alone by your fear. The world knows enough of your career; but how little do they understand your intriguery, treachery, villainy, and the deep, dark plotting of your hell-stained life! And yet, and oh! how strange! this woman who has suffered all the tortures of misplaced affection, abusive words, kicks and cuffs at your hand, still clings to you with such heroic devotion, and seals her lips to all the sufferings of her poor, broken heart, her downtrodden life? and were you less than what you are, as I said before—a fiend of the blackest dye—you could appreciate it, and, for the sake of this love that has withstood the volcanic ruptures of those evil passions of yours, and from the sincerity of her heart, so often prayed 'Father forgive him,' and as often sealed her own pardon of these wrongs with a kiss, you would from this moment lead a different life. But kindness is of no avail with such a one as you, who heeds only the whiplash of the law. And I assure you, the sobs and entreaties of her whom you so ill-treat is all the reason it has not been applied before; so let this be an incentive to a better life, or you may reap the reward of your doings before you are aware; for there are hounds on your track, and it is only the good spirits of your household that keep them at bay."

CHAPTER XXXIV.

"O, mamma!" said little Blanche, "it is my birthday, and I am nine years old; the violets are in blossom. May brother and I go to the woods? I want to gather some of those pretty flowers for a wreath and a crown, for the concert is to-night, and I am to be queen."

"You to be queen!" said her mother, while she drew her up fondly and gave her a kiss. "I hope my little daughter is deserving the honor." And a proud and happy feeling stole through the heart of Elice, as her eyes rested upon the countenance of the child radiant with hope and pleasure.

"Yes, won't it be nice? You see, they always choose the best singers for the place, and those who can perform the most difficult part of the music, and so they have chosen me; and not because I am beautiful. I—I—well, I do wish I was. Now Maude Green is so handsome that every one stops in the street as she passes, to get another look at her. Am I very homely, mamma? Rosie Sharon said I was the worst looking person she ever saw, and that if I were to be queen, it was only because my father was rich, and not because I was pretty or any better than she. But she was mad, because she wants to boss everything, and every one to do just as she says ; but she'll find out! The teacher heard her growl, and she came near being turned out of the play. I wish she had been."

"No, no, dear, you do not wish so. Don't you know how wrong that is? We must do unto others as we would have them do to us ; we must love our enemies."

"Love our enemies?   Well, I don't love any one that don't love me; do you?"

"It is hard sometimes, but you know our blessed Saviour prayed for them, and we must try to imitate his example. Now if to-night, when you say your little prayer, you ask God to bless Rosie, and then to-morrow speak kindly to her, and friendly of her to your schoolmates, I believe she would treat you differently.   You retaliate, don't you? that is, when she says hateful things, reply in the same spirit,—you quarrel with her."

"Of course! You bet I don't take any of her impudence! Why, she has made me so mad before now, I have told her I'd lick her; and I will! why; mamma, she sassed little cousin Johnnie, and snatched away his books, one day, and kicked him; and I went straight up to her, and—and—"

"And what?   Tell me, Blanche."

"Why, I pushed her off the big stone at the back of the school house, and she rolled from the top of the hill to the bottom.   I was scared; but it didn't hurt her much; I didn't mean to hurt her, but then she must let us alone, that's all, or she'll catch it!"

"Is that what you learn at Sunday school?"

"No, it isn't, I s'pose."

"What was the Golden Text for last Sabbath?"

"'If a man smite thee on one cheek, turn the other also!' What does that mean?"

"How did your teacher explain it?"

"I don't just know, only she said we were never to quarrel or fight with our little brothers or sisters, and that we had better keep out of the company of all those boys and girls that were not peaceable; that, if they were naughty and struck us, God would punish them for it.   But I told her God was so good I was afraid He wouldn't give them half what they deserved; and then, He'd be so long may be in doing it, that if ever they should take a notion to pound me, or pull my hair like they did to others sometimes, I would prefer to lick 'em myself, and then they'd never meddle with me again. But I would not think of touching any one that was good to me; do you believe I would, mamma? But now may we go to the woods?"

"Yes, but not stay too long."

"And how are we to know?"

"You keep near the edge of the woods; that is where the prettiest of the flowers grow, and then, when the time is up, I will ring the bell for you."

"Oh! sweetest, best of all mothers, you are so good! Come, Charlie, get your hat and let's away."

Some of the school children met them at the door, among them, Sammie Wilmington with his sister, and a few others of Blanche's favorites; and they were soon treading on pretty mosses, through the huckleberry and other bright green shrubbery, in quest of flowers that were scattered in rich profusion all through the leafy covert—the beautiful, shady home of the squirrel and chipmunk, the blue bird, and linnet. Never were there happier children. Sammie gathered all the largest and brightest of the violets and gave them to Blanche. He hardly knew why he did so, but some way he liked the smile she gave him whenever he tossed to her lap those little beauties; and he would rather she would have them than any one else, or to keep them himself. But when the others remonstrated with him for showing partiality, he simply said, "But if you were to be queen to-night, then I might pluck them for you; but, as it is, she must not be eclipsed."

They all acquiesced, chatted, sung and made merry, while their little hearts seemed brimful and running over with happiness till the bell rang that was to call them home.

Evening arrives; the beautiful park is illuminated; the seats all taken. It is the children's concert; and so the parents, older brothers and sisters are much interested. The play was Leopold and Leonora—a prince and a child queen. It was fabulous, and composed for the occasion. She was betrothed to him; but young as she was, in anticipation she felt the yoke of bondage that was to tighten about her neck. She despised her lover, while he adored her. By many years her senior, he felt a strange mingling of pride and ambition, as he looked forward to the time when her little jeweled hand should be placed in his and she should become his wife; and, but for her aversion, they would have been married at once. She never thought to avert the doom that awaited her, until she saw a peasant lad about her age that won her love all unconsciously, as she met him, or rather, passed him in the grand old park, where she often rode surrounded by a retinue of lords and ladies, when he would always be playing on a beautiful harp, oftentimes accompanying the instrument with his voice, while the rich, sweet tones of both fell upon her ears, entrancing her senses, as the ethereal strains of some heavenly spirit. Once, and once only, their eyes met, and in that gaze, the whole story was told: he knew he was loved, and never was the warbling of the summer birds more beautiful than the harmonious tones that dropped from his fingers and lips, and was wafted on the balmy breath of the morning air to that little girl arrayed in the most costly silks, glittering with jewels, as her fair head nestled lightly upon the white satin folds that lined the elegant carriage in which she rode, drawn by four snow-white horses. Oh! bliss beyond all description, to feel the sunlight of a sweet smile, and from such a source! not that he was unaware there lay a gulf between them as wide and long as the pit of the grave, which he never expected to pass; but that he could have one kindly thought from that being whom he considered one of the sweetest of earthly mould. Leopold saw it all, however, feared the result and determined to put the boy out of the way. He had annoyed them before, he said mentally; the best way would be to meet him alone; with one hand he could tie the scoundrel that dared to take even a kind look from his affianced. He would hurl him to the abyss that gaped and strained for victims not a hundred yards away. And then he bethought himself that he could not do it, but would league with some of the soldiers to entice him into their ranks and let an accidental shot put an end to his existence. He was jealous of the love of his darling; not that he thought she would prove disloyal to him, but that look did not just suit him, and woe to the man that dared stand in his way!

Having, however, overheard the plot, disguised as a peasant, Leonora went in search of Alfonson Alzino, the youth of whom we have spoken. She told him of his danger and advised him to have nothing to do with the soldiers, and then was gone. Alfonson could not believe he had seen the idol of all his fondest dreams and had almost come to the conclusion that it was an apparition—that an angel had appeared to him; when one of the soldiers, tapping him on the shoulder, asked him to come and play at court; that Prince Leopold had been so entranced by his songs that he had gained him admittance to entertain the queen with the high lords and ladies.

He thought of the words of the peasant girl, how she had warned him; but still he said he would run the chance; to be where he could daily see the angel of his visions would be heaven to him, and he would look out for treachery.

It was May: Leonora had bought several baskets of beautiful wild violets of a little flower girl; and, to gratify a strange whim of hers, she had been allowed to be arrayed in these for the evening. Her diamonds were left off, and instead, a crown was made of these "little woodland nymphs," as she called them. There were the deep blue, the white, the straw colored; and she was decked from head to foot with nature's own jewels; and, what no one knew but herself and Alfonson, was his little gift.

He came. He knew why she had done this; it was for his sake. Oh! could it be, he was so loved? He improvised a song. It said nothing of the queen; but it was all about a spirit that had winged its way from the skies and bent its flight to beds of mosses and wild flowers; who, after decking itself with them, went around as a ministering angel breaking them off and strewing them by the side of the sick, the down-trod-den and the weary of the earth; and then, after a time, was received into heaven. And all the time he kept his eyes on the beautiful Leonora—he could not help it, for he was spell-bound. Leopold saw this; and, constraining his rage no longer, rushed on him with his sword, and thrust it through his heart. He fell; but when he died, there was a piercing cry of agony went up from other lips: they were the queen's, and she, too, was dead.

This was the play. Blanche Clayton personated Leonora; Sammie Wilmington the musician, and Alfred Gray the prince. Other boys and girls were the lords and ladies. They were applauded and applauded again; it seemed so real. The people said they never thought Blanche handsome before; but the radiance of her countenance, the bewitching softness of her large, black eyes, the silvery sweetness of her voice, made her very attractive. And there was something more than play about those tell-tale blushes that occasionally tinted the alabaster whiteness of the fair face of Sammie with the most delicate pink, which only lent a charm to his high and handsome brow and deep blue eyes.

"Do you know what Alfred Gray says about you?" said little Mabel Wilmington, addressing herself to Sammie.

"I do not;—nothing good, I suppose."

"He hates you, and says if he ever sees you making up to Blanche Clayton, he will kick you into the middle of next week. These were his words; he was talking to some other boys."

"Was that all?"

"No, he would like to thrash you; and he would, sometime; you were nothing but a pauper; would have been in the poor house if it had not been for my father."

"That's nothing, Mabel. I wonder what makes him so angry at me."

"I don't know; only he said Sam thought he was somebody

when he was playing piano last evening ; but if 'old Clayton' knew how he was trying to shine up to Blanche, he wouldn't wonder if he'd come to a fate as bad as Alfonson who had the audacity to court the queen. I stood it as long as I could, and then I walked straight up to him and told him you were my brother ; and that you were able to thrash any boy like him, anytime, and he better keep his hands off of you. Now, Sammie, won't you please to give him a good lickin' when you see him, and let him know he shall not be talkin' about you in this way ? "

" I shall let him alone, little pet," he said kissing the plump, rosy cheek of the child, "unless he makes me too mad, and pitches into me first ; and then I suppose I couldn't help taking my own part."

" And if you don't, you are a fool, so there ; and I won't own you any longer for my sweet, good brother."

" Halloo ! " cried a voice a few evenings afterward, "is that you, Sammie Wilmington ? " and Alfred Gray made his way up to his side and was soon in conversation with him, "Come down to the river and fish with me."

" No, I cannot ; my lessons are hard for this week ; we are on a review and I must study evenings."

" But you shall ! " and he took hold of his arm and gave it a pull.

" You must let me alone, Alfred Gray," said Sammie, "you must not think you can brow-beat me after this style ; for I will not stand it."

" You ! who are you ? "

" I try to mind my own business ; and if I was born of wealthy parents like you, I would have striven hard, if they were living, not to disgrace them by getting intoxicated."

Alfred Gray drew himself up ; a large diamond glittered on his finger, and one on his shirt bosom, showing how lavish his friends had been with him. "See here, pauper brat, you don't want to say I'm drunk, or I'll make way with you ! "

"I do not want to fight, you will please let me alone."

"But what do you go to Clayton's for?   He says he will put you out, if he ever sees you inside his house again."

"Does he?"

"And, furthermore, he must never hear of your speaking to Blanche again.   He was raging when he found out you were lovers just in the play; for he said it seemed too much reality, and you were too low born.   And so you are—your father was a dirty sot, and your mother—"

"Hold!" cried Sammie, his face white with rage; "I can bear all the insults you may please to heap upon me, but my sainted mother's name shall not be desecrated.   Take that, Alfred Gray!" and he felled him to the ground and held him there, and pounded him till he cried for mercy.

Blanche and her mother happened to be passing that way at the time, and heard the whole conversation and knew just what the row was about.

Blanche said, "Alfred was to blame, and I shall never speak to him again; and I am so glad that Sammie got the best of him."

Her mamma replied, "It hurts my feelings so much to see children quarreling and fighting; and I am very sorry that two members of the academy, as well as the Sabbath school, should become so angry at each other."

"But Alfred deserved the 'whaling' so bad; and I'm glad he got it!"

Sammie was from that moment a great hero, in her estimation.   He had dared to stand up for his rights; to battle for his friends against such odds.   A man in years, as she thought, for he was seventeen, while Sammie was only twelve; and how he did it, she didn't know; but God helps the weak, and so He helped him.

CHAPTER XXXV.

Walter Clayton was satisfied with housekeeping, and although the hardest matter in the world, even when convinced of an error, to admit it, yet in his own mind he thought a woman after all had considerable to do to keep the house in order, to cook the meals, and was never again known to argue the matter with any person.

"I must have a servant girl," he said, "who will it be? Of course, Hettie is the very best girl in the world—I do not know her equal, and I wish she would come back, but that will never do after her going into the church and telling what she has—people would wonder and wonder, and take me for an idiot for harboring a thief in my house. Hettie meant no harm, did not even think she was pilfering, I know, and if I could induce her to return, now she has her eyes opened, it would be a nice thing. Well, Hettie was a grand girl—had not a fault as I could see, not a single one. To be sure she was considerable cross to the children sometimes, but they are so very trying she could not help that. Blazes, I wonder how many times I slapped them for saucing her. Well, they no business to do it—ought to be pounded if they did not mind every word she said. Elice maybe would not want her to work for us any more, but she has nothing to say about it; I am master of my own house, I guess; and when it comes to such a pass that I have to ask my wife what servant we shall have, I'll break up housekeeping altogether."

Hettie would not go again to Walter Clayton's, although he used all the persuasive arguments of which he was master to induce her, but was not long in finding another—Susan Smith—and one quite to his notion as far as he knew—who proved on a few days trial to be bold, impudent, intriguing, thievish creature, without one particle of honor in any respect. All of which did not worry Walter Clayton very much, as she managed to be very pleasant when he was around, and in a good natured way to get his help in taking and holding the reins of government; after a time to carry a despotic queenly sway over the house.

The children were misused, but after informing their father, ceased altogether to tell him, as it did no good—only incurring his wrath and displeasure, and as for Elice, she must have no voice in the matter. If she made an attempt to expostulate Walter would say "you are everlastingly finding fault; you ought to do the work yourself and shall, if you kick up a row. Susan is a splendid girl. We never have a servant to please you."

"Do you want your children to be cuffed around by that girl?" Elice would sometimes enquire.

"They don't dare to tell me Susan strikes them."

"Nevertheless she gave Charlie that black eye."

"I don't believe it. Why didn't he say so when I asked him?"

"Did you not tell him not to come to you with tales about Susan? That you would punish him if he did?"

"Well, yes! for I found out they were getting to be as bad as yourself—never telling the truth. Now I know Susan too well to think she would do anything very wrong—so let this end the matter."

CHAPTER XXXVI.

Susan has now been in her place for more than a year. She has succeeded without detection, in obtaining keys that will unlock every drawer, bureau, trunk, etc., in the house; and in the absence of the inmates, satisfies her curiosity in examining their contents, reading private papers and letters, but being very careful to replace them properly, that she may not be discovered.   As yet she has purloined nothing lest she should lose the opportunity of securing something of far greater value that might be deposited; only taking that which chanced to be carelessly left around, where it would as soon be laid to the children as to herself.

Blanche having one morning occasion to return from school for a book, found her looking over her box of letters.   She had taken out twelve bearing the signature of Sammie Wilmington and expected to peruse them here in her little bedroom unmolested.

"What do you mean?" said Blanche in great wrath; "I'll inform my mamma of all your dirty tricks, and have you discharged."

"And I'll tell your father you've been gettin' love-letters from the feller that he forbid you 'sociatin' with.   Now, my little miss, you better not be too upstropulus, that's the long and short of it, or he'll hear a thing or two."

"You are a thief, a liar and a mischief-maker; and I hate you worse than I do any one else in the world!"

" I'm hired, for telling, you know ; I get fifty cents on a week mor'n I would if it wa'n't for that ; and it's likely I'd see anything go wrong in this house without tellin' the master ; besides I think he orto know. Now, if you'll give me that pretty gold locket and chain of yourn and say you lost it, I'll keep still. You know you'd git a terrible thrashin' if you be a girl. I'd hate to see you licked, now that's so. Do, that's a good girl, and I'll never tell if you git a thousand like 'em ; and I'll help you too—carry mail for you ; mebbe you'll need me sometimes."

Blanche wrung her hands and cried; she knew she had been told never to speak to Sammie, and she feared it would go hard with her if he found out she had been holding correspondence with him ; but to part with that precious gift from her dear, dead mamma, was a hard blow for her ; she did not feel as if she could do it. At last she said, "That coral necklace and those pretty charms—won't they do ? "

" No, they will not—the gold one or none," and Susan held the box firmly, saying, "I will take them all to your father as soon as he comes here unless you give it to me."

"Well, there it is, then ; now, how much will you ask me, and I will buy it back, just as soon as I can save money enough."

"All right. Now you can depend upon it, anybody can do anything they want to, if they'll pay me for it."

Susan managed to keep one of the letters, however, when, after tearing off the signature, she dropped it where Mr. Clayton would find it.

It was just dinner hour: all the family were seated around the table, when, stopping suddenly, he remarked that he had found a very funny letter ; he thought it beat all the love letters he ever saw ; but as there did not happen to be any names mentioned, it would be hard to tell to whom it belonged; it was evidently from some young lad. He read aloud, while the face of Blanche first turned to deep crimson, and then to ashy whiteness.

"'My Darling: You know I love you a great deal better than any girl I ever saw. There never was a person lived that could begin to come up with you; well, yes, there was one once—you know whom I mean—but she has gone to Heaven, and there is nobody left for me to love but you. Sometime, I presume, we will get married. You know what you told me: that you would never have any one but me. If I thought you would, it would kill me; but I know you will not, will you? You remember when we gathered the flowers—how beautiful they were; but you were the sweetest of them all; and I wanted to tell you then how much—how very much I loved you, but could not—'" The rest was torn off.

"I'd like to know what silly little upstart wrote that," said Mr. Clayton. "If I knew of any boy sending such trash to you, Miss Blanche, I'd thrash you both. Never let me catch you at such nonsense, You'll find it will not be well for you."

Blanche said nothing. She would not tell a lie; she would not deceive him. By this time she had regained her composure, so he did not seem to mistrust her.

Susan was in an adjoining room, chuckling over her little trick, as she called it, which she played on Blanche, "just to see," she said, "how skart she would be."

"What do you think of it?" she said as soon as she found Blanche alone. "Do you see what you'd got, if I'd told on you? Now, see here, your father showed me that very letter and asked me if I thought Blanche was correspondin' with the boys, and I told him, 'No, not a bit of it; I saw Belle Stratton drop it out of her pocket when she came for you to go to school with her.' Now, if you hadn't give me nothin' you don't expect I'd keep your secrets for you, and tell a wicked lie to git you out of your scrapes—no, sir, not I; but I'm a friend to you, and, as long as you don't tread on my toes, all right. You understand?"

"Yes, I do? but I don't see how I'm ever to get so much money to pay you. I don't have five cents a week, hardly, and you ask me five dollars for the chain, and you know it's mine, Susan. It was my dear, dead mother's. Do, for her sake, let me have it again, and I'll give you every penny I can get for all winter."

Susan flew into a rage. "You can have it," she said, "but of course the letters are locked up in my trunk; I could show them any 'time."

"Well, then keep it; I will do the best I can; but for the love of mercy, don't let my father see them."

"No, not if you do as you promised."

Blanche went to her room and threw herself upon her bed in an agony of despair. "Oh!" she cried, "what am I to do? Where will I get the money? And supposing father should ask to see the miniature, as he sometimes does, and I could not produce it; he would then wish to know where it was, and I could not tell a lie!"

Susan had followed her, unperceived; and, as soon as the door was locked, she slipped to the keyhole and listened. She heard her sobs, and knew just what they were about, and was determined to involve her in still greater difficulty. She rapped gently at the door. It was opened and she was bidden to enter.

"I've got a plan for you; I don't want to be too hard on nobody, and it'll help you all out."

"What is it?" answered Blanche, brightening.

"You know you sleep in the next room to your papa's. Now, climb up when he is asleep, take the key out of his pocket, bring it to me, and I'll help you to unlock his safe where you could git as much as a hundred dollars, if you wanted to."

"Supposing he should find it out?" Blanche answered, wishing to lead her on.

"He never would mistrust us. He couldn't be made believe I would do such a thing; he's an old miser, anyway, and don't treat none of you none the best. He jaws you for what you don't never do, and acts like an old heathen around here. He thinks I'm 'bout right, though. You see, I've a great knack of throwin' sand in folks' eyes if I've a mind to. What do you say?"

"I'll never do it. He might whip me to death first for the letters; but steal, I will not!"

"But that wouldn't be stealin', you big ninny, for no law could touch you, even if it was found out, which would never be."

"Susan, I'd die before I'd be guilty of the crime! so talk to me no more about it."

"Well, fool, then you won't tell on me, will you? If you should, you know how easy it will be for me to deny it; and I stand ten to one in your father's estimation for honesty, truth and everything else angelic to what any the rest on you do; and, furthermore, you see if I wouldn't make a big breeze between your father and you—I'm capable!"

"I know that; you are a devil. Where do you expect to go when you die?"

"I ha'n't thought nothin' about that yet; there's time enough for that; but be careful what kind of names you call me, miss, for you remember you are still in my power."

"Yes, but I'll be even with you some day—now see!"

"Look out how you cross my path; I'm your friend now. You have an easy life—nothing to do but go to school; all you want to eat, I s'pose; clothes comfortable enough; nothing to what I'd have if I was a millionaire's only dotter, though, I've heard folks remark that you nor none on the rest on you was dressed decent; but that's not here nor there: you have quite a little heaven here to what you would if I got after you."

"You are after me now, I should think," replied Blanche forcing a smile; she knew her words were true. "Better have her good will, if possible," she thought. "You are pretty good sometimes: I will keep quiet."

14

"So you better," and Susan left the room.

"That money must be raised: I've a plan," Blanche said, mentally, after she again bolted the door and found herself alone. "The scholar in our class who writes the best essay receives a present of two dollars; and the one that stands first in his studies one of five dollars. Now I mean to have them both. I can if I study hard, I know; but oh! I shall have to work to get ahead of those three boys, for they have now a good deal better knowledge of their books than myself. But I'll sit up nights, but what I will accomplish it! I know now; I will get mamma to write the composition, and then I will surely succeed—no, no, that will never do—that would be deception and next to stealing to palm this off as my own, and so cheat the deserving pupils out of the prize; I cannot nor will not do so treacherous an act, and, besides, I know her too well; she could not be coaxed to write it; but she will assist me, I am sure; she will give me a nice subject and ideas—that would be right, I guess, I'll ask her. Dear, sweet mamma! she never failed me in my troubles, but always helped me out if she could. I tell her everything, for she never scolds me even though I am deserving; but papa storms and raves; I dare not make a confidant of him. Oh! how I wish I could go to him as I do to her, throw my arms around his neck and ask his forgiveness when I do anything wrong. But I can't; he frightens me so. Now he ought not to be angry about those letters; I am sure there can be no harm for me to love Sammie and for him to love me, for I cannot help that. How could I when he has carried me to school every winter for years, on his large sled, trudging through great heaps of snow, tucking my shawl snugly around me, and carrying my dinner basket; and then, when the spring came, and the great blinding showers of rain, and the sun shone out warm melting the snow, and making the roads so very bad, and the nice stone walks in the academy grounds, got bits of board and sticks of wood and laid over the bad places so that I need not soil my feet nor fall into the mud?

Of course I love Sammie, and where is the harm? I love my brothers, and my father when he is kind to me ; but when he is cross, and unreasonable, and tyrannical, and snappish, and oh! just as hateful and ugly as can be, why—I hate him—I guess— yes, I can't call it anything else, for I wish he was dead, and myself too!"

CHAPTER XXXVII.

Examination day came and passed ; both prizes were awarded to Blanche ; but oh! how many headaches, sleepless nights and days of toil they had cost her. She had oftentimes studied by the light of a little lamp in her room till the wee hours of morning. The excitement had kept her up, but now it was over ; her overstrained nerves began to react, and her pale face showed how far she had gone beyond her strength.

The money she gave to Susan, and in return received the chain ; but when she came to look over her letters, she found several of them missing ; thus there was a whip held over her to still lacerate the tender flesh, and cut deep into her heart. She felt it keenly, and remonstrated with this fiend, who only replied that she had given her all that she ever had. It was, of course, useless to argue the case with her, and so Blanche gave it up ; but all the time felt that there was a volcano beneath her feet that might burst at any time and immerse her with its boiling lava. "I am only twelve but I have seen trouble," she said. "I believe I will go to my mother and tell her all about these letters now," she said, holding them in her hand; "and if she thinks best, I will take them to papa, and tell him I meant no wrong; but, if I have committed sin by disobedience, I crave his forgiveness; but, then, I should have to tell him that I did still keep my acquaintance with Sammie; that I held conversation with him every chance I got,—and I cannot do it; for he would surely make me promise never to speak to him again; and that would break my heart, I believe.   O, spirit of my mother, come down from Heaven and help me!   Why did I not die before these dark days came?   People imagine children should be as happy as the little birds that sing the whole day long.   But they never allow a snake to coil around their nests, and nestle in them, ready to bite their wee ones whenever they get a chance ; but here we have an adder in our house, and oh! how many times we have all felt its sting.   But papa thinks she is good—of course he does, or he would not keep her; but I know all about her.   If I should tell him what I have seen, he would not believe it; she has such a pretty way of getting out of everything, and throwing the blame all on some one else, and so, she would manage with me.   O blessed Jesus!   I'll go to Him and rely upon Him—that's what mamma has told me so much ; but it seems as though I did not know just how.   But there is one thing I can do : I will ask Him to send this dreadful woman out of the house; for, if He does not, I shall die."

At that moment Susan entered her room—all smiles.   She said she had found those letters, and had come to give them all up.   "Oh, you are so good!"   Blanche answered,   "and then I shall not worry so."

"You are a fool to let them trouble you, any how: that's nothin' to have some one tell you that he loves you, and they can't help it ; and you musn't speak to no other boys but him. You orto see some I've got.   Now what do you s'pose I care who knows it; but then I thought I'd come and jest tell you if these letters would be of any account to you, I'd give every one on them up if you'd just give me that pretty bird of paradise you have worn now on your hat for all last winter ; you have kept it as good as new, and ye see I'm going to uncle's next week, and I want to take some presents to them, so to make them good-natured ; so I'd like to take that bird to my cousin, for one thing."

"Why! my grandmother gave me that, and what would she say?"

"Fiddlesticks! let her say. She won't know it. Tell her you wore your hat to school one day, and a big boy came into the entry and stole it—that's reasonable enough, ain't it?"

"But you can't get me to tell that lie; besides I've paid you for them all, once."

"Your father was talking about that letter again he found, and wanted to know of me if I thought Blanche had anything to say to Sammie any more. I told him no, I knowd she didn't, and stuck up for you good. Now, spos'n' I'd jest hauled out these pretty love 'pistles, as your father calls them, and showed him! You might as well be struck by thunder, I guess; you might as well say your prayers and prepare to leave!"

"He wouldn't kill me?"

"No, not as bad as that, I s'pose; but I'd 'bout as liv be murdered outright, as to have him know about it, if I was you; for you'd think a whole swarm of bees was let loose 'round your ears, I guess, for the next six months; there would be such a terrible uproar. He's awful, ain't he, Blanche?"

"He is worse if he has some one like you to set him up, and you are all the time hatching up a fuss."

"That's my business, to be sure. You see, he pays me for telling, and the rest pay me for keeping still; so, betwixt you all, I manage to be kept in pin money."

"If I was mamma, I'd put you out, for you are all the while getting her into trouble. You think I don't know it, I suppose."

"She knows better. I'm the best friend she has got."

"But who told papa the falsehood about her getting mad and burning up all my first mamma's dresses?"

"I didn't."

"I heard you! And furthermore you stole those very articles. I might inform them!"

"I never done it, nor you nor no saint could make them think so."

"But I saw you take them."

"But you dassant tell. Who did I see talking together after school in the academy yard, and what did you say? You told Sammie you'd love him forever; now didn't you? You couldn't deny it, for you ain't jest like me—you wouldn't tell a lie. Now give me the bird, and I'll say quits; you might as well, for if we have a fight and play the fool, why, my head is a little the longest, for it's the oldest, and 'twould be you, miss, that would come out the little end of the horn, and not me, you are wise enough to see, yourself."

"Well, here is the bird."

"All hunkey! Here's them letters, and no mistake. Ain't I good? Good night, Blanche, I shall not see you again very soon, as I start to-night on the midnight train for uncle's."

CHAPTER XXXVIII.

It is autumn—glorious season! The bright green leaves are tinged with gold and crimson; the frosts have commenced to drape the flowers in its modest but beautiful robe of white, while the husbandman is still gathering in his hoarded wealth of ripened grain and fruit.

Elice is once more seated in the little arbor, wrapt in contemplation, and wondering, with all this loveliness spread out in nature—these precious gifts—that man should be so unthank·ful, and unhappy; while her heart goes out to the Great Giver, in sweet praises for life and health.

She took a letter from her pocket, that she had received a week previous, to again peruse. It was from her mother, and not the first time that she had stolen away by herself to enjoy those blessed words that were such a comfort to her in trials and afflictions, for each time it seemed as if she had actually seen and held sweet converse with her, in not only that which pertained to her temporal, but spiritual welfare.

''My Darling Child:—You cannot imagine how happy I am to be able, after a tedious illness, to address you. I have been very near the door of death, I suppose, but thanks to Him who rules in the armies above as well as on earth, that to-day, for the first, I went into my flower garden and sat for an hour under the grape vines' shade. A thousand remembrances stole over me of the past. And to whom, dearest, did my thoughts wander out in quest? A little one robed in blue or white, running to and fro among the flowers, as happy as the birds the live-long day—grown now to womanhood, and away, oh! so far away that my heart aches to think of the distance; hoping, but fearing that her life is not what it was, or what it seemed—a dream of bliss, to whom the troubles of childhood never came. I am afraid you are not so happy now; but we must not expect too much in this world, for here we shall have tribulation, but in the bright beyond—peace. Live for Christ, darling; lay up treasures in Heaven; set not your affections on things below, for a crown surely awaiteth, if you are faithful to God. I am so longing to see your dear face. Come home; do not delay long; the apple trees are loaded with fruit; the grape vines pend with their weight; the fragrance of the wild roses lends a charm, and the odor of the new mown hay is sweet and invigorating.

"Your father sends his love with a thousand kisses, and says, 'Tell Elice to be sure and come and stay through all the lovely autumn;' now don't disappoint him, for he looks forward to your visit as the happiest days of all the year. His health is failing; but his hope in Christ grows brighter and still brighter as he nears the beautiful land—the Holy City of salvation.

"That we may be ready to meet the king of terrors—death, is the prayer of your mother and friend,

"Mary Woodville."

Elice had scarcely finished this loving epistle before a telegram was handed her. It was from her father:—

"We fear your mother is dying—hasten!"

"My mother! my dear, dear mother! Oh! it cannot be!" she murmured, and fell fainting to the ground.

When she recovered, she picked up the telegram. "It must be a dream!" she thought. "No, no, there it is, in black and white; 'your mother is dying!' It must be true; it must be true. Sweetest, best of all parents, shall I never see thee again alive? Oh! for one word from those blessed lips, to tell me how I am loved; and my spirit would take its flight with thine. Sorrow has alone 'been my lot since we separated; and now, with my head upon thy breast, within thy grave I would lay me down and rest, sweet, sweet mother!"   She lifted her eyes heavenward with this prayer :

"Father, forgive my lack of submission and give me strength to sustain me through all my sorrows that have come so suddenly upon me."

She then arose and started for the house; several times, however, she leaned against the fence for support, and, although she tried so hard to have no will in the matter, to give it all into the hands of thê Eternal; yet, as her thoughts wandered to the sick couch of the dearest earthly friend that she ever had, or ever expected to possess, she could not help wishing and hoping that she might recover from disease and be able to visit with her, on her arrival; that it was a mistake; that excitement had led her father to his sad conclusion respecting her. She met her husband at the door, who, seeing the pallor of her face said, "What is the matter?"

She handed him the telegram and then broke forth into piteous moans and sobs that would have melted a heart of stone.

"And you intend to go?" he said; "you cannot do any good."

"Oh! papa, I must start on the first train!"

"Yes, yes," said little Blanche, "if it were you, papa, wouldn't you want Charlie and little Robin and I with you if you died?"

"Well, I s'pose you'd have to go, if it took the last cent I had—here it is then."

"And alone! Must I go alone? Will you not accompany me? Oh! such a terrible pain here!" and she pressed her hands tightly over her burning brow.

"No, I will not; it's enough for you to spend money unnecessarily, without wanting me to; and as for your folks, I never did like them, your mother especially."

"Oh, my mother! sweet mother, so dear to me! a thousand times could I die in her stead!"

"Papa, I love her," said little Blanche. "Don't you know how she used, when she was here, to sit up till midnight, and mend our clothes, and make dresses for me? I wish she would get well. Tell her, mamma, I want to see her and I hope she won't die, and take her such lots of kisses—poor grandmama!" and herewith the tears ran down her cheeks like rain.

Elice prepared hastily for her journey, and was ready at the depot to take the express train bound for New York when it came. All the passengers noticed the quivering lips, and ashy paleness, like death, of her countenance, and said among themselves that she was too sick to be travelling alone; while her head reeled, and she thought, at times, she never would reach the end of her journey. But strength came, from the sweet fountain where it always had; for, after taking some wine that a lady offered her, then laying her weary head for a time upon a pillow that the kind hearted conductor procured for her, she felt much better; and when she reached the home of her parents, was better prepared to meet the trouble that awaited her than when at the door she parted with her cruel and tyrannical husband, whose very presence sent a thrill of dread and fear to her heart, and in that ratio weakened her nerves and induced sickness.

"My mother!" were her first words, as she entered the house.

"In there," said her father pointing to a large room on the east side of the building. "She is delirious; is now calling your name."

"And not dead?" Oh, thank God, not dead!"

"No, darling, your mother still lives to give you her dying blessing," he said, folding her to his breast. "Go in, now, she may know you."

She hastened to her beside; reason, for a few moments asserted its right. "My child! my child! I am so glad you are here! The sands of my life have been lashed by the waves of death; each one comes nearer to me. I must leave you; but Jesus, my friend, is with me, and in his precious arms he will bear me over the tide, where myriads of angels are waiting on the other shore to welcome me. Don't you see them? Hark! I hear their hallelujahs. Sweet, sweet, Christ! my all and in all! Who would not be a Christian? who would not love the Lord? 'Though I walk through the valley and shadow of death, I will fear no evil, for Thou art with me, Thy rod and Thy staff they comfort me.' 'He breaketh the bands of death in sunder.' Praise His holy name!" A smile then overspread her countenance. "Farewell!" she whispered, "I am entering the beautiful city;" and breathed her last in the arms of her husband.

It was a consolation above all things to know that she died so peacefully; that she fell asleep in Christ; that she would be raised incorruptible in the morning of the glorious resurrection; but yet that home was desolate without the sweet words of hope that ever dropped from her lips; that came as manna to the barren desert of many a poor heart that had listened to her counsellings; that had been blessed both spiritually and temporally by this kind-hearted woman.

The moonlight streamed through the closed shutters of that chamber of death, where the mother of Elice had been laid; the same little room where they had been together so much; where the family had gathered in prayer; and this loved one so many times asked God to give her all of her dear children to go with her to that Happy Land: and, entering, Elice sat there long hours with folded hands and streaming eyes, watching by the side of the sleeper, and wishing that she was as free from sin as her darling mother had been, and desiring above all things that she could lead as blameless a life. She thought of the vacant chair at the table; the seat at church, where she had been in attendance so many years; the vacuum at the altar of prayer; the loss of her strengthening influences; the touch of that dear, administering hand in sickness; and a sense of lone-liness and desolation swept over her, that she had never—no, never felt in all her life, before. And she hoped that God, in his precious love, would see fit, at not a far distant time, to call her hence from her troubles; that together they would rest so sweetly under the beautiful maples that were so soon to over-shadow her mother; where she would be free from the oppres-sions that had converted a happy life into one of anxiety and sorrow; for the mildew had already gathered upon her young heart, withering its flowers in the spring time of their freshness; each rivulet of happiness frozen beneath the icicles of terror and fear; and the foliage of its brightest vegetation blackened by despair.

She started up; she pressed kisses upon the brow, the cheeks, the lips of her dead; she laid her face to hers; she took her hands, while her thoughts again went upwards:—

"O Thou to whom this heart ne'er yet
Turned, in anguish or regret,
The past forgive; the future spare;
Sweet Spirit, hear my prayer!
Oh! leave me not alone in grief;
Send this blighted heart relief;
Make Thou my life Thy future care;
Sweet Spirit, hear my prayer!"

She then went to her room—to her couch; but not to sleep; for all night long an upturned face was before her, radiant as that of an angel, white as the drapery of frost that hung at this time upon every living thing under the broad, blue sky; and a grave—a new made grave not a hundred rods away, where the winds were now moaning out a requiem for the departed. And so, when morning came, she had never closed her eyes to slum-ber. The next day she was buried. Before Elice left for her western home, which she did on the coming day she strewed flowers upon her grave, and bade her farewell with these words: "Dearest, best, kindest of mothers, by the aid of the power that watches over all our movements; by that grace which God sees fit to shower upon His creatures here below, we will meet thee again, when our life's pilgrimage is at a close, and Christ by his ministering angels shall say, 'It is enough; thy work upon earth is accomplished.' "

For months Elice never slept but she dreamed of her mother; and scarcely a moment passed but she was in her mind.

The following poem will describe her feelings, written the winter after her death:

> "Fierce, fierce, are the winds !
> Their icy breath binds
> All the green, grassy plains
> With their cold, icy chains.
> Out, out, in the storm,
> There lies a loved form,
> Where the pale moonbeams lay ;
> Through the tall maples play.
> Under the snow,
> Low, very low;
> With a brow pure and white,
> As the frosts of the night ;
> And clasped hands as cold,
> As the drapery fold
>
> That long ago covered the beautiful flowers ;
> That long ago spread over summer's green bowers ;
> There, there, where the storm-cloud this bitter night sweeps,
> My best beloved lies—there she sleeps, sweetly sleeps.
> All the light shut away from her soft hazel eyes,
> There she lies ! there she lies ! my dear mother lies.
>
> There, there is her bed ;
> For, oh ! she is dead.
> And will she not come if I call ?
> Her dear gentle hand let it fall,
> So softly again
> On my brow of pain ?
> Never more, never more,
> Will her voice as of yore
> Sweetly fall on my ear
> My sad spirit to cheer?
>
> Never more, never more her blessed songs be heard,
> More dear to my heart than the notes of a bird ?
> Never more, never more a smile light her brow ;
> Has she gone, and forever gone from me now ?
> Never more, never more my weary life bless
> With a fond kiss of love—with a caress ?
> To the kind, loving hearts that await her at home,
> Will she come never more, never more will she come ?

Through the darkness of night, from the fathomless shore,
Ring out the sad words, '' Never more, never more !''
But from her cold grave the moss rose shall rear
It's beautiful head, when spring shall appear ;
And the violet sweet, and the lily shall bloom
On her green grassy grave, now an ice-fettered tomb.''

CHAPTER XXXIX.

Susan did not go to her uncle's, as she expected. Mr. Clayton told her she could not be spared in the absence of his wife; so she gave up her trip for another year; she would then be twenty-one, she thought, and would make her home among her friends: then her chances would be better for carrying on some of her diabolical schemes, as the mistress kept too close a watch over her proceedings, when she was around. Once aware that she would not scruple at any time and place to steal whatever lay in her way, sure of her acquittal by her husband, and not having the power to dismiss her, Elice had been doubly cautious; feeling assured that something would turn up that he would be as glad as she to rid himself of this obnoxious person.

Mr. Clayton was nervous and excited. He had received a telegram that a lawsuit in which thousands of dollars were involved, had been lost; and instead of placing his pocketbook containing a large amount of money in the chamber secured by the combination lock, he put it into one of the little drawers outside.

Susan watched every movement—was ready to avail herself of this bit of carelessness on his part, and to set at work to obtain the money as soon as there was a fitting opportunity. She had one of his keys to the outside door of the safe—had found it in his bedroom one morning when sweeping—which he had not missed.

The clock struck twelve. Listening at the door of the

apartment where he slept.; his heavy breathing fell upon her ears. "Now is my time," she thought, and, going to the safe, she unlocked it and was soon in possession of all the money here deposited. The next thing she did was to hide it in some safe place, go cautiously to the outside door, open it, throw all the papers around the safe, and then set up a hideous cry of "thieves! robbers!" to awaken the master of the house.

All this was so successfully managed, that he actually thought he had been robbed by skillful burglars, and that they had made good their escape. So, long before morning, a hundred men were in search of these villains, looking in every direction. There had been no train out of the place since the depredation; so they must be secreted in the woods or some other hiding place, and of course, they were sure to be found, so they said. But when the next evening came and the men were in from all the points assigned them, they had gained no clue to the thieves, and it seemed quite probable that Mr. Clayton would never know what had become of his money. But, gathering up the best knowledge that could be gained after listening to the story of the servant girl, and putting all manner of questions to her, the "local" furnished this thrilling report for the *Herald* of the following morning:

"DARING ROBBERY!

"Three masked men, armed with bowie knives and revolvers, entered the residence of our wealthy townsman, Walter Clayton, Esq., and, while the family were sleeping soundly in their beds—no doubt sweetly dreaming of peace and repose—succeeded in taking three thousand dollars from his safe. It is supposed the family were all chloroformed excepting Susan, the servant, who slept in a little room adjoining, which was not visited by them, but who, in awakening, showed the most unbounded bravery in screaming at the top of her voice for the master of the house and assistance, while they threatened to shoot her if she did not keep quiet. Why they did not, is the mystery; but probably they were anxious to expedite business, and did not care to link themselves, if ever caught, with the double crime of robbery and murder. The girl should be rewarded, for, of course, she did her best to avert the theft, even at the peril of her own life. We trust the rogues will be discovered and brought to justice."

Susan did not seem at peace; she was continually asking when Mrs. Clayton was to return, and alleging that she had several letters from her uncle, asking her to hasten her visit; that she would like to go very soon. She feared her money was not in a secure place, and her desire was to leave before she was suspected. Getting up one morning, she said she would be obliged to start on the noon express; for she had received a telegram and a horse and carriage were to be sent to the station, a distance of eight miles to meet her at her arrival; and she did not want to disappoint her kind friends. By a great deal of persuasion, however, Mr. Clayton got her to remain another week, by telling her he would send them word himself, and apprise them of her different arrangements.

That evening Elice returned from her mother's funeral; she had been gone two weeks, only, from home; but in that time flowers had been removed from her bonnets, velvet ribbons ripped from her dresses; while several articles were missing; silver spoons she had put away so carefully, gone; and what she had prized as one of her dearest treasures—a miniature of little Robin when a baby, in a lovely case—no where to be found. She was sick at heart, but said nothing.

Susan had a little trunk that she always kept locked, that Elice thought she would visit on the first opportunity. She knew it would not be worth while to divulge her plan to her husband, for he would pay no attention to her, unless it was to accuse her of fault-finding; so, one evening, in the absence of the servant girl, she went to her room, and, with a key she had procured for the occasion, opened it; and here she not only found all the missing articles, but little Blanche's locket and chain, the same she had toiled so hard to earn money enough to buy back of her; then the bird of paradise, together with silver and gold coin that had been given the children, which they supposed were now safely stored away in their little banks.

She suspected that this girl was now in possession of the missing money, and she set about to detect her if possible. So, one day after all the family had left the house, Susan could not withstand the temptation to again count her treasured pile and gloat her eyes over her ill-gotten gains. Elice had a key to her room, and, coming back suddenly, she unlocked the door and there found her just putting it all back in its hiding place, which was in the straw of her bed. She found she was caught and offered compromise.

" I'll give you half if you won't tell ; I'll kill you if you do. Here swear—on this Bible ! " and sprang and locked her in. Elice smiled. She saw she had a part to play, for, here alone with this girl, who seemed now a very demon, with twice her strength, a fear of detection and a desire to save her treasures, she knew not what might happen.

" You—you broke into my trunk yesterday—somebody did, and I b'l'eve 'twas you ! I'll put you where the dogs won't bite you, I believe, any how ! "

" But you wouldn't harm me, Susan. I never wronged you ; besides, you would be hung."

"Don't keer! don't keer! I wouldn't nuther, because old Clayton wouldn't let me ; he hates you, and would be glad if you's out of the way, so he would."

Susan sprang and grasped a revolver that she had concealed —another one of the missing articles belonging to the house— and held it at her head.

" You say you'll swear ? "

" I'll tell you what I'll do," said Elice, with the greatest composure ; "but you must sit down ; I have a capital plan for us both."

" And then you won't tell ? "

" I'll do just as I say. Did I ever tell you a lie ? "

" You didn't—no, you didn't," and she sat down quietly.

Some minutes elapsed. Elice said, "I have been to your trunk and found many missing articles. Will you replace everything if I will keep your secret?" But with two bits of rope which she found on the floor, she was preparing a noose to entrap her, in case she would not conform to her wishes.

"I'll give you all but the money; and you shall help me to get off to my uncle's. You won't lie; your word's better than that are book," pointing to the Bible. "Will you?"

"You must give up the money, too, Susan."

"No, I won't. You don't want to git me too mad, or you'll be sorry!" and with these words she stood erect, her hands clasped behind her, while she still held the revolver, but this time with the trigger in readiness to pull.

Elice knew there was danger, but her trap was ready, and, quick as thought, and before the girl was aware what she was doing, she had slid the rope over her hands, drawn up the knot, and with the other end, in which there too was a loop, had thrown it over the post of an old fashioned bedstead and secured the prisoner. Susan, wild with fright, begged for mercy, promising everything if she would but liberate her; but Elice unlocking the door, hurried as fast as she could for an officer. Meeting Mr. and Mrs. Ashton, who were out for a morning walk, she told them all the circumstances, and asked them to come as witnesses, which they willingly did. The four entered the apartment where the servant girl was secured.

"Will you give me the key to your truuk?" said Elice.

"Here it is, then. What do you want of it?" she answered sullenly.

Elice handed it to the officer. He opened the trunk, and, as we heretofore said, the most of the stolen articles taken from each member of the family since she came to the house were there found.

Mrs. Ashton espied the chain and locket—the same that Elice had been accused of trading to a peddler for silverware; about which reports had gone forth through the whole town; and a few had sympathized with Mr. Clayton about it, saying it was hard to have his first wife's likeness stolen; and that Elice had no business to do such a mean thing, if she was jealous of her. But here it was, and Mrs. Ashton said, "ought not to be given him at all, for he had no right to keep thievish servants in the family and then lay his losses on an innocent wife."

Just as they had taken the last article from the trunk, and after Susan had delivered up the money, confessing everything, Mr. Clayton came in. . "What is all this row about?" were his first words.

"I suppose you will be pleased to know," said the officer, "that all your lost property has been found and your money returned."

"I looked for you," said Elice, "and you were nowhere to be found; and, as I felt the necessity of hurrying up matters, I took this business upon myself."

"Why!—how?—you don't mean to say that Susan is the thief? I don't believe it."

"But it nevertheless is true," replied the officer; "she has owned it."

"And here is your missing miniature and chain," said Elice, reproachfully, "for which I have been compelled to suffer so much."

"Which," added Mrs. Ashton, "you told me and others were stolen by your wife, when it was that cringing, trembling beast of prey that for the past three years has hovered over your house like the locusts of Egypt, ready to destroy every green thing that might have grown up in your household; and you knew it, and yet, you keep her for a pest to your family, who dared not open their lips lest oaths and imprecations should be heaped upon them. Shame! You both ought to be in prison."

Mr. Clayton at his request was left alone with the prisoner.

"What are you going to do?" said Susan.

"Why, nothing. I have my money; that is all I want;" and he sat down and commenced counting it.

"It's all there.   No use of that.   I only took it for a joke."

"I presume so; mighty big one, though!"

"I didn't know but you'd send me to prison, that is, if you da—st; but I didn't bel'eve you dast, for—you know—and I wasn't no big fool nuther; weze in the same boat. You remember that big lie I swore to for you? And you swore to the same thing; and I was kalkerlating, if you found me out, and made a muss with me, I was going to be even anyhow; and if I had to look through one pigeon hole, why! it wouldn't matter much, for you'd be looking through another at the same time."

"Do you want to start for your uncle's to-day?"

"Yes, if you'll give me five hundred dollars to go with."

"I won't do it."

"Well, then, s'posin' I tell some of the things what I know?"

"No one would believe you."

"If I swore, wouldn't they?"

"Not with my oath against yours."

"But what if I can bring two or three what knows the same thing?"

"Who are they?"

"You know well enough all about it—my father and mother; and they'd be glad to have a chance to swear against you. Will you give me the money? If you will, I'll never trouble you again. I know a heap, and have a good tongue to let out on you; and no one ken hender me."

He counted it out to her, and helped her away on the evening express.

CHAPTER XL.

Six years have passed. The dim twilight is fading into night. The birds have hushed their notes and gone to their dreams; while the gentle breath of a beautiful summer evening fans the cheeks of two as ardent lovers as the world ever produced— Sammie Wilmington and Blanche Clayton. They had come to this day through great tribulation, but are now as happy in each other's society as it is possible under the circumstances; and, seated side by side, they talk of their future prospects and form plans, exchange words of endearment and encouragement, hoping their troubles are nearly at an end and the time not far distant when the dearest hopes of their lives will be consummated.

"In a year more I shall graduate," Sammie remarked, "and then, darling, I shall come and claim you as my own. Oh, happy day to you and me! I am not rich, as you know, but am offered a professorship in the college where I have been attending. I can support you; and a good living is all that is necessary for the present. By and by, when we get older, we will have luxuries, perhaps; but let come what may, these willing hands will work for one who has been my idol through all the past years of my life. What say you?"

"But if papa should not give his consent?"

"He will, dearest. What objection can he bring to our union? I know he used to dislike me, but I thought that was all past."

"He even hates you.   Through all the years of my acquaint-ance, I have never dared to invite you to our house."

"I know, and haye felt grieved; but you have always had some good excuse for our meeting at other places than your home, and never hinted at this truth.   But I will go to him at once, tell him how essential it is to our happiness for him to feel differently; to acquiesce in our plans; and then I see of no other obstacle in the way of our union.   I cannot return to my lessons until I know all."

Blanche shook like the leaves over their heads.   She dreaded to have Sammie say anything to her father, for she knew how terrible his wrath had been at different times when he had heard hints of the relationship that existed between them; how he had stormed, and threatened, and raved; but that was long ago, and he had scarcely mentioned his name in her presence since.   Once or twice, however, when some one had spoken of his high literary attainment, she had heard him say, "Humph! that fellow is nobody, nor ever will be.   I don't like that pau-per blood of his;" and she felt that it would be almost useless to say anything to him; and feared an open insult to Sammie, if he should venture to approach him; so she said, "I will speak to papa myself, about the matter."

"Your wishes are my law, Blanche.   He surely will listen to you," and here they parted for the night.

Going up to him the next morning, Blanche laid her hand on his shoulder, and, smiling, said, "Papa, I have a few words to say to you.   Can I see you in my room?"

"I guess so," he answered drily, "what do you want?"

After she had led the way to her own little room up stairs, she told him of her feelings respecting Sammie; plead his cause eloquently with her tears, and the strongest language love could assume.   Said she: "I know of his poverty; but for this I do not care, he has splendid habits, and great tal-ents; and I am sure you will never have cause to regret that you have given your consent to our marriage."

"What is all this about?" he said in great wrath; "you don't mean that you really love that low born idiot; that he has dared to aspire to your hand? Never—never shall you marry him! I would see the sod open and swallow you up first! Where is he? I thought that tomfoolery of yours was at an end, and it has only broken out fresh again; that he had gone away from the place, and was not troubling my head any more about him! Blanche, you must never speak to him again; but, should you be foolish enough to join your destiny with his, I'll disown you: I'll cut you off without a cent! Where is he now? The villain! the villain! Loafing around town, some-where, I presume. I'll go and find him, and give him a good thrashing!"

"O papa! please do not get so angry. Indeed, you have no cause to pour out your wrath upon Sammie, who never did a mean act in his life; whose only crime—if that be one—is his poverty. Once you were poor; and boastingly I have heard you speak of the first money you ever earned. You then seemed as proud as a king to be reckoned among the self-made men of your age."

"I know not why, but I despised him from the time he came begging at my door, when a little boy. I hate beggars."

"You mean when he came with the flowers to sell, when his poor mother lay dying? I have heard mamma tell the whole story?"

"The same. But what was that but begging? His flowers were not worth anything."

"The act was not only laudable, but praiseworthy. Have you seen him lately?"

"Not since he went away four years ago; but I hate him—I always did and I always shall!"

"You have no reason to."

"His father was a drunkard, his mother a vile woman. What good comes of such?"

"You speak of that you know nothing."

"But that is the story; and I wonder that he was ever adopted by Professor Wilmington. But he has no money to give him—is one of those persons who live from hand to mouth —nothing but a schoolmaster. Beautiful legacy to leave a child —a few books, a dog and a cat,—a horse and carriage, perhaps! Why, he does not even own the house he lives in."

"But Sammie may one day be rich like yourself. Should he be—"

"Plead his cause no longer. I have told you what you may depend upon, and I will not change my mind."

"O papa, reconsider! Let me invite him to our house, and then you can judge for yourself respecting him; he has changed so much and for the better since you saw him last!"

"Never! never! I have already selected a husband for you —rich and powerful. Marry him, and a large fortune shall be yours; dare to thwart my wishes, and I will leave you a beggar —now choose." Saying this, he left the room muttering curses upon the poor orphan that had dared to come between him and his fondest wishes.

Blanche sat down. She was pale, and in the greatest state of excitement and anxiety; for she felt that her father's words were irrevocable; that he would carry out the threat that he had made irrespective of her feelings; and so trembled as she thought of the future; and sorrowed as one without hope when she saw all of the bright castles she had raised in her imagination demolished; and, so far as she could see, no kindly beaming star of hope ever to arise that could banish the mists of darkness which had been scattered around her young life by the cruel and bitter words of her tyrannical father; for she had never known anything in her life but submission to his strong will. And she knew not how 'to go to work to sever the great iron chain that had been growing stronger and stronger for years; that seemed always to come between her and everything she most desired, hedging up her way, and making her life miserable.

Evening came. Sammie was passing through the park ; his steps were slow, for he was thinking of the school days spent in the old academy, when, day after day, he was permitted to behold and even to hold conversation with one who had always occupied the highest seat in his affections. And he felt a strange fear that they must be separated, perhaps forever. He believed that all was not right, and oh ! if this should prove true, what would his ambition amount to ? for, with all his hopes for future greatness there was mingled a sweet voice cheering him on : through all his persecutions about his birth and parentage there was always one strong defender of his rights—Blanche. If she should fail him ? What would he do ?

" It must not be ! it must not be ! I'll go to her father, myself. He surely is not the cruel man to wish to sacrifice her happiness for all her life on the shrine of mammon."

Blanche was passing at this hour, on her way to the house of a friend who lived just outside of the academy ground, and as it was much the nearer, she had entered the enclosure and was hurrying as fast as she could to her place of destination. She did not see Sammie until he called her name.

" I am so glad for this blessed moment; for, do you know, darling, I have been entertaining vague and incomprehensible fears ; I have been thinking—but I will not say. Did you speak to your father ? "

"I did. O Sammie ! " and she turned her face away that he might not see its paleness.

" Tell me the worst."

" He forbids my speaking to you again under the penalty of witholding my portion of his property from me."

" That is nothing. We will not need it."

" Worse than that—he is going to oblige me to marry a man I hate."

" Oblige you ! Can he do it ! "

" I have always obeyed him ; I have never dared to do otherwise—he is my father, you know."

" And you will accede to his wishes?"

Blanche had not time to reply before another form was seen treading the stone pavement, who, coming closer, she recognized as her father.

"Villain! pauper! knave!" he roared. "You have stolen my daughter's affections and now you would ruin her?" and he sprang and grasped him by the throat. With one firm grip, Sammie grasped the hand of his antagonist and loosened it: then in a mild voice said, "Mr. Clayton, I see no good reason for this assault; for Heaven knows I would not harm one hair of your daughter's head. If you do not like me, it is no reason you should abuse me; if I am not rich, I am at least honorable. We met by accident. I had started for my boarding place—she, for the house of Mr. Miller just through that gate; so do not blame her for this meeting."

Mr. Clayton mistook his game. He had looked upon Sammie as a mere boy, and he was surprised and awed to find in him, not only an equal in courage, but more in strength; and he believed, in spite of his mild language, that it would not do to trust too much to his good nature. So he said coolly, "I want no fuss, sir, and if it is as you say, you are excusable; but I had forbidden Blanche having anything to do with you for reasons best known to myself."

"Will you please tell me your prejudices? I am not aware of having merited censure, and I assure you, I shall ever strive to be worthy of so estimable an acquaintance and friend as your daughter."

"Since you have asked me, I will be plain. You have sought her society when you knew it was in direct opposition to my wishes; won her affections, and asked her hand in marriage? Do you deny it?"

"No, sir, and yet I fail to see myself a culprit. I love her; I would make her my wife. Is there anything discreditable about that?"

Mr. Clayton's hot temper again gained the mastery of him.

He forgot the diplomacy—that it were better to keep cool and collected, than saucy and arrogant; and so answered Sammie according to the folly of a purse-proud tyrant who knows of no other rule with which to measure the world around him than the money they may chance to possess.

"Sir, you are a pauper. She is my child; and do you know what that means?—a possessor of unbounded wealth at some future time, if she marries according to my wishes; if she varies from this, she may trail her weary footsteps along the highway and starve; I would not help her to a crust of bread."

"Demon!"

"What! what, sir! do you insult me, you vagabond child of infamy?"

"What did you say?" roared Sammie.

"That your father was a drunkard; your mother a harlot. Dare to speak or say it is not so, and I'll swoop you to the ground with one blow!" and with these words he clasped his throat, forgetting again in his wild frenzy that it was not a child with whom he had to deal; but a full-grown man, that would avenge the wrongs of his sainted mother, in any spot and place, if possible.

Sammie once more unloosed his hold. "Call me what you like, but let my parents rest in peace;" and before he was scarcely aware, Walter Clayton lay upon the stone pavement, not harmed materially by the blow upon his temples. justly given, which he received from the hands of his opponent; but, like some wild beast, infuriated beyond description, when it finds itself wounded and worsted in a fray to secure its prey. But still, it was some minutes before he had recovered sufficiently from the shock to rise. When he did, he grasped his revolver and looked around; vowing vengeance upon that lad who had dared to insult him, as he said, without cause or provocation. He roamed the park for his victim, but he was not to be found. Instead he came upon a group of boys who immediately fled; but crying as loud as they could:

"Served you right, old fool! What business had you to meddle with that feller jest goin' 'long mindin' his own business? Guess you won't want to tackle a daysent boy agin; and if he couldn't licked you, we was goin' to help him—afther all he didn't know it, though."

Walter Clayton fired his pistol, but it did no damage.

"Sure! we must git out of this or be shot," they said, still running with their utmost speed. "He'd as live kill sum one as not, he's so mad." "And still, he dassan't," said one of the most courageous of the band; "I dare face him," and, turning about, he waited for Mr. Clayton to come up. But instead, he turned his steps homeward, hoping and praying that the time was not far distant when he could be avenged on the boy that had dared to take his own part, or speak a word in his own defense.

Maddened almost to desperation, he went home—then up stairs to the door of his daughter's room, where she was sitting, and turned the lock. "There ma'am, you are a prisoner until I release you!" he muttered, then went to his room breathing cruel threats upon her; which, of course, she did not hear. But there was one who did, and that was Elice. She asked him what was the matter, and told him kindly that he had no right to treat a child after this manner; that in nine cases out of ten it only tended to fix her mind more firmly; and if he did not wish her to associate with Sammie Wilmington, to tell her the why and wherefore, and do it in a fatherly way. "If he is not a fit companion for her, prove it to her; and when she knows the truth of the statement, she will drop him of her own accord."

He would not listen to reason, however, and vowed she should remain there all the longer, now that Elice had interfered, and, further, she should be kept on bread and water. But we will now leave her and look for Sammie.

After his skirmish with Mr. Clayton he hurriedly passed out of the park and went directly to the grave of his beloved mother, and there, beneath the shadows of the willows that his tiny hands had planted immediately after her burial, whose branches now drooped gracefully over the pure white monument, he threw himself down in very agony of spirit, wishing and pray-ing that the life which seemed destined to so much bitterness would speedily come to an end, and he might join that friend in the skies ; whose love he *feared* was the only one to prove true, and whose eyes seemed now to be looking out from among the stars reprovingly—from that heaven of eternal beauty and happiness where her pure spirit had found a resting place. And then a voice from out the depths of that same beau-tiful beyond whispering to his heart, " ' Vengeance is mine ; I will repay, saith the Lord.' 'A soft answer turneth away wrath, but grievous words stir up anger.' O, Sammie, my son, my son ! Grieve not, for do you not know I am above the reproach of the enemy ?" And then he felt how much better it would have been for him had he fled upon the first assault from his adversary, and resolved he would never again let his passion rise to a pitch so uncontrollable. Then he thought of the gulf between him and Blanche ; how it had widened and deepened in the past hour ; and probably when her father told her his exaggerated story concerning the fray, that she would never speak to him again. If such were the case he would enlist in the army or quit the country at once, where he would never be heard of by her ; bend all his energies to business, and never come back until he had amassed a fortune equal to that of her father. Then, turning once more to the statuette of his mother, which now in the light of the full round moon, looked so lifelike and more lovely to his fevered imagination than it ever did before, said " Adieu ! beloved one, but for thy spirit-ual interference, my hands might one day be imbued in the blood of the wretch that dared to heap calumny upon thy inno-cent head ; but for thy sake I will strive to rise above the un-just remarks of all my enemies, ferret out thy history and prove to them their baseness. I know I can do it, and will with the help of that God who loves mercy, and aids the innocent in all their laudable undertakings."

The next morning, in accordance with his terrible fears, he received the following letter:

"Mr. Wilmington:—In view of your base treatment of my father, I wish from this moment to drop our acquaintance; and right glad am I to have had an opportunity, before matters progressed further, to ascertain your real character. There were several in the park at the time—men of standing and worth, who would not prevaricate—that told me all about your ungentlemanly assault; how, without the slightest cause, you commenced your raid upon him who, when kindly endeavoring to make explanations, was leveled to the earth by your brutal hand, whom you intended to murder, and would, had your cowardice not prevented. You must never intrude yourself into my presence again; and henceforward let my name never be uttered by lips as vile as yours.

"I do not ask you to reply, nor desire you to do so. The very fact of what we were to each other sends a thrill of horror to my soul. You, a would-be murderer! which of itself is sufficient to sever the very last link of friendship between us; and would say, go thousands of miles away from here, and be happy, if you can, with all this stain of guilt upon your heart.

"Yours truly, BLANCHE CLAYTON."

"Falsehood! treachery!" exclaimed Sammie, when he had finished reading the letter. "What enemies of mine have filled the ears of my affianced to change her heart, so loving, so true, so gentle, to one of stone? Oh! could she but know the truth, she would not chide, but pity me—I who have always striven to do right; that have struggled so hard against stern fortune; and now, as life had commenced to brighten, to see it overshadowed by the vile breath of slander and misrepresentation. Must I bear it? No, I will not; but, alas! there are such fearful odds: Mr. Clayton with a fortune to spend, if he choses, and yet not be impoverished, upon men many of whom for the paltry sum of five dollars would corroborate any falsehood he might utter—even more,—testify, if he desired, to the same; and I—poor—without friends—without a dollar to defend my good name. I would go to Blanche; but it would do no good: of course, she believes him with those 'men of worth,' as she affirms, that have told her the same story as himself respecting our combat. So, once more to thy grave, beloved mother, to kiss the green sod that covers thy mortal remains—to gather some of the flowers that blossom above thy head, which I will place with thy miniature that I have always worn upon my breast; which shall henceforward serve me as a talisman to keep me from yielding to temptation; and then, I will roam, who cares whither?—any place but this is preferable, where, just in sight of love's golden chalice, with my hand upon the cup, it has been dashed aside."

16

CHAPTER XLI.

The next day found Sammie Wilmington seated in the cars bound for New York, intending to take the next vessel out of port sailing for Liverpool.

"Any place but Lavarre," he thought, "where I am so painfully reminded of the past—the birth as well as the burial place of my hopes of happiness in this world. If my betrothed had only proved true, I could have borne the rest ; but she has told me to quit the country, and if my presence has become so offensive to her, to see her, and not hold any communication is worse than death ; and I will strive with all the powers both of mind and body to bury all record of the past into oblivion, and to go so far away that my tormentors shall never hear of me again."

Sadly did his eyes linger on the tall old trees that shaded the academy, that he perhaps would never again behold. Then, as the cars rolled past the cemetery, a monument rose above all the rest of these time-stained stones, that had covered the remains of one who had never been treacherous, who, had she lived, would have loved him to the last. Then there was the river, whose waves seemed to sing out a sad good bye as they rippled over the smooth and shining stones at the bottom ; the lake with its wealth of water lilies that were bending and nod-ding in the delightful breezes of this summer morning, where, in company with his beloved Blanche, in those little row boats now tied to the beach, he had skimmed its glassy surface, gathering armfuls of these flowers, which he then felt were no fresher nor purer than the heart that throbbed within her bosom. And oh! how happy they had been in each other's society; how swiftly the hours had winged away, as she had sung to him some of his favorite songs, while her sweet voice was echoed back from the chasms near, long after her words had died upon her lips! Would he ever know or realize such bliss again? while another voice from out the future seemed to answer, "no." Then, there was the little hut where he had been fondled in the lap of poverty and starvation. Even this had a charm for him; for he recalled his early trainings in truth and integrity, which he trusted would abide with him through all the days of his weary life. But, as he gazed upon the half-demolished rustic seat beneath the huge willow, although he strove to be calm, his whole frame shook with the most violent agitation; for he remembered the ghastly paleness of one whom death had already claimed for its victim, and the last words ever uttered by his dying mother; for here it was that she had told him for the first time that she must leave him, and warned him with her latest breath against the vices to which his father had fallen a victim—drunkenness and debauchery. It was here that she knelt in the lovely summer evening, and asked God to bless the poor boy, so soon to be an orphan—so soon to be thrown out upon the charities of the cold and heartless world, —so soon to be bereft of the last earthly friend that he possessed; to be a father to the fatherless; to take him beneath the shadow of his loving wing; keep him from all the evils that surrounded his life ; from yielding to the temptations that might come to him in this world, and at last receive him into Heaven.

But on, on, sped the cars, and woodland, river, fields and flowers were far in the distance,—a vapory mist flitted before his eyes; his head was dizzy, and, had he undertaken to arise from his seat, he would have staggered and fallen. He picked up a book and tried to read. It was Macaulay's entertaining History of England ; but he failed to interest himself. He then

took from his valise a volume of poems—the same that he and
Blanche had perused together so often; there were the passages,
marked with her own hand; but these too, had lost their charm,
only as he recalled the dear hand that had turned over the
pages, the voice that had read to him so many of those beautiful lines from his favorite author—Thomas Moore, those eyes
that had so often melted to bewitching softness, and even tears
at the recital of different parts of this elegant work—"Lalla
Rookh," "Paradise and the Peri," and other parts equally as
charming; and so this was put aside. And then laying his
weary head upon his hands, he tried so hard to come to a forget-
fulness of all the past; to believe that the future would yet
smile propitiously, and that time would heal his wounded and
crushed spirit.

He arrived in New York the next morning, and, as the
steamer "Atlantic" was about to be launched, took passage
immediately. The day was fine. It was his first experience
with the wind and the wave of the broad ocean, and, as the
white-capped surges lashed the shore, and the ship, like a thing
of life, commenced plowing the vasty deep, hope, though ever
so faintly, whispered to his soul; for some way they seemed
to him a connecting link in the chain that was to solve
the mysteries that had enveloped his parents' life, to clear
up the mists that now hung over his whole being. And he
was not sorry that he started upon this journey, although he
felt how hard it would be for a young man without means to
make his way in a foreign clime unaided by friends, unassisted
by the influence that wealth always carries with it.

Several days had passed; he had made no acquaintances, and
hardly spoken to any person; he was too busy with his own
thoughts to note what was passing around him. Only one
gentleman had given him any attention, and that was through
his little daughter who had fancied him her uncle, and called
him so; and who each day, so soon as she was awake in the
morning, begged her papa to let her go and see him: and so,

the prattle of this little child, her sunny smile and mirth, took him out for a time from his deep melancholy and gloom; and he learned to love her society, and look upon her coming as one might look upon the sunshine after a terrific thunderstorm, the flowers and the birds, the balmy breath 'of the beautiful spring, after a cold and cheerless winter. One day she had strayed away from her father and bent her steps to the upper deck. Sammie saw her, but, being busy writing a letter at the time and supposing her father close at hand, paid no further attention until he heard he heard her cries, when, with lightening rapidity, he started off in the direction of the sound and just in time to see a man hurl her over the railing into the deep below.

"O God!—help, help!" the villain exclaimed. "I tried to save her, but was a moment too late."

Sammie, without waiting a moment, plunged into the foaming spray. With one strong arm he grasped the child, and held her head above the water. By this time her father and others had come to the scene of distress. A huge rope was lowered, and Sammie and she were brought forth from what might have been a watery grave. He told his story, which the man who did the terrible deed stoutly denied. The little girl corroborating this statement—said, "Ze bid man flung me into ze water; thed he's doin to drown me!"

"Yes, I see—I see it all; he is my deadly enemy. Several times he has tried to murder me, but was foiled in his attempt; and now he wreaks his vengeance on my innocent child."

The wretch that perpetrated the deed, was placed in irons, to be handed over to the proper authorities so soon as they should arrive in port. Sammie was rewarded with the generous smiles of the ladies and gentlemen on shipboard, to several of whom he was introduced by the child's father; and this was not all. Mr. Mayville—for that was his name—handed him a check for one thousand dollars, payable to his order, which, however, he would not accept. It was urged upon him, but to no avail.

"It was simply an act of humanity and love," he said, "and if I have done a praiseworthy deed, I am amply repaid in the consciousness of saving a human being from death, and of doing right,"—then to himself—"As my beloved mother would have bidden me, if she could have spoken to me that moment from out the blue—through the parting clouds that floated so gracefully above our heads."

The ship sailed smoothly on, and at last cast anchor at Liverpool. There had been no storms—no fierce, savage hurricanes of wind to toss the gallant vessel; nor fires to demolish—to lay waste this beautiful structure; deaths none. The voyage had been as pleasant as a lovely summer sky, with its soft fleecy clouds by day, the never ending, never ceasing music of the waves; the silver moon and the stars by night which seemed to look out from on high as sentinels to assist the mariner on his lonely way through the trackless ocean, and to afford light and comfort to the traveller upon the broad waste of waters.

In the bustle of landing the past was for a time forgotten. Mr. Mayville, however, did not forget the great service rendered by the young stranger; but shook him cordially by the hand on parting, and said, "Young man, if you ever need assistance come to me. I shall remember with tears of joy that noble and heroic deed, which was the salvation of my sweet Lilla, through my life long; for, when I look upon her now in the flush of health, when I clasp her to my heart, when I stoop to receive her fond caresses, when I grow so happy in her sweet society, and when with all my weight of care the merry notes of my little bird shall fall upon my ears to relieve my depressed spirit, I shall draw the contrast between this, and a cheerless, dreary life which would have been mine, had it not been for your prompt assistance in the hour of her peril. Accept my blessing, and forget not if ever you are in trouble to give me a call." He then handed him one of his business cards and bade him adieu.

Sammie went directly to London. He then looked around

for a boarding place.   He did not wish to go to the most fashionable house, for this he knew his means would not allow; and
yet he wished to avoid one that was not held in good repute.
At last he found comfortable quarters and at a very reasonable
price; but even here he knew he could not abide long unless
he was fortunate enough to procure business.

Several weeks passed.   He had met promptly all his bills—
washing, board, fuel and light; but his money was nearly exhausted and what he was to do in the future was unknown to
him, for he had not been able to obtain employment of any description.   He sat down and commenced unpacking his valise;
he hardly knew why he did it, for he felt that it would be but a
day or so longer that he could remain where he was; and there
was nothing there that if pawned, would bring him the price
of a week's board; but yet, he proceeded to his task.   Each
article of clothing and each book was laid upon the little
table before him; and when he came to the last one, as he
opened it to peruse again those lines marked by that loved one,
now in a far off country, which he had not ventured to look at
since he put it away while traveling in the cars, resolving in his
own mind that its pages should never again be read by him, a
paper fell out; which, on looking at, he discovered to be the
same check on one of the leading banks of the city, payable to
his order, presented to him but refused on shipboard, and which
Mr. Mayville must have found a chance to place inside the book
in his little hand trunk.   No,—that was not it; he remembered
having lent him the book of poems.   It must have found its
way inside by carelessness or accident; at all events he would
not draw it; he would beg or starve first; he would seek the
owner and return it to him.   He looked again at the card presented by the stranger at Liverpool.   His office must be but a
few squares away.   He went out on the street; he passed on
and on by the great blocks which towered high above his head,
through the motley throng that nearly blockaded the thorough-

fare, when he came to the right street and number; and with palpitating heart went in and enquired for the proprietor.

The gentleman addressed gave him a look which said plainer than words, "Are you not mistaken, young man?" but replied at last, "Mr. Mayville seldom admits any person into his office unless on the most important business, which cannot be done by any of his agents. You see he is the proprietor of this mammoth silk establishment, and has no time to spare in business hours."·

"But please take this to him," Sammie said, handing the card presented by Mr. Mayville, with his own name written on the other side. "He will remember. I will detain him but a moment."

"But I have no right, sir; it is against the rules; and I should be reprimanded if I did—perhaps lose my situation."

At that moment Mr. Mayville entered. He had not been at the office this morning; had been detained for some time at his home. He knew Sammie, and, grasping his hand, shook it cordially; then invited him to a seat in a room fitted up luxuriously for his own especial benefit. He saw he looked sorrowful, and thought he had something to communicate, and hesitated to speak; so he said, "Can I do anything for you?" Sammie handed him the check over which he had worried so much, and told his story.

"It is yours: I will see that it is cashed."

Sammie felt all the pride of his mother's family arise in his bosom, and said, "I did not come, Mr. Mayville, to ask alms at your kind and generous hand, nor can I accept it; but to see if you had not a situation to give me, or something that I could do. I am willing to take any position, and think I can please you."

"True, true, sir. Are you a good accountant? I need another book-keeper in place of the faithful man who died in my absence. You shall take his place."

Sammie's heart bounded for joy as he heard these words;

and, after thanking his kind friend, he went to his boarding place with a much lighter step than when he passed out a few hours previous, thinking how hard he would try to please his employer, who must be a strange sort of a man to allow a person without recommendations or friends in his establishment. But Mr. Mayville, an over cautious man, did not think so, for he reasoned after this manner : that a man must be honorable, indeed, to do as Mr. Wilmington had done; and liked the noble dignity of him who was willing to do anything that was honorable, so that he might gain a competency for himself and be independent of his friends. So, next morning, Sammie might have been seen at the hour appointed, at the grand establishment of Mayville & Co., awaiting their orders.

CHAPTER XLII.

But we will retrace our steps over the trackless desert of waters—the broad Atlantic—and go to the little chamber where Blanche was made prisoner by her father.

She dreamed that night that Sammie came to the door of their house with a basket of flowers ; he was in the act of giving them to her, when a huge serpent came forth from those beautiful blossoms and coiled its slimy length about her. Sammie sprang for a club to kill the venomous reptile, but before he reached her it had fastened its fangs in her flesh. She screamed with terror. The sound of her own bitter wailings awoke her, and she sprang from her bed in a perfect paroxysm of fear. Being naturally of a superstitious frame of mind, it made a deep impression upon her, and she trembled as she thought of the chances of being torn from her idol, and she feared that they would yet be separated for all coming time. As soon as it was light, she dressed and started to go down stairs, but found her door locked. She wondered what it could mean, but said nothing, thinking after a time some person would come up and then she would know all. Several hours passed ; she heard footsteps upon the stairway, then a key turn in the door. Soon her father stood before her. She saw he was angry, and her instinct told her it was about Sammie; that it was for no other purpose that he had come but to reprimand her and to heap anathemas upon her lover. But, assuming cheerfulness and pretending not to notice his appearance, and remembering, too, the text of the worthy parson of the Sabbath previous, "A soft answer turneth away wrath," she smilingly said, "Up early, papa; how is that ?"

"Never slept a wink last night. No wonder; if ever a man has trouble it is I. Such a family! Such children!"

"What now?"

"Enough—was waylaid and robbed of several hundred dollars—knocked down and money taken from my pocketbook while I lay insensible on the hard pavement."

"What! what!" exclaimed Blanche in astonishment.

"True! true!" said he, "and by your lover—your devil! but the officers of justice are on his track, and another day will find him lodged in our county jail to await trial for his misdemeanors."

"Oh! oh!" cried Blanche, "it is not so! it cannot be!" and reeling fell upon the floor at the feet of her father.

But even her agony did not draw him aside from his purpose, and he had not so much as a single misgiving that he had gone forth even at a late hour of the night and secured the services of a rascal, as deeply dyed in sin and vice as himself, to forge the letter that drove Sammie to a foreign country—a pretended missive from his affianced.

After Blanche had recovered, she said, "Do you mean to say papa, that you have sent a sheriff for Sammie, and that you intend to send him to prison?"

"I do—that is where he belongs. He is not fit for a civilized community."

"He is not guilty."

"What! do I lie? Is that what you mean? I have ample proof—but see here: I will release him if he will leave the town, and if you will swear in this little book, you never will speak to him again."

"What! take an oath, and never speak to Sammie again? I'd beg, I'd die first!" Her father's hot blood had gained the ascendancy in her veins: she knew he had uttered falsehood; for she had stood at a distance. and, although unperceived by either party, been an eye witness to ;the drama of the evening previous; and she would confront the world for Sammie, if the gallows were raised in the distance to hang her.

"It's untrue—it's basely false; and I will testify, when the time comes for me so to do, to its fabrication!"

"Against your father?"

"Against injustice and a dishonorable lie."

She was now disarmed of all fear of him—him whose very voice had caused her oftentimes to tremble; and could Sammie have seen her now in her anger defending him, he would have looked upon her as one might look upon a beautiful clinging vine, transformed suddenly by the tempest, into a towering oak capable of withstanding the lightning's dart and the savage hurricanes.

"Then you propose to assist the rascal?"

"Were that forlorn pauper that asked a crust of bread but yesterday falsely accused, and I knew it, I would bear testimony for him against the world, if necessary. I do intend to aid him to the extent of my ability; furthermore, there were several beside myself in the park who know all."

"And who?"

"I am not at liberty to tell; time enough when they are obliged to speak."

Mr. Clayton changed his tactics; he said, "You remember that elegant watch and chain that you admired so much?"

"Very well?"

"I will send for it to-morrow, if you will make me one promise."

"What is it?"

"That you will marry Rowland Gray. He has been looking at some lovely diamonds; intends to give you a set estimated at several thousand as your bridal gift. You are to go directly to Paris as soon as you are married, where he has some business to attend to, make the tour of Europe, and then return to settle

down in his elegant country residence but a few miles from
Philadelphia.   He is worth at least three millions."

"Is just thrice my age."

"That is nothing."

"But I don't love him."

"But you cannot help it when you see how lavish he is with
his money to make you happy.   Please me now, dear Blanche.
I will make my will before the sun goes down; a hundred thousand dollars shall be yours, and no person on earth will wrest
it from you."

"I cannot make the sacrifice."

"You will not do it?"

"Never! never!   Not if it were in his power to bequeath
the famous necklace of diamonds presented to the daughter of
one of our great generals by an Egyptian prince—not if you
gave me all you are worth, which is no small amount, I know.
Sell myself for gold?   O, papa! for the love of mercy never
present the subject to me again, for it will do you no good."

"You will rue it—now mark me.   I can make your life a
hard one."

"I never yet have lain upon a bed of roses."

"But you may toss upon one of thorns."

"So be it.   I will have an easy conscience, if a hard lot."

"You are ungrateful—ungrateful!"

"I do not mean to be either."

"You are a very tigress; but I can and will tame you—now
see!   I'll show you!" and he went out and locked the door
after him.

Blanche sat mute and motionless, her purposes unchanged,
her mind set; and as soon move the everlasting hills, as to de-
coy her from the path she had marked out.   She was not to be
bought, neither was she to be frightened into an acquiescence
with her father's plans.   He might perform all his threats, drive
her from home, disown her; but marry Rowland Gray she
never would.

CHAPTER XLIII.

Mr. Tattum sat in the corner smoking his meerschaum; his wife was at the table supping her tea.

"I say, Mary Ann," said he, "hev you heerd the news?"

"What news?"

"'Bout old Clayton and Sammie Wilmington."

"What about it?"

"Why, Clayton kicked up a big row with him, pertended he'd stole a heap o' money from him, (mebbe he did, for all I know), and he's run away, or so they say; but I s'pose the sum o' the matter is, that he's done this on purpose to make a fuss between him and Blanche."

"Whom all but Walter Clayton have known for a long time were engaged to be married," said Minnie, looking up from her embroidery. "I am so sorry for Blanche, for she feels so badly."

"Yes, yes, they have had a terrible fuss all around, I hear; but I don't care, I'm glad enough to have something come to that girl to bring her down a peg or two. Why! they say her father has her locked up for two or three days, and fed her on bread and water only."

"Poor, dear child!" said Mrs. Glenn; "I can hardly believe he would do such a thing, and she an only daughter."

"Do! do such a thing? Yes he would, an' a heap wuss," Hezekiah answered.

"Served her right!"

"Oh, how can you say so, mother? she is such a sweet, good

girl; and I consider it a great misfortune for her to have such a father."

"Bad enough for any one but her. But the little upstart carries her head a little too high to suit me—and then, is so impudent."

"I never thought so."

"See how she used me after my accident."

"What!" said Minnie, "have you had an accident? I did not know it."

"Why, when I slid into the ditch over there."

"You mean when you broke the ice to receive your second baptism after you had that spell of sickness in church that time?" Minnie replied, her eyes brimful of merriment, while she looked more steadily at her work and plied her needle the faster. "What did Blanche Clayton do?"

"You vixen! you are as bad as she any time."

"But what did she do? tell us now."

"Why, she had the impudence to say, 'Mrs. Tattum, did you hurt you much, falling into that water?' and then looked over at the girls with her, and grinned, and then they all ran oft laughing."

"And you ran after them."

"I'll bet; and if I'd caught them, I'd sauced them, you may be sure. I'd, I'd knocked them flat into a mud hole!"

"But you got the worst of it and fell down: and one of the party hallooed back, 'Come here, Sister Tattum, and I'll pick you up;' but remember she was only about nine years old at that time, and children must be children."

"Hard set, all on 'em—hull family of Claytons; don't want to tread on any o' their toes, I tell you, now then," said Hezekiah; "but you ain't heard the wust yet."

"Well, what can be any worse, father dear?"

"Why, them are two boys run after me one day in the street, as hard as they could, and ses, 'Mr. Tattum, halloo, Mr. Tattum;' and I turns 'round and, ses I, 'Wot, boys?' thought mebbe their father wanted me for somethin' or uther, and they commenced to sneeker like; and I ses again, but purty sharp this time, 'What do you want?' 'Why,' ses Charlie, 'I wanted to ax you if your dog got his tail hurted a good deal, when Sister Tattum tramped on it,' and, 'I wouldn't let my dog go to meetin' again, if I was you. Do yer want to sell him? How much will you take?' 'Why, yes,' ses I, 'of course. Do you want to bay?' And he ses 'No, sir, I don't; but I heerd father say tother day after he'd come home from meetin', that that preacher ought to have Sister Tattum and her dog for a congregation to keep the rest awake; and he believed he'd buy it for him. How much do you ax?'"

Minnie laughed till her head ached, while Mrs. Tattum called them all sorts of names, interspersing her language, now and then, with an oath.

"But do not be so angry, mother dear," said Mrs. Glenn, "for you know they were little children at that time; but now are perfect gentlemen."

"I dare say, perfect little d——ls; I hate the whole posse!"

"You do? Mrs. Clayton, and all?"

"She's the best of the clique, but she's not a Clayton."

" And grandmamma Clayton?"

"She's an old vixen—the worst of any of them."

"If she'd come here in just a minnit, you'd eat her up," said Hezekiah, dryly; "I hate so much desate. Here now, you b'long to the church over there, and you do heeps of things wot I couldn't."

"What do I do that you could not?"

"Well, you speak bigger words sometimes than I dast."

"What words, you old fool?"

"Duz that become a church member to call their husband a fool?"

"Yes, if he is one."

"I'm a mighty notion to tell the preacher on you—he'd excommunicate you; and if I do, I'll tell as how you did take them are things from Clayton's hired girl, which was just as wuss as stealin', any time."

"If I did, you were glad to help eat them."

"I don't go to meetin' every Sunday and make b'leve I'm a saint, and then when the pasture comes, put a long, solemn face on; and when he axes me how I'm gittin' along in religion, tell him I'm strivin' to serve the Lord to the best of my ability, ax him to pray with us afore he leaves; and when he aint more'n out of sight, git mad and call the hull on you such awful names, and boss everything around. No, sir, that aint me—Hezekier Tattum. I'm plain and outspoken, don't tell lize 'bout nothin', let my neighbors alone; mind my own business; don't go inter a church and swear to somethin' I know aint so 'bout the brethren and sisterns; don't bother myself 'tall 'bout their meeting; and I'll not git half so hot a corner, when I die, as you will, now Mary Ann. Why, you've b'longed fifty years, ain't you? and what good has it done you? No more good than for you to keep me up the most of the night when the gals used to have boze— you killed 'em all by kindness. Oh, I remember, and shall till my latest breath, how one cold, raw night the wind was howlin' in the tree tops like so many wildcats let loose; the snows come down as thick and fast as though you'd been shakin out your feather bed, when a knock was heerd at the front door which proved to be Adolphus Jordon—wisht he'd been t'other side uv Jordon, the way it turned out."

"Oh! speak out, most worthy—what next?"

"Why, it waz when one uv Minnie's boze wuz here and he wuz goin to set up with her, for he come regular three times a week. Well, what did you have me do but kindle fires in the parlor; then say I must set up to see to the fires (wished it had singed him the way it turned out), and the feller didn't go home till four o'clock in the mornin'! It was fust, Hezekier split a leetle more wood, (I b'leve the rascal tried to see how much he could burn), then, go crack 'em butternuts; then, pop some

17

corn, while you blistered your face over the fire making molassus candy for 'em.   But this didn't satisfy you, you had to send me out in the blusterin winds and storms to git peanuts, and then insisted for me to crack 'em.   Well, just to please you, I cracked the pesky things, and then you wanted me to take 'em in and pass 'em 'round, instead uv lettin the gal come out and git 'em.   So this I dun to please you, and by that time the fires had purty much gone out; and then I hed to jest button up that old army cloak 'round me and sally out agin after wood; and he never cum agin.   I tell you, Mary Ann, a man's a man; you don't want 'em to know that you are in a kinder uv hurry to gid rid uv your gals; you don't want to feed 'em on nicknacks; you don't want to flatter 'em up much; you don't want to let 'em know that all they want to do is to ask, for then you'll be sure not to marry off your darters; for then they'll think there's somethin' wrong—they'll git sick and disgusted like.   I'll tell you it's about like as if you had a big melon patch; well, if they are nice, and beautiful, and ripe, and sweet and good like, why, you put a big snarling dog at the gate and enclose them in with a high fence.   Wall, where on arth did yer ever see a lot uv boys er men but what would manage to break into it?   Why, they'd do it if it broke their necks, because they think they are good.   But sposin' they didn't have no dogs 'round nor fences, but hired somebody to shell peanuts by the peck to feed 'em on.   'Twouldn't be no go; they'd think them watermelons wan't good fur nuthin, and they wouldn't tech 'em. Why, Mary Ann, have you lived to be so old, and don't know yit how a man goes by contraries?"

"It's all so," said Minnie, coming in at that moment. Mother has made me blush many a time by being so officious. Of course gentlemen would think she wanted to get rid of her daughter badly."

"Always finding fault with me, some of you; I believe I'll hang myself."

"Shall I git a rope, Mary Ann?"

"I don't want to reprimand you," said Minnie, laughing, "for you are one of the very best of mothers, only you want to do too much for us; and if I live to be a very old maid, it will be none of your fault, that you did not try your prettiest to get me a husband—I never shall blame you. Come now, dry your tears, and listen to this letter; perhaps my name will be changed yet."

"Whom is it from?"

"That same young gentleman you are speaking of. I guess the nicknacks won him, after all.

"My Dear Minnie: Unavoidable were the circumstances that took me from you so unexpectedly, and that have kept me away for the past five years; but every obstacle is now removed, and if your hand is still disengaged, I shall claim it.

I wrote you several letters, but received no answer. There was a deep-laid plot to separate us forever. I cannot tell you now, but will explain all when I see you. The ways of Providence are so mysterious and our lives are such an enigma. Will be at your home to-morrow eve.

"Your old friend and lover,

ADOLPHUS JORDON."

CHAPTER XLIV.

"Your mother is quite sick," said the elder Mr. Clayton, addressing his son Walter. "We think consumption already seated. If so, there can be no reason for hoping she can recover. I hardly know what we are to do, she is so irritable; her sickness has shattered her nerves wonderfully—is not the same woman that she was."

This conversation was held at the residence of Walter Clayton, where Mrs. Tattum had repaired an hour previous, to relate some little scandal she had 'heard, and to obtain the loan of some groceries until she could find the time to dress to go for them.

"Ought to be sick," she muttered. "I ain't sorry for her, and nobody would care much if she should die;" and then she looked at Elice, thinking her words would have a full echo in her thoughts and feelings, but instead, Mrs. Clayton replied: "Whatever people's follies or faults may have been, I sympathize with them in affliction."

"I could see some people hung!"

"Forgive as ye would be forgiven. Do unto others even as ye would that others should do unto you."

"That's all well enough to talk, but who practices it? Do as you are done by—that's my silver rule. I hate that woman."

"Not a week since I saw you shake her cordially by the hand and invite her to your house."

"But that was for a purpose. I wanted to find out something. Funny you should advocate her cause when she's always been your worst enemy. You'd stand ten to one in the estimation of people, if it had not been for her. Why, maybe you are not aware how she has been around from house to house slandering you."

"I know everything, I believe, or should by this time. I have learned to my sorrow of more than one Judas Iscariot; have been a recipient of their kisses and smiles, as well as their murderous attacks upon my good name, which they vainly thought were of so secret a character that I would never feel the sting, or know the author of this mischief. But ah! how much will they have to account for in the great day when God himself shall arraign them for this sin, before His tribunal, and they will have to answer to Him, when He shall judge the world in righteousness. Let me be oppressed if it must be, sinned against; if I only preserve a stainless soul If I am injured by the designing, they will get their punishment in the next world, if not in this. But sometimes we reap the reward of our fol lies in this life."

"You are a saint," she answered ironically. "Don't you never feel like pounding somebody when ,they say something awful mean and provoking? I do. Why that old woman has said some very hateful things about you."

Elice did not reply, but passed out of her room into the front hall where her husband and father-in-law were still holding conversation, the hand of the latter on the knob of the door as if ready for departure. She enquired very kindly in reference to the health of her mother-in-law, and asked if she could not do something for her.

"If she could only have some person to sit by her bedside through the day and give her medicine, it would be a great relief to me; I am weary of watching nights. I don't believe she will last long."

The great heart of Elice was bursting with sympathy as she saw how haggard the old man looked; and she cast her eyes imploringly at Walter, and said, "Can't I be spared to assist them, papa?"

"You are not strong enough," the old man replied; and then he thought, too, of all the unkind remarks his wife had made, and feared it would place Elice in a disagreeable position; and, as she had not buried her weapons of warfare so thoroughly but that she sometimes at the present said hateful things concerning her, he felt that he would not like to subject her to the pain she even now might inflict in some of her moody states.

Elice seemed to divine his thoughts. "Father," she said, looking up into his tearful eyes. "I think when she sees what good care I take of her, she will drop her prejudices—perhaps love me a little."

"You never gave her any reason to do otherwise. I wonder, oh! I wonder she has taken the course she has."

"Please, father, don't speak of it; let by-bones be by-gones; soon all will be buried with the lifeless form beneath the clods of the valley. It will be my greatest pleasure to smooth her pathway thither. Do not deny me, for I request it; and oh! if she changes her mind in that brief lapse of time, I shall be thrice blessed."

The old man's feelings at last overcame him, and, bowing his head and leaning more heavily upon his cane, tears fell even to his feet, while he could only gasp, "You are good—too good; oh! how could one expect this of you, you poor downtrodden, sorrowful child, abused and oppressed. But God will reward you."

"That is all I want," said Elice, and put her arms around his neck and kissed him, just as she would her own dear father, and bade him cheer up, assuring him that it made not the slightest difference what had been said in the past; that she should only look to the comfort of his poor sick wife, if she would permit her, and do all in her power to lessen her suffering.

"Some one has come to take care of you," the old man said, on entering the room where his wife lay sick.

"Who?" she feebly enquired.

Elice approached the bed and extended her hand: "I will stay with you for a time, if you desire it."

There was a visible frown upon her countenance; but she bowed assent, and then enquired for her own daughter.

"She was too busy to-day; was expecting company; but says she will be up to-morrow."

"And couldn't leave to watch with her sick mother?"

"You must remember she is worn out—has sat up night and day."

"Oh, yes, 'tis time, she is a good child; but I was just thinking that no person could keep me from her, if she was in my condition."

Elice remained four weeks; and when that time had elapsed, no one could do anything to please her half so well. Her medicine must all pass through her hands, her pillows be adjusted by her; and she alone could be entrusted to comb her hair or get her meals. One day she looked unusually perplexed; she was evidently growing each hour more and more feeble, and felt that she soon must die; and there seemed a great weight upon her mind. Elice was bending over her, bathing her temples and stroking back the gray tresses that now and then fell over her pale, thin face; when she drew her down and kissed her, murmuring, "Oh! my good angel, after all—all. How kind you are to me, and I,—oh! I have been so unworthy—am so unworthy still of the blessings bestowed daily by you dear hands." The hot tears fell in a moment from the eyes of Elice on the face of her mother-in-law, but she could not reply.

"Oh! can you—can you forgive me, before I go hence? I know not why I was so persistent in my persecution of you, for you certainly had never wronged me; but such evil influences were all the while at work with my naturally perverse disposition. Mrs. Tattum—false-hearted, untrue, deceptive to the last—I listened too long to her. She lived so near you I thought she must know, but I have found her out. You have not told me you forgive me."

"I have nothing to forgive. If we err, if we wrong a fellow-man, we sin against the high and holy God; and it is to Him we should go for absolution. Calm yourself, dear mother; forget all in the past that is painful to you."

"But you must have suffered so much."

"Jesus sustained me; and now He has made all things right. I have prayed for this hour of reconciliation, and am happy beyond measure that it has come; and if you have at last learned to love me, if you have found out your mistaken judgment in reference to my character, I am satisfied."

"Love you?—as much as my poor feeble heart is capable. Now I have confessed to you I shall die easier."

When the sun had gone down, she had passed to another world. But the last act of her life was to take the hand of Elice and put it to her lips; the last name she was heard to whisper was hers.

CHAPTER XLV.

Elice, weary from watching so long by the bedside of her mother-in-law, had thrown herself upon the couch to rest. She had overtaxed her strength, and felt she needed quiet to recuperate her depressed faculties of mind as well as of body; for, in the past four weeks of solicitude and toil, a marked change had come over her, and she feared the utter prostration that might follow unless she took the greatest care of herself.

She had a servant in every way trustworthy, and thought she would give the whole care of the house into her hands until she regained her strength.

It is a cold December day; the winds are howling without, and the snow beating wildly against the window panes. More desolate than ever seem the bare branches of the trees, the leafless shrubbery and the climbing rose vines that make such a pretty shade over the windows of her room in the bright summer, a spot so inviting; for death has been in the family, and, although she has not been beloved as she desired, she missed the voice that usually had spoken kindly to her, whatever tone it might have assumed away from her immediate presence; and Elice was so glad when she thought of her mother-in-law as laid away with friends in the cemetery, that she had been capable of bringing about a change in her feelings; that she had seen how erroneous had been her judgments, and not only come to a full reconciliation and appreciation, but actually to love her presence in her sick room; and she returned thanks to the Father of mercies and truth for this bless-ing, hoping she might yet be enabled to win over all her enemies ; for it had been such a bitter draught to her sensitive mind to feel that she had been misjudged, while scarcely a per-son whom she met took her for what she really was—capable of any sacrifice to add happiness to the lives of her friends; and foregoing any pleasures if it only helped fill the cup of joy for a loved one. But there was this to comfort Elice :—those who knew her best, loved her most; and God, the Searcher of all hearts, who could look from His lofty throne into their very depths, knew that she .desired above all things to lead a pure and spotless life, and, knowingly, would not commit an offense against a living creature under the sun or break any of the precious Commandments.

While Elice was musing, she fell into a sleep. She dreamed her room was filled with heavenly spirits. One of them bend-ing lower than the rest, whispered in her ears, ''Sorrowful daughter of earth, thou art yet doomed to still greater disap-pointments ; but Christ shall give His angels charge concerning thee. Goaded to the very verge of despair, thou shalt wish to flee from this sin-stained earth ; but there is yet work for thee, beloved one ; put thy shoulder to the wheel, and Jesus will help to bear thy burdens. Wear meekly thy crown of thorns, for it will turn to a diadem of never-fading flowers. Thou shalt yet 'tread upon the lion and the adder.' 'Though thou pass-eth through the furnace, the smell of fire shall not rest upon thy garments.' Thou hast seen affliction; but through this, death shall be robbed of its terror ; the crown of everlasting life glitter more radiantly upon thy brow ; thy harp awaken to more ecstatic music in that beautiful land whither thou journey-est. Be patient; be forbearing ; love thy enemies ; do good unto them who despitefully use you and persecute you."

Ere it had ceased speaking, she was awakened by the merry sound of laughter in the rear of the building, and then scuffling. She thought little of this, as her servant was given to those frolicsome pastimes whenever Robin and Charlie, who had now grown to ages of fourteen and sixteen, wished to engage in these athletic sports. A model servant in every other respect, and thinking no evil or rudeness in this, but proud of her supe- . riority of strength, she embraced every opportunity of showing them, with all their boasted powers, that she was more than a match for them, and if they were able to handle boys, as they had often affirmed, much older and larger than themselves, they had no business in her hands ; and in spite of the remonstrance of the heads of the family to desist from these rude sports, would seize the time of their absence to pursue their favorite amusements. Accustomed from childhood to this, as strange as it may seem, it was a part and parcel of her being, and she could no more resist the temptation than the inebriate could pass the grog-shop with its long rows of sparkling decanters without indulging his appetite.

The day had nearly passed; the twilight began to throw its dim shadows over the world. Nora (this was the servant's name) had been full of mirthfulness and happiness, from early morning until the present hour, singing a portion of one song, then another, as she busied herself in the kitchen; and at any time, a person might look upon her as a stray sunbeam, she was so cheerful and pleasant; and, although she had never made an open profession of religion, there was an undercurrent of piety that permeated her life; for she talked much about Christianity, and wished so many times that she might be a faithful follower of our Lord and Master. She was a girl of more than ordinary intelligence—such a person as would claim a degree of attention, no matter in what station she was found, and one who could never fail of winning respect; in no wise handsome, but honorable, trusty, kind hearted, and respectable.

Elice felt that indeed she had found a treasure, while Nora never failed of setting forth her good qualities to all her friends and acquaintances, often expressing herself after this manner : ''She is the best woman I ever saw. I never worked in a family I liked half so well;   have a splendid home where I shall remain as long as I live, unless, perhaps," smiling, "I sometime conclude to take one of my own."

The day of which we have been speaking she had been unusually cheerful.   It was Saturday: she had more to do on this day than usual, but was nearly through, when, coming to the room of her mistress, she knocked at the door which when opened, she asked permission to have a little chat, as she had something upon her mind about which she wished to seek advice, and it was to her, and her alone, she would entrust the secrets of her life, for she felt they would be in safe keeping.

"Certainly, Nora," the mistress answered.   It was then three o'clock, afternoon.

"Would it be right to break an engagement with a gentleman providing his presence had become odious?"

"What! are you engaged?" Elice asked.

"Not exactly.   I have never told Mr. Brown I would marry him; but I know he expects me to."

"Not by words, but by actions?"

"Yes, that is just it.   I have given him to understand that I would, and that is what troubles me.   I know he loves me and has made many sacrifices for me; but under it all, I have discovered a very selfish nature.   He is unkind to his widowed mother; now and then takes a glass of whisky.   He has many faults: I never could be happy with him."

"Then why did you encourage him.   It is positively a sin to come out in false colors.   The affections are not to be trifled with.   It has brought utter ruin to many a person whose heart has been bounding with the brightest hopes and expectations. Care and discretion should always be exercised.   If one cannot reciprocate an attachment, she can spare the pain of inflicting a deeper wound by blindly leading a gentleman on to *define* his position."

"I regret it all. I have never intended to do wrong; but must I lead a life of misery for this one error?"

"If you wish to break off further connection with him, go to him frankly, tell him the state of your feelings; that you have not meant to deceive him, and are sorry for what you have done. Do it without ostentation or pride. He should feel willing to give you up. That is the best you can do under the circumstances."

"That would be Christian-like. Oh! you are so good! how I wish, like you, I could ask the blessings of God upon all my undertakings! Sometime I mean to get religion and join the church."

"My dear child, religion is not something to get, but to do; and joining the church never yet saved a person. True 'tis a great assistance, and yet, we may attend upon all its ordinances and feel none of the divine fervor in our hearts. We must deal justly, love mercy and truth, exercise charity toward all men, and then the wings of salvation will overspread us like a banner; without these, we are as 'sounding brass or tinkling cymbals.'"

"I see it all. Oh! won't you remember me in your prayers at the throne of grace, that your dear Saviour may be my Saviour, and that I may get to Heaven at last? I have longed for this time to tell you the true state of my feelings. You have heard me laugh and sing and never imagined, I presume, that I thought of the hereafter; but there is not a night passes, but I kneel a my bedside, and ask God to forgive my sins of the day."

"And do you not think He sometimes answers your petition?"

"I know He does."

"Continue to ask Him, and He will give you the witness of His spirit. He will speak to you with such a voice that you cannot mistake. Jesus stands ready to fold you to His blessed bosom—trust Him."

"Oh! I will, I do," she answered, and left the room.

Once more in the kitchen, she hurried up the work. Seven or eight pies were taken from the oven, and put upon a large table until they should cool sufficiently to put them away.

Robin came in, picked up a knife, and proceeded to help himself to a piece of one.

"Give me that knife," she said.

"Not unless you are the stronger, Miss Nora," he answered laughing.

"I'll show you that I am," she replied in the same good-natured way which always characterized her, and proceeded to wrest it from him. Neither thinking of danger, and both determined to win the victory, each made the utmost effort to succeed. "I have it now!" she would repeat. "No, it's mine," Robin would answer. Lacking discretion, they wrestled for a few moments, when she, being the stronger, threw him upon the floor. Her weight was heavy, and she consequently went with great force—sufficient to send the knife handle first through the wall, then into the apertures between the laths, while its sharp point made an incision into the main artery of her neck. She uttered one cry, and said, "I've cut myself," when Robin ran immediately to his mother's room.

"What is the matter?" she enquired.

"Nora has cut herself!"

They both then hastened to the kitchen, when, terrible to relate, the poor girl had succeeded in gaining the door where she was standing, as if to obtain the air, and the blood flowing profusely from the wound.

"How did you do this!" Elice asked.

"Send for a doctor, and be quick—I'm fainting!" was her only reply; when Elice, seeing she was about to fall, clasped her arms about her and endeavored to seat her in a chair close at hand; but it was of no avail, she was not strong enough to effect her object; and so Nora, after reeling and staggering for a moment or so, came down heavily upon the floor. She rallied, however, and got upon her knees. She had not then lost all consciousness. Still she could not speak.

Elice, feeling that she could do nothing for her, hastened for assistance. A man was passing and she called him in. Another one, hearing the cry of distress, offered his services. "Poor, dear, suffering girl!" Elice murmured; "carry her to bed." They laid her upon the bed. By this time, Robin entered with the doctor. He had mounted a horse at the first thought of danger, and hurried for a physician, who pronounced the wound fatal and said she was dying.

By this time the house was filled with people talking, conjecturing, and wondering how the accident came about. Robin told his simple, childish story, which all there seemed to believe, as he was too young, if he wished, to think of fabricating a falsehood. Elice, covered with blood caused by throwing her arms around about the girl when she strove to assist her, faint, and sick at heart at the sight of so much distress, was laid, too, upon a couch in her room. In just twenty minutes from the infliction of the wound, Nora was dead.

In that motley throng, there congregated, the vicious were mingled. Then it came into the mind of the Evil One to stir up his subjects and set them at his foul and dirty work. A person most fitted for the business, one of the offscourings of the town—a drunken profligate, by reputation—Joe Gordon by name, took this upon himself. "I will arouse suspicion," he said mentally, "against Robin Clayton. His father is immensely rich and will pay a large sum to turn the scales in his favor. I am capable of stirring up strife; anything but this ceaseless toil to earn a livelihood. I could see any man, woman, or child hang if it would be the means of keeping me through this cold winter, so I need not be a drudge. Work, work, work, work—that is the poor man's lot—work or die."

"But have you no conscience," a voice whispered.

He started. "It would not be right; but there are a good many things that are wrong in this world. It always was turned upside down from the beginning. Now, why should old Clayton have all the money and I none? Ha! ha! 'disgorge! disgorge!' shall be my watchword, and he will do it or the blood of some of his family will be spilt. I wish I could see the halter around his neck—I'd place it there myself if I had a chance, for a few thousand, and no one would find it out. Oh! the cursed law. If it wan't for the law, I'd waylay that man and rob him some of these dark nights—not him particularly, but anybody that has money. Why am I poor and others rich? I hate the rich; wish they were all compelled to divide with me—but that's not to the point. How is the thing to be commenced? Of course the public mind must be soured, and, as the scum is always the first to foment, I'll set up all my cronies. Am kind of a king amongst the vile of this town, and I can rule pretty well in my kingdom. Drunkards, thieves, liars compose it, but I don't care. My brass buttons are my passport, policeman is my name; but yet the position does not get me a living. I have to work—curse the work!"

The room where he was sitting was filled with people.

"I believe," he whispered, "that there has been foul play; that boy that seems so innocent has murdered that girl."

"Preposterous! What do you mean, Joe Gordon?" spoke one.

"P'raps 'tis so," said one of his fiendish chums; "looks jist zactly as if he might hav' dun't—have him risted."

"Wretch! what are you talking about? that child guilty of so foul a crime!" said a third.

"Serve a warrant on him, boss, serve him right," his favorite replied.

Soon he was in the hands of the law to answer to the terrible crime of murder. It was a time never to be forgotten. Weeping eyes were there, that scarcely ever shed a tear before, sorrowing hearts for the early dead—a victim to her own love of amusement; an innocent child branded with shame, accused of the most terrible offense that could be committed—a young boy that had always from the time that he could speak, turned away with an agonizing face at the sight of distress, that was never known to take the life of the most humble creature in the great creation of the Almighty God, but guarded to the extent of his power all the birds' nests built in the great maples that surrounded his father's house against that class of urchins whose delight was to rob them, sought out the poor ragged boys of the place, bestowing upon them all of his clothes that he had outgrown, and buying many a little luxury for a sick one with what money he could earn in various ways.

" I know not what my children would have done, had it not been for him the past three or four winters," said a very poor woman. " It was none of the very best he gave them, but all he could spare, and it covered them and kept them warm. I verily believe they would have frozen to death but for his kindness ; and it's many a time he has brought some nick-nack, two or three eggs, or a bit of cake for our sick little Charlie, who would have died for the want of something nourishing. Poor little soul ! It's so cruel to think he must be arraigned for that dreadful deed, when he's as innocent as the angels in Heaven."

" True! true!" answered a second, a third, and a fourth; " he never did it." One old lady, an Irish woman by descent, sat in the corner wringing her hands for some minutes and weeping most bitterly, then broke forth, at last, into a bitter wail; and, going up to this policeman, Joe Gordon, said, "Curse yez! curse yez! ye divil. All holy saints and angels curse yez! and the blissed Virgin curse yez ; and every person that takes sides against that blissed child, curse them! fer didn't he go over the ice whin it cracked under his feet, and drag Patsie from the waters whin he wid have drownded, sure ? " And then going up to little Robin, while tears from her honest eyes fell faster and faster as she spoke, said, " Courage, darlint. The law niver can harm the likes of yees. O Holy Virgin save yez from all those blood-thirsty hounds!"

18

Robin, paralyzed with grief at the death of this true hearted .
servant girl, could scarcely repeat his story which he was compelled to give under oath, but which, when he had finished, had
impressed the great throng there gathered, as being true as
that blessed book which the dear boy raised so reverently to
his lips.

The faith of Elice for a moment wavered, and she inwardly
ejaculated, "Oh ! where is God, that He thus permits the wicked to triumph?" Then she thought of the vision of the
day, and the same voice came back to her: "He shall give His
angels charge concerning thee," and felt that it was the Eternal
One who had spoken through His angels; and she laid her hand
upon her throbbing heart and said, "Be still! be still! Though
Thou slay me, yet will I trust in Thee."

"Don't you see," said Joe Gordon, this most obedient of
Satan's subjects, "how pale she is?" pointing to Elice, "and
how haggard and how besmeared with blood? Now she must
have had a hand in this, and I'll sift it to the bottom. She may
have the power to pay me a large sum of money to let her
alone. Let's work this up, Reuben Thurston," this being the
name of his favorite. "Now, you know you were the second
man on the spot. Zounds! if you had been the first, then we
would have them; but it's that old feller, Woodbergh, that will
tell the whole truth—couldn't bribe him to treachery or falsehood; but then, we'll do the best we can for all that. Let her
alone for a few days; we will first establish the fact that it is
murder and then we will feel our way along; we will throw out
our little hints and see how the public receives it, for if we
should boldly assert our belief in her guilt, we might receive a
dressing of tar and feathers; for you know she has a great
many friends, and they rank among the most influential in the
city. The newspaper is the most powerful weapon we can use,
and this old printer up here would use his infernal machinery to
send a man to hell for a five dollar bill."

"Capital! I know now you're prime minister from that infernal region. I'll help you all I know."

"And that ain't much!" Gordon answered laughing; "but as far as you do know you'll answer; but when you come to swearing, we'll cook that up. I want to tell you what to say inasmuch as you'd just as live swear to one thing as another."

"Providing——"

"I understand. Of 'course all the money we make out of this thing shall be divided even with every one in the ring."

"All right, I'm at your service."

CHAPTER XLVI.

At early dawn Elice stole into the room where the servant girl lay in her winding sheet, once more to gaze upon her lovely features, and, stooping down, she kissed those marble lips that had never for a single time in her presence spoken but in gentleness and kindness; and as the last words of their conversation of the day previous came to mind:—"I will, I do trust my Saviour,"—she could not help feeling that she was now in the society of "just men made perfect;" that her pure soul was drinking from those everlasting fountains of joy that flow in the paradise of God; and how rejoiced she was that, although exhausted, feeble and sick, she had permitted her to come to her room, and unfold her mind; for now she felt assured that, she slept the sweet sleep of peace—she reposed in the arms of Jesus and would awake in the morning of the resurrection, incorruptible. And she thought, oh! could she but tell her tale, how soon the mystified senses of unbelievers would discover the cause of her death, and how glad would she be to clear that innocent boy whom she had learned to love as a brother, and who had so very often assisted her in her work when he had seen her flag with weariness or she was hastening to get through with business for a ride, a walk, church or party. Severing a tress of her beautiful golden hair which she desired for a keepsake from one who had rendered her so many kind services—through indisposition and otherwise—she said, "Farewell, dear child; in Heaven we'll meet again; till then a last farewell—farewell!"

Robin went about as one beside himself, neither eating nor sleeping for several days and nights in succession.

"O mamma!" he said, "if we had only been obedient to your wishes, that accident would not have happened."

"No, darling," she answered, "whenever we break the laws of God, we suffer for it; and you know that is an express command: 'Children, obey your parents.'"

"I know—that is what I learned long ago at Sunday school, and if I had only heeded it, we might have been saved so much sorrow of heart, so much trouble, and Nora would now be living, and we would all be so happy."

"Let it teach you a lesson, dear—the sight of that cold clay form which, but for ignorance and folly, might now be in our midst flushed with the hue of health and happiness; and remember that a violation of those precepts laid down in the Bible brings misery and death. But go now to God in prayer, ask his forgiveness for the great sin which you have committed, as well as all of the sins which embitter your life, if, perchance, He will relieve you of the burden that oppresses your agonized soul."

Then Elice, with her hands upon the head of little Robin, upon her bended knees, poured out her thoughts to the only source from which they could derive one ray of comfort at this trying hour; and oh! how earnestly she besought Him that this sad circumstance might be the means of bringing him while yet in the springtime of his life to seek the face of Deity; that the blossom of true piety might grow up in the garden of his heart; and that his after life might show that he was indeed a child of the most High; that there might be no tares to separate from the wheat, and when the beautiful harvest should at last come, he might hear it said, "Well done, thou good and faithful servant, enter thou into the joy of thy Lord."

"O mamma!" he said, "why do they wish to lay this terrible deed to me? I would die myself, before I would have harmed her in the least."

"I believe you would, but this is one of the great trials that God permits; and perhaps it is for your good. His ways are often mysterious and past finding out; but we shall know if we are ever so happy as to enter through the golden gates into the celestial city."

"I wish I could understand," the child said, rubbing his forehead, "now in one of our lessons was this verse. 'Ye must be born again, or ye can in no wise enter into the kingdom of heaven.' The teacher explained it, but some way I could not see just how it was."

"It is simply this: we must have all evil, such as envy, malice, hatred, and pride, rooted from our hearts; love all mankind, and try to do them good, and love the great God above who sent His beloved Son into the world to die for us poor fellow creatures that we through Him might have everlasting life."

"And if we fail to do this, we cannot go to Heaven—is that it? Now I don't see how I am to love Joe Gordon, who is trying so hard to make me out a murderer, and would like to see me hung for what I am not guilty. O mamma, impossible! I hate him with all my heart, for he is so vile, such a wicked, cruel wretch to want to make us all so much trouble. Does God love him?"

"Even if they brought in false testimony at last to condemn you, it would be no worse treatment than our Saviour received at the hands of his supposed friends who, when He was pointing them to the way of life, making so many sacrifices to do them good, was arraigned before Pontius Pilate to answer to charges of which He was never guilty; at last compelled to wear a crown of thorns, bear the cross, and in the face of a cruel mob was crucified."

"And He loved them?"

"He prayed when He was suspended between the heavens and the earth, when they were taunting Him with cruel words, the nails being driven through his hands and feet, and the blood flowing from his wounds, 'Father, forgive them, they know not what they do?'"

"But He is God, mamma, there is not so much expected of us."

"Don't you know in the Lord's Prayer, the most beautiful ever uttered or taught on earth, are these words: 'Forgive us our trespasses as we forgive those who trespass against us'?"

Robin looked up into her pale and sorrowful face, "I cannot, they have made you such suffering ; if it were only myself, I might."

"But you will try?"

"Yes, yes, for your sake, if you say so."

"Not mine but your own—Christ Jesus help my poor, dear boy!"

CHAPTER XLVII.

Mr. and Mrs. Clayton had retired for the night. They had not yet been asleep when the old fashioned clock that hung in the dining-room struck twelve.

A loud knock was heard at the door.

"Who can be here at this time," said Elice.

"I cannot imagine," her husband replied, "but I will know;' and, hurrying out, he was soon face to face with Joe Gordon and Ben Brown; the latter being a detective from a neighboring city, and employed by this vile policeman to work up the case.

"I have a warrant for the arrest of your wife."

"What is the charge?"

"A very grave one, sir—as accomplice with your son in the murder of her servant girl, on the 29th of December last; and we came for the purpose of taking the body. We want her to come with us to the hotel, where we shall take charge of her through the night, thence to Cambden on the early train, to answer to the crime committed."

Elice heard a part of the conversation but, wild with terror, inquired of her husband if she must be dragged from the house by these ruffians at that hour of the night; and asked him if he could not protect her from these pitiless rascals.

"I told them I would be responsible," he said, "for your appearance; and with this assurance they consented to let you remain where you are. But go back to bed; sleep if you can, for to-morrow at an early hour, in the custody of these officers, you are to go to Cambden, where you are to have an examination by the district attorney before a justice of the peace; and if found guilty, to be committed to jail, there to await the opening of court, when you will have your last and final trial before the high judge of the county; then convicted or cleared, as can be shown by evidence whether you are innocent or guilty.

"But I can prove my innocence, you know, papa."

"You have no right to bring witnesses at all, it is a one-sided thing, and the worst feature in the case is, it is unbailable."

"Oh, the injustice! cruel, false injustice!"

"Yes, that is true, but law is law, and we cannot alter it; we must abide by its decision every time."

The heart of Elice throbbed wildly when she thought of the chances she sustained of being handcuffed and taken to prison; for she felt she was in the hands of a cruel mob that would probably bear witness to anything to condemn her; and it seemed beyond the power of human wisdom to aid her, or her friends to do much good.

She went up stairs and tapped gently at the door of her sister's room, who had heard all that had transpired, and was now on her bended knees, asking God to protect and make a way for the escape of the innocent. She arose when Elice entered, her face radiant with hope that had been so strengthened through her supplication at the throne of grace.

"O, my darling sister," she said, "God will come to your succor; though all earthly friends forsake, yet He will not forsake His children. Can you trust Him?"

"Yes, yes, I do."

They then opened the large Bible—a gift to Elice from her dear departed father—to see what God would speak by the mouth of His prophets, feeling that this was their only rock of refuge, their only source of comfort in this terrible hour of agony and distress. The first chapter they turned to was about the wonderful deliverance of Paul and Silas from a dark and gloomy prison ; how their bonds were loosed and they were set at liberty by the Great Jehovah, whom they feared and served. The next, of Daniel ; how God sent His angels and closed the mouths of the lions that they did him no harm. Then the Hebrew children, with whose history every child is familiar ; and oh ! how their hearts bounded with joy and praise that God was the Judge and not man ; and that He is able now as then to show His power and goodness ; and they believed He would do it in shielding Elice from any harm that a wicked mob might devise, and they thanked Him again and again and lifted up their voices in praise to Him who, they felt, would show the designing that He could rule on earth as well as in the heavens, and that all things could be consumed by the breath of His nostrils. And arising from their knees with tears of gladness trickling down their cheeks, that their kind Father had deigned thus to show His smiling face to His poor, sinful worms, kissed each other a final good night, while each repaired to her bed and slept a sweet, peaceful sleep, feeling that angels were watching over them to deliver from evil.

The next morning the news of the arrest of Elice spread like wild fire, while her friends flocked around her *en masse*, each anxious to do something for her. Among them was the beautiful and accomplished daughter of a wealthy banker of the city, whose ears were ever open to the cry of distress.

"O Mrs. Clayton," said she in the most sympathetic of tones, "what can I do? I would willingly go to Cambden on foot if it would do any good, and plead with those in authority, with tears, to release you. No respectable citizen of this place believes the sad story concerning you; all know it to be a base fabrication to draw money from your pocket. Do not be disheartened; do not let it trouble you, for you will surely triumph over all your foes and be acquitted at last, for the prayers of all the good that have learned the sad news of your shameful arrest will go up from their altars this morning; and we trust that God who hears and answers prayer."

"Yes," said Elice, "praise His great and holy name. He leadeth us by a way that we know not, but we must follow Him."

Many accompanied her to the depot; and, as she waved a good-bye from the platform where she stood until the moving of the train, all looked after her with moistened eyes, and turned again toward their homes with sorrowing hearts.

Mrs. Leland, arriving at her father's princely mansion, sat down with a goodly number of friends and foes already collected to discuss the only question thought or spoken of in town at the present hour—whether Mrs. Clayton was innocent or guilty of the alleged crime of murder, and held them spellbound for more than an hour with her eloquent words spoken in defense of her absent friend; and if any there had a shadow of a doubt before her touching appeal for the right, it was dissipated before her weighty arguments, that would have been complimentary to a lawyer pleading for the life of his client. "I know she is innocent as the angels above, and you know it, but the lie has already been heralded to the world: among strangers, she bears the mark of Cain, and it must be washed away."

She then got paper and pencil and wrote the following:

"REMONSTRANCE.

"Being personally acquainted with Mrs. Elice Clayton, and always knowing her to be a woman of untarnished reputation, and standing high in the estimation of her friends as regards everything that is purely religious or moral, of a tender, sympathetic, kind-hearted nature; we, the undersigned, with a full belief in her innocence respecting the atrocious crime of murder; also in that of her son who is now but a mere child, of whom we can truly say that cruelty bears no part in his nature; but, on the contrary, there have many instances come under our observation of his seeking out, among the poor and needy, a sufferer and relieving his necessities, kindly bestowing upon him the last farthing he possessed; assisting many a poor wayfarer who had enlisted his sympathy by his tales of poverty and distress, by an intercession with some friend to give him a night's lodging, a meal of victuals, or clothes to keep him from freezing to death through the biting frosts of winter,—wish to publish these facts in the city newspaper, from which we hope they will be copied far and wide, that every shadow may vanish that has come to those fair names through the rascally villains whose only object, we believe, is to make money by the deep plotted intrigues and falsehoods which they have caused to be put in circulation against them."

After this was completed, she read it to those there assembled, when all in the room, including her good father and mother, attached their names to the paper. She then went to the clergy, all of whom were glad of the privilege of doing her the favor; then to the most of the respectable citizens of the place, who, without the least hesitation, followed their example. It was then published, that every one might see for himself the great respect in which they were held by the community in which they had so long been citizens.

The cars by this time had borne Elice, her husband, sister and the officers into Cambden, and they were seated in the old court house, on Sixth street, to await further developments. Elice went before the judge, waived examination, and gave bail for her appearance at court. In the meanwhile a large concourse of people were assembled at a good-sized hall, hired especially by the justice of the peace, as his was too small to hold the crowd that had gathered to listen to the examination of the prisoners. They were all waiting with breathless expectancy to see them enter. The time came for them to make their appearance, but they did not come. Half an hour elapsed, the mob held their breath in suspense; while all the people wondered what it meant. There was mingling of voices asking why they tarried; what was the matter; while the justice, who seemed to feel the dignity of his calling, with his mind already made up without the hearing; who, with the filth and rubbish of Lavarre—in other words, the prosecutors and witnesses in the case—in prospective saw their towns-woman committed to jail; and gloried to see her there behind the iron grates and locked away from the sight of her friends. But she would come, and no mistake, they all said. In a moment the detective entered, bearing a paper from the court, which freed her from all further molestation until the time of her trial; and she was free to roam whither she would.

"The bird has flown, eh?" said the justice sneeringly, suddenly precipitated from his throne of dignity; for he had forgotten there was any power in the State but his own; and coveted so much the honor of passing judgment upon his victim; so crafty to receive his fees, and so anxious to please the low-bred mob that employed him.

"Was ever the like known?" said a person sitting by the side of an old man whose hair was already whitened by the frosts of many years.

"Yes, eighteen hundred years ago there was a certain man, Peter, who was thrown into prison, bound with chains and sleeping between two soldiers; and behold the angel of the Lord came upon him, and a light shone into the prison, and he smote Peter on the side, and bade him arise; and his chains fell off. He told him to bind on his sandals and follow him, and he did so. He accompanied him even to the iron gate that leads into the city, which opened to them of its own accord. He was miraculously delivered, as you see, by the great God above; and simply because he feared and served Him. So with the prisoner whom you have so longed to gloat your eyes upon this day; whom, if your nature could be satisfied, you would love to hang upon some of those lofty shades just outside this building. But she is released; the cords you bound her with are rotten; your power has been set at naught."

The mob dispersed; but not without oaths and bitter threats. Some of them, in their drunken frenzy, were taken into custody by the police.

One of the party, wishing to annoy the friends of Elice at home, sent a telegram that she was lodged in jail, not to be released until her trial; and great pains were taken to bear the news to the family, especially to little Robin, whose cup of agony was now so full that not one drop could be added.

"O my mother! my mother!" he exclaimed in tones of the deepest grief, "I could stay in the gloomy cell for years rather than you should remain there one night."

CHAPTER XLVIII.

When Elice returned home, she found Mrs. Rockville, a pious old lady of over sixty years, seated in her room waiting to receive her. Taking her hand in both of hers she said, "This is what I have prayed for. God is good, my child. And so the jail is not your abiding-place for the night as some have predicted."

"No," answered Elice. "Did ever a child have more reason to be thankful to a kind and tender parent, than I to my beloved Heavenly Father this day—for he has delivered me from all my enemies."

"Do not fear, all will be right in the end—you can never be condemned. Though the way may appear dark and your enemies beset you on every hand, there is a steady unwavering light that can lead you safely through. You trust it?"

"How can I help it after what I have passed through? I do, indeed—but you know the innocent oftentimes suffer."

"But you believe God hears and answers prayer? To-day I have prayed as I never before have done that the truth might shine forth to the world concerning this great calamity—that you might be cleared of every stain, and I felt assured it was the witness of the Spirit when I heard as it were a voice saying: 'As your faith, so be it unto you,'—and I am so glad to-night to see you so calm under such distressing circumstances."

Elice could only answer: "God is good—so good in giving me so faithful an advocate of my cause, but, Mrs. Rockwell, were I condemned to die, this same beautiful light of which you have spoken would illumine the dark precincts of the tomb, and I should only get home a little sooner. The only terrible thought about it is that I should be branded as a murderer and the cruel disgrace fall upon my children."

"Did you know I saw you at the train this morning? I went for the purpose of giving you encouragement, but when I got there, my heart was too full for utterance. Like our Saviour, you were in the midst of a mob guarded by officers. Did you, like Him, my child, feel like praying: 'Father, forgive them, for they know not what they do'?"

"I hardly thought of my position. I was lifted above and beyond—it was the same as though spirits of justice and love floated between them and me, with flaming swords to keep me from injury, and thus they have kept their places until the present, and my unwavering trust in my Divine Master tells me that all their efforts against me will be useless."

The good old mother in Israel whose face was now illuminated with the light of love divine commenced singing:

> "Praise God from whom all blessings flow,
> Praise Him all creatures here below,
> Praise Him above ye Heavenly Host,—
> Praise Father, Son, and Holy Ghost."

in which Elice joined heartily.

She then said: "Oh that every one could have this childlike simplicity and faith. Whatever your fate might be, I believe you could meet it calmly."

"My Saviour has taken away the sting of the grave."

"Yes! yes! he has lain there before us, and he arose in all the beauty of incorruptibility. It will be sweet for me to follow where he leads."

"For he will conduct us to glory and immortality."

"To mansions fair that he hath fitted up for those who love Him."

"And we shall never hunger and thirst any more, for we shall continually eat of the fruit and drink of the fountain that give to us everlasting life. It is not a sad picture—the death of the Christian. A life-boat filled with angels bearing him steadily on over the dark and turbid waters of death, and carrying him through pearly gates into Heaven."

Mrs. Rockwell then shaking Elice by the hand, imprinting a kiss upon the pale face, went home, praying all the way that her faith, which was so strong, fail her not, through the terrible ordeal which she yet·must pass.

19

CHAPTER XLIX.

The next day was communion in the church of which Elice was a member; and oh! with what pleasure, and real happiness did she look forward to the moment when she with her friends might kneel around the altar, and partake of the symbols of the suffering and death of her dear Redeemer.

She would then be among those who would not look upon her with suspicious eyes, but as a member of the great family who would throw their protecting arms about her, and shield her from the calumnious breath of the outside world, and encourage her with words of hope in her great tribulation.

Her mind wandered out to the garden of Gethsemane, and she thought of the agony Christ must have endured to cause him to sweat great drops of blood; and how keen his anguish, when he was betrayed by a bosom friend with a kiss on his cheek, and none of these things have or will happen to me—they were my foes, and not my friends in the church. If I should be thus treated, I would lose all faith I believe in Christianity—for no Christian would or could treat another Christian after this manner.

True they have not been to visit me, but as yet they have had no opportunity, only this beloved mother, Mrs. Rockwell, who is a very pillar in the church, active in doing good in every spot and place, and I have learned from her lips that all with whom she has conversed considered me innocent, and incapable of so horrid a deed. The minister also has placed with his own hands his signature to the remonstrance drawn up in my favor.

Oh! my beloved pastor—like as a hen gathereth her chickens under her wings to shield them from the coming storm, or as a good shepherd watches over his flock to keep away the wolves who 'might tear them in pieces and destroy them utterly, so doth he look after the lowliest of his flock over which he has been appointed by his Master above, and how sweet, how incomparably sweet—though hell rages without, and the adversary would swallow us up, we may seek the dear little nest, receive the smiles of kindred spirits and feel that we are not by them misapprehended.

Soon a knock was heard at the door—she opened it—her pastor stood before her.

Oh! how her heart bounded with joy to think that though the winds were howling without, he had, unmindful of the storm, come to comfort her—how kind and considerate he was of her feelings.

He did not offer his hand—he did not call her sister as was his wont, but coldly said, "Good morning, madam," with no demonstration of kindly feeling.

"Will you be seated?" said Elice, overwhelmed with grief caused by the frigidity of his manner.

"I have but a moment to stay," he replied, "have been sent by the church, who ask as a favor at your hands, that you withdraw. It is a painful duty that has been imposed upon me, but one which I feel that I owe, inasmuch as I am its pastor—and when I explain it to you, of course, you must see it is the wisest course for all."

"How so?" said Elice, trying to be calm.

"Well, please understand me, in the first place, there is not a single member who does not believe you innocent, and a Christian. But that is not it—we are in debt, a portion of which we expect to liquidate through outsiders—these people who do not belong to any church but go where they desire, and many of them have taken a decided stand against you, and declare if you remain in the church they shall go elsewhere. They pay liberally—so you see how we would cripple ourselves financially if we allowed them to go away. As a Christian woman you would not wish it?"

"If you were by the wayside and saw a poor little lamb that had been assaulted by brutal hands, and beaten until it was nearly dead—still struggling for its life—would you put your foot upon it?"

"No, I could not be thus cruel."

"If you saw a child about to be run over by a locomotive, and it was in your power to save it, would you do so?"

"Certainly—I would try."

"Financially that could not hurt you—to show the better part of your nature—to be a man. 'If ye but give a cup of cold water in My name to one of those who believe in Me, verily I say unto you, ye shall not lose your reward.' "

Mr. Monell saw the point at which Elice aimed, and becoming exceedingly angry, at last said, "I cannot see how it is going to hurt you to withdraw from the church—while it will do us an infinite amount of good."

"You represent the church, and they have sent you? Is this the mind of the whole body?"

"Well, yes—no—I don't know as it is, but I believe it is for the best."

"I cannot acquiesce."

"Then we will turn you out," he said, and left the house.

For the second time since the great trouble the faith of Elice wavered, and she exclaimed in bitterness—"Where is God? Where is God?"

With the knowledge of but few of the church, and without their consent, the name of Elice was stricken from their books, to the wonder and amazement of all the Christian churches and ministers of the place, as well as most of the residents of the city.

In striving to make himself popular, Mr. Monell became exceedingly *un*popular, while the star of his church was in the wane for several years, and he left the conference of which he was a member lest he should be excommunicated for this violation of their rules.

CHAPTER L.

Just after the departure of the pastor Mrs. Ashton and her daughter called upon her.

Both threw their arms around her neck and wept with her—their tears of genuine sympathy and joy to find her safely at home once more—hers, at remembrance of the painful interview she had just had, with a—supposed—Christian friend.

Mrs. Ashton led Elice to a chair—with her soft hands stroked her forehead, brushed away the tears that were still falling upon her pale cheeks and kissed her affectionately.

"My more than friend," Elice murmured, "my mother—my sister—how can I repay you for the great interest you have taken in my welfare—but God will reward."

She then told her to be of good cheer; that she had friends—enough of them—most loyal, and not to think they would forsake her—that her husband started for Cambden on the very next train out, after the news came of her shameful confinement in jail, to tell the sheriff to give her all the privileges of the house—to spare no pains to make her comfortable—a seat at their own table, and if there were any bills to settle he would willingly attend to it.

At this announcement a dizziness came over Elice—a mist floated before her eyes—she was about to faint, for she felt herself torn in spirit from all the creeds and dogmas of the church, even to doubt their right to be called Christians, as they had showed themselves so uncharitable, for she could not help drawing the contrast between this man of the world, who made no pretensions of religion and Christianity, and him who represented the church—him who had just now wished to turn her from the shelter of the fold, when the storms of persecution were raging wildly around, and the wolves had left their coverts in the forest to pounce upon their prey as soon as the unfaithful shepherd had let down the bars, and with his own hands had hurled to them the victim.

"I thought I was a bearer of good news," said Mrs. Ashton.

"Indeed! indeed, you are, but life, religion, everything has become so mystified, and I cannot see my way through the darkness which envelops me. I feel myself struggling on the waves of unbelief, and I fear I must sink yet into the dark abyss of hopeless despair, with all the light and knowledge which I supposed I possessed."

"I do not know what religion is, but it occurs to me that the greater good that comes to me, the more trust I should feel in the watchful care of Providence. I cannot understand why you should lack faith. From my standpoint I discovered, in your happy release to-day, the dove sent forth from the windows of Heaven and bearing to your poor wounded spirit the olive branch of peace—a current from the Eternal which must take you into the harbor of rest at last. It is strange you do not see it."

Elice then told her friend all that had occurred between her and her pastor, and said it was this that puzzled and perplexed her.

"I understand now," she said. "It is not all gold that glitters. You have had your heart too much bound up in the church—you have mistaken the shell for the sweet kernel inside."

Elice bowed her head in meekness. She was willing, yea, even glad to be taught, although it was not by the old orthodox method.

"I know, I am perfectly incapable of unfolding the Scriptures to such a one as you—who all your life have lived under the sound of the Gospel—in strict attendance upon public worship, Sabbath school, Bible class, prayer and class meetings—observing every form of the church, but if you will allow me to illustrate without taking offense, I will do so—the truth of which has just flashed athwart my mind from some source—I think from a pure one—and suits your case.

"When Peter was sailing with kindred companions upon a calm and undisturbed sea, he saw only the light house—thought only of the life-boat that would be sent out should a terrible tempest come furiously upon them. But when the winds blew high, the ship commenced rocking to and fro, the big waves leap, and lash her sides as though they would swallow her up, his faith in human aid was shaken; for no one ventured out to his rescue, and while he battled bravely to save his crew, and was not expecting it any other way than the one heretofore spoken of, he did not recognize his Divine Master walking toward him on the waters, and not until he had commenced sinking, did he cry out, 'Lord, save, or I perish.' Like you he had trusted too much in human agencies. Call it forms and ceremonies if you like; or, perhaps you had become a Jonah to the pious captain,—this may be a better version.''

Elice smiled: "I think this one will do, inasmuch as I was cast overboard."

"And now you will not be above your Master, but willing to eat with publicans and sinners. Orthodoxy sees no heaven, no Christianity, only through its own church, while Christ gathered his followers from poor illiterate fishermen—from the humble, everywhere. I do not profess to be good. I know I am very sinful, but if I ever do have religion, I hope it will be after His style."

The eyes of Elice were opened; she saw in her friend's remarks a just rebuke for her former blind folly—felt that whether in the church or out of it people were alone to be judged by their fruits.

CHAPTER LI.

All nature had commenced smiling sweetly. The balmy breath of the beautiful spring had awakened the flowers to life; the young lambs were skipping on the plains, the green grass already covered the broad fields, while woodland, river and rivulet, beasts, birds and sparkling fountains each in its way sung the glad song of a happy release from the tyrannical chains of a hard and despotic winter.

The day had at last come—the seventh of May, when Elice and her son were to be tried for their lives, and as they stepped into the carriage that bore them to the depot, could not help observing the cloudlessness of the sky, for not a floating speck seemed for a moment to shut out the bright sunlight.

"Do you see," said Elice, "God is smiling. Happy omen, for prisoners bound."

"But He has kept you from being confined by the slightest cord," remarked her sister.

" Except in spirit, dear sister, but they have even then rested so lightly, when I have felt them lacerating my heart, His own dear hands have come between them and the tender flesh, and have saved the pain they otherwise might have inflicted, and I shall be disappointed if this trial is not one of deliverance and we permitted to sing the sweet songs of our Great Deliverer. I have no fears, not even a shadow of doubt crosses my mind so great faith have I in His dear and precious promises."

Groups of men and boys of every class and grade had gathered on the rude benches in front of stores, or were standing discussing the great topic—the arrest—the trial that was so soon to take place, while many were watching the prisoners from their homes with tearful eyes. They thought of the chances there might be of their conviction, as they held in their hands the morning paper, containing the doings of the grand jury, who on the day preceding had found a true bill against Elice— murder in the first degree. The same excitement prevailed in Cambden on their arrival, only many of them, perfectly unacquainted, knowing only by the stories that had been in circulation, had more curiosity to get a look at the monsters who could so deliberately assassinate a human being without cause or provocation.

Elice was at last acquitted, when the case of her son was soon taken up and ended with the same happy result.

CHAPTER LII.

"Will you and your daughters join our fishing party, Mrs. Tattum? The lake is as smooth as glass to-day; it looks like a storm, however. Should there be one to-night, I anticipate fine luck to-morrow," said Mrs. Carlyle.

"I am afraid of the water, never having been out in a row-boat."

"But they are perfectly safe. I have been on the lake a thousand times, and no accident ever yet occurred. Come, don't be afraid. We will go in the morning, and gather in the beautiful trout—in the afternoon, cross over, and pick huckle-berries. They say there are oceans of them on the mountain."

"O mother! do let us go; it will be so delightful. Only to think of having a large basket of that delicious fruit, and all at once! Who all are going?" said Augusta.

"Just a few—Mrs. Jenks and our teamster. Take them along to do the work mostly, that is, to row and help carry the berries and fish."

"Capital! it takes you for contrivance. I suppose they think it is for obligation's sake, because they helped us along so nicely with our church trial. Well, of course, they were of great assistance. By the mouth of so many witnesses, how could we help but conquer our foes?"

"A wicked, terrible lie! As bad as I am you couldn't get me to swear for you," said Hezekiah.

"Oh, ease up! be quiet! You are always coming around

when you are not wanted, to say something disagreeable," his wife replied.

"Won't you go along, Mr. Tattum?" said Mrs. Carlyle.

"Not I, nary a bit o' it.   Should expect to be swallowed up by a wale—boat and all—to go in sich a crowd."

"Hush up, now do!" Mrs. Carlyle answered, laughing; "you are pretty good; you never gave us away to the church, for all you have been very angry at times with us both."

"It's a purty funny kind o' an old bird that would pick the feathers all off o' his young birds, Mrs. Carlyle.   I wouldn't never want to lift up my head, ef I'd be guilty of sich a thing. What folks can't find out for themselves, they'll never know from old Hezekier."

"You will go to Heaven, I think."

"If so, shan't see you thar."

"How so?   Don't be so hard on me.   The most of people consider me a saint, even to the minister."

"That may be; but its 'cause he ain't 'quainted like I am."

"You flatter me exceedingly."   Then turning to Mrs. Tattum and daughter, "Be on hand early, as soon as six."

Next morning a little party of five,—Mrs. Carlyle, Mr. Carlton, Mrs. Jenks, Mrs. Tattum and Augusta (Minnie could not go for some reason), might be seen seated in a little boat, skimming over the smooth surface of the lake, apparently as happy and fearless as the birds around them, which now and then touched the waves with their golden breasts, as they winged their flight over and around this lovely sheet of water, while the party sang, shouted and made merry, as they threw in their hooks and drew up the living treasures of the deep—now and then a spotted bass, then a pike or pickerel, until they thought they had caught enough for one day, when they rowed for the opposite shore to procure their berries.   They were soon there and gathered all their baskets full, and were returning home, well pleased with their day's work.   They turned out of their course, however, to pluck some water lilies, Augusta saying she

would not go without them; for these she designed as a · present to the minister's wife, for whom she had been making some
of the same kind in wax.

"Oh! yes," said Mrs. Carlyle, "and half of my fish, also
berries, will go to the same place."

"Indeed!" Mrs. Tattum answered; "but I was intending to
give them nearly all we got; for you understand he favors us
very much whenever we get in a tight place."

"He knows we are too good to do anything wrong, mother,"
said Augusta, laughing—"gifts are binding."

They noticed by this time the small, black cloud that had
been visible in the west, which they had not thought worth
heeding, had grown very large, while streaks of lightening
had commenced darting from it, one after the other in rapid
succession, and they thought best to pull for the shore with all
possible alacrity; but the winds commenced blowing and beat
so wildly against the little boat they could not make much
progress, while the storm beat piteously upon their unsheltered
heads. But Mark was a good oarsman and had been out upon
larger lakes than this, in rough gales, and told them not to be
frightened; that he knew he could bring them safely to land;
to trust to him: but when they looked upon the sheet of water,
so smooth and placid in the morning, piled up with fierce, angry
waves, some of which every moment threatened to upset them,
they lost all confidence in human aid, and dropped upon their
knees in wild terror, asking rescue and pardon for all those terrible sins they had committed, which now in this hour of agony
and death, arose before them in all of their true and real light;
and there was no show, no hypocrisy, in those burning words
that fell from that party, who so soon expected to sink beneath
those turbulent waves, while a voice seemed to their disturbed
consciences to whisper, "As ye sow, so shall ye reap." And
they could not but feel, that, if they were lost, it was but a just
retribution for all their past follies and sins; and thought that

if they ever reached shore they would make some confession—would lead an entirely different life.

"If I could only manage to get out of these troughs," Mark said, "and face toward land, then I might succeed in bringing the craft through."

Just as these words were spoken, another wave swept over them ; the boat was overturned, and all for a few moments were lost to sight.   Then wild cries for help, mingled with the dirge-like tones of the fierce storm, being heard only by Him into whose ears, as a last recourse for salvation from a watery grave, they had poured forth their prayers in sincerity, with a faint hope of pardon after a whole life spent in cruel mockery of those great truths that Christ came into the world to establish—a hollow profession of religion without the shadow of reality; and what was worse, by their unchristian example, been the means of turning many poor sinners from the cross—from leaving the ways of sin for those of righteousness.   But they all went down at last, excepting Mark, who succeeded in clinging to the boat until the storm passed ; and then, being an expert swimmer, through the greatest exertion gained the shore.

Toward eventide the next day, the bodies were found and conveyed to their homes.   The grief of the heart-stricken families and relatives can be imagined, perhaps, but not told. Even Deacon Smith and wife, and Mrs. Col. Thompson were deeply moved, as they gazed upon the lifeless forms of those whom they had once so despised, who had been capable of doing them all so great a wrong, but whose lips could never again utter untruths; and if they had revealed their thoughts as they turned away from the house of death, which seemed so solemn—so sad—they would each in his turn have whispered, "I forgive you." And shall we, can we, would we say, that the ears of Jehovah had not been opened to their entreaties? that He, the Father, the friend, to all the fallen ones of earth ; to the lowly, to the poor, as well as the rich, could not be as merciful? We commit their souls into the hands of Him who doeth all things well. The ways of Providence are mysterious and past finding out, and who knows but His all discerning eye discovered, in this judgment, the only way of bringing those sinners to true repentance and Heaven at last?

Minnie, overburdened with grief, sought consolation at the foot of the cross. Here she found her Saviour ready to bless her, and through her happy experience, felt that it was not so hard, after all, to tread those sweet paths of peace and holiness. All that was required, was to obey the commands of God and to heed the Spirit's warning voice whenever it spoke to her soul. "This is the way, walk ye in it."

Her father, hitherto an unbeliever in Christianity, began to feel that anything that could transform the nature of a person as Minnie's had been since the death of her friends, must be real; and, after he had seen her go about so patiently bearing life's burdens, and sacrificing herself for the good of others, attending to all his wants, proving herself to be a true and dutiful daughter, he abstained from drunkenness, and asked to be taught the ways of life; and, as he ever after until his death —which occurred in about two years—lived up to the highest light of which his uncultured mind was susceptible, we have no doubt but the judgment day will disclose his robes washed and made white in the blood of the Lamb.

CHAPTER LIII.

Sammie Wilmington has succeeded one of the deceased partners in the firm of Mayville & Co. His indefatigable industry, honesty, polished manners, and truly gentlemanly deportment since he came to the establishment, won for him the situation, as well as the good will of all therein concerned. He is a favorite of the beautiful and accomplished daughter of the senior partner, Mr. Mayville, to whose elegant mansion he is often an invited guest, where they play upon the piano and sing by the hour together, he always choosing the pathetic, sometimes the really melancholy, as these accord so fully and truly with his own feelings—she the gay, dashing, charming airs that find so ready a response in her own happy heart and lively imagination, and wonders at the strange taste of her friend.

One evening playfully inquiring of him why he was always gathering together and selecting all the solemn pieces from her music, he replied after her own manner, not caring to have her read any of his sad history through any of his own careless words or acts :

"For very contrast, Miss Mayville, with your own inspiring, bewitching and brilliant songs. Does the setting sun lose aught of its glory by occasionally going from our sight beneath the blackest clouds ? Do not the flowers send forth more fragrance by sometimes being drenched in the rain ? And may not our lives become better by accustoming ourselves to its sorrows as well as joys—even to the tracing out the history of some poor unfortunate who has lived to see every lingering ray of hope die out of his breast? While we can love the day with all its light and beauty, yet we could not well do without its counterpart, the night, when we seek our rest and sleep, and enjoy the keen pleasures, oftentimes, of delicious visions. Then it is our loved ones come back to earth and converse with us, those we have laid away in the chilling grave; and we live again the happy days of the past in their sweet society; we are children sometimes, roaming through wildwood and glen in quest of the gay butterfly with its gorgeous wings, and drinking happiness as freely as the air we breathe; or the buttercups beneath our feet, the invigorating dew. It takes the sorrows, the crosses of life, to give us a keen relish for its pleasures."

Miss Mayville did not reply; but commenced reading aloud:

> "Come back, ye gay tints of the morning
> That shone on my childhood,
> So richly the hillside adorning,
> The mosses, the wildwood;
> Breathing love, breathing life, to the young bubbling fountain,
> The fresh bursting buds on the crest of the mountain,
> Or the sunflower, even, that grew at my door,
> That life-giving influence thou deignedst to pour.
> Onward, onward, thy course o'er land and o'er sea,
> While the world, smiling, gave a welcome to thee.
> How now, gentle light, if ye e'er come at all
> To my hearth, to my home, so dimly ye fall?
>
> It is not but each morning I shine just the same
> On the palace, and cottage, and hut in the lane;
> But thine eyes have grown dim by the reason of weeping,
> Deep shadows of woe to thy dreary life creeping,
> Shutting out from thy care-stricken heart, gentle one,
> All the beauteous rays of the bright morning sun!"

"Some of those sentiments are quite true, Miss Mayville. People are apt to imagine there are fewer joys in the present, and are continually fault-finding and wondering why it is so, never thinking that the selfishness of their natures, nursed for many a long year, has at last become a bar to shut away the sunlight of happiness that they have themselves experienced before their dispositions soured, and they had encased in this coat of steel all their best and noblest feelings—true sympathy and love for mankind."

"So our own actions are the means of bringing us pleasure or misery? Ah! a great deal of heart-rending anguish comes to us often that we could not have averted, even had we seen it beforehand. Man is born to trouble. You never saw me shed a tear, never otherwise than happy, and think I am not capable of sympathetic thought or feeling—have nothing in common with those less blessed than myself, with home and friends."

"And wealth and luxuries and everything possible to bring joy to a person, who, like you, has just launched, as it were, his bark on the silver-crested spray of life's glittering sea. No, no, Miss Mayville I know you better than you think. You are not the thoughtless devotee of fashion for which some might take you; for underneath all this, you have a heart that beats in true sympathy with the fallen and crushed ones of earth. That shabbily dressed child that you fed and clothed but yesterday could corroborate my words."

"How did you know anything about that?"

"She was hurt down here as she attempted to cross the street. I took her in my arms and carried her over. She could not walk home, and I ordered a hackman to drive to her quarters. I went along fearing she might be more seriously injured than was thought for. She told me her little story." After a few moments' pause in the conversation, he said, "Would you not like to take a ride to-morrow morning? I am up usually very early and walk several miles before going to my business; but thought I would change the order, that is, if you would accompany me."

"But it must be after my fleet and beautiful coal black steeds, and myself the driver, eh?" and she looked so irresistible he felt that he could scarcely refuse her anything she might ask; and so he said:

"Any way to please you, Miss Mayville; I have no will in the matter."

"Then we will drive to Summerset Castle on the Thames, a magnificent old country-seat owned by Lord Parloe, who has become very old and feeble and is not expected to survive a great while. Papa tells quite a romantic little incident that is said to have taken place years ago at that castle. They had a young and lovely daughter whom they nearly idolized, who fell in love with a gentleman beneath her rank, to whom she was forbidden to speak on penalty of being made a prisoner within ts walls. She found means, however, as any true-hearted girl might if she chose, and not only communicated with her lover, ibut held clandestine meetings. Her father found it out, and actually locked her in her own room, never allowing her out except with an attendant. The lover being informed how matters stood, bribed a servant to bear a note to her, asking her to elope with him on a certain night; and told her just how to manage, which was, I believe, to let herself down from a window with a rope that he had sent to the top of a ladder, which he had placed beneath, where he would stand to receive her in his arms, assist her down, and then they would fly together to parts unknown, and so be rid of their cruel tormentors. In this she fully acquiesced, and, although it was many a long year ago, they have never heard from her since."

"And they made no search?"

"Oh, yes, were nearly distracted; and had detectives out looking for the missing pair, but all to no avail. All that they could gather was, that they were married by an obscure curate at his residence, in the presence of two or three witnesses who happened to be there at the time."

"And gave their real names?"

"Yes, but their disguise was so perfect that, although he had often heard of them both, took them for peasants, or, so he said; probably the truth being that he was bribed, and it was all understood between them beforehand."

When she had finished speaking, Sammie was as pale as death, and felt that he had been listening to a tale more interesting to him than he would care to have her know, and went back to his own home with a determination to sift the matter to the very bottom; for he fully believed that he had a clew that would help him unravel the mysteries that had hung over his early life, and when, in the morning, they rode past the magnificent old castle, and saw an aged pair sitting on the upper piazza in earnest conversation, he felt his heart strangely warming toward them; for something told him he looked upon his own grandparents, and he longed to clasp them both in a fond embrace; show them the miniature that he still wore next his heart, and tell them all he knew about their beautiful but truant daughter. But pride then came to his aid, and he thought that he never would give them an opportunity to repulse him as they undoubtedly would on his father's account.

CHAPTER LIV.

Sammie Wilmington is now in good circumstances, surrounded with a host of friends, and has no reason to waste time, poring over any former troubles, or passing sleepless nights on the account of his ungratified boyish wishes. If he had loved Blanche and she had turned the cold shoulder upon him, if she had been so unstable in her affections, which her haste to censure him had proven, that was no reason why there were not other bright eyes in the world as well as hers, and that would shine with more steady light if their hearts were enlisted.

Belle Mayville was very sweet and bewitching with her slight form, mild blue eyes, and golden hair which she usually did up in a soft coil upon her head, or let fall in a large braid down her hack, sometimes looping it up with a lovely pin made of solid gold, in the form of a large cross and set with costly diamonds. When had he seen so inspiring a vision as she, when he last visited her, the next evening after their ride to Summerset Castle? who might very well remind one of a fairy rather than a human being as she sat by the side of him, engaged in conversation, dressed in a light airy robe of pure white, in full blaze of the light of the chandelier that shone out every evening and illumined the grand parlors of her father's elegant mansion. But although Sammie loved the society of this dear girl, he did not look upon her in the light that the reader might imagine, perhaps. She permitted him to call her sister; and he felt life would be far more drear without her; yet his former love was not so fully obliterated but the germs still remained, which only needed a little light and nursing to cause to spring forth once again into fresh and beautiful blossoms; and although he tried to erase her image, he found that there it was in spite of all other visions in which grace, refinement, or wealth were so deeply mixed, and was likely to remain, when even the names of the proud heiress or captivating belles of the gay city of London were entirely forgotten.

It was a holiday, and Sammie thought he would take a stroll away by himself; so he turned his footsteps toward Summerset Castle; for, although he never intended to make himself known to its inmates, yet there was a strange fascination about this place; and it would have been pleasure beyond what he ever expected to enjoy to roam within the enclosure of those sacred grounds, or to sit within those walls that had once resounded with the merry laughter of his darling, who was now sleeping the peaceful sleep of death in a far off land.

He had walked within a mile of this place, when he saw horses attached to an elegant carriage running toward him with all possible speed. On, on they madly, wildly dashed, until within a few rods of him, when, without waiting to think of the consequences, he jumped directly in front of them, grasped each by his bits, vainly thinking to arrest them in their course; but they were strong and powerful, and wild from fright, and in a moment, loosing themselves, they sped on until coming to a tree the carriage ran against it and was overturned. Sammie was left behind in the road, senseless, and to all appearances a mangled corpse. The coachman just in sight was soon there and on his knees, hat in hand, meekly asking forgiveness for the accident, and promising to do better in the future. The inmates of the carriage, Lord and Lady Parloe, who had only been very slightly injured, in a moment had alighted and were hovering about the stranger, who had come to such a shocking death, pitifully bewailing his sad fate, when a slight twitching of the lips told them life was not as yet extinct; and after the carriage was righted and things restored to order, a pillow was made of one of the cushions for the bruised head, and he was placed inside the coach, where they, too, entered, after having given orders to the coachman to drive with all possible dispatch to the castle, and then go quickly for a physician.

Arriving there, he was carried in and laid upon a bed, and everything done to restore him to consciousness, when, after hours of faithful perseverance, he awakened from his death-like stupor and opened his eyes, though still in that dreamy, bewildered state that one often feels between waking and sleeping, without any distinct knowledge of anything that was passing around him; and it was several days before he seemed to realize his situation, not even knowing then where he was, or for just what reason he was prostrated on this bed, unable to move or rise to his feet.   He could see enough, however, to know he was surrounded with all the elegance that wealth could bring— books, statuary, pictures, and mirrors that reached from the ceiling nearly to the floor, costly carpets, and beautifully frescoed walls, while the gentle zephyr's breath wafted to his partially benumbed senses the delicious aroma of flowers through open windows and closed blinds.

But he was not likely to remain in ignorance a great while; for Lady Parloe, who had been much interested, and attracted to him from the first sight for the chivalrous deed he had done at the risk of his own life, had staid in the room most of the time since he had been brought thither, to see that every want should be gratified, and to watch with a mother's loving care a return of reason, and strength, and life; if, indeed, he could be restored, which the doctor said was doubtful; and only the best nursing would bring him through alive.   And now, discerning his curiosity, she slipped up to his bedside and told him all the circumstances that had brought him hither, and bade him not to fear; that he would soon be able to sit up, then go out on the gounds to walk—till then, his comfort should be paramount in her thoughts.   A week or more passed.   He was now so far recovered as to be able to walk to the window with assistance, and sit for an hour or more: and as he watched the boats gliding over the beautiful Thames, and looked about upon the scenery, he could not help thinking of a time long gone by, when other eyes, and those his own blessed mother's, had felt the same enthusiasm as himself; and taking out her miniature, he gazed long and sadly upon it, wishing from his inmost heart that the dear old lady to whose tenderness he owed his life knew just the relationship that existed between them.   He was startled from his reverie, however, by the approach of one of the servants, bearing a picture in his hands.   A few changes were to be made in the rooms, and this was ordered to be hung up at the foot of his bed.   It was a large oil painting of a young and lovely girl of about sixteen; and, as the eyes of Sammie wandered to it, he uttered a scream of delight and surprise, for it was his mother's portrait; he knew he could not be mistaken, and in his excitement he dropped the little jeweled locket he held in his hand.

Lady Parloe coming in at this moment, espied it, and approaching him, opened it.

It was now her turn to be surprised.   Trembling with agitation, scarcely able to control herself, she hurried to him with the inquiry: "Where did this come from?"   Then placing it to her lips, while tears commenced to flow freely, and run down her furrowed cheek, "Oh! I remember so well a birthday gift to Frederica, my lost darling, my pet, my beautiful child.   But where, oh, where did you get it?"

Sammie now felt that the time had come when he must make explanations, or sink in the estimation of those people who had deigned to show him such consideration; and keeping nothing back, he told her his whole history, and showed her the diary with which the reader was made acquainted in a preceding chapter.

"Your looks might have told me as much," she said, "and although indefinable feelings arose all the time, saying the blood of the Parloes run in your veins, I did not heed them; for I did not see how it could be. But I believe all you have told me, and henceforth you shall be as a son to me."

She then went to the room of her husband, carrying with her these proofs she had in her possession respecting Sammie, and asked him if he could not forgive his daughter for her undutiful act, and take her child to his heart and home.

"Certainly," he replied, "but not until a more thorough investigation of matters. You know there is so much deception in the world. He might turn out another 'Baronet's son.'"

"And then if you knew for reality that he is indeed her own child—our precious, sweet, dear, lost Frederica?"

"He is then our heir, and successor to Summerset Castle," he said enthusiastically.

She had feared that pride would stand in his way, and that he would refuse to recognize the offspring of a man whom he had considered beneath them; and her susceptible woman's heart was so happy when she found he was willing to give up former prejudices and recognize the young stranger. He seeing her feelings, immediately said, "Do not allow your expectations to arise too high as regards this young man. I must become acquainted with his antecedents, know all about his character and reputation he now bears: we must not allow ourselves to be deceived."

"That is easy told. An inquiry of the firm of 'Mayville & Co.,' will show us all we wish to know in that direction. He said he was partner; you remember Mr. Mayville has been to see him several times."

"I know, I know—presume it is all right; and oh, how blessed," he thought after she had left the room, "to have a son once more! too good to be true. Poor Frederica! little lost darling, how sad her fate!" and here he groaned aloud, as the past came rushing upon him with all its vivid reality; but he quieted his excited feelings as soon as possible; for he knew that in his feeble condition he must be calm or take to a sick bed, from which it were doubtful if he would ever again rise.

An investigation was soon made, and not a stone left unturned to get at the truth of all that they had heard.

Once satisfied that there had been no deception practiced on the part of him of whom they heard such favorable reports, they desired him to settle up his affairs with the firm of Mayville & Co., come to Summerset Castle, and live with them altogether; recognizing him at once as the rightful heir of all that belonged to them.

Two months later, and Summerset Castle was literally covered with crape; long columns of all the leading newspapers were devoted to an obituary notice of the deceased Lord Parloe, while all who knew him mourned for him as for a dear friend— all the servants gathering themselves together every evening for a long time afterwards, talking over the good qualities of their late master, and weeping as many would not for a father.

On the demise of Lord Parloe, with the exception of a large yearly annuity that was to go to sustain several different institutions of charity, another for the church of which he was a member, then a library that he had established, not forgetting all of his faithful servants that had been in his employ so many years; Sammie became heir of all his wealth, which amounted to several millions ; and right glad was Lady Parloe to have so competent an arm upon which to lean in her old age, so good a counsellor as she found in him—honest, true, and kind-hearted to the last.

CHAPTER LV.

"Mr. and Mrs. Ashton, Lavarre, Pa., U. S. A."

"What does this mean?" said Sammie, as he glanced at a card handed him by one of the bell boys at the Grand Park Hotel, where he was a boarder, whereon were inscribed the above names.

" Friends, sah, down in the pahlah, wishing to see you, sah," the servant answered meekly.

Without waiting to ask any more questions, Sammie hastened to the large reception room, and was soon face to face with those whom of all the world, (with one exception, whose name we will leave the reader to guess) he was the most delighted to see—the friends of his childhood and youth; who in all the trying hours of his sorrows never came in contact with him but gave him a word of cheer and bade him hope for a bright future.

Charlie Clayton had come to London, too, on very important business, for an extensive manufactory of some kind where he had been employed for several years at a large salary, and now desiring to establish a branch business in a foreign country they knew of no one with whom they felt they could so well intrust matters as with him; and in looking over the advertisements in one of the leading papers after his arrival, he noticed the name of Sammie Wilmington, and called the attention of his friends to it, not thinking for a moment that it could be one and the same gentleman with whom he had once been so well acquainted. But Mr. and Mrs. Ashton thought it quite probable; as they always had a good opinion of his abilities to push his own way among the very best; and so, ascertaining his boarding place, thought they would call, and were as much gratified to see him as though he had been of near kin to them, and heartily pleased to think, in spite of all opposition, he should so far exceed their expectations.

They chatted for an hour or more, Mrs. Ashton expecting something would be said about Blanche, and was prepared to tell him all she knew, and if possible, to effect a reconciliation between them. and bring them together once more. But, as Sammie did not mention her name, she hardly knew how to commence. Finally she said, "You did not know Charlie Clayton accompanied us, and is now in the city?"

Sammie turned pale and became terribly agitated upon hearing once more that familiar name; but striving to keep back the deep feelings that it had aroused, he answered calmly, "And why did he not call? or has the hatred of the father extended to him?"

"He thinks you treated his sister shabbily, and says he wants nothing to do with such a person."

"Then he does not know of the letter? Perhaps none of you do?"

"We know all about it; have heard Walter Clayton laugh over his trick several times. Blanche never wrote it—a forgery of his."

"What! what!" Sammie scarcely knew what he said or did; for a new revelation had dawned upon his bewildered senses; but before they were scarcely aware, he had been to his trunk and brought down the time-stained, tear-blotted missive and handed to them to peruse. "Is not that her autograph?"

"A close resemblance, but not her's. Oh, if you knew of all her sorrow on your account! She is not the same girl she was five years ago. Then the roses faded from her cheeks, and people thought she was going into a decline which would wind up her days. She has never been well since you left for parts unknown."

"Did she hear of her father's baseness?"

"She found it out lately, I believe, and I think had she known your address, would have written you."

"And not married? Loves me still? Tell me truly, Mrs. Ashton. Oh! I never expected to hear so much."

"We are intimate friends. She trusts me with all her secrets, and I know you have never been forgotten."

"I will write immediately and tell her all. No, this will not do; for her father will intercept my letters; this would make more trouble for Blanche."

"I will be glad to make necessary explanations; for it will make her so happy, I know," said Mrs. Ashton.

But it was too long for Sammie to wait; the mails would be all too slow; so next morning he informed his friends that business called him away for a few weeks to his old home, Lavarre. After taking fond leave of his dear old grandmother, telling her all, and getting her to consent to his plans, he set sail the next day for America.

"Is the boy insane?" enquired Mr. Ashton of his wife, "to go away so soon, and not so much as say goodby?"

"Indeed, you wrong him; for he was at our rooms several times to see us; but you were out."

"A little love affair; hope really it will not turn his brain. Well, joy go with him, and success crown his visit. Blanche is a dear, good girl."

"And as deeply enlisted as himself. But how will he get along with the father? There will be trouble again. Look at that article," handing him a newspaper, in which the whole matter was made public about the will of Lord Parloe, the newly found heir, etc., to Summerset Castle and all that belonged to the late master, with a few exceptions.

"If old Walter just knew of this, he would be as meek as a

kitten, and coaxing and sweet as a puppy for a bone. Otherwise—I pity Sammie."

"Everybody is talking of the good fortune that has so lately come to this stranger, as they call him; but Sammie Wilmington is not the one to cringe to Walter Clayton, nor even to tell him anything. I wonder how he will get along with him?"

"I would like to be a mouse in the wall and here all that is said."

"I've hit on a good plan! Send all these different papers to the old mammon worshiper, and write him a letter about what you have seen and heard. It will save time and trouble."

"He might not believe; and I hate to interfere in other people's matters. But it shall be as you think best. I presume, however, he would not like Blanche to know of this streak of luck until he sees her, and hears from her own lips a renewal of those vows of former days."

"Lest she should marry him for money? Oh, Sammie knows her too well. Did she not love him and promise to become his wife, when a poor lad?"

The letter was written and dispatched with all other proof that could be obtained, and reached their destination one week in advance of Sammie, he being detained that length of time in New York on account of sickness; and when he arrived at Lavarre Walter Clayton was the first to take his hand and welcome him, saying, "I was hasty, Mr. Wilmington, in our fray of years ago, and am really sorry that we ever had any trouble; but I see things in a different light from what I used to. You must give us a call. How long do you intend to remain at Lavarre?"

Sammie wondered, but thought that, as changes oftentimes came over people for the better, perhaps Mr. Clayton was one of that sort, not attributing his blandness to the right cause, for he thought he never could have found out about his good fortune, as he nor any person else there knew of his whereabouts since he had left the home of his childhood."

Walter Clayton went home and told Blanche that Sammie Wilmington had arrived; that he had grown from an awkward boy to a handsome man; that he had seen, made up friends with, and invited him to call; that he would be in that evening.

" Is it indeed true, papa?" and she looked incredulously.

"Yes, yes, it is all so; and if—well, if he says anything about your former engagement—about—about—well, you know what I mean, Blanche, of course I will not keep him a great while in suspense; because—because—I know you love him truly, and always have, and I would like to see you happy. Am sorry for what happened in the past; but I was hasty, and thought it would be the best for you to marry Rowland Gray; for you know he was then very wealthy. But I see that riches are liable to take to themselves wings, as in this instance, and a man becomes poor in a day; and it is best after all to take a companion for his good qualities, and brains, than for gold; and I would advise a person to marry for love, and nothing else. So, if Sammie says anything to you, don't hang back on my account."

Happiness is but a poor word to describe the feelings of Blanche at this moment. Her whole soul was permeated with a new life, and a change commenced from this time, in both mind and body.

"O papa, how kind you are!" she said, immediately bursting into a flood of tears; then throwing her arms about his neck, kissed him. Her father knew well the cause of this demonstration, but, pretending ignorance, asked if she was sorry he had come.

"No, oh, no," she answered, wiping her eyes, "for I love Sammie with my whole heart; but it overflows with joy, surprise, and thankfulness. I did not expect it. Papa, you are so good!"

"How easily the child is deceived," thought Walter Clayton. "If she knew my secret, she would lay the whole thing to my craftiness to obtain a rich son-in-law. So far, so good. I am sharp enough to keep matters to myself."

An hour had scarcely elapsed before Sammie Wilmington stood in the presence of Blanche.

Reader, their meeting is too sacred for intrusion. God and angels, alone, may witness the rapture of each, as they make explanations and pledge to each other once more vows never to be broken; and Walter Clayton was as proud as any conqueror, when he gave his daughter to the noble youth who had hastened to her side upon the very first revelation of her faithfulness to him, and her sacrifice. And Sammy was too happy to remember old grudges, much less to speak of the past; and not till they were married did he tell Blanche anything respecting his fortune, and then, folding her to his heart, said, "Dearest, you loved me in my poverty, and you surely will not think the less of me now that I am able to surround you with every luxury of life. I know all about your refusal of the costly diamonds, and for my sake, yes, for my sake; but you shall not lose your reward."

Sammy had not been at Lavarre a week before he received a telegram apprising him of the illness of Lady Parloe, with a desire for him to hasten to London with all possible dispatch. So he and Blanche were not long in getting ready; for, when the next train was due, bound for New York, they were at the depot awaiting it, Walter Clayton, Elice and Robin accompanying them; and not till the last "farewell," "God bless you, my darling," had been listened to through the car window, did Blanche realize what it was to go so far away from those who loved her so dearly—from the home of her childhood, where she had spent pleasant as well as sad hours; her dear, darling mamma, who had taught her to lean upon that high Arm that was able to support her in all her deep trials; that had kept her heart from sinking into utter despair, when sorrows like a great cloud swept over her young life, and she had felt no other wish than to die and leave a world so full of misery and woe. But

her disturbed feelings were soon quieted by the kind words of
her husband, who assumed cheerfulness for her sake, and would
have been as happy now as mortal can be, had it not been for
the sad intelligence that had that morning reached him respecting the dear one far away whom he had learned to love with all
the fondness one might feel for a mother.

But we will pass over all incidents that occurred upon their
journey, and will simply tell you how very pleasant it was and
interesting, particularly to Blanche, who had never before been
on this wide waste of waters, the Atlantic; and how glad they
were that their dispatch had reached their friends, Mr. and Mrs.
Ashton and Charlie Clayton, all of whom were waiting at Liverpool to receive them, the latter being entirely reconciled to his
new brother, as was evidenced by his cordiality.

Inviting Sammie to a seat by the side of him on the way to
the metropolis, he enquired of him if he was acquainted with
Miss Belle Mayville.

"A warm friend of mine—a daughter, you know, of one of
our firm. Have you ever met her?"

"Was introduced to her a year ago at her uncle's, in New
York, a gentleman with whom I expect to enter into partnership, that is, if I choose. I prefer, however, to work awhile
on my salary, as there can be no risks. Five thousand per year,
you know, will support me nicely."

"And a partner, eh? Tell me, Charlie."

"Miss Mayville may answer all your questions."

In four weeks from that day, there was a grand wedding at
St. Peter's Church—such a one as might well accord with the
notions of the wealthy and aristocratic families of gay old London,—that of Belle Mayville and Charlie Clayton.

A few months, only, had elapsed, when grief of a serious
nature came once more to Summerset Castle. Lady Parloe
breathed her last, her life going out as a beautiful sunset day so
undisturbed and peaceful, and she so happy, she said, that her
dear old home had fallen into such good hands.

A letter written by Blanche a time after her installment as mistress of Summerset Castle will show how she felt about her good fortune; and, although she was now surrounded by wealth and grandeur, yet she was the same dear, dutiful, loving child as before, ministering to the sick, and giving of her means to make life happy for many a poor, downtrodden son and daughter of Eve.

"My Darling Mamma: I scarcely can tell you of my great happiness, nor describe the joy I feel in my new home; and it is not that I am raised above every care in life by our unbounded wealth, which is by far more than papa can boast; but that with all this, which is a blessing and a great one, I know, inasmuch as we can make others happy by the means; but that my husband is so kind, so loving, so true, and does everything for my pleasure; that he has become a devoted follower of the dear Saviour whom you, my sweet, sweet mamma, taught me to love, not only speaking by precept, but more by your example, your untiring patience through all your tribulations in life— through your great persecutions.

"I will tell you how to spend a portion of our time, for we do not allow a moment to go to waste, feeling that we must give an account of this, even at the great day. In the morning Sammie calls all the servants together and reads a portion of the Scripture and explains it to them; all then kneel, while he petitions the throne of grace and mercy, asking God to shed abroad his precious love in the hearts of these children. The consequence is that He has heard his prayers, and they are all hopefully converted. You ask me how I know;—simply by the peaceable fruits of righteousness in them manifested—patience, love, forbearance. We then breakfast and walk, row or ride, for two or three hours, all over the grounds, through the park, on the carriage road that winds along for several miles by the beautiful Thames; then taking a different direction, through lofty shades, we find ourselves after a while once more at the castle, of which I will some time give you a description, but not now, for I have not the time; the hours that intervene are filled by practicing music. Afternoons:—directly after dinner a professor gives us lessons—Sammie on different 'instruments. It seems as if there were no need of this; for to my mind, he surpasses his teacher in sweetness of tone, in everything already; and I tell him so, but he says I am prejudiced in his favor and am not capable of distinguishing piano from fortissimo, and laughing, I say that may be so in 'your case. I receive instructions on guitar and piano.

"Next, there are a great many of his tenants who have been unable to maintain their families for awhile on account of sickness. These we visit every day; and while we bestow our temporal gifts, think not we forget to break to their poor benighted souls the 'bread of life.' Evenings we spend mostly in reading. How I wish you could take a peep into our elegant library; there is nothing upon which you would wish to feast your mind but you would find here.

"I shall look for a visit from you, papa, and Robin the coming summer. Promise me, darling mamma.
With much love,
Your BLANCHE."

Another written a year after the marriage of Blanche and Sammie :

"MY SWEET MAMMA: Congratulate me. I am able once more to go out, and have just come in from a ride, feeling refreshed and invigorated. Thank God with me that my perils are passed. I am well once more; and nestling away in its downy nest is a little darling with the brightest eyes of blue, which have opened enough for me to know are just like its papa's; while we can brush its flaxen hair into the dearest little ringlets all over its head; this, too, when it becomes a few years old, will be just the color of Sammie's. Do not laugh at my enthusiasm, when I say still further that it is very beautiful, and only two months old; but you know, darling mamma, for you once had a little heart throbbing against yours that was all your own, that to a mother, a child has peculiar attractions that no one else can see ; may be in this case.

"Sammie is delighted, of course, and says it shall be called after its two grandmammas, Frederica Elice. Will that please you ? I need not ask, for the pleasure and good of your children were always paramount in your thoughts. I shall teach my little Elice unselfishness, and, if her character should one day shine conspicuously in that respect like her whose name she bears, I shall be so proud of her. Still, I will breathe into your ears, darling mamma, my great happiness. I told you in other letters of the mission Sabbath school, of which Sammie was superintendent. Charlie and Belle have now enlisted as teachers, and so much good is being done, it fills my heart with joy. I know it will yours to hear of it.

Still I am praying for dear papa, and firmly believe that all of those prayers of faith that have gone forth from your lips since I can remember, for him, will not be unanswered.

"Good-bye for the present. BLANCHE."

CHAPTER LVI.

A few extracts from the diary of Elice, and letters received and sent a time previous to her death, will show more plainly than any words of our own, that Christ has power to sustain the Christian whose trust is in Him alone, even after their feet, weary of treading this vale below, have stepped into the Jordan and they are passed all recovery.

"July 1st.—My birthday. I shall never live to see another; for the physicians say I must die—must die; and what does this imply? A separation simply of soul and body—a life, a beautiful, glorious life in the beyond. Shall I then repine? True, I must leave some of my dear ones behind, but they will come to me. Oh, I have faith that I shall see them all at last in the kingdom of Heaven."

August 2nd.—A letter from Charlie: dear boy, how I love him! and to know he is indeed converted—his heart changed, and actually laboring in a mission Sabbath school, striving to win hearts to God, is bliss indescribable! Oh! we shall meet bye and bye up yonder, if not on earth, sweet child; but I do hope to see him and Blanche yet before I pass away. I have never told them my condition, or how quickly they would fly to me; but I dislike to distress them, still in my next letter they shall know all. How sweet to know that, through all the opposition that has assailed my life, the misjudgments, that the minds of those dear children have not been embittered against me. But this was another one of the blessings bestowed, for which I thank my Father above. But I must stop scribbling and read the letter:"

"Mamma, dear, do you feel neglected because three weeks have passed, and you have not heard from me? You will not when I tell you that Belle has been ill and I have watched by her bedside night and day, fearing that each moment would be her last; and now that she is slowly recovering, I thought I could take the time to write you. Although I am happy—for my sweet wife is all the world to me—yet I miss your dear voice; and your kind counsellings. You have had a rough life; but I trust those days are over, and you will be happier than you ever have been. I have now entered into partnership with the firm for whom I have done business so long, and am making money very fast; but think not I set my heart upon wealth; there are higher enjoyments than the accumulation of gold, and I have found them in the service of the Master above.

You cannot tell how badly I wish to see you, and think Belle and I will make a trip to America soon. You will not forget us in your prayers, I know.

"Your affectionate son,

CHARLIE CLAYTON."

"Such a letter is consoling; such words are sweet to me; my life after all has been a triumph; my pathway is gilded to the tomb; I have suffered persecution, but heaven and immortality await me and mine."

"August 25th.—It is the storm and the wind as well as the sunlight that has unfolded the leaves of this beautiful rose. Had there been no clouds, no rain, the tree must have died with the heat of these summer days; but now its fragrance is wafted by every passing breeze that blows. So with Christ's followers; the storms of persecution, trouble, sorrow, of every name and nature, as well as the sun and dew of gentleness, kindness, and love, unfold their Christian character, and cause it to yield the blossoms of true piety. Let my life, blessed

Father, be such that no stain may rest upon it; my example accord with my profession."

"September 1st.—My life is ebbing fast away. I shall probably never see another anniversary of my wedding day. How the winds whistled and howled around my father's cottage, uprooting the shade trees, and demolishing all the vines that had hitherto clung to the lattice—a warning prophecy of my future. I could not see it then, for Walter was there and had thrown around me his arms of affection. 'Twas enough. How I loved him! And happiness smiled upon me even from the wrecks the winter storms had made. My tears are falling fast, as I recall the hours; but they will all soon be dried upon my Saviour's loving bosom. How I wish Walter was a child of the Most High—was treading in the beautiful paths of righteousness! Still I have faith that some time in the future he will be a praying man."

"September 5th.—At the sight of the hectic flush upon my cheek, with the knowledge that the sod must soon cover me, he taunts me with cruel words. How unjust, how hard! when I have always done so much for his comfort and happiness; but Walter will sometime visit my grave with regrets, and be made to see, through his own affliction, how he embittered my life. God is an avenger of wrongs, as well as a justifier of good deeds.

"September 6th.—I read among the arrivals, those of Hon. A. S. Ashton and wife; just returned from a tour in Europe. Joy, joy, my dear friends! Yes, more than that has she been to me—sister, mother, counsellor, everything. But here they come. I thought they would hasten to visit me; they will tell me all about my darlings over the Atlantic. It will be so good to hear from their honest lips, of their happiness and prosperity.

Come and gone! I did not think the meeting would so affect them; but it was the sight of my distress. She could scarcely converse for tears and sobs. Dear, kind, ministering angel, she will come again, and will grow calm when I tell her of the peace I feel in my soul; when I speak to her of that rest that is to be

mine; of the tree of life, under whose broad branches I shall
soon be sheltered, and for aye; away from the storms of life—
sorrow, persecution, envy, malice, scathings of evil, lying, deceitful tongues, all, all, and safe in my Father's fold; He the
Shepherd.

"September 7th.—A letter from Blanche:

Sweet Mamma: Tell me not that you must die; for I fear I
shall grow sinful and rebel. Every moment since I read your
letter bearing the painful news, I have prayed for submission,
and still it comes not. You who watched so tenderly over my
early life; that so readily forgave all my wrong doings; that
came to my side with pleasant smiles, and cheerful words, when
my feet had already slid into the mires of despondency; that
dragged me from a seemingly hopeless grief, and bade me look
away beyond the clouds for comfort. O mamma, my agonizing tears blot my words; I can write no more. Sammie says
we will start for America on the next vessel out of port. I
must see you soon. How can I wait?

"Your affectionate daughter,

Blanche."

"Poor, dear Blanche! she does indeed love me truly. God
sustain her!"

"September 8th.—A telegram from Charlie. He and Belle
are also coming home. How good God is! I shall once more
be permitted to see all my children."

"September 9th.—Walter has promised I shall lie with my
kindred on the banks of the Cohocton. That was kind, and in
part makes amend for his ill treatment. How glad I am that I
can so freely forgive all the wrongs he has done me! Another
life how different from this! Heaven, sweet heaven, my eternal
home! No revengeful feelings will there stir up our hearts; no
malicious, envious strife come to dispel the serenity of our joys.
Peace, peace, everlasting peace! I am so contented to die."

"September 18th.—Another telegram. The children will be
home on the evening train; they will see my life go out. I

never thought the pillow of death could be so downy; but the arms of Christ are around me. Sweet, sweet Saviour, how blessed am I !"

These were the last words ever penned by Elice Clayton. She died as calmly as though she were going to sleep; was buried at Woodville by the side of her loved ones. A monument of surpassing beauty towers above her head; on it the simple inscription :

"*Our Mamma. A pledge of affection from ' Those Orphans,' who loved her so dearly in life—in death did not forget her.*"

In another book entitled, "His Other Wife," which we expect soon to publish, we will tell you more of Walter Clayton; his wicked life, and sad death.

The·End.

www.ingramcontent.com/pod-product-compliance
Lightning Source LLC
Chambersburg PA
CBHW031138120726
47905CB00006B/1731